D1624156

Dietz, W.

When duty calls.

WHEN DUTY CALLS

WHEN DUTY CALLS

CALLS

WILLIAM C. DIETZ

ACE BOOKS, NEW YORK

Science Fiction

Muskegon Area District Library

THE BERKLEY PUBLISHING GROUP
Published by the Penguin Group
Penguin Group (USA) Inc.
375 Hudson Street, New York, New York 10014, USA
Penguin Group (Canada), 90 Eglinton Avenue East, Suite 700, Toronto, Ontario M4P 2Y3, Canada
(a division of Pearson Penguin Canada Inc.)
Penguin Books Ltd., 80 Strand, London WC2R 0RL, England
Penguin Group Ireland, 25 St. Stephen's Green, Dublin 2, Ireland (a division of Penguin Books Ltd.)
Penguin Group (Australia), 250 Camberwell Road, Camberwell, Victoria 3124, Australia
(a division of Pearson Australia Group Pty. Ltd.)
Penguin Books India Pvt. Ltd., 11 Community Centre, Panchsheel Park, New Delhi—110 017, India
Penguin Group (NZ), 67 Apollo Drive, Rosedale, North Shore 0632, New Zealand
(a division of Pearson New Zealand Ltd.)
Penguin Books (South Africa) (Pty.) Ltd., 24 Sturdee Avenue, Rosebank, Johannesburg 2196,
South Africa

Penguin Books Ltd., Registered Offices: 80 Strand, London WC2R 0RL, England

This is an original publication of The Berkley Publishing Group.

First edition: October 2008

Library of Congress Cataloging-in-Publication Data

Dietz, William C.
    When duty calls / William C. Dietz.—1st ed.
        p.   cm.
    ISBN 978-0-441-01632-7
1. Space warfare—Fiction. I. Title.
    PS3554.I388W46   2008
    813'.54—dc22
    2008030836

PRINTED IN THE UNITED STATES OF AMERICA

10   9   8   7   6   5   4   3   2   1

For Allison Elizabeth Dietz,
in recognition of her courage, and determination.

WHEN DUTY CALLS

1

PLANET ORON IV, THE CONFEDERACY OF SENTIENT BEINGS

Captain Antonio Santana, Commanding Officer of Alpha Company, 2nd Battalion, 1st REC, felt a noticeable jerk as the CF-10 Assault Boat fell free of the Troop Transport *Cynthia Harmon* and began a gradual descent toward the nearly airless planet below. The lightly armed landing craft was accompanied by four Dagger 184 aerospace fighters. That knowledge brought the cavalry officer scant comfort, however, because he knew that once his largely untried company hit the surface of Oron IV, the navy wouldn't be able to do much more than cheer them on. Or mourn their deaths.

Santana felt his body float up off the surface of the jump seat, or try to, but a six-point harness held him in place. Behind the officer, back in the CF-10's crowded cargo bay, sixteen space-armored bio bods and nineteen cyborgs shared the heady combination of fear and excitement that precedes *any* combat insertion. And this one was worse than most. Because not only was half the company fresh from basic training, and had never been in combat before, but the raid was the type of mission normally reserved for the Marine Corps. Except there was a shortage of jarheads at the moment—which was why the Legion had been ordered to stand in for them. Making a bad situation worse was the fact that Major Liam Quinlan had assumed command of the 2nd Battalion while Santana was on leave. And for some reason the new CO was determined to find fault with everything the officer did, a fact that had become obvious to the entire company and made the veterans resentful.

But Santana had dealt with difficult commanding officers before and been able to win most of them over by doing a good job. With that in mind, the cavalry officer put all of his other concerns aside to focus on the task at hand. The pale orange planet seemed to swell as the CF-10 entered an atmosphere thick with methane, carbon dioxide, and nitrous oxide. Which was why the world was considered worthless, or had been until recently, when the war between the Ramanthian Empire and the Confederacy of Sentient Beings had begun. Suddenly everything was in flux as old enemies became new friends, a new faster-than-ship communications technology began to reshape the way future wars would be fought, and planets like Oron IV were suddenly significant. Not as places for people to live, but as strategic jump points, where supplies could be pre-positioned for battles yet to come. Because, as Military Chief of Staff General Bill Booly liked to point out, supplies are the lifeblood of *any* army.

Which, assuming the intelligence people were correct, was why the insectoid Ramanthians had chosen to establish a presence on Oron IV, a planet that lay well within the Confederacy's gradually shrinking borders, was generally inhospitable to life, and rarely received visitors. All of which made it the perfect place for the bugs to hide a whole shitload of supplies while they got ready for the next big push. "Are you sure the chits are down there?" the copilot inquired dubiously. "There are no signs of electronic activity so far. . . . Maybe they went home."

"That would be nice," Santana replied over his suit radio.

"But odds are the bastards are lying low. That's what I would do if I were them."

All radio communications were being routed through the company-level Integrated Tactical Command (ITC) system, which meant that Major Quinlan could monitor the company's progress from the well-padded comfort of the *Harmon*'s Command & Control Center (C&C) and participate in any conversation he chose to. "I don't think any of us care what *you* would do if you were a Ramanthian," Quinlan commented caustically. "So, stow the bullshit, and stick to your job."

The copilot looked back over her shoulder as if to apologize, and Santana shrugged, as if to say, "Don't worry about it."

Meanwhile, back in the cargo bay, Master Sergeant Dice Dietrich frowned. The hollow-cheeked noncom had served with Santana before. First on LaNor, where a consortium of off-world governments had been forced to battle the Claw, and then on Savas, where elements of the 1st REC took part in a raid that required them to traverse hundreds of miles of hostile territory. So Dietrich not only knew what the cavalry officer was capable of, but was familiar with Santana's combat record, which included *two* Medals for Valor and a Distinguished Service Cross. Complete with a newly added star. And, being a decorated veteran himself, Dietrich knew how divisive an officer like Quinlan could be. Divisive, and if they weren't careful, *dead.* Because it was the noncom's opinion that every garden requires an occasional weeding.

Both of the company's quads were back by the loading ramp, where they could hit the ground first, backed by seventeen ten-foot-tall Trooper IIs, all of whom were clamped to the bulkheads, and fifteen bio bods, many of whom were looking at the "Top," trying to gauge his reaction to Quinlan's comment. Mindful of the fact that the major could hear anything he said, Dietrich grinned menacingly from behind his faceplate and aimed a one-fingered salute up toward space.

The legionnaires seated around the noncom laughed,

and even though both of Santana's platoon leaders witnessed the gesture, they were careful to ignore it. Partly because they had no love for Quinlan themselves, but mostly
because they were afraid to get crosswise of the hard-eyed
sergeant, and the veterans who were loyal to him. The net
effect was to break the tension and simultaneously restore
the company's confidence in Santana. Because if Dietrich
had faith in the captain, then it was obvious that they should,
too.

The assault boat and its sleek escorts bucked their way
down through multiple layers of turbulent gas until they
could skim the planet's arid surface. There wasn't much to
see other than frequent outcroppings of gray rock, dry
riverbeds, and occasional forests of what looked like petri-
fied trees. Then, after ten minutes or so, the landing craft's
boxy shadow rippled over the only man-made structures on
the planet's surface. The complex consisted of a rusty dome,
a clutch of globular tanks, and a sand-drifted landing pad.
The words "Madsen Mining" were still legible on the cracked
duracrete if one looked hard enough. The entire facility was
nestled within the open arms of three interlocking hills,
which the map provided by Madsen Mining referred to as the
Three Amigos.

"Bingo!" the copilot said excitedly, as she stared at the
readouts arrayed in front of her. "That sucker is radiating
way too much heat. . . . It looks like the chits took over the
mine! Maybe we should tell the Dags to bomb 'em."

"They're too deep," Santana replied wearily. "In fact,
based on the schematic that Madsen Mining gave us, it looks
like some of the major galleries are more than a thousand feet
below the surface. Besides, there's a war on, and some of
those supplies could come in handy. . . . Put us down one
mile to the west. Who knows what kind of weapons systems
and booby traps the bugs have in place around the landing
pad."

Quinlan's response came so quickly it was as if he'd been
waiting to make it. "That's a negative Alpha Six. Why give

the enemy time to prepare? You will land on the pad—and do so immediately. Over."

The pilot looked back over his shoulder as if to say, "What now?"

Santana swore under his breath. He'd been hoping to avoid conflict, but if that was what it was going to take to protect his legionnaires, then that's the way it would have to be. "Alpha Six to Zulu Six. I'm sorry, sir, but there's a lot of interference down here, and you're breaking up. Over."

The pilot grinned as Quinlan began to rant and rave. "You're lying, Santana. . . . And disobeying a direct order! I'm going to—"

But whatever the major was going to do was forever lost as the copilot flicked a switch, and the relay went dead. "Sorry, sir," she said, knowing that the flight recorder would capture her words. "It looks like we have some sort of com problem."

"See what you can do with it," the pilot replied calmly, as he brought the boat's nose up and fired the repellers. "I have a ship to land. Thirty to dirt . . ."

Santana was already up out of his seat and making his way back into the cargo bay when the assault boat's skids thumped down, the rear hatch whirred open, and the entire ship shook as Private Ivan Lupo lumbered down the ramp onto Oron IV's reddish soil. The cyborg stood twenty-five feet tall, weighed fifty tons, and was supported by four massive legs. It was no accident that the so-called quad was the first legionnaire to hit dirt, because not only were Lupo's sensors superior to those carried by the bipedal Trooper IIs (T-2s), but his gang-mounted energy cannons were more than a match for anything up to and including a Ramanthian battle tank. Not that Alpha Company was likely to encounter enemy armor on a backwater crud ball like Oron IV. Of course Lupo knew that ". . . assumptions can get you killed." That's what he and his buddies had been taught back in basic, and having already been executed for murder, the ex-con had no desire to die again. Not so soon at any rate.

Lupo assumed a defensive position about a hundred yards west of the landing craft, as Private Simy Xiong exited the ship and took up a similar position off to the east. As the second quad settled over her legs, Santana sent First Lieutenant Lucy Amoyo's platoon out to secure the rest of the perimeter. For many of the legionnaires it was the first time they had set foot on a potentially hostile planet, so even though there weren't any visible signs of life, the entire outfit was amped.

Amoyo, one of the few members of Alpha Company who *had* seen combat, was no exception as she rode her ten-foot-tall T-2 out onto Oron's arid surface. From where the officer stood, high on the cyborg's back, she had an excellent field of vision. More than that, she was free to focus most of her attention on the first platoon rather than negotiate the raw terrain. *That* chore fell to Sergeant Amy Matos, formerly *Corporal* Amy Matos, who had been killed in action two years previously, and given a chance to re-up as a cyborg. Which was really no choice at all since Matos couldn't afford even the cheapest cybernetic civbod, a vehicle that would allow her to *look* human even if certain biological functions were forever lost to her.

So Matos brought her weapons systems to condition-five readiness and cranked her sensors to high gain, as she circled the newly created perimeter. The cyborg could run at speeds up to fifty miles per hour, operate in Class I through Class IX gas atmospheres, and fight in a complete vacuum if necessary. And, thanks to her fast-recovery laser cannon, air-cooled .50-caliber machine gun, and optional missile launchers, the T-2's firepower equaled that of eight fully armed bio bods. Having completed a full circuit of the perimeter, and being satisfied with the way her troops were positioned, Amoyo ordered Matos to pull up. "Alpha One-Six to Alpha Six. Over."

Had Santana felt free to do so, he would have been the first bio bod off the ship. But the entire company was watching, and the officer knew he couldn't disembark with the first platoon lest the action be interpreted as a ~~~~ Lieutenant Amoyo's judgment. And, given t ~~~~ was his executive officer (XO) as well as the ~~~~ leader, it was important to build her rep. S ~~~~ standing in the cargo bay, monitoring the h ~~~~ (HUD) on the inside surface of his visor, when the call came in. "This is Six," Santana replied calmly. "Go. Over."

"The landing zone is secure, sir," the platoon leader reported flatly. "Over."

"Roger, that, One-Six," Santana replied. "Keep your eyes peeled. Out."

Based on previous experience, Santana knew that his other platoon commander, a young second lieutenant named Gregory Zolkin, had a tendency to be excessively wordy where his reports were concerned. He hoped the untried officer had been paying attention to Amoyo's succinct style as the two of them made eye contact. Both were sealed inside full body armor, so what might have otherwise been a casual interchange was made more formal by the need to use radio procedure, which was required whenever a conversation took place on the company-level push.

"Alpha Six to Bravo One-Six," Santana said. "Based on the amount of heat that's escaping from the mine shaft, there's a very real possibility that the bugs are hiding out below, waiting to see if we'll go away. You and I will take the first squad and knock on the front door. Meanwhile, Alpha Six-Two will take the second squad and circle around behind the hills. His job will be to locate the back door. And believe me—there is one. Do you have any questions? Over."

Zolkin had *lots* of questions. Not the least of which was would he make an ass of himself, shit his suit, or get killed? But, being unable to actually ask those questions, the lieutenant gave the only answer he could. "Sir, no, sir. Bravo One-Six out."

Santana hadn't discussed the plan with Dietrich in advance, but such was the relationship between the two men at the noncom had anticipated such an assignment, and was ready for it. Because if a substantial number of chits were allowed to surface in the wrong place, the results could be disastrous. And rather than download the task to Zolkin, Santana had given the job to his company sergeant, knowing Dietrich had more than enough experience to handle it. "Okay," Santana said evenly. "Let's hit the dirt. Six out."

More than a thousand feet below Oron IV's harsh surface, Subcommander Sig Byap sat within a pressurized chamber and watched the Confederacy ship lift. It was just what he'd been hoping for, except that rather than take the alien soldiers along with it, the reentry-scarred vessel had deposited them on the surface, where the ugly-looking creatures were pumping air into a field hab.

The Ramanthian swore as the assault boat hovered for a moment and stirred up a vortex of dust before crossing the defensive perimeter and accelerating away. Then, as a large knot continued to form in his belly, the officer watched a four-legged cyborg turn and "look" his way. Missile racks appeared along both sides of the quad's hull—and there was a momentary flash of light as one of them fired. Camera 36 went dark a fraction of a second later. Having missed the carefully concealed surcams during initial sweeps of the area, it appeared that subsequent efforts had been more successful, as 92 percent of Byap's surveillance devices were taken offline. That meant the eggless scum *knew* about the subsurface storage facility and intended to capture or destroy it, which the degenerates would very likely be able to accomplish thanks to the amount of firepower they had.

However, given that Byap was a sworn member of the *Nira*, a fanatical group of officers for whom surrender was unthinkable, there was only one choice: fight to the death. Not something Byap lusted after the way some Ramanthians did, but a perfectly acceptable outcome given the needs of his people. Because with five billion newly hatched citizens to care for, the empire was in need of everything. Especially real estate. Which was how the war had begun—and why he and his troops were about to die.

The Ramanthians preferred to live underground, so while somewhat monotonous, life inside the mine had been acceptable up until that point. Video screens, most of which had been rendered dark, covered a rocky wall. They were fronted by a curved control console, five saddle chairs, and the same number of technicians.

Byap was seated behind them, and swiveled around to face a heavily armed file leader named Beeb Nohar. Having responded to the general alarm, the officer was dressed in power-assisted space armor that would not only protect the soldier from a complete vacuum, but enable him to rip a legionnaire's head off should that be necessary. The helmet that Nohar held clutched in the crook of his right arm incorporated side-mounted black portals through which his compound eyes would be able to see, and a hook-shaped protuberance designed to accommodate his parrotlike beak. The file leader listened impassively as Byap spoke. "The automatic defenses located in the vicinity of the main lock won't be sufficient to stop them," the subcommander predicted. "Confront the animals in the main corridor and show no mercy. I will take File Two, exit through the escape shaft, and attack the troops on the surface."

The plan made sense, given the circumstances, even though it couldn't possibly succeed. But both of Nohar's mates had been killed on Infama VI, and he was eager to join them in paradise. "It shall be as you say," the file leader agreed stoically, and came to the Ramanthian equivalent of attention.

Byap stood. "You are a fine officer," the subcommander said feelingly. "The Queen would be proud. Dismissed."

Once Nohar was gone, and the technicians had been released to rejoin their units, Byap shuffled over to the control console, where he removed the wafer-shaped device that dangled from his neck and slipped the object into a waiting slot. A gentle *whir* could be heard as a remote appeared, and the officer took possession of it. There wasn't a single member of his command who wasn't aware of the strategically located demolition charges that had been pre-positioned throughout the mine. But being aware of a potential calamity, and *knowing* it's about to occur, are two different things. So the officer thought it best to pocket the device when none of his subordinates were present to see him do so. Especially given the fact that once the charges went off, the entire mine would collapse, killing everyone inside.

From all appearances it looked as if someone or something had bypassed the dome's heavy-duty lock by hacking a huge hole in the habitat's metal skin. The Ramanthians? Possibly, although Santana had his doubts, as Sergeant Omi Dekar carried him through the ragged opening. There wasn't much to see as the T-2's headlight swept back and forth across the nearly empty interior. In fact, it looked as if the place had been gutted years before. By humans most likely, looking to strip the mothballed facility of electronics, or anything else that could be sold on the black market.

Having found nothing of interest inside the dome, the legionnaires made their way toward the small blocky building that served as the entry point to the mine below. The terrain, not to mention piles of rusty pipe and pieces of old mining equipment, conspired to funnel the squad through a narrow passageway. Was that a matter of chance, Santana wondered? Or the result of careful planning? "Take it slow," the cavalry officer cautioned. "And keep your eyes peeled for booby traps."

That was good advice, as soon became apparent, when Staff Sergeant Carol Yanty spotted two pieces of pipe that stuck up out of the ground like gateposts and motioned for those behind her to stop. What caught her attention was the fact that anyone who wanted to approach the main lock would have to pass between the head-high pylons. The NCO dropped to the ground, made her way over to a pile of scrap, and selected a small piece of sheet metal. Harsh sunlight glinted off the object as it sailed between the pipes. Lieutenant Zolkin, who had been somewhat skeptical until then, watched in slack-jawed astonishment as a bolt of bright blue electricity jumped from one pole to the other and punched a hole through the scrap of sheet metal as it did so. Then, having completed its task, the system returned to standby.

The platoon leader couldn't hear the *sizzle* from inside his suit, but there was nothing wrong with his imagination, so he could easily visualize what would have occurred had he been allowed to lead the rest of the squad through the narrow passageway. Would his armor have been sufficient to protect him from such a device? Maybe, Zolkin concluded, and maybe not.

The electrified posts were quickly slagged by the T-2s, thus allowing the entire team to pass unharmed. "Okay," Santana said over the squad-level com channel. "That confirms what we already knew. . . . The bugs are in residence, so stay sharp."

And they *were* sharp, or as sharp as they could be, but some traps are difficult to detect. As the legionnaires learned when Private Mak Matal put his full weight on a sand-swept pressure plate and triggered a carefully shaped charge. The explosion blew both the T-2 and his rider into a thousand fragments. They soared upwards until gravity took over and began to pull them back down. The bloody confetti had a tendency to bond with anything that it came in contact with. Including the legionnaires themselves.

The disaster was so unexpected that even Santana was shocked, especially since he, Zolkin, Yanty, and their T-2s had safely crossed the very same spot only moments before. Killing the fourth person, or in this case *persons* to pass over the mine was a tactic intended to inflict casualties, sow the seeds of doubt, *and* terrorize those who survived. That was bad enough, but having lost one-third of Yanty's squad, Santana was even more concerned about the unit's ability to defend itself as the survivors came together in front of the main lock. "Check the hatch for booby traps," Santana ordered tersely. "And, if it comes up clean, blow it."

Zolkin felt as if he should be giving orders, or helping somehow, but found that it was difficult to see. So he reached up to wipe the muck off his face shield, realized what the bloody sludge was, and threw up in his helmet. The vomit ran down the officer's chin, found its way past his neck seal, and dribbled into his suit. The stench was sickening, and Zolkin felt an intense sense of shame, as his stomach heaved yet again.

"Get away from the hatch," Santana ordered, as Yanty slapped a charge against the metal door and stepped to one side. All of the soldiers took cover as Yanty flipped a safety switch and thumbed the remote. There was a flash of light as the charge went off, followed by a cloud of dust, as air was expelled and an equivalent amount of Oron IV's atmosphere rushed in to replace it. That was Private Oneeye Knifeplay's cue to fire six grenades into the black hole in an effort to kill any chits that were waiting within.

Santana couldn't hear the explosions, but he could see flashes as the grenades went off, and sent pieces of razor-sharp shrapnel flying in every direction. And even though the wait was only a few seconds long, there was still enough time to feel the fear seep into his belly. *Matal and Bisby died the first time they went into combat,* the soldier told himself. *But even though you've been in combat dozens of times, you're still alive. Why is that? And how many more doors can you walk through before your luck runs out?*

There was no answer, just as Santana knew there wouldn't be, and for some reason it was an image of Christine Vanderveen's face that the cavalry officer saw as he entered the swirling smoke. It might have been Camerone, in 1863, or Dien Bien Phu in 1953, or any of a thousand actions since, as the company commander waved his legionnaires forward. "What the hell are you waiting for?" Sergeant Yanty wanted to know, as the remainder of her squad stood frozen in place. "A frigging invitation? Let's kill some bugs!"

Four bio bods and four T-2s entered the mine, and followed the gradually sloping shaft downwards, as their lights played across the rough-hewn rock walls. And that, according to File Leader Beeb Nohar's way of thinking, was just fine.

It was a long way from the control cavern to the escape hatch located on the other side of the hills above, so Byap and the twelve troopers who accompanied him still had a ways to go, when they received word that the aliens had entered the mine. A price had been paid, however, a bloody price, and that gave the Ramanthian pleasure as he urged his soldiers forward. Blobs of light swung back and forth across rocky walls, and badly faded alien hieroglyphics could be seen here and there, as the Ramanthians shuffled past a side gallery crammed floor to ceiling with army rations.

Finally, after five minutes of additional travel, the file was forced to a stop in front of the emergency exit. Having checked to ensure that the lock's surcam was operational, Byap took the time necessary to scan the external environment before proceeding any farther. Because once out in the open, the subcommander knew that his tiny force would be vulnerable to enemy cyborgs *and* the Confederacy's aerospace fighters. But the surcam revealed nothing other than a cloudless sky and the steep scree-covered slope that led to the iron-oxide-stained plain below.

Confident that the immediate area was safe, Byap led his troopers into the lock and tapped a series of numbers into the human-style keypad. Sunlight splashed the lock's interior and threw shadows against the back wall as the hatch cycled open. As Byap led the file out onto the treacherous hillside, he knew speed was of the essence if he and his troops were to circle around and take the enemy by surprise. The Ramanthian knew that the ensuing battle would constitute little more than a gesture, but he wanted to die with honor.

Such were Subcommander Byap's thoughts as a .50-caliber bullet left the barrel of Private Mary Volin's sniper rifle, sped through the air, and snatched a trooper off his feet. "That was a good one," Dietrich commented, as he stood. The noncom's face shield made the binos more difficult to use, but the dappled body armor that the chits wore was easy to spot against the light gray scree.

Byap saw the trooper spin away, knew the bullet had originated from somewhere below, and spotted movement as a tiny figure rose to look up at him. "There!" the officer said, as he pointed at the alien below. "Kill him!"

And the Ramanthian troopers tried, but the second squad was more than a thousand yards away, which put the legionnaires well beyond the effective range of the Ramanthian Negar assault weapons. That left Volin free to peer into the 10X scope, pick her next target, and send a second armor-piercing slug spinning upslope.

Byap swore as *another* trooper went down. Then, knowing that he had no choice but retreat, the subcommander turned and began to scramble uphill. The movement brought the officer to Dietrich's attention. "See the bug who's leading the rest of them uphill?" the noncom inquired conversationally. "Kill him."

And Volin tried. But a sudden breeze came in from the west and gave the speeding bullet a tiny nudge. Not much, but enough to knock the slug off course, and momentarily save Byap's life. But the 706.7-grain projectile still took the subcommander's left arm off, turned him around, and dumped him onto the scree. And it was then, while staring up into an alien sky, that Byap remembered the remote. Time seemed to slow as the Ramanthian fumbled for the object and finally found it.

The suit had sealed itself by that time, cauterized the terrible wound that he had suffered, and was busy pumping drugs into the officer's circulatory system. That made it hard to think, but the officer forced himself to focus, as he struggled to break the remote's safety tab. A simple task given *two* pincers, but difficult with only one, especially when the enemy was shooting at you. Finally, having made use of a neighboring rock to break the tab off, Byap gave the device a squeeze.

There was no response at first, or that was the way it seemed to the Ramanthian, as troopers continued to fall all around him. But then the earth shook, the entire air lock was blown out of the hillside, and the scree began to move. That was when Byap knew his efforts had been successful—and that the gates of paradise would open before him.

Having forced his way into the mine, Santana expected to encounter stiff resistance from the Ramanthians and was surprised when nothing of that sort occurred. There was something oppressive about the rock walls that closed in around the legionnaires as the throatlike passageway took them deeper underground. What little bit of comfort there was stemmed from the fact that while small, his force packed plenty of firepower. Occasional lights cast an ominous greenish glow over tool-ripped walls as the floor sloped steadily downwards.

As the squad pushed deeper into the mine, and his T-2's powerful headlamp pushed its way into various nooks and crannies, Santana was careful to record everything his suitcam "saw." That included the Ramanthian-made vehicles that were parked in turnouts, "bug" script that had been spray-painted onto the walls, and occasional sorties into side caverns stuffed with supplies. All of which would be of interest to Intel.

But all the while the company commander couldn't escape the feeling that he and his companions were under surveillance as the T-2s monitored their sensors and their lights probed the murk ahead. But there was nothing to see until the trap closed around them. The mine was a maze of cross tunnels and vertical access shafts. So by hiding two levels above the main tunnel, and dropping spiderlike into the main passageway, the Ramanthians were able to land *behind* the legionnaires and thereby block their escape route. That was the plan anyway, and it would have been successful, had it not been for Lieutenant Zolkin. Having been assigned the drag position, and given strict orders to ". . . Watch our six," the officer's T-2 had been forced to walk backwards much of the time.

Even so, if the officer hadn't been so clumsy as to drop a bag of grenades, which he was then forced to jump down and retrieve, Nohar might have been able to land his file undetected. But such was not the case as Zolkin lifted the sack, saw a space-armored Ramanthian appear out of nowhere, and threw a grenade up corridor. All without pausing to think about it. The enemy trooper was blown to smithereens, and Zolkin was back on Tebo before the rest of the squad could respond. The sequence of actions earned the platoon leader a precious "well done" from Santana.

Thanks to the early warning, the legionnaires were able to fight their way back toward the main lock even as a dozen heavily armed troopers fell on them, and the interior of the mine shaft was transformed into a hellish nightmare of strobing muzzle flashes, exploding grenades, and wildly swinging lights. "Form on me!" Santana ordered. "Pull back toward the lock!"

Having only a small force of T-2s, and facing an unknown number of enemy troops, Santana knew he was in trouble. The decision to enter the mine had been a gamble, one he regretted, so it was time to salvage what he could.

Once the ambush site was behind them, the officer ordered the T-2s to turn and fire as a group, before making a run for the lock. And it was then, as the cyborgs began to pick up speed, that the ground started to shake. Clouds of dust and smoke were injected into the main tunnel even as slabs of rock fell from above and holes opened in the floor. And that's where Staff Sergeant Carol Yanty and her T-2 went, as a fissure appeared in front of them, and Private Su Hopson stepped into the hole.

Santana, who had intentionally stationed himself at the tail end of the fleeing column, swore as the twosome disappeared and daylight appeared up ahead. "Run!" the officer shouted, as a wall of smoke, dust, and flying debris began to overtake the legionnaires from behind. "Run like hell!"

But the T-2s needed no urging, and were already moving as quickly as they could when the final charges went off, and a plug of poisonous air helped expel them from the mine. It was dark inside the dust cloud, but the cyborgs could "see" with their sensors and were able to keep going until the smoke finally cleared and it was possible to stop. Dekar turned to look back, which meant Santana did as well, not that there was much to see. A pile of rubble marked the spot where the entry lock had been. The dust cloud was starting to disperse and the hill off to the right had been scarred by a new landslide.

The essence of the mission, which was to confirm that the Ramanthians were present, and dislodge or kill them, had been achieved. But at what cost? Half the squad had been killed, and thousands of tons of potentially useful supplies were buried in the mine. All of which left Santana feeling more than a little depressed as he led his troops back toward the company's temporary base. Stars started to twinkle as the sun set, darkness claimed the land, and the long bloody day came to an end.

ABOARD THE TROOP TRANSPORT *CYNTHIA HARMON*

More than one standard day had passed since the battle inside the mine, the loss of four legionnaires and thousands of tons of supplies. All of which weighed heavily on Santana as he made his way down the ship's main corridor to the cabin assigned to Battalion Commander Liam Quinlan. Where he expected to get his ass royally chewed. Or, worse yet, face formal charges.

Private Kay Kaimo had been assigned to stand guard outside Quinlan's door. The legionnaire came to attention as her company commander approached and rendered a rifle salute with her CA-10. Santana responded with a salute of his own, rapped his knuckles on the knock block next to the hatch, and waited for a response. It came quickly. "Enter!"

Santana took three paces forward, executed a smart right face, and took one additional step. That put him directly in front of the Battalion Commander as he came to attention. It was widely known that Quinlan was fifty-six years old, had been passed over for lieutenant colonel on two different occasions, and would have been forced into retirement had it not been for the war. As the Confederacy's armed forces began to ramp up in order to deal with the Ramanthians, there was a desperate shortage of experienced officers. That meant Quinlan, and others like him, were likely to be promoted. Santana's eyes were focused on a point about six inches above the other man's head, but he could still see quite a bit. The man in front of him had small, piggy eyes, prissy lips, and pendent jowls. His uniform was at least half a size too small for him and tight where a potbelly pushed against it. Quinlan nodded politely. "At ease, Captain. Have a seat."

The invitation came as something of a surprise to Santana, who fully expected to receive his tongue-lashing in the vertical position, consistent with long-standing tradition. The navy had provided two guest chairs, both of which were bolted to the deck, and Santana chose the one on the right. The cabin was three times larger than the box assigned to him and was intended to serve Quinlan as office, conference room, and sleeping quarters all rolled into one.

However, unlike most of the Legion's senior officers, who saw no reason to personalize a space soon to be left behind, Quinlan was known to travel with a trunkful of personal items calculated to make his tent, hab, or stateroom more comfortable. For that reason all manner of photos, plaques, and memorabilia were on display, items that would quickly be transformed into a galaxy of floating trash were the *Harmon*'s argrav generators to drop off-line.

But that wasn't Santana's problem, so the company commander kept his mouth shut as Quinlan selected an old-fashioned swagger stick from the items on the top of his desk and began to twirl it about. "So," the major began. "I read your after-action report, and while it was essentially correct, it was my opinion that you were excessively hard on yourself."

Santana, who was still in the process of recovering from what he considered to be a flawed performance, was astounded. "If you say so, sir," the cavalry officer replied cautiously. "But I continue to feel that our casualties were too high—and I regret the loss of those supplies."

"Nonsense," Quinlan said dismissively. "The Navy will dig the supplies out in a matter of weeks. You did all anyone reasonably could. . . . That's why I took the liberty of rewriting certain sections of your report, which I would like you to read and sign. Go ahead," the senior officer said invitingly, as he made use of the swagger stick to push the hard copy in Santana's direction. "Take a look."

Quinlan tapped his right cheek with the leather-clad stick as Santana skimmed the words in front of him. The essence of the situation quickly became clear. While ostensibly changing the report so as to benefit one of his subordinates, Quinlan was actually taking care of himself! Because he would remain as *acting* battalion commander until such time as his promotion to lieutenant colonel came through. And even though that was pretty much a done deal, it wouldn't hurt to pump some positive field reports into BUPERS while he was waiting. Especially if the incoming data addressed the area where the major's résumé was the thinnest. Which was actual combat.

While Santana knew Quinlan had never gone down to the planet's surface, those who read the report would assume he had, and would give the portly officer at least partial credit for what would appear to be a successful mission after Santana's self-critical comments had been removed. When the cavalry officer's eyes came up off the last page, Quinlan's were waiting for him. "So," the major said mildly. "Unless you spotted a factual error of some sort, I would appreciate your signature."

Santana wanted to object—but had no grounds to do so other than his suspicions. Which, were he to voice them, would sound churlish and ungrateful. So, there was nothing he could say or do, other than to sign the report and return the stylus to Quinlan's obsessively neat desk. "Excellent," the other man said, as he took the hard copy and put it aside. "Now that we have that out of the way we can talk off the record. Man-to-man if you will. Beginning with your proclivity for insubordination."

It was at that point that Santana understood how skillfully he had been manipulated. Though unwilling to cast the outcome of the mission in a negative light where official records were concerned, lest that spoil his long-awaited promotion, Quinlan was free to *say* whatever he chose. The hatch was open too, which meant Private Kaimo was intended to hear, so she could share the high-level drama with her peers. "Yes," the major continued, as if in response to an unvoiced objection from Santana. "Gross insubordination. Which, if it weren't for the pressures of combat, I would feel compelled to put into writing."

My God, Santana thought to himself. *He's speaking for the record! On the chance that I'm recording him!*

"But it's my hope that a verbal warning will suffice," Quinlan said reasonably. "When I give orders, I expect them to be obeyed, regardless of the circumstances. Understood?"

There was only one answer that the cavalry officer could give. "Sir, yes sir."

"Good," Quinlan said contentedly. "It's my hope that you will prove to be a more reliable leader than your father was."

The surprise that Santana felt must have been visible on his face because the other officer reacted to it. "Yes," Quinlan confirmed. "Back when I was a newly hatched lieutenant, and your father was a staff sergeant, we served together. Unfortunately, I found Sergeant Santana to be a somewhat hardheaded young man who was frequently disrespectful and occasionally insubordinate. Which is, I suppose, how *you* came by it."

"Top" Santana had been killed fighting the Thraks inside the Clone Hegemony. During the years prior to being admitted to the academy, Santana had spent very little time with his father. No more than twelve months spread over eighteen years. Just one of the many disadvantages of being born into a military family. But Santana remembered the man with the hard eyes, knew what he expected from the officers he reported to, and could imagine the extent to which Second Lieutenant Quinlan had fallen short. "Yes," the cavalry officer replied gravely. "My father made a strong impression on me."

"Enough said," the major replied, as if conferring a favor. "We'll be back on Adobe six days from now—where we can build on this experience to make the battalion even more effective. Dismissed."

Most of us are going back, Santana thought to himself. *But four of our legionnaires will remain here.* The dark-haired officer rose and saluted.

Quinlan made use of his swagger stick to acknowledge the gesture, let the back of the chair absorb his considerable weight, and watched Santana leave. *I own you,* the officer thought to himself. *And, when the need arises, I will spend you as I see fit.*

2

And a great pestilence will be upon the stars, as billions are born, and billions must die.

—*Author unknown*
The Pooonara Book of Prophecies
Standard year 1010 B.C.

ABOARD THE RAMANTHIAN CARRIER *SWARM*

The carrier was in hyperspace, so the enormous hangar bay was pressurized as General Oro Akoto looked out over the two thousand eight hundred members of the *Death Hammer* Regiment. The *Hammer*, as it was popularly known, consisted of three battalions of crack troopers who were all standing at attention as they waited for the new Queen to appear. They were dressed in ceremonial attire, rather than combat armor, and stood with their wings respectfully vertical. The air was thick with the combined odors of chitin wax, cold metal, and ozone.

Akoto's division included two other regiments as well, each on its own ship, as a Ramanthian Battle Group that consisted of more than fifty vessels prepared to strike deep into the Clone Hegemony. A powerful force, or that's how it appeared, but the general knew better. The truth was that only one-third of the division, the regiment now before him, was truly battle-ready. The other regiments had been cobbled together from support battalions, reserve units, and so-called veteran volunteers. Meaning middle-aged warriors who were fit for garrison duty but not much else. However, the choice to use such a force was not motivated by desperation, but the Queen's belief that it would be adequate for the job, even if Akoto wasn't so sure. Would the previous sovereign have overridden his judgment? No, the old warrior didn't believe so, but the new Queen was very different from the "great mother," the much-loved monarch who had sacrificed herself in order to bring more than five billion new citizens into the galaxy.

Akoto's thoughts were interrupted by a ceremonial blare of foot-powered battle horns as the Queen shuffled up a ramp to join him on the speaker's platform. In marked contrast to the great mother, who had been incapacitated by her egg-swollen body during the final years of her life, the new monarch was not only extremely fit but dressed in spotless combat armor, signifying her intention to take the same risks her subjects did. It was a decision that horrified her advisors and thrilled the Ramanthian populace.

As the so-called warrior queen arrived on the platform, and Akoto bent a knee, the officer felt his body respond to the cloud of pheromones that surrounded the royal. The chemicals caused him and every other Ramanthian who came into contact with them to feel protective, receptive, and willingly subservient. The royal's space black eyes glittered with intelligence as she motioned for the officer to rise. "Good morning, General. . . . Or is it afternoon? It's hard to tell sealed inside this ship."

It was a simple joke. But one that made her seem more accessible. The banter was captured by the hovering fly cams that were present to record the moment for both historical and propaganda purposes. It was just one of the many tasks for which Chancellor Itnor Ubatha had responsibility. The civilian followed the monarch out onto the platform, took his place behind her, and felt a sense of satisfaction as he looked out over the warriors arrayed in front of the royal. Ramanthian citizens everywhere would feel a sense of pride as they watched their Queen address her troops prior to battle.

"Greetings," the Queen said, as she stepped up to the mike. And that was the moment when the members of the *Hammer* realized that the royal was wearing armor identical to theirs. The high honor elicited a loud *clack* of approval as 5,600 pincers opened and closed at the same time.

"Seek approval, and enjoy its warmth, but under no circumstances come to rely on it." That was one of the many teachings that the Queen had learned from her predecessor, which was why she made a conscious effort to discount the applause, and went straight to the point. Her much-amplified voice was piped into every nook and cranny of the ship. "By this time tomorrow, you will be on the surface of Gamma-014 doing battle with the Clone Hegemony," the royal said. "There are two reasons for this. First, because the clones are human and will inevitably be drawn to their own kind. And second, because Gamma-014 is rich in a mineral called iridium, which we need for a multiplicity of applications."

Ubatha had heard both arguments before but remained unconvinced. Yes, the clones came from human stock, but they believed themselves to be both morally and physically superior to the rest of the "free-breeding" species. That meant there was an opportunity to drive a wedge between the two groups, or would have been, had the royal been willing to pursue diplomacy rather than war. And there were plenty of other planets with significant deposits of corrosion-resistant iridium, so why go after Gamma-014? Unless there was a *third* reason for the unprovoked attack, something the Queen wasn't ready to share with even her most senior advisors—but would prove compelling once it was understood. Ubatha hoped so. Because the alternative was to conclude that the new sovereign wasn't all that bright. A depressing thought indeed.

"You will have the element of surprise," the Queen assured her troops. "And you will outnumber clone military forces two to one. But most importantly, you will be armed with the inherent superiority of the Ramanthian race, which is destined to rule the galaxy." That was the line the regiment's political officers had been waiting for, and they took the lead as a resounding *clack* echoed between durasteel bulkheads.

"Finally," the monarch concluded. "Know this. When *you* land on Gamma-014, *I* will land with you."

That statement resulted in a storm of frenzied clacking, which continued even after the royal had left the platform and made her way down to the deck below. The people of Gamma-014 didn't know it yet, but death was on the way.

PLANET GAMMA-014, THE CLONE HEGEMONY

The Ramanthian attack came without warning as dozens of warships emerged from hyperspace, quickly destroyed the tiny contingent of navy vessels that were in orbit around the planet, and spewed hundreds of aerospace fighters into the atmosphere. There were no pronouncements from space and no requests for surrender, as the sleek aircraft began a carefully planned series of surgical strikes. Precision-guided bombs hit government buildings, leveled power plants, and flattened the main military base. The targeting data had been gathered by Ramanthian, Thraki, and Drac merchants during the preceding year.

But, thanks to careful planning on the part of General Akoto, certain airfields, roads, and bridges were spared. The reason for that strategy soon became apparent as a swarm of assault boats dropped out of space, bucked their way down through the planet's frigid atmosphere, and sought their preassigned landing zones. There were only twenty-three major cities on the sparsely settled planet, so it wasn't long before they were in enemy pincers, as the Queen landed and symbolically entered the rubble-strewn capital. The fact that she was carrying an assault rifle wasn't lost on the population of the Ramanthian home planet when they saw the video less than an hour later. The propaganda coup would have been impossible back when messages were carried aboard ships or faster-than-light (FTL) message torpedoes. But now, thanks to the new hypercom technology that had been developed by Ramanthian scientists, real-time communication over interstellar distances was an everyday reality.

Decisive though the alien victory was, there were holdouts. One was a clone officer named Colonel Jonathan Alan Seebo-62,666, who, like all of the soldiers both above and below him, was a genetic replica of a dead hero who was said to have embodied all of the military virtues. Which was why the original Seebo had been chosen by founder Carolyn Hosokowa to "father" an entire army.

This approach, when replicated across *all* professions, was intended to produce ideal citizens, each playing his or her part in a nearly perfect society. But even though their genes were identical, each clone had different experiences, which made them individuals. Some of whom, like the increasing number of people who favored "free breeding," threatened to bring the carefully designed social structure crashing down around them. For there was no place for so-called accidental people in a strictly hereditary society. Or that's the way Colonel Six and other social conservatives saw it.

Of course all such concerns were placed on the back burner when the Ramanthians attacked. Once it became clear that the planet's orbital defenses had been crushed, and the Ramanthians were landing in force, "Colonel Six," as most people called him, took immediate action. The officer was in charge of the army's Cold Weather Survival school located at the foot of a rugged mountain range. It was a military facility that had been used to train thousands of troops over the years but was currently on hiatus until the *really* cold weather set in. That meant only forty-six instructors and support personnel were present. That was the bad news. The *good* news was that all the Seebos under the colonel's command were battle-hardened veterans who knew how to survive in a wintry environment and fight a guerrilla-style war, which was what the clone officer fully intended to do.

And, thanks to the fact that Six was in charge of a facility that was both remote and intentionally primitive, the bugs left the Spartan base alone as the Seebos took all of the supplies they could carry, loaded them onto genetically engineered pack animals, and disappeared into the mountains. It was a seemingly meaningless event in the grand scheme of things, but one that would cost the Ramanthians dearly over the days and weeks to come. For there was only one thing more dangerous than winter on Gamma-014, and that was Colonel Six.

PLANET ALPHA-001, THE CLONE HEGEMONY

A significant portion of the spaceport had been sealed off from regular traffic, flags snapped in a stiff breeze, and rows of Jonathan Alan Seebos stood at attention as the spotless shuttle settled onto its skids. As the main hatch began to cycle open, a band comprised of nearly identical musicians struck up "All Hail to the Confederacy," which seemed pretty unlikely as the Ramanthians won battle after battle, and the government was forced to go looking for new allies. The once-hostile Hudathans were on board, but the Clone Hegemony considered itself to be nonaligned, something President Marcott Nankool was determined to change as he stepped out into bright sunlight.

A receiving line that consisted of senior government officials was waiting to greet Nankool and his staff as they stepped onto the blast-scarred tarmac. The clones who had met the president on previous occasions took note of the fact that he was at least forty pounds lighter since his stint in a Ramanthian POW camp.

Precedence is important where diplomatic matters are concerned, so Christine Vanderveen found herself toward the tail end of the Confederacy's delegation, in spite of her recent promotion from Foreign Service Officer (FSO)-3 to FSO-2. It involved a significant increase in authority and responsibility that was partly the result of the manner in which she had distinguished herself while on Jericho. An experience shared with Nankool, who had been on his way to visit the Hegemony, when captured by the enemy.

But rather than resent her relatively low status in the delegation, Vanderveen relished it, knowing that very little would be expected of her until actual negotiations got under way. That meant she had more time to look around and absorb the atmosphere as her superiors shook hands with peers, told lies about how wonderful the Hegemony was, and began what was sure to be a high-stakes round of negotiations. Because without help from the Hegemony, which was to say hundreds of thousands of Seebos, there was a very real possibility that the Confederacy would dissolve into its component parts, all of whom would vie with each other to cut a deal with the Ramanthians.

As Vanderveen made her way down the receiving line, one of the first people she ran into was Ewen Ishimoto-Nine, the Hegemony's ambassador to the Confederacy. He was normally stationed on Algeron, where the Confederacy's government had taken up temporary residence, but was home because of the visit. Rather than kiss her on the cheek, as the diplomat normally would, Vanderveen's counterpart was careful to shake her hand instead. Because kissing, like all other aspects of free-breeder sex, was officially frowned upon. "Christine," Ishimoto-Nine said warmly. "I was so very happy to hear of your safe return."

Vanderveen said, "Thank you," and wanted to talk more but was forced to move on. That was when she was introduced to Henry Hyde-Fifteen, the deputy secretary of state, as well as his boss, Carly Chambers-Ten, the secretary of state, both of whom were friendly if somewhat distant. Normally at least one of the Hegemony's three Alpha Clones would have been present to receive a head of state, but none were. Was that an intentional snub? Or a manifestation of how busy they were? There was no way to know.

The bar codes that all of the clones wore on their foreheads took some getting used to, as did the fact that when Vanderveen looked over at the band, the only factor that distinguished one musician from the next was their relative ages. But there wasn't all that much time for reflection as the receiving line spit her out and the officer in charge of Nankool's security detail herded the VIPs toward a convoy of six-wheeled limos, each of which flew a small Confederacy flag from whip-style antennae. The legionnaire didn't look the least bit like Santana but had a similar manner and served to remind the diplomat of the leave the two of them had shared on Earth. Where was he, she wondered? Back on Adobe? Or on his way to some other hellhole? It wasn't easy maintaining a relationship when both of them were on the move and a war was under way.

Orders were given, doors slammed, and the convoy departed. Having found herself in a car with three administrative assistants, Vanderveen took advantage of her new rank and maintained a lordly silence. Bio bods mounted on Trooper IIs jogged alongside the vehicles, weapons at the ready, as the motorcade left the spaceport and entered the city beyond. The metroplex was a study in symmetry. Grid-style streets met each other at right angles, box-shaped buildings stood in orderly rows, and a cookie-cutter park occupied every sixth block.

But, having read the fifty-page intelligence summary that Madam Xanith's people had prepared for Nankool and his staff, Vanderveen knew that the city was actually less orderly than it appeared. Tensions were seething just below the surface—including the discontent being voiced by a nascent opposition party. Young people, for the most part, some of whom were rumored to be "naturals," and hoped to overthrow the hereditary dictatorship in favor of a democracy. The opposition consisted of social conservatives and secret death squads that might or might not include members of the police.

As if summoned by her thoughts, two clone policemen,

both riding gyro-stabilized unicycles, pulled even with Vanderveen's limo. Both wore white helmets equipped with face shields, black body armor, and combat boots. One of the clones looked straight at the diplomat, and she felt a chill run down her spine, as he nodded and accelerated away.

The motorcade turned onto a tree-lined boulevard shortly after that. Ranks of citizens lined both sides of the street. They had been ordered to come out and welcome Nankool to Alpha-001 whether they wanted to or not. And because the Hegemony's citizens had been prevented from intermarrying, and reproducing in what Vanderveen considered to be the normal manner, they stood in the racial groupings that coincided with their professions. Computer technicians here, dental assistants there, and so forth all according to a plan handed down from on high. *What are they thinking?* the diplomat wondered, as the black, brown, and white faces slid by. *Do they favor an alliance with us? Would they prefer to go it alone?* There was no way to tell because, in keeping with the orderly nature of clone society, citizens weren't allowed to cheer, hurl insults, or pepper the motorcade with rotten fruit. All the clones could do was wait for the foreign dignitaries to roll past, then return to their jobs.

By peering past the driver, Vanderveen could see the low, boxlike structure that lay ahead. It was topped with a dome and soon proved to be the motorcade's destination as the lead vehicle swept around a circular driveway and paused under a formal portico, where a clutch of ominous T-2s stood waiting. Many of the cyborgs wore the machine equivalent of tattoos—some of which were quite fanciful.

It took a while for the more senior officials to exit their cars, but Vanderveen's opportunity eventually came, and the diplomat followed a gaggle of talkative undersecretaries into the capitol building. A formal reception area led to a short flight of stairs and the corridor beyond. Heels clicked on stone, and voices echoed between barren walls, as a guide led the presidential party past a checkpoint and into the Chamber of Governmental Process.

It was a large circular room with a highly polished white floor. Triangles of shiny black marble pointed in toward the center of the space, where a beautiful green-and-blue double helix served as both pillar and sculpture. Vanderveen knew the column was intended to represent a single molecule of a chemical substance called deoxyribonucleic acid, or DNA, which is the basic building block of all living organisms. The symbol had religious as well as scientific significance for the clones.

The sculpture shimmered as bars of light representing the four chemical compounds called bases floated upwards and disappeared into the ceiling. A circular table fronted the column, and a man rose to greet them. The Alpha Clone went by the name Antonio Seven. His hair had once been black, and shiny with pomade, but that was long ago. Now it was white, and what remained of once-thick curls circled the ruler's head like a silver crown. What hadn't changed were the almost military manner in which he held his body, the Spartan black tunic that he favored, and the matching pantaloon-style pants. His bare feet made a *slapping* sound as he came forward to embrace Nankool. "Greetings old friend!" the Alpha Clone said warmly. "I'm afraid that Marcus is too sick to join us, and Pietro sends his apologies. The demands of government require his presence elsewhere." That was a lie, since Pietro rarely did much of anything anymore, preferring to sit on his veranda and paint. But Antonio saw no reason to disclose that, both because it would have been disloyal to do so, and because it suited his purposes to conceal the extent to which he ran the government.

The next forty-five minutes or so were spent making introductions, and consuming a seemingly endless procession of appetizers, as both sides began to jockey for position. This was a rather chaotic process in which Vanderveen found herself going one-on-one with a clone general. The topic of conversation was the pros and cons of Ramanthian assault rifles, a subject about which the military man was surprised to learn the young woman was quite knowledgeable.

Meanwhile, unbeknownst to all but those gathered around Nankool and Antonio, a messenger arrived. After scanning the piece of paper that had been handed to him the Alpha Clone frowned. Nankool could sense that something important was in the offing and was paying close attention when the other man opened his mouth to speak. "My apologies, ladies and gentlemen," Antonio said gravely. "But I just received word that Gamma-014 has been attacked by the Ramanthian Empire. And, based on preliminary reports, it appears the planet has fallen."

Gasps of surprise were heard, along with expressions of incredulity, as everyone sought to absorb the terrible news. Except that Nankool, who should have been sad, felt wildly jubilant instead. Because here it was! A heaven-sent opportunity to secure the alliance he so desperately needed! But none of that was visible on the politician's face as he offered his condolences. "I'm very sorry to hear that," the head of state said soberly. "And I'm sure I speak for the entire Confederacy when I say that we stand ready to fight side by side with people of the Hegemony to stop Ramanthian aggression."

Vanderveen, who was close enough to hear, was impressed by the way the chief executive had been able not only to seize upon the unexpected opportunity but to do so in such a graceful manner. Meanwhile Antonio, who was increasingly burdened by his age, felt an impending sense of doom. Because not only was there the fate of Gamma-014 to consider but it was likely that troublemakers within the Hegemony would use the Ramanthian attack to advance their demands for change. But it would have been a mistake to say any of those things out loud, or to accept Nankool's offer of assistance without giving such an alliance careful thought, so Antonio sought to push the matter off. "Thank you for your condolences," the Alpha Clone said feelingly. "We appreciate your kind thoughts. Now, if you will excuse us, my staff and I have work to do. I'm sure you understand."

"Of course," Nankool replied kindly. "Thank you for your hospitality."

Antonio departed a few minutes later—with most of his senior officials in tow. Given all the time they had spent together on Jericho, there was a special bond between Nankool and Vanderveen. A relationship the diplomat sought to downplay for the most part—but allowed her to address the president directly when she chose to do so. "So what do you think?" the foreign service officer inquired, as she appeared at Nankool's elbow.

"I think the bugs are going to be sorry," the president of the Confederacy of Sentient Beings said grimly, as he popped a ripe olive into his mouth. "Very sorry indeed."

PLANET ADOBE, THE CONFEDERACY OF SENTIENT BEINGS

The robot army attacked at night, when their sensors would give them a significant advantage over the Legion's bio bods, at least half of whom would probably be asleep. And, because Major Liam Quinlan had placed Alpha Company, 2nd Battalion, 1st REC along the front edge of the desert escarpment, they were the ones who took the brunt of the assault as the oncoming horde sought to break through the defenders and reach the power plant beyond.

There were three types of robots, starting with skeletal androids, who stood six feet tall and carried assault weapons. Then came so-called rollers, which traveled on four fat tires but were equipped with six, and built in such a manner that they could perform somersaults and keep on going. Behind them were the aptly named slabs, which were low, heavily armed tanklike vehicles, specifically designed to engage the Legion's quads, who were armed with machine guns, energy cannons, *and* missiles. They unleashed a barrage of fire that swept across the top of the escarpment as hundreds of robots rushed forward to close with the enemy.

Santana heard the explosions, rolled off his air mattress, and was exiting the command bunker when a simulated rocket landed not ten feet away. There was a flash of light, followed by a loud *bang*, and something analogous to a mild electric shock as the indicator light attached to his body armor went from green to red. As that took place Santana's name vanished off the ITC, and First Lieutenant Lucy Amoyo was put in command.

All of which was readily apparent to General Mortimer Kobbi, who was seated in the command quad five miles to the rear, watching to see how the battalion would deal with the unexpected onslaught. It was disappointing to lose Santana early on, but that was often the way of things, and having served with the cavalry officer on Savas, the general was already acquainted with the young man's capabilities. So it was with considerable interest that Kobbi watched Amoyo rally the badly mauled company as the first wave of androids boiled up over the escarpment, a development Kobbi could monitor by listening to the company push and switching between the various video feeds that continued to pour in from bio bods and cyborgs alike.

Meanwhile Santana, who was no longer allowed to interact with his subordinates, went in search of a place to sit and watch the action without getting in the way. Having found a flat rock, and placed his back against a boulder, Santana alternated between scanning the highly codified data available on his helmet's HUD and the fireworks going off all around him. A line of simulated explosions rippled along the face of the escarpment as Dietrich triggered the mines placed there the evening before, and static rattled through the cavalry officer's helmet speakers as electronic counter measures (ECM) took roughly 10 percent of the aggressor bots off-line.

Dozens of robots had been neutralized by that time and would remain right where they were until reactivated at the end of the exercise. But there were more of them, and Alpha Company was soon forced to fall back, as a tidal wave of androids and rollers came up over the ten-foot-high embankment. The battle was very realistic. So much so that Santana felt a moment of fear as a squad of robots stalked past him, their heads swiveling back and forth, their weapons at port arms. His heat signature was clear to see, but so was his indicator light, so the hostiles left Santana alone as a flare went off high above them. The eerie light threw harsh shadows toward the west, as the survivors of Alpha Company were forced to fall back on the rest of the battalion, and the fake power plant beyond.

Which raised a rather interesting question. . . . Where was the normally assertive Major Quinlan? Because so far, in spite of repeated calls from Amoyo, there had been no contact with Bat HQ other than with the CO's radio tech (RT), who was busy routing everything to Captain Mitch Mays of Bravo Company because the XO had theoretically been "killed" by an infiltrator.

It was a question that was of interest to General Kobbi as well, since Quinlan was still "alive" according to the ITC, but literally missing in action. There was a pause in the fighting as Mays allowed the surviving members of Alpha Company to pass through his lines, followed by eerie screams as a flight of unseen fly-forms swept in to provide close air support. Thunder rolled across the arid landscape as electronic "bombs" fell on the horde, flashed as they went off, and left dozens of machines motionless on the battlefield. That was when Quinlan's voice was finally heard. It sounded thick, as if the officer had just awoken, and was a bit disoriented. "This is Zulu Six. . . . Alpha, no Bravo Company, will pull back to the defensive wall and hold. Over."

"No!" Santana said out loud. "There's no way *through* the wall! The robots will crush Bravo Company against it!"

Of course Captain Mays was no fool, and could see the same thing, since the very real steel wall that protected the fake power plant was twelve feet high, and the only entrance to the enclosure was on the southern rather than the northern perimeter. So the officer objected, was immediately put down, and forced to obey Quinlan's orders. With predictable results. Half an hour later, just as the sun started to peek up over the eastern horizon, the last member of the 2nd Battalion, 1st REC was officially killed. His name was Liam Quinlan—and his promotion to lieutenant colonel came through later that same day.

PLANET JERICHO, THE RAMANTHIAN EMPIRE

As the imperial battleship *Merciless* and her escorts dropped into orbit around the Planet Jericho, the Queen was in the control room to witness the event. Not because the regent hadn't seen a ship make planet fall before, but because the world below was of particular interest to her. Viewed from space, it was a beautiful planet, one of a number of such worlds granted to the empire in partial restitution for damage suffered during the Hudathan wars. It was a Hive-normal planet, which meant it was Earth-normal, too, and had been home to an advanced civilization long before her race had risen to sentience. Evidence of that could still be seen in the ruins scattered about the world's emerald green surface.

But that was ancient and therefore boring history as far as the royal was concerned. Because her purpose in visiting Jericho was to assess the condition of the Ramanthian nymphs that had been hatched there over the last few months, thousands of whom had been left to fend for themselves in the wake of a commando-style raid by Confederacy forces. It was a calamity that she, as their moral, if not actual, parent, was obliged to mitigate.

Five hours later the Queen shuffled down a ramp and onto the surface of Jericho. The airstrip, which had only recently been carved out of the forest some twenty miles west of what had been Jericho Prime, was protected by guard towers and an electrified fence. The air immediately around the royal yacht was heavy with the acrid stench of ozone, and a series of loud *pings* was heard, as hot metal started to cool. Moments later an entire file of heavily armed Raman-thian troopers moved in to protect the royal, not from alien soldiers, but an equally potent threat.

The officer in charge of the so-called reorientation center had been a largely unknown military functionary prior to being put in charge of the experimental facility. And, not having met a member of the royal family before, never mind the Queen herself, was understandably nervous as he bent a leg. "Welcome to Jericho, Majesty. Commander Sool Fobor, at your service."

"What are the fences for?" the royal inquired bluntly. "Do animals attack the airstrip?"

Fobor looked from the Queen to Chancellor Ubatha as if beseeching him for help. One of the problems traditionally associated with the tercentennial birthing was that after mil-lions of nymphs were born, the youngsters went through a wilding state during which they hunted in packs, killing and eating anything they came across before gradually becoming more biddable. It was a process that had been extremely hard on both Hive and Ramanthian society over the past 200,000-plus years. Which was why the great mother ordered her sub-ordinates to acquire planets like Jericho and seed them with eggs. And with predictable results. Because once hatched, the voracious predators began to roam Jericho like blood-crazed beasts, killing everything they encountered—members of their own species included. So, never having dealt with a royal be-fore, Fobor didn't know how to respond. Ubatha came to his rescue. "The fences are positioned to keep the nymphs out, Your Excellency," the Chancellor put in carefully. "They can be quite violent as you know."

"Not anymore," the Queen objected staunchly, as she eyed the tree line. "The wilding should have been over weeks ago."

"True," Ubatha replied patiently. "Except that once the aliens destroyed the processing centers, the nymphs were left on their own. And, in the absence of proper socializa-tion, some of them turned feral."

"We're doing the best we can," Fobor said defensively. "But having missed the point in their neurological development where the nymphs are most biddable, it's been very difficult to work with them. Perhaps her majesty would allow me to show her one of the holding pens?"

The Queen thought the term "holding pen" was objectionable, but rather than strike out at the officer the way she wanted to, she managed to keep her temper in check. "Show me," she grated.

So the royal entourage was invited to board armored cars, which passed through a gate and followed a dirt road into the jungle. Though unable to look up through the metal roof, the royal ordered the driver to open the vehicle's windows. That allowed the Queen to peer out into the sun-dappled depths of the triple-canopy forest that surrounded them. It was an environment very similar to the equatorial zone on Hive, where the Ramanthian race had risen to sentience. The process had been heavily influenced by the fact that the species had been gifted with *two* types of females. Most females could lay a maximum of *three* eggs, thereby replacing one three-person family unit, while a small number, like the Queen herself, were physiologically capable of producing *billions* of new citizens. Just as her predecessor had. Not frequently, but every three hundred years or so, as the overall population began to level off or decline.

The general effect of that phenomenon was to push the race forward, but at the expense of social turmoil, and terrible famines. *But not anymore,* the royal thought to herself. *Now we can hatch our eggs on planets like this one and protect the citizens of Hive from harm.* That was the plan anyway, but owing to a series of unforeseen events, the local maturation process had been compromised.

There was a commotion as the convoy came to a halt, and troopers were deployed to form a protective ring around the Queen and her entourage as the visitors exited their vehicles. It was hot and humid, so the royal removed her green cloak, and threw it into the back of the armored car. That left her wearing light body armor over a sleek bodysuit. Not the sort of outfit the great mother would have approved of.

By that time Ubatha, as well as the rest of the royal party, had become aware of the acrid scent of urine and a low-pitched *gibbering* sound that emanated from someplace nearby. "Please follow me," Commander Fobor instructed, and led the Queen's entourage along a path that wound through the trees. Moments later the group emerged into a clearing in which heavy equipment had been used to dig three enormous pits. Each was about two hundred feet across, roughly fifty feet deep, and covered with wire mesh so the inmates couldn't escape by using their wings. The ever-present fly cams darted out to capture shots of the facility, but were soon recalled, since it wasn't the sort of video deemed appropriate for the empire's citizens to see.

An observation platform had been constructed next to Pit One, and the rest of the party followed as Fobor shuffled up onto the flat surface. Meanwhile, down in the muddy cavity below, a pair of sharp-beaked nymphs were fighting to see which one of them would get to consume a chunk of raw meat. The rest of the prisoners, some twenty in all, made growling sounds and appeared ready to rush in if there was an opportunity to advantage themselves. "We capture them out in the jungle," Fobor explained helpfully. "Then we bring them here, where our sociologists begin to work with them. Once a particular individual begins to demonstrate the right sort of behaviors, he or she is transferred to Pit Two, where further socialization takes place. Then it's on to Pit Three, graduation into a crèche, and formal schooling."

Fobor was obviously very proud of the system, and perhaps rightfully so, but when one of the combatants tore the other's throat out, that was more than the Queen could take. There was a soft *thump* as the royal jumped down onto the ground, shuffled over to the gate, and ordered the guard to open it. And, being a foot soldier, the trooper did as he was told. That enabled the monarch to pass through the first checkpoint unimpeded and begin the circular journey down to the second and last gate before anyone could stop her. Fobor was horrified and began to shout orders to his troops. "Don't let her through! Prepare to fire on the prisoners! If you hit the Queen, I'll kill you myself!"

But Ubatha, who knew the Queen as well as anyone did, had noticed a change down in the pit. Not only were the juveniles staring at her majesty—they were strangely silent. "Keep your troops on standby," the Chancellor instructed. "But allow the Queen to enter."

"But the nymphs will tear her apart!" the soldier objected.

"Do what I say, or you'll regret it," Ubatha grated. And suddenly Fobor became conscious of the fact that while some of the royal's bodyguards were aiming their weapons at the nymphs—others were pointing their assault rifles at him!

Meanwhile, as the sovereign arrived in front of gate two, she was not only unaware of the drama playing itself out up on the surface but completely focused on the young Ramanthians in the pit. She could smell the acrid odor of their urine, see the intelligence in their shiny black eyes, and *feel* the blood-bond she shared with them.

Fobor gave the only orders he could, the gate swung open, and the Queen entered the pit. The nymphs were motionless at first, and seemingly unaware of the targeting lasers that roamed their bodies as the regent plowed her way through six inches of urine, feces, and mud to reach the very center of the pit. Then, as the juveniles absorbed the rich amalgam of pheromones that surrounded the royal, a seemingly miraculous change came over them. A soft *humming* sound was heard as heads dropped, wings seemed to sag, and they shuffled inwards. It soon became clear that rather than attack the monarch, as Fobor feared, each juvenile hoped to make physical contact with her. And as the Queen reached out to touch her adopted children, she sang to them in a language as old as the first nest, and filled the air with the chemicals that they needed and wanted.

It was the most amazing thing Fobor had ever seen, and he said as much. "Yes," Ubatha agreed thoughtfully, as the royal worked her magic. "We are truly blessed."

3

The few active rebels must have the qualities of speed and endurance, ubiquity and independence of arteries of supply. They must have the technical equipment to destroy or paralyze the enemy's organized communications.

—T. E. Lawrence
"The Science of Guerrilla Warfare"
Standard year 1929

PLANET GAMMA-014, THE CLONE HEGEMONY

The town of Strat's Deep was located at the foot of the Hebron mountain range, right on top of a large deposit of nickel, about forty miles north of Tow-Tok Pass. There were a number of ways to reach the settlement, but given the fact that the Ramanthians were patrolling both the sky and the roads, Colonel Six and his men chose to approach the mining community via an old foot trail. Having arrived on a broad machine-carved ledge high above the town, the officer ordered his troops to take cover in an abandoned mine shaft, and scanned Strat's Deep through his binoculars.

The town consisted of forty identical homes, all of which were bunched together on the west side of the railroad track that had been built to haul iridium away. Though no expert on the subject, Six knew iridium was a by-product of nickel and that there were two ways to extract the element from the planet's crust. The first approach was called open-cut mining, which wasn't practical given the steep terrain, and the fact that the ore was deep underground. For that reason a series of side-by-side shafts had been driven deep into the mountainside where the newly mined material was loaded onto the low-profile tunnel trucks that were used to bring the ore down to the processing plant. And, judging from what Six could see through his binoculars, the mine was still in operation. Was that because Ramanthians had occupied the town and were forcing the humans to work? Or because the locals hadn't received instructions to shut the operation down? The latter was certainly possible given all the confusion.

The answer soon became apparent as the officer heard a loud *thrumming* sound and ducked as a Ramanthian shuttle passed overhead. The transport completed one circuit of the settlement before putting down at the center of the shabby town square. Six was still recovering from the shock associated with the aircraft's sudden appearance when a squad of Ramanthians emerged from the administration building and herded a group of humans toward the shuttle. Meanwhile, what might have been boxes of rations or ammo were being unloaded and placed on the ground. Once that task was completed, the prisoners were forced to board the alien ship, which lifted off a few moments later. Six was hidden in a cluster of boulders by the time the shuttle passed overhead and departed for the south.

The officer waited for a full five minutes to make sure that the aircraft wouldn't circle back before leaving his hiding place and crossing the ledge. Two heavily armed Seebos were on guard just inside the entrance to the mine and nodded to their CO as he entered. The rest of the company was camped about a hundred feet back and well out of sight. Lieutenant Seebo-790,444, better known to the troops as Four-Four, looked up from the pot he was tending. The junior officer looked much as Six had twenty years earlier. "Pull up a rock, sir. Your tea will be ready in a minute."

It felt good to sit down, and as Six held his hands out to collect some of the fuel tab's excess heat, he knew the chill in the air was nothing compared to what winter would bring. "So," the younger officer ventured. "How does it look?"

"The town is crawling with bugs," Six answered gloomily. "It's my guess that they were dropped in during the early hours of the invasion."

"So you were right," Lieutenant-44 mused, as he poured steaming-hot water into a metal mug. "They're after the iridium."

"It's the only thing that makes sense," Colonel Six observed as he accepted his share of the tea. "I can't think of any other reason to attack this slush ball."

Four-Four took a tentative sip from his mug, found the brew to his liking, and cupped the container with both hands. His breath fogged the air. "So what's the plan?"

"We'll wait for nightfall, go down into the valley, and kill every chit we find," Six replied coldly.

The junior officer raised an eyebrow. "And then?"

"And then we'll cut the tracks, blow the processing plant, and seal the mine. Winter's coming, so it will be a good six months before the Ramanthians can reopen the facility. Assuming we don't kick their assess off the planet before then."

Lieutenant-44 was silent for a moment as if considering what his superior had said. "What about the workers?" he inquired seriously. "There could be reprisals."

Colonel Six remembered the townspeople who had been loaded onto the Ramanthian shuttle for transportation to who knows where. "Yes," he answered soberly. "Based on reports from inside the Confederacy, reprisals are extremely likely. Those who can fight will be asked to join us. Those who can't will create places to hide in old mine shafts like this one. And the locals know where they are."

Four-Four wasn't sure how people would survive something like that but was careful to keep his thoughts to himself.

The clones spent the afternoon catching up on sleep, cooking a communal meal, and maintaining their gear. Once the

sun had set, the guerrilla fighters followed their commanding officer out of the mine shaft and down a weather-eroded
access road toward the dimly lit town below. Thanks to the
night-vision goggles they wore, everything had a greenish
glow, but the soldiers were used to that, and quickly split into
platoons. The first platoon, under Colonel Six, made its way
toward the administration building. Meanwhile the second
platoon, under Lieutenant-44, was headed for the processing
plant.

Having had the town under observation all afternoon,
the Seebos had a pretty good idea where most of the Ramanthians were, but there were other problems to cope
with. Not the least of which was the necessity to eliminate
all resistance without giving the bugs a chance to call in reinforcements. Fortunately, the clones had the element of
surprise working in their favor. But they had something else
going for them as well—and that was the strange, almost
supernatural, relationship that existed between them. Because having been created from the same DNA, and raised
with replicas of themselves, the Seebos were like fingers on
the same hand as they ghosted between the town's mostly
darkened buildings.

There was little more than a series of soft *pops* as the sentries stationed outside the administration building fell, and
the clones rushed to surround the structure. The clones knew
that the facility had two entrances, and once both of them
were covered, Six led a squad up onto the front porch. The
door seemed to open on its own as one of the bugs sought to
exit. So the officer shot him in the face and pushed his way
into the vestibule beyond.

A second door opened onto a reception area, and three
Ramanthians were already headed his way as Colonel Six entered. The officer took them down with short bursts from
his submachine gun (SMG) and shouted, "Kill the radio!" as
the rest of the squad came in behind him.

"Got it, sir!" a corporal replied as he fired three rounds
into the rugged com set that occupied one of the desks. The

alien RT took exception to that, produced a pistol, and was trying to bring the weapon to bear when the corporal fired again. The bug jerked spastically, fell over sideways, and began to leak green digestive goo onto the floor.

"Good work," Six said grimly. "Find the rest of them."

"You came!" a female voice said gratefully, as the rest of the squad went looking for additional chits. "Thanks be to the founder!"

That was when Colonel Six turned to see that half a dozen townspeople had been tied to chairs that lined one of the walls. The individual who had spoken was a member of the Mogundo line and therefore an administrator. The rest were Ortovs. A hardy line commonly used for industrial applications. "How many of you are there?" the officer demanded brusquely.

"Twenty-six," the woman replied crisply. She had brown skin, flashing black eyes, and a full figure. The officer imagined what she would look like without any clothes on, felt the usual response, and pushed the image away. Such thoughts were less frequent than they had been twenty years earlier but still plagued him.

The sound of muted gunfire interrupted the officer's thoughts as the second platoon dealt with the Ramanthians in the processing plant. "Please! Stop the fighting!" one of the Ortovs pleaded. "They have our children!"

"She's right," the administrator put in, as a soldier cut her loose. "The Ramanthians took hostages earlier today."

Six nodded. "Yes, I know. And I'm sorry. But there's nothing I can do about it. Gather your people together. . . . Tell them to pack cold-weather gear, plus food that won't spoil, and bring it here. But only what they can carry on their backs. Because the bugs will return, and when they do, they'll kill everyone they find."

"But what about our children?" the Ortov sobbed. "The ones they took?"

Under normal circumstances, on planets like Alpha-001, clone children were raised in crèchelike institutions where they could be properly socialized. But that wasn't always possible on less-developed planets like Gamma-014, where children were occasionally assigned to an appropriate community at the age of two, to be raised within the embrace of the profession to which they would one day belong. But that practice could lead to unacceptably strong bonds between individual adults and children, as was clearly the case where the distraught Ortov was concerned. Because even though she hadn't given birth to a child, she clearly *felt* as if she had, and that was wrong.

"Maybe the children will survive," Colonel Six allowed, as the Ortov was freed. "But I doubt it. The Ramanthians regard mercy as a weakness, and if we're going to beat them, we'll have to be just as hard as they are. Now stop crying, get your things, and hurry back. I plan to pull out thirty minutes from now."

The woman began to sob, and might have remained right where she was, had two of her companions not taken the miner between them and half carried her away.

"We have some explosives," the administrator said helpfully. She was determined, and Six liked that.

"Good," the Seebo replied. "That means we can save what we have. Perhaps one of your people would show us where to place them?"

The process of placing the charges, and pulling the civilians out of Strat's Deep, took the better part of an hour, rather than the thirty minutes that Six had been hoping for. But it went smoothly, and once both the townspeople and the Seebos were assembled on the ledge above town, it was safe to trigger the charges. A series of muffled *thuds* was heard, and the onlookers felt the explosions through the soles of their boots, as a rockslide clattered down a neighboring slope. "All right," Colonel Six said grimly. "The bugs will come looking for us tomorrow. Let's find a place to hide." And with that, 150 people vanished into the night.

Seven hours later, when the Ramanthians assigned to hold Strat's Deep failed to check in as they were supposed to, and attempts to contact them failed, a quick-reaction force was dispatched. It wasn't possible to assess the amount of damage inflicted on the mine shafts from the air. But there was no mistaking the fact that the railroad tracks had been severed—and the processing plant had been reduced to a pile of smoking rubble.

And when members of the elite *Hammer* regiment hit the ground, the town was empty except for the row of twenty-six Ramanthian bodies laid out in front of the admin building, and the large numbers scrawled across the facade. The paint was red, the numerals were "666," and none of the troopers knew what they meant.

A report was written, approved, and passed up through the chain of command. And, when it appeared on Okoto's computer screen, the general actually read it, a fact that would have amazed the lowly file leader who authored it.

The numbers "666" held no particular meaning for Okoto, but the officer was a student of human warfare, and widely read. Which is why he went looking for a certain file, brought it on-screen, and scanned for the passage he had in mind. It read:

"Many people think it is impossible for guerrillas to exist for long in the enemy's rear. Such a belief reveals lack of comprehension of the relationship that should exist between the people and the troops. The farmer may be likened to water and the latter to the fish who inhabit it."

The text had been authored by a man named Mao Tse-Tung. And he had been dead for a long, long time. But Okoto could tell that someone else was familiar with the revolutionary's writings as well. Someone who was very, very dangerous.

PLANET ALPHA-001, THE CLONE HEGEMONY

President Marcott Nankool and his staff were quartered in the equivalent of a large if not especially posh hotel, which the Hegemony's State Department ran for both the convenience of visiting dignitaries and its own intelligence service. The entire building was bugged, including conference rooms like the one that the visitors had been forced to meet in, which was why all of them were shooting the breeze, catching up on administrative tasks via their data pads, or simply staring into space as a team of four military technicians worked to sanitize the room. No doubt the clones would disapprove of the cleansing, but they couldn't very well complain about it without admitting that they had been spying on their guests.

The conference room was a long, rectangular space that had no architectural interest whatsoever, except for the gigantic floor-to-ceiling window that took up most of the south wall and allowed Christine Vanderveen to look out over an angular cityscape. Thanks to a very effective weather-management system, it rarely rained during the day. That meant the founder's architects had been able to count on generous amounts of natural light and calculate the way that shadows would caress their buildings before constructing them—all of which was unique to clone society insofar as Vanderveen knew.

Having located all the audio pickups, neutralized the photosensitive wall paint, and eradicated the tiny pinhead-sized robo cams that had been roaming the room, a harried-looking naval tech approached Legion General and Military Chief of Staff Bill Booly III. Although Vanderveen didn't know the officer well, she had seen him on many occasions over the years, and was surprised to see how much older he looked. He still had his mother's gray eyes and his father's athletic body. But his hair was shot with streaks of white, lines were etched into his face, and his skin was very pale, like someone who rarely gets any sun. "The room is clean, General," the tech told him. "But we can't guarantee that it will stay that way for more than an hour or so. The clones are sure to launch some sort of counterattack through the ventilation system."

Booly nodded. "That should be sufficient. Thanks for all the hard work."

The tech didn't receive many "thank-yous," especially from senior officers, and was clearly pleased as he returned to the back of the room. Vanderveen watched the general walk over and say a few words to Nankool. *Here we go,* the diplomat thought to herself, as the president nodded. All of the small talk quickly came to an end as Nankool stood. "Okay, everybody," the chief executive said, as he eyed the people assembled before him. "We have a counter from the Hegemony—so let's get to it. There's some good news and some bad news."

The announcement produced a chorus of groans, which Nankool acknowledged with a good-natured grin. "I'll give you the good news first. Alpha Clone Antonio-Seven has agreed to a military alliance with the Confederacy. Beginning with a joint task force to liberate Gamma-014."

Vanderveen joined the rest of the staff in a loud cheer. But Booly, who harbored serious misgivings about the new alliance, was noticeably silent. "And the bad news?" the officer inquired cynically, as the noise died away. "How bad is *bad*?"

It was the moment that Nankool had been dreading. There was nothing he could do but tell the truth. "Given that Gamma-014 is one of their planets, and that roughly sixty percent of the joint task force will consist of clone troops, the Hegemony wants to put one of their generals in overall command."

Booly looked down at the floor as if to momentarily hide his expression before bringing his eyes back up. Everyone in the room knew that the joint chiefs opposed such an arrangement, and for some very good reasons. Although the Hegemony's soldiers were good, the Seebos had little if any experience where joint operations were concerned. That, combined with a general air of superiority, and the very real possibility that clone officers would show favoritism toward their own kind, meant things could and probably would go wrong—the kinds of things that could cause a whole lot of casualties for the Confederacy. So, even though Booly's voice was neutral, there was no question as to how the general felt. "And your position, Mr. President?"

Booly had been loyal to Nankool, *very* loyal, and was a bona fide war hero to boot. Not to mention the fact that his wife, Maylo Chien-Chu, was the billionaire president of the star-spanning company that her uncle Sergi Chien-Chu had founded, and was therefore quite influential. So the politician wanted to make the general happy. But the alliance was important, *critically* important, even if the price was high. So there was nothing Nankool could do but look Booly in the eye and say what he believed. "I wish it were otherwise, General, but we need this alliance, and I believe we should agree to it. I promise you that *after* we take Gamma-014, the joint chiefs will be in control of the campaigns that follow."

A lump had formed in the back of Booly's throat, but he managed to swallow it. The president's mind was made up, that was clear, and given the extent of his wartime powers, Nankool had the authority to create such alliances when necessary. The Senate would have to ratify the agreement, but that would take months, and chances were that the battle for Gamma-014 would be over by the time they got around to it. For better or for worse. "Sir, yes sir," Booly said dutifully. "Has a general been chosen?"

Vanderveen saw Nankool's expression brighten as it became clear that Booly wasn't going to challenge his authority. "Why, yes," the politician answered cheerfully. "The officer the Hegemony put forward is General Seebo-785,453. Do you know him?"

Booly winced, and the staff officers seated around him were heard to *groan*. "I'll take that as a 'yes,' " Nankool responded grimly. "And I'm sorry you don't approve. But that's how it is—so we'll have to make do. Besides, once you and your staff put your minds to it, I'm sure you'll find ways to manage him the same way that you manage me!"

That got a laugh from the civilian staff, but Vanderveen could tell that the officers were disappointed, and felt sorry for them. Because now that she knew a soldier the way she knew Santana, the diplomat had a much deeper appreciation of the way in which the military was often squeezed between the vagaries of political necessity, and the realities of war.

With the alliance in place and the question of command having been settled, it was time to address logistics. The Confederacy was already hard-pressed, and the need to dedicate scarce resources to Gamma-014 meant military assets would have to be withdrawn from some other location. But which one? Each possibility entailed risk.

Eventually, all of the arguments and counterarguments began to blur, and Vanderveen's attention began to wander. Her eyes were inevitably drawn to the window at the far end of the conference room and the cityscape beyond. That was when the diplomat noticed the people on the roof across the street. And as she watched, they muscled a long cylindrical object up onto the waist-high wall in front of them. Then, having secured both sides of whatever the object was to the building, they pushed it over the side. As the roll of plastic fell free, a blue banner was revealed. The white letters were at least six feet high, and spelled out the words "FREEDOM NOW!"

Given its location, there was no doubt about whom the protesters were trying to communicate with, and since no one else seemed to be paying any attention to the sign, Vanderveen raised a hand. "Excuse me, Mr. President," the diplomat said. "But it appears as though someone is trying to send you a message."

The entire group followed Vanderveen's pointing finger over to the opposite building and not a moment too soon. Clone security agents were already on the roof by that point. It took less than five minutes for the secret police to arrest the protesters, pull the banner back up, and disappear from sight. All of which was both interesting and disturbing. Because as the Confederacy sought to prop the Hegemony up—there was the very real possibility that it had already started to crumble.

PLANET ADOBE, THE CONFEDERACY OF SENTIENT BEINGS

The Legion's base on Adobe had been constructed after the first Hudathan war, and was laid out in concentric circles, with the spaceport, which was designated A-1, located at the very center of the sprawling facility. Santana was supposed to meet General Kobbi on C-2, Sector 3, which was dedicated to supply, a simple word that embraced everything from mess kits to the state-of-the-art NAVCOMPS that naval vessels required to find their way through hyperspace. Rather than hike all the way in from F-3, where the 1st REC was quartered, or try to requisition a vehicle, Santana had chosen to ride Sergeant Omi Deker instead. It was a very good decision since the T-2 knew his way around the base.

So as the cyborg jogged along one of the main roads that radiated out from A-1, the helmeted officer was free to look around. It was not only hellishly hot, but eternally dusty, despite the water the big tanker trucks laid down four times a day. Inflatable habs lined the streets. They looked like half cylinders laid on their sides, and in spite of the fact that they weren't intended for permanent use, some of them had been there for ten or even fifteen years.

And, if there were plenty of things to see, there were plenty of things to hear as well. As the two legionnaires passed through territory that belonged to a variety of different commands, they were exposed to a cacophony of sound as power wrenches *chattered*, servos *whined*, engines *rumbled*, and a series of sonic *booms* rolled across the land. Discordant and chaotic though the base seemed to be, Santana could feel the underlying sense of purpose that bound everything together. Because even the lowliest private knew that one of the Hegemony's planets had been taken by the Ramanthians, and that the clones had agreed to an alliance, which meant many of them would wind up as part of the task force being assembled to take Gamma-014 back.

The announcement received mixed reviews in the O club,

because, in spite of the fact that most officers understood the importance of the alliance, many of them had doubts about the Hegemony's military prowess. Except for Santana, that is, who had been sent to one of the clone worlds immediately after graduating from the academy, and fought side by side with the Seebos on LaNor years later. The cavalry officer's train of thought was interrupted as Deker took a right onto C-2. "We're almost there," the noncom announced over the intercom. "That's the hab up ahead."

The Supply Command structure wasn't much to look at, and was far too small to house much more than a few desks, but a quick check confirmed that they were in the right place. Once the T-2 came to a halt, Santana removed his helmet, left it on a hook intended for that purpose, and jumped to the ground. A cloud of fine red dust billowed up around his boots as he pulled a garrison-style cloth "piss cutter" onto his head in lieu of the bulky blue *kepi* Legion officers normally wore. "Take a break, Sergeant. I'll contact you via my pocket com when it's time to leave."

"Roger that, sir," the T-2 replied. Deker had friends everywhere—and Supply was no exception. And maybe, just maybe, the cyborg could beg, borrow, or steal a pair of knee couplers. Because even though it was against regs to hoard parts, some items were harder to get than others, and couplers were in short supply. And Deker had no intention of trying to fight the Ramanthians with one or both of his knees locked in place.

Once inside the hab, Santana discovered that the interior was not only blessedly cool, but reasonably free of dust, which was something of a miracle. A corporal showed the cavalry officer into an office where both General Kobbi and a middle-aged colonel were seated. The supply officer had bushy eyebrows, flinty eyes, and a horizontal slash for a mouth. Kobbi made the introductions as the staff officer stood. "Colonel Hamby, this is Captain Santana. He was one of my platoon leaders on Savas."

Everyone knew about the raid on Savas, and Hamby's respect for the tall, dark-haired officer went up a notch at the mere mention of it. "Glad to meet you, Captain," the supply officer said gruffly as the two men shook hands. "Welcome to Regimental SupCom."

Santana said, "Thank you, sir," and waited to hear why he had been summoned.

But no explanation was forthcoming as Kobbi stood, and said, "Come on. There's something we want to show you."

So Santana had little choice but to follow the other officers down a short hallway to a bank of elevators. Suddenly the cavalry officer understood why the surface hab was so small. The supplies were underground, an arrangement that reminded the officer of Oron IV, as the elevator lowered them down into the interconnected caverns that lay below the C-Ring. When the platform came to a stop, and the door slid open, they entered the subterranean equivalent of a gigantic warehouse. Or that portion of the ring-shaped underground storage facility assigned to the Legion—since both the navy and Marine Corps controlled portions of the facility as well. Lights marked off regular intervals above them, a small army of specially equipped androids whirred about, and the air temperature verged on frigid.

An electric-powered cart was waiting for them. Hamby slipped behind the controls, and Kobbi sat in the passenger seat, which left Santana to jump in the back. He braced himself and hung on as the supply officer put his foot to the floor. The vehicle *whirred* loudly as it carried them past twenty-foot-tall storage racks, into a maze of neatly stacked cargo modules, and past a battalion of shrink-wrapped T-2 war forms.

Finally, just as Santana was beginning to wonder when the journey would end, Hamby turned into a side corridor and came to an abrupt stop. The senior officers got out, so Santana did likewise, and followed them over to a line of tables. What looked like a full kit had been laid out, starting with uniforms, boots, and body armor, followed by night-vision equipment, weapons, com gear, and much, much more. In short, everything that a bio bod would require for combat.

But Santana was mystified. After all, why would a general and a colonel bring him all the way down into an underground storage facility, just to look at gear that he and every other legionnaire were already familiar with? Kobbi nodded as if able to read the younger officer's mind. "So, Captain," he said. "Knowing full well that we are about to take a little trip to Gamma-014, and having done your homework, what's wrong with this picture?"

Both of the senior officers watched expectantly as Santana ran a critical eye over the kit. That was when the cavalry officer remembered what he had read about the Hegemony planet and put one and one together. "It's going to be winter when we land," Santana said. "And the uniforms on the table were designed for desert use."

"Bingo," Hamby said grimly. "And, because LEGCOM informs me that we won't be able to get any winter gear until after the campaign begins, I'd say that the 1st REC is going to freeze its collective ass off."

"As if we don't have enough problems," Kobbi put in gloomily.

"Now," the supply officer said, as he motioned for the other two to follow him. "Take a look at *this!*"

Santana arrived at the very last table to find that a complete set of cold-weather camos had been laid out on the table, including thermal underwear, heated socks, insulated vests, wind- and snow-resistant outerwear, and heavy-duty boots. All of which were identical to what the Legion would issue to its bio bods except for one important detail: Rather than the white-gray camo pattern that the Legion preferred, the uniforms spread out in front of the cavalry officer were white and *black*, which was the iteration the navy issued to its personnel when they were forced to work on wintry planets like Algeron. Just one of the ways in which the various branches sought to preserve their precious identities. But what, if anything, did that have to do with Santana? He was mystified. "That's some nice-looking gear, sir. Naval issue if I'm not mistaken."

"No, you're correct," Hamby responded evenly. "Ironically, given our situation, the navy storage facility on the far side of the C-Ring has tons of that stuff. More than they will be able to use during the next five years."

"But they don't want to give it to us," Kobbi said disgustedly. "Because an unforeseen emergency could arise—and a certain admiral wants to cover his ass."

By that time the *true* purpose of the meeting was starting to become apparent. Having attempted to obtain the cold-weather gear through official channels, and having been refused—Kobbi and the regimental supply officer were contemplating a so-called midnight requisition. And, rather than order Santana to steal the supplies, which would be illegal, they were informing him of the need in hopes that he would take it upon himself to effect the necessary "transfer."

The unofficial assignment was a compliment of sorts, since it implied a great deal of trust on Kobbi's part, but it was also unfair. Since the Legion could court-martial Santana if he was caught—while the more senior officers would probably go free. He could say "no," of course, by simply ignoring the entire conversation, which was clearly the smart thing to do. Even if that meant losing Kobbi's sponsorship.

But that would mean that the 1st REC's bio bods would hit the dirt on Gamma-014 dressed for a summer stroll just as the temperature started to drop and snow fell out of the sky. The result would be unnecessary casualties. Which was why Santana was going to do the wrong thing for what he believed to be the right reasons. Kobbi detected the slight hardening of the cavalry officer's features and knew he had the right man. "That's unfortunate, sir," Santana said evenly. "Thank you for the briefing. Is there anything else?"

Hamby looked over to Kobbi, saw the general shake his head, and looked back again. "No, Captain. There isn't.

Come on. I have a bottle of Scotch stashed in my desk—and there's no reason to save it."

The Legion had strict rules about who could legitimately have sex with whom, but there was always someone who chose to violate such regulations, even though the penalties could be quite severe. One such individual was Staff Sergeant Lin Schira who, having successfully seduced one of the clerks that reported to him, enjoyed having sex with her in the storage room adjacent to the office they shared with three other people. A rather mechanical process in which the lance corporal was required to drop her pants, bend over, and hang on to a storage rack while Schira took her from behind.

And, because the sergeant liked to have sex just prior to lunch, everyone knew better than to enter the storage room at 1130 hours. Everyone except Company Sergeant Dice Dietrich that is, who had been aware of the daily assignation for some time, but had chosen to mind his own business.

But that was then, and this was now, as the rangy noncom entered the BatSup office, ordered all of the enlisted people to "take ten," and made his way over to the door labeled "Storeroom." Plastic buckled as Dietrich kicked the door in and a girlish scream was heard as the hard-eyed noncom entered with camera in hand. Schira swore as the flash strobed, and there was a good deal of scuffling as the lovers hurried to pull their pants up. "Yeah, yeah," Dietrich said heartlessly. "Life sucks. But that's how God wants it! Now, assuming you would like to own this camera, there are some things you'll need to do for me. Or, I can send this puppy up to the general, who will pull your stripes and send you to a billet even worse than Adobe. So, what'll it be? The choice is yours."

Even though Navy Master Chief Yas Ruha could have spent the entire watch sitting on his can, while the twenty-one bio bods and robots under his command did all the work, he liked to pilot the bright yellow CH-60 loaders and took pride in his ability to do so. That was why the lifer was strapped into one of the fifteen-foot-tall exoskeletons, busy plucking cargo modules off the "three" shelf, when a "train" load of cargo modules arrived at the bottom of the four-lane access ramp. Which, in keeping with standing orders, his subordinates were quick to report.

Having placed the last module onto an outgoing power pallet, Ruha guided the huge walker over to the vast in-processing area, where newly arrived supplies were routinely scanned into the tracking system, prior to being stored on the appropriate racks. Two neatly uniformed navy supply techs were waiting to greet the master chief as he put the CH-60 on standby and hit his harness release. Rather than use the built-in steps the way some newbie would, Ruha dropped onto an actuator, and wrapped his arms around a steel leg. Then, with a confidence that stemmed from years of practice, he slid to the floor. "Good afternoon," the diminutive master chief said as he crossed the pavement to where the other two men were waiting. "So what can *you* do for *me*?"

The joke was sufficient to elicit a chuckle from both the dark-haired chief petty officer and the hollow-cheeked first-class who stood at his side. "A whole shitload of space armor just came off the *Epsilon Indi*," Santana answered genially. And it's supposed to go aboard the *Cygnus* pronto. Unfortunately the *Cygy* isn't going to drop hyper until o-dark-thirty. So we need a place to stash the stuff until tomorrow, when we can boost it back up. All the tracking data should be in-system."

" 'Should be,' and 'is,' are two different things," Ruha said cynically. "So it never hurts to check." So saying, the master chief drew a pistol-shaped scanner from the holster on his right thigh and made his way past the tractor. As soon as he was level with the first cargo module, the noncom ran the scanner over the bar code plastered across the side of the box and eyeballed the tiny screen.

Santana held his breath. Sergeant Schira swore that while it was almost impossible to *remove* supplies from the system without triggering lots of alarms, it was relatively easy to *add* items, since thieves would have no motive to do so. That was the theory anyway—but would it work? Or would the little master chief realize something was wrong and call the shore patrol? Because if that occurred, it would soon become apparent that Dietrich and he were imposters.

But, based on the way Ruha was acting, it looked like Schira's theory was correct. Because the petty officer was walking along next to the train, and each time he scanned a bar code, the noncom would nod as if satisfied with what he saw. Had the master chief been paying attention to anything other than the numbers on his scanner, he might have noticed that all of the cargo modules had been freshly painted and equipped with the type of Legion-style grab bars that would enable T-2s to move them around.

Thankfully, Ruha wasn't attuned to such matters, so once the cargo was checked in, all the imposters had to do was get a receipt, and turn some very small robots loose on their way out. Once on the surface it was a simple matter to abandon the stolen tractor, enter a waiting quad, and wait for the hatch to close before changing back into their Legion uniforms. Then, having sought fold-down seats in the otherwise empty cargo compartment, it was time to fish a cold beer out of a cooler and start to worry. Phase one of the plan was complete—but what about phase two? The quad began to pitch and sway as it made its way through busy streets—and the day wore on.

There was no light within the cargo module, but that didn't bother Sergeant Omi Deker, thanks to the fact that the cyborg could chat with Sergeant Amy Matos, Corporal Stacy Subee, and Private Ka Nhan on a low-power squad-level push that the swabbies weren't likely to monitor. And, even if they did, all the mop swingers would hear was some legionnaires telling war stories.

Having been in the module for more than eight hours, it was time for Deker to activate his work light, open the specially rigged latches, and emerge from hiding, an activity that would go undetected assuming Captain Santana and Top Dietrich had successfully deployed the pinhead-sized robots. The robots were programmable machines that the Legion's special ops people used to neutralize video surveillance during raids. A servo *whined* as Deker pushed the cargo module's lid upwards and peered out through the resulting gap. The cavern was lit around the clock, but largely inactive between midnight and 0400, which was why 0130 had been chosen as the best time to strike.

Confident that it was reasonably safe to exit the cargo module, Deker gave the rest of the team permission to go before pushing the lid up out of the way and crawling out of the box. It would have been impossible, not to mention impractical, to hide T-2s in the cargo module. That was why the cyborgs had chosen to wear the small, very agile "bodies" known as spider forms instead. The electromechanical bodies were quick and strong, which made them ideal for the mission the cyborgs had volunteered for.

Meanwhile, as the legionnaires spidered out onto the floor, the cameras mounted on the massive support columns went off-line. That produced a low-level technical alert that went into the maintenance queue and would be dealt with later that morning.

That left the cyborgs free to work which, thanks to an elaborate run-through two days earlier, they were able to do with a minimum of communication. Even though the big CH-60 loaders were designed for the convenience of bio bods, the spider forms were *very* adaptable, and it wasn't long before Deker and Matos were busy plucking cargo modules off shelves like shoppers in a supermarket. Then, once a sufficient amount of space had been cleared, it was time to reverse the process by replacing the stolen containers with the units Santana and Dietrich had brought down from the surface the day before. While all of that was going on, Subee and Nhan were kept busy replacing the bar codes on newly delivered units with copies of those on the containers that they planned to steal. That strategy should keep Master Chief

Ruha happy until someone opened one of the modules only to discover it was half-filled with sand—the one thing that everyone on Adobe already had lots of.

The whole process took about an hour, and once the switch was complete, it was time for the cyborgs to hide in the same modules they had arrived in. Time passed slowly after that, *very* slowly, but uneventfully as well. So that, when Santana and Dietrich arrived at 0730, they were allowed to pull the entire trainload of cargo modules up onto Adobe's surface, where they were soon lost in traffic.

Later that night, in the 1st REC's maintenance facility, the cargo modules were painted olive drab, retagged, and stored with the rest of the equipment that would soon accompany the regiment into space. When Santana was finally able to return to his quarters, it was to find a sealed envelope resting on his pillow. The handwritten note inside read: "To Captain Antonio Santana. Thank you for a job well-done. Warmest regards, General Mortimer Kobbi."

4

For how can tyrants safe govern home, Unless abroad they purchase great alliance?

—*William Shakespeare*
King Henry VI, Part III
Standard year 1591

ABOARD THE BATTLESHIP *REGULUS,* OFF PLANET NOCTOR, THE RAMANTHIAN EMPIRE

Like Jericho, Noctor was a so-called nursery planet, except in this case the maturation process was proceeding according to plan, as millions of juveniles were removed from the wilds and the process of socializing them began. So while the Queen stood with her back to a huge viewport, the cloud-wrapped planet made a fitting background as the royal addressed the most senior members of her staff.

"The attack on Gamma-014 was an unqualified success," the Queen began matter-of-factly, as she surveyed the faces in front of her. "Our forces are in complete control of the planet. Meanwhile, based on intelligence provided by Thraki agents in the Clone Hegemony, it appears that an alliance has been struck. It will take the humans time to assemble a joint task force and launch a counterattack on Gamma-014. Once they do, our naval forces will fade away allowing the allies to land in force."

"Now," the monarch added meaningfully, as her compound eyes swept the compartment, "iridium is important, but let's discuss the *true* purpose of the attack on Gamma-014, and what we stand to gain."

Ubatha felt a surge of satisfaction. His instincts had been correct! The attack on Gamma-014 had a greater purpose. But what was it? The answer came as a complete shock. "The attack on Gamma-014 is a feint," the monarch explained, as a holographic star map blossomed behind her. It showed a class-five star orbited by eight planets and some smaller planetoids. "In fact, the entire campaign is a diversion intended to draw military assets away from the *real* target, which is *Earth.* While a number of species belong to the Confederacy, it's the humans who hold the organization together, and therefore represent the greatest threat to our people. So by attacking their home world, we attack the heart of the Confederacy."

There was a long moment of silence as the compartment full of functionaries sought to absorb what they had just heard. That was followed by the staccato *rattle* of pincers as all but one of the government officials communicated their approval. The single exception was Chancellor Ubatha, who, though ever eager to please the Queen, was unwilling to signal approval he didn't actually feel. Her majesty noticed this immediately. "I'm glad so many of you approve," the monarch said tactfully. "But I expect more from my advisors than applause. Chancellor Ubatha? I sense you have doubts."

The invitation could constitute a trap, a way to draw Ubatha out into the open, then take his head off. The functionary knew that, but had risen to high office by offering honest counsel, and was constitutionally unable to do otherwise. "Yes, Majesty," Ubatha replied solemnly, as he came to his feet. "While what Your Highness said regarding the humans is true—there are other factors to consider as well. Based on intelligence reports, as well as media analysis, we know only a third of Earth's population truly supports the war. Primarily because the conflict is so distant and has yet to touch their daily lives. But I fear that an attack like the one you describe will shatter their sense of complacency and serve to rally both the animals who live on Earth *and* the hundreds of millions who dwell elsewhere. Thereby *strengthening* the opposition rather than weakening it."

Ubatha paused to look around before taking his argument to its logical conclusion. "So I oppose an attack on Earth," the functionary concluded gravely. "But if overruled on this matter, I recommend that we *glass* the planet, rather than simply occupy it. Because by rendering the world uninhabitable, we will strike the sort of psychological blow that you visualize, but without being required to commit any troops. Soldiers we will need when the surviving humans seek revenge. Thank you for the opportunity to speak."

Only one pair of pincers was heard to *clack*. But they belonged to the Queen, who understood how difficult such a speech was, especially given the political risk involved. "Thank you," the monarch said sincerely, as the rest of her advisors watched the drama unfold. "You make some excellent points. But I am going to overrule you—for the following reasons. First, the same intelligence reports that you referred to make it clear that even as the more adventurous members of the human species left for the stars, there was a marked tendency for lazy, self-satisfied, and privileged members of the race to remain on Earth. Which means the planet will be relatively easy to pacify.

"Secondly, were we to glass the planet as you suggest that we should, it could cause the surviving humans to launch another attack on Hive. The last one killed 1.7 million Ramanthian citizens—so how many would the next assault kill?" she demanded rhetorically.

"Thirdly, rather than render Earth uninhabitable, I want to use the planet as a bargaining chip. A tidbit that we can negotiate over for the next twenty years. Then, when all five billion of the great mother's children reach adulthood, we will sweep through the Confederacy and eradicate the animals once and for all!"

The plan was so audacious, and so farsighted, that all of Ubatha's doubts were swept away. "Thank you, Majesty," the Chancellor said humbly. "I have seen the future, and it is ours."

PLANET GAMMA-014, THE CLONE HEGEMONY

The sky was lead gray, and the temperature hovered just above freezing, as Mama Dee led her ragged flock of followers west along the two-lane highway. A bitterly cold wind pressed against their scarf-wrapped faces as a heavily loaded Ramanthian convoy passed them headed in the opposite direction. The humans could feel the wash of heat produced by the alien power plants and hear the *rattle* of click-speech as one of the troop transports passed them. The bugs might have stopped the band of humans had it not been for the "truce stick" clutched in their leader's left hand.

Dee was a big-boned woman who looked a lot like her broad-faced Ortov mother. Although some of her Chan-line father's DNA could be seen in the shape of her eyes and the breadth of her nose, most of her body was concealed by an ankle-length gray cloak that was cinched around her waist with a length of rope. All manner of items dangled from the makeshift belt, and they appeared to dance as she turned to look over her shoulder. Then, having assured herself that the group was intact, Dee faced the wind.

Like most free breeders the "Children of Nature," as they called themselves, had been forced to eke out a living high in the mountains or risk sanctions from the "true breeders" who lived on arable land at lower elevations. Founder folk, which was to say bigots, who continued to believe in the nonsense Dr. Carolyn Anne Hosokawa put forward, in spite of how absurd the theory of rational design obviously was. Such hostility made life difficult, very difficult, but now Dee and her flock were faced with *another* problem. Because only three days after seizing control of the planet, a squad of heavily armed Ramanthians had appeared in their village and ordered the Children of Nature to walk all the way to the city of Ship Down, where a civilian POW camp had been established. And, to make sure the humans did as they were told, the aliens destroyed the collection of stone huts that constituted the village even as the refugees left.

Of course Dee and her two dozen followers had no desire to enter a camp, especially one populated by founder folk. But they hadn't been able to come up with a realistic alternative. The truce stick was actually a tracking device shaped like a staff, which provided the Ramanthians with real-time data regarding the family, and where it was going. In fact it could actually "see" them, and their surroundings, or so the bugs claimed. They could dump the device of course, but that would cause the chits to send a shuttle. And Dee knew what would happen next. The Ramanthian aircraft would locate her family and put all of them to death. That left Mama Dee with no alternative but to trudge toward the dimly seen afternoon sun and hope for the best.

Having moved into position during the hours of darkness, and having found cover on a rocky ledge, there had been little for Colonel Six and two of his Seebos to do but hunker down in their sleeping bags, and take turns trying to sleep. But it was difficult due to the pervasive cold, the muted *roar* of the river below them, and the occasional *whine* of turbines as Ramanthian convoys crossed the bridge nearby. The light arrived gradually, as if hesitant to replace the darkness, and was filtered by a thick layer of clouds. A fire was out of the question, but Six gave permission for one of the Seebos to heat some water with a carefully shielded fuel tab.

Having brushed his teeth, and taken a somewhat awkward piss, the officer crawled forward to the point where he could place his back against a rock and peer through a screen of lacy vegetation. The target was an arched bridge. It was about half a mile away and still shrouded in mist. The vapor began to dissipate as the air warmed and vehicles loaded with troops, heavy weapons, and supplies continued to cross it.

All were viewed from an angle, since the clone's vantage point was down canyon, looking toward the southeast. Meanwhile, directly below the bridge, river 78, 241.2 jumped and boiled as if eager to escape the mountains and travel to more hospitable climes below.

Six heard a *scraping* sound and turned to find that Corporal One-O, as his comrades called him, had arrived with a mug of steaming tea. It had been necessary for the Seebo to duckwalk, and though a small amount of the precious liquid had been lost during the trip, most of it still remained. "Here you are, sir," One-O said cheerfully. "Are two sugars enough?"

"That's plenty," Six replied gratefully. "Thank you. Once you've had your tea, pack up the gear, and tell Niner to bring the launcher. We'll wait for a heavily loaded convoy, dump the bridge into the canyon, and haul ass."

"That'll show the bastards," One-O said approvingly. "Don't worry—we'll be ready."

"Good," Colonel Six responded, and allowed the lichen-covered rock to accept his full weight. The mug warmed his hands, the bridge drew his eyes, and the officer wondered how many bugs he would kill on that particular day.

"Okay, squirt," Mama Dee said, as she scooped the child up off the road. "How 'bout a ride?"

"I'm tired," the little girl complained. Her nose was running, and she wiped it with a sleeve.

"I know you are," Dee said sympathetically. "But look down there! See the bridge? Once we cross it, we'll stop for lunch. How does that sound?"

"Can I have a cookie?" the child wanted to know.

"Yes, you can," Mama Dee assured her, and started downhill. Treacherous though the truce stick might be, it made a good staff, and gave off a solid *thump* each time it made contact with the ground. There weren't any vehicles on the road at the moment, which was just as well, as the civilians followed a series of steep switchbacks down to the steel bridge. That was the moment when Colonel Six spotted the group, made a minute adjustment to his binos, and swore as the faces rolled into focus. A couple of them looked familiar, but most were unique, and therefore suspect. Corporal One-O and Private-469 had come forward by then and were ready to fire the rocket launcher. The pincer-operated controls were a bit strange, but Nine was confident that he could fire the weapon, and was clearly eager to do so. Having heard Colonel Six swear, One-O was curious. "What have we got, sir?" the noncom inquired. "A problem?"

"A group of mongrels," Six replied disgustedly. "That's what we've got. All headed for lower ground."

A high-pitched *whine* was heard, and Six panned the binos to the right, just in time to see a vehicle appear at the west end of the bridge. The troop carrier paused, and the shrill sound of a whistle was heard as a squad of Ramanthian troopers shuffled forward to inspect the structure, a precaution Six hadn't seen before. Did that mean other convoys had been ambushed? *Yes,* the officer thought to himself. *If the possibility of guerrilla warfare occurred to me, it would occur to my brother officers as well.*

One of the Ramanthian troopers paused to dump his gear onto the bridge deck, before spreading his wings and slowly taking to the air. It was a rarely seen sight and an excellent reminder of what the bugs could do. The soldier soared out over the gorge, entered a downward spiral, and disappeared under the span—the place where demolition charges if any were most likely to be found.

"Get ready," Six said, without turning toward the men crouched beside him. "I don't know what's lined up behind that troop carrier—but I have a feeling it's the kind of target we want. We'll wait until the bridge deck is full before firing the first rocket. Load the second one as fast as you can."

"Sir, yes sir," One-O said obediently. "But what about the civilians?"

Six swung the binos left just in time to see the group of free breeders arrive at the bottom of the opposite slope and step onto the far end of the bridge. The truth was that he had forgotten all about the degenerates until One-O's reminder. And now, as they started to cross the span, the first vehicle of the Ramanthian convoy rolled onto the structure from the west. Had the civilians been members of a recognized line, Six would have been compelled to cancel the attack. But this was different because the ragged-looking creatures were *accidental* people—random beings that had no recognized place within the founder's plan. Whereas the Ramanthian troop truck, two tank carriers, and the support vehicle that were halfway across the span had tremendous value. Especially to the enemy. So as the two groups came into alignment, and the final seconds ticked away, Six made his decision. "Clear your safeties. Prepare to fire. *Fire!*"

Had one of the Legion's officers given the order to a legionnaire, it was quite possible that the man or woman operating the weapon would have refused to obey. Because legionnaires were *supposed* to disobey what they knew to be illegal orders. But such was the relationship between the Seebos that most of the clones couldn't even conceive of refusing an order from one of their brothers. So Nine gave the firing bulb a hearty squeeze, felt the tube resting on his shoulder jump, and heard a loud *whoosh* as the alien missile raced away. The warhead hit the center of the bridge, produced a flash of light, and a *boom* that echoed through the canyon. Smoke swirled, and a single chunk of concrete fell free, but the overall structure remained intact.

Mama Dee and her tiny charge had been thrown face-down by the force of the blast. But the clan leader was quick to regain her feet. The child was crying, as Dee plucked the tyke off the debris-strewn pavement, and yelled, "Run!" The west end of the bridge was about a hundred feet away. It looked like a mile.

"Put the next missile on the last truck!" Six shouted, as

the smoke cleared. The Ramanthians were firing wildly by then, being unsure of where the first rocket had come from, but hoping to suppress the incoming fire.

Private-469 did as he was told, saw the rocket fly straight and true, and had the satisfaction of witnessing a direct hit. There was a tremendous *roar* as the boxy vehicle blew up, cut the bridge in half, and dumped both tank carriers into the raging waters below. Six noted that the first truck, the one loaded with troops, was on the far side of the gorge. That was unfortunate—but couldn't be helped.

Meanwhile Mama Dee and roughly half her family stood at the west end of the broken span and stared down into the wreckage-choked canyon. All of the free breeders were sobbing except for Dee, who was too angry to cry. Slowly, and with a precision that sent a chill down Colonel Six's spine, the deviant turned to look into his eyes. Because the woman on the bridge *knew* the rockets had been fired by one or more Seebos, *knew* her people had been sacrificed, and *knew* someone was looking at her.

Finding it impossible to look the woman in the eye, Colonel Six lowered the binoculars, and scowled. "Throw the launcher into the gorge, and let's get out of here," he growled. Another blow had been struck—and another price had been paid.

PLANET ALPHA-001, THE CLONE HEGEMONY

The Plaza of the Immortals was half a mile wide and a mile long. The arena was oriented to the planet's north pole so that each point of the compass was represented by a formal entrance. Thousands upon thousands of tiered seats slanted up away from the plaza, and all of them were filled. Not randomly, but according to genetic lines, which meant that office workers were seated with office workers, construction workers with construction workers, and so forth. And each section of seats was backed by a towering statue of the "immortal" from whom that particular line of DNA had been copied. So it appeared as if hundreds of gods were present to preside over what took place within the plaza, each stern-faced visage staring out over its progeny, as if able to see something that mere mortals couldn't comprehend.

It made for a very impressive spectacle as Alpha Clones Antonio, Pietro, and even the ailing Marcus sat atop the three-story-high reviewing stand just below likenesses of *their* progenitors. And one level below them, in seats reserved for foreign dignitaries, President Nankool and his staff were present as well, something the millions of clones who had been ordered to watch video of the ceremony on their dormitory screens could plainly see.

The carefully planned extravaganza began with a low-altitude flyover by six wing-to-wing fighters—and martial music so loud that Vanderveen was forced to cover her ears at times. That was followed by the ceremonial entrance of the famed Lightning Brigade, who ironically enough *weren't* slated to lift for Gamma-014, but were present to lead the rest of the troops onto the plaza.

And as music played, and flags snapped in the breeze, Vanderveen couldn't help but be impressed as thousands of combat-ready Jonathan Alan Seebos marched into the long rectangular arena, split into company-sized groups, and turned the plaza into what looked like a gigantic chessboard.

But then, as groups of clones who didn't look a bit like the Jonathan Alan Seebos began to enter the arena, Vanderveen heard exclamations of dismay from the more senior officials seated around her. "They're conscripts!" the secretary of the navy was heard to say. "The bastards are sending civilians to fight the Ramanthians!"

Vanderveen was far too junior to be seated next to the president, but she could see him, and knew the man well enough to recognize the anger on his face as General Booly leaned in to whisper something into his superior's ear. Because rather than contribute crack troops, the way they were supposed to, it was clear that clones intended to pad their force with people drawn from nonmilitary genetic lines.

But there was nothing that Nankool, Booly, and the rest of the staff could do but sit and watch as the last of the conscripts took their places, and everyone in the arena was subjected to a thunderous noise as a formation of aerospace shuttles swept in to hover just above the parade ground. Then, with a degree of precision that bespoke countless hours of practice, the transports settled into the squares not occupied by people. It was an extremely impressive maneuver that was calculated to impress the citizens of the Confederacy, many of whom were watching the live feed via the new hypercom technology.

No sooner were the shuttles on the ground, and their engines silenced, than the speeches began. Speeches by workers, minor officials, major officials, Alpha Clone Antonio, and finally Marcott Nankool. Who, though furious at the Hegemony's leaders, had no choice but to join them on the reviewing stand and praise the alliance.

As music played, and the audience cheered, thousands of troops entered their shuttles, took their seats, and strapped in. Once the loading process was complete, the transports took off the same way they had landed, in unison.

Then, as part of a carefully choreographed aerial ballet, the shuttles peeled away from the formation one at a time, accelerated upwards, and were soon lost to sight as their contrails merged to form an arrow that pointed upwards. That was the cue for the members of the Lightning Brigade to come to attention, march out through the exits, and return whence they had come.

Vanderveen was happy to see them go. Finally, after more than four hours of sitting in a chair, it felt good to stand and follow her "betters" down to ground level, where a formal reception was about to begin. It was the sort of function that would normally be quite boring, but might become rather heated, given the way in which the Confederacy had been snookered. Vanderveen was understandably curious regarding how Nankool would handle the situation, so she began to shadow the chief executive as the party began. That strategy quickly paid off as the president and the Alpha Clones came together. Marcus had been forced to leave, due to his health, but Antonio and Pietro greeted Nankool like old friends. And Nankool responded in kind.

But then, as soon as he reasonably could, the president spoke his mind. The words were measured, but his jaw was tight, and his eyes were bright with repressed anger. "That was a very impressive ceremony, gentlemen. But I was surprised to see a substantial number of civilians mustered on the plaza. It was my understanding that the Hegemony would contribute crack troops."

Given the fact that Alpha Clone Antonio had consistently spoken for the Hegemony up until that point—Vanderveen found it interesting that it was Pietro who chose to respond. He had light brown skin, flashing black eyes, and perfect teeth. The clone was wearing a well-draped toga with his trademark pin on the left shoulder. And, judging from Antonio's expression, it seemed as though the first Alpha Clone was annoyed by his brother's tardy participation. "Yes," Pietro said blandly, "that *was* our intention, until General-453 entered into the discussions. It's his opinion that the Legion, combined with our brave Seebos, and members of the newly formed Civilian Volunteer Army (CVA), will trounce the Ramanthians within a matter of weeks. . . . Isn't that right, General?"

As if on cue, General Jonathan Alan Seebo-785,453 materialized out of the crowd. The officer possessed his line's manly good looks, but there was something slightly dissipated about the way his features sagged, and the puffiness of a body that hadn't been required to march anywhere in a long time. But even if Four-fifty-three didn't cut a soldierly figure, he was a skilled bureaucrat, and could be quite charming.

"President Nankool!" the general said heartily. "And General Booly . . . This *is* an honor. It's a pleasure to meet you."

"Yes," the clone officer continued, as he looked from face to face. "I took the liberty of making some rather timely changes based on intelligence received over the last few days. Given the size of the force at our disposal, and the relatively small number of Ramanthians on Gamma-014, we should be able to overwhelm the ugly beasts in no time at all. So rather than commit too many of my brethren to the task, thereby weakening the Hegemony's defenses elsewhere, I chose to send a CVA regiment along instead. Not in direct combat roles, mind you, but to provide engineering, logistics, and medical support."

"That plan assumes a conventional war," Booly said pointedly. "What makes you so sure the bugs will fight that way? The Ramanthians will be well entrenched and could come at us from all directions."

General-453 wasn't used to having his orders questioned, or so it appeared from the blood that rushed to his face, and the way his fists were clenched. "First," Four-fifty-three replied icily, "I believe it is customary to address a superior officer as '*sir*.' An honorific to which I, as commanding general, am clearly entitled.

"Secondly, while the Legion is no doubt extremely knowledgeable where the Confederacy is concerned, Gamma-014 lies within the Hegemony, which means I am in the best position to judge what is and isn't appropriate."

"Except that Gamma-014 lies within the Ramanthian Empire at this point," Booly observed pointedly. "Which is where it's likely to remain unless we send enough troops to take it. *Sir*."

"Please," Alpha Clone Pietro said, as he held up his hands. "Save your energy for the Ramanthians! We are allies, and I'm sure that command differences, if any, can be resolved over some good food! Come, let's eat."

Nankool wanted to continue the debate, as did Booly,

but it would have seemed boorish to do so. Therefore, both the president and his top general were forced to follow Pietro as he led them to a table loaded with refreshments. And Vanderveen, who knew Santana might be among the legionnaires sent to Gamma-014, was left to worry. The knowledge brought scant comfort—but the first stage of the counter offensive was under way.

ABOARD THE CONFEDERACY'S TROOP TRANSPORT *ENCELADUS,* JUST OFF PLANET GAMMA-014, THE CLONE HEGEMONY

In spite of the fact that the *Enceladus* was a large ship, and specifically designed for transporting troops, the vessel was so crammed with people that Captain Antonio Santana had to maneuver around marines who were camped in the main corridor, and squeeze past the boxes of rations that were stacked along the lesser passageways, before being able to enter the warren of compartments reserved for the 1st REC. A bio bod shouted, "Attention on deck!" as the officer appeared, but Santana said, "As you were," before most of the legionnaires could respond.

It was too warm for comfort as Santana entered a fuggy miasma made up of equal parts perspiration, gun oil, and ozone. Greetings came from all sides as he worked his way back through the maze of lockers and bunks toward the area set aside for noncoms. Because of the heat, most of the bio bods were walking around in T-shirts and shorts.

Their war forms were stored below, adjacent to the hangar bay, so the cyborgs were equipped with spider forms. And thanks to their extraordinary mobility, the borgs had been able to colonize the overhead, where a maze of exposed girders, pipes, and ductwork provided a habitat no one else could take advantage of.

Meanwhile, down at deck level, the bio bods were listening to music, watching vids, playing cards, repairing their gear, cleaning weapons, doing push-ups, or just shooting the shit. "Whatcha got for us, sir?" Staff Sergeant Briggs wanted to know, as he looked up from his hand comp. "Are we headed dirtside?"

It had been noisy till then, but the sound level dropped by 50 percent as everyone waited to see what Santana would say. "We'll hit the dirt soon," the company commander predicted. "But not today. . . . The bugs had quite a welcoming party waiting for the navy—and the swabbies are still in the process of kicking their ugly butts. Then, once the heavy lifting is over, we'll go down and tidy up."

That produced a chorus of chuckles, and the legionnaires went back to whatever they had been doing as Santana weaved his way through the crowded compartment and made his way back to where Company Sergeant Dice Dietrich was seated on the deck. The noncom had his back to a corner, his eyes were closed, and it appeared that he was asleep. But when Santana entered the area, Dietrich's eyes snapped open, and he was suddenly on his feet. "Good morning, sir," the noncom said. "And welcome to the sauna."

Santana grinned. "Thanks, Top. . . . I don't know which is worse. This, or the two-person cabin I'm sharing with three of my fellow officers. Here's hoping we get dirtside before we all go crazy. In the meantime I have a job for you. . . . It seems Private Bora-Sa got into a game of Rockets and Stars with some jarheads, came to the conclusion that he was being cheated, and put five of them in the sick bay. There weren't any fatalities, thank God," the officer added gratefully. "But the brig is overcrowded, so the jarheads are willing to release the idiot into our custody, so long as we promise to keep him here."

Like all Hudathans Bora-Sa was *huge*, and Dietrich couldn't help but smile, as he imagined marines flying in every direction. "Yes, sir. I'll go get him."

"Thank you," Santana replied. "And tell the private that he's going to pull every shit detail that Sergeant Telveca can come up with for the next thirty days."

"I'll tell him," Dietrich agreed grimly. Then, having eyeballed the officer's flawless Class B uniform, the noncom raised an eyebrow. "You're looking pretty sharp today, sir. . . . If you don't mind my saying so."

Santana knew that was Dietrich's roundabout way of asking where he was going, whom he was about to see, and ultimately why. "It seems that the commanding general is flying from ship to ship in an effort to meet as many senior officers as he can," the legionnaire explained. "Colonel Quinlan was invited, and since the XO isn't available, General Kobbi tapped me to sit in for him."

Dietrich nodded. The XO had been injured in a vehicle accident back on Adobe—and had therefore been unable to lift with the rest of the regiment. Most of the enlisted people thought Santana should be named acting XO, but no announcement had been made, and now it looked as though Kobbi might be about to force the issue. All of which was well above Dietrich's pay grade, so the noncom was careful to keep his face expressionless, as he made his reply. "Sounds like fun, sir. Have a good time."

Santana had a deep and abiding hatred of meet-and-greet evolutions, a fact that Dietrich was well aware of. Which was why the officer said, "Screw you, Top," before executing a neat about-face, and exiting the compartment.

Meanwhile, all of those who had been busy listening to the conversation witnessed the interchange, saw Dietrich smile, and chuckled appreciatively. Entertainment was in short supply aboard the *Enceladus*—so any diversion was welcome.

Crowded though conditions were on the troopship, battalion commanders had been given cabins of their own so they would have a place to meet with subordinates. When Santana arrived outside Quinlan's quarters, the officer saw that the hatch was closed and assumed another visitor was inside. Military courtesy required him to knock three times and wait for an invitation to enter. When nothing happened he knocked again and counted to thirty.

Still not having received a response, and expecting to find that Quinlan had departed without him, the officer palmed the entry switch just in case. Much to his surprise the hatch cycled open. A few tentative steps carried Santana inside. And there, slumped over his fold-down desk, was Colonel Liam Quinlan.

The officer was drunk, judging from the half-empty bottle of gin at his elbow, and completely motionless. "Colonel?" Santana said experimentally as he reached out to touch the battalion commander's arm. "Can you hear me?" Quinlan attempted to lift his head, mumbled something incomprehensible, and began to snore.

Conscious of how the scene would look should someone pass by, Santana hit the door switch, and waited for the hatch to close before returning to the desk. The colonel was in love with meetings, especially ones where he could clock some face time with his superiors, so why was the bastard drunk?

Having noted that the battalion commander was facedown on a sheet of official-looking hard copy, Santana placed a hand on top of the other officer's nearly bald skull, hooked his fingers over Quinlan's forehead, and pulled upwards. That freed the piece of paper, which the legionnaire removed prior to lowering the other man's head onto the desk.

The BuPers printout, because that's where it had originated, was a bit blurry where some of Quinlan's gin had come into contact with the ink, but still readable. As with all such messages, it was brief, formal, and brutally direct: "Dear Colonel Liam Quinlan," the message began. "It pains us to inform you that your daughter, Lieutenant Junior Grade Nancy Ann Quinlan, was killed in action off CR-0654 in the Rebor Cluster. Please accept our heartfelt condolences regarding this terrible loss. More details regarding Lieutenant Quinlan's death, plus remains, if any, will be forwarded to your address of record. Sincerely, Major Hiram Fogles, Commanding Officer ComSec, BuPers."

Santana swore softly as he put the printout down and looked at a picture he hadn't had any reason to pay attention to until then. The face that looked back at him was young, surprisingly pretty given her father's porcine features, and locked in an eternal smile. The possibility that Quinlan might have a family, and have feelings toward them, had never occurred to Santana.

It wasn't easy to drag the portly colonel over to his bunk, roll him onto it, and arrange his body so that he looked reasonably comfortable. Then, having thrown a blanket over the officer and dimmed the lights, Santana slipped out into the corridor. There was a gentle hissing sound as the hatch closed, and the red "Do not enter," sign appeared over the entry.

The meet and greet with General-453 was already under way by the time Santana entered the ship's wardroom. Kobbi was seated at the far end of the compartment and shot the company commander a questioning look as he slipped into the room. But there was no chance to talk as a marine colonel rose to pose a question. "What about weather, sir?" the grizzled leatherneck wanted to know. "I understand winter's on the way—and we don't have the proper equipment."

Santana was seated next to Kobbi by that time, and the two men exchanged glances, both thinking the same thing. The cold-weather gear that Santana and Dietrich had "requisitioned" from the navy was aboard, but wouldn't be issued until the very last minute, lest the swabbies find out what was going on.

Meanwhile, General-453 was perched on the corner of the head table and seemed to enjoy the interaction with his subordinates. "I understand the nature of your concern, Colonel," he said smoothly. "Gamma-014 is well-known for the severity of its winters. Fortunately, our forces will be able to land and eradicate the bugs *before* the really nasty weather sets in. It may be necessary to leave an occupying force behind of course—but the Hegemony will supply them with whatever they need. Is there anything else?"

"Yes," Kobbi said, as he came to his feet. "I wonder if the

general could provide us with more information regarding the capabilities of the Civilian Volunteer Army. . . . Specifically, how much training they've had, what role they will play, and for which units?"

General-453 didn't like the question, as was clear from the expression on his face and the contemptuous way in which his response was worded. "Kobbi is it? Well, *General* Kobbi. . . . Had you taken time to read the *Plan of Battle*, especially the subsection titled 'The Role of Civilian Volunteers,' you would already know the answer to your question. But, since you didn't, I will reply by saying that each volunteer is genetically qualified to fulfill his or her role, is already an expert in one of three clearly defined support specialties, and has been through four weeks of rigorous military orientation. That training includes familiarization with the chain of command, roles and responsibilities for each rank, and the appropriate protocols."

Everyone watched as Kobbi, who was still on his feet, nodded respectfully. "Sir, yes sir. . . . But can they fight?"

That produced a nervous titter, followed by a series of coughs, and a rustling noise as some of the officers repositioned themselves. The clone, who was visibly angry by that time, seemed to spit out his words one at a time. "Yes, General. The CVA can fight if need be. But if you, and your troops, do the job properly, they won't have to. Will they?"

The caustic interchange might have continued had it not been for one of Four-fifty-three's aides, who took the opportunity to intervene. "I'm sorry to interrupt gentlemen, but the general is due aboard the *Mimas* two hours from now, and his shuttle is waiting."

The meeting broke up shortly after that, and Santana was forced to wait as more than a dozen officers stopped by to thank Kobbi for asking about the CVA, before filing out into the corridor. Finally, once they were alone, Santana had the opportunity to tell Kobbi about Quinlan's daughter. The senior officer winced and shook his head sadly. "I'm afraid things aren't going well, Tony—not well at all."

Was Kobbi referring to Quinlan's daughter? General-453's arrogant leadership style? Or to the conduct of the entire war? There was no way to be sure—and Santana knew better than to ask.

5

There is no better fate than a glorious death in the face of insurmountable odds for the sake of one's clan.

—Grand Marshal Hisep Rula-Ka
The Warrior's Way
Standard year 2590

ABOARD THE BATTLESHIP *STERN-KRIEGER*, NEAR PLANET EARTH, THE CONFEDERACY OF SENTIENT BEINGS

Except for the LEDs on Fleet Admiral Cory Trimble's workstation, vid screen, and bedside clock, it was pitch-black inside her cabin as the com began to *chirp*. Trimble swore as she surfaced from a deep sleep, fumbled for the handset, and brought it up to her ear. "Yes?"

The voice on the other end of the line belonged to Flag Captain Hol Baraki. The two officers had known each other for more than twenty years, so when Trimble heard the tightness in his voice, she knew something was wrong. "I'm sorry to disturb you, Admiral," Baraki said formally. "But we need you on the bridge. The first elements of what we assume to be a Ramanthian fleet dropped hyper five minutes ago."

Trimble felt an iron fist grab hold of her insides and start to squeeze. Here was one of the scenarios that she and her staff had warned the Joint Chiefs about when President Nankool took 10 percent of the already-anemic home fleet and sent it off to take part in the attack on Gamma-014. But the knowledge that she and her staff had been correct brought

Trimble no pleasure as she said, "I'll be right there," and put the handset down.

Klaxons had begun to *bleat* by that time, but could barely be heard within Trimble's tightly sealed cabin, as the ship's crew went to battle stations. The *Stern-Krieger* (Star Warrior), was a sister ship to the famous *Gladiator*, which had been lost to a Ramanthian ambush only months before. Her five-mile-long hull was protected by energy shields, thick armor, and an arsenal of weapons that included both energy cannons and missile launchers. And, like any vessel her size, the *Krieg* was accompanied by more than two dozen escorts, including a couple of heavy cruisers, a medium-sized carrier, six destroyers, and a variety of smaller warships, supply vessels, and a fleet tug. All of which *sounded* impressive, but was only one-third of the force assigned to protect Earth prior to a long series of peacetime budget cuts, increasing apathy on the part of the planet's citizens, and the steady erosion of assets associated with the war.

But there wasn't a damned thing Trimble could do about that as she took the time necessary to apply some makeup before donning a fresh uniform. Not because she was vain, but because it was important to look the way she usually did, especially during a time of crisis. The face in the mirror had a high forehead, wide-set hazel eyes, and lips that were too thin to be sexy. It was a flaw the officer had always intended to fix, but never gotten around to, like so many things related to her personal life. Her hair, which was silvery, barely touched her collar.

Once dressed, Trimble took one last look in the mirror, threw her shoulders back, and left the cabin. A pair of marine guards came to attention, offered rifle salutes, and followed the admiral up the corridor toward the bridge. It was a short trip, and intended to be, since her sleeping cabin was located just aft of the control room.

The battleship's primary Command & Control (C&C) computer was generally referred to as Gertrude for reasons lost to history—and was currently making use of one-billionth of her considerable capabilities to communicate with the *Krieg's* crew. "This is not a drill. . . . Secure all gear, check space armor, and strap in. Primary weapons systems, secondary weapons systems, and tertiary weapons systems have been armed. All fighter aircraft are prepared for immediate launch. . . ."

The two smartly uniformed marines posted just outside the control room crashed to attention as the admiral approached, and remained in that position until the hatch *hissed* open, and Trimble entered the bridge. The marines assigned to protect her remained outside.

An ensign shouted, "Attention on deck!" but Trimble waved the honor off, and made her way down a gently sloping ramp toward the center of the dimly lit control room. It consisted of a huge windowlike vid screen, that was largely useless at the moment, since there was nothing to look at except a couple of escorts that were half-lit by the sun. So Trimble went straight to the 3-D holo tank located at the center of the bridge, where Baraki and two members of his staff were monitoring the Ramanthian incursion.

The entire solar system could be seen floating inside the containment, including a miniature sun, eight realistic-looking planets, their moons, numerous planetoids, asteroids, comets, and even the larger pieces of man-made junk—like the abandoned hab in orbit around Venus. And there, headed toward Jupiter, were the green geometrical shapes that represented the home fleet. The other officers looked up as Trimble stepped into the glow that surrounded the holo tank. Their faces were lit from below, and their expressions were grim. "So, how does it look?" the admiral inquired hopefully.

"Not good," Baraki said darkly. The flag captain had neatly combed dark hair, serious brown eyes, and a long face. "Especially now. . . . Look at what popped out of hyperspace two minutes ago."

The enemy fleet was represented by geometric symbols. Each signified a particular type of ship, and all of them were red. However, the incoming object that Baraki had referred to didn't conform to any known classification of warship. It was too big for one thing, shaped like a sphere, and seemingly under the protection of the bug battle group that was clustered around it. "I see it," Trimble acknowledged. "But what *is* it?"

"We're not absolutely sure yet," the other officer answered cautiously. "But it looks like the Ramanthians strapped a hyperdrive to a small planetoid, and are using pressor beams to nudge it toward Earth. Kind of like a soccer game."

"My God!" Trimble exclaimed, as the implication of that became clear. "They plan to push the planetoid in, hit the planet, and lay waste to the surface!"

"Yes," Baraki agreed bleakly. "That's the way it looks."

"Well, they aren't going to succeed," Trimble said grimly, as she brought a fist down on the rail that circled the holo tank. "We're going to hit that thing with everything we have, knock it off course, and send those bastards to hell! Notify the escorts, accelerate to flank speed, and prepare to engage."

Baraki nodded. "Aye, aye, ma'am." Then, having turned to his XO, the flag captain growled, "You heard the admiral. Let's grease the bastards."

ABOARD THE BATTLESHIP *REGULUS,* NEAR PLANET EARTH, THE CONFEDERACY OF SENTIENT BEINGS

In marked contrast to human warships, where the bridge was often located toward the vessel's bow, Ramanthian architects preferred to bury their control rooms deep inside the hull, where they were that much safer. So that was where the newly promoted Admiral Ru Lorko was, standing in front of a floating holo, with pincers clasped behind his wings. The naval officer had large compound eyes, a pair of antennae that projected from the top of his head, a hooked beak, and an elongated exoskeleton that had been holed in battle and patched with a metal plate. A shiny rectangle that was the genesis of the nickname, "Old Iron Back," and of which he was secretly proud.

Though once considered too eccentric for promotion to higher rank, Lorko was the officer who had been responsible for the destruction of the *Gladiator* and her entire battle group. The victory had brought the commodore to the Queen's attention, catapulted the often-irascible officer to the rank of admiral, and led to his latest mission: Attack, occupy, and govern Earth. A difficult task under the best of circumstances, but made even more so by the presence of the warrior queen, who was forever asking questions, making unsolicited comments, and offering gratuitous advice. And now, as the enemy came out to meet him, she was there at Lorko's side. "You were correct," the royal said unnecessarily. "They took the bait."

The naval officer's response was little more than the Ramanthian equivalent of a grunt. But the Queen had been briefed regarding Lorko's personality and took no offense. Because to her way of thinking, the admiral and the rest of her staff were tools, and so long as the tools functioned as they were supposed to, nothing else mattered.

Even though the two fleets were coming at each other at incredible speed, many hours were to pass before the leading elements of each battle group would make contact. There were plenty of things for Trimble to do at first. But eventually, after the proper notifications had been made, all the admiral could do was wait as the distance between the two fleets continued to diminish. Finally, after what felt like an eternity, the Ramanthians were within range. The first missiles were fired, and even though Trimble knew most of them would be intercepted, she was looking forward to drawing first blood. But then, just as the first weapons neared their targets, the enemy fleet disappeared!

Both the Admiral and the other officers who were gathered around the holo tank assumed they were looking at a technical glitch, until Gertrude's calm, nearly inflectionless voice came over the PA system. "With the exception of the spherical object, presently designated as P-1, all other enemy vessels reentered hyperspace. Destination unknown."

The immediate response was a loud cheer, as the bridge crew celebrated what looked like a rout, as the fleet continued to close with P-1. But Trimble felt something cold trickle into the pit of her stomach as the Ramanthian planetoid continued to grow larger. No damage had been inflicted. No casualties had been suffered. So why abandon the field of battle? There had to be a reason. A strategy of some sort. But what was it?

That was the moment when the planetoid exploded, a new sun was born, and 72 percent of the home fleet was destroyed as successive rings of white-hot plasma radiated out to vaporize everything they touched. One moment the *Stern-Krieger* was there, and the next moment she wasn't, as both the flagship and most of her escorts ceased to exist. The *roar* of static filled the ether, and the debris field continued to expand outwards, all without the loss of a single Ramanthian life. And there, with practically nothing to protect it, lay planet Earth.

PLANET GAMMA-014, THE CLONE HEGEMONY

Night had fallen hours before, but having nothing to fear from above, the Ramanthian base was lit up like a double helix on Founder's Day. That made it easy for Colonel Six and his men to see what was going on inside the razor wire and pick targets for their 81mm mortars. The weapons had a range of approximately six thousand yards, which meant they would be able to reach everything within the perimeter.

To prevent such an attack, groups of civilian POWs had been placed adjacent to, and in some cases right on top of, key targets, including the command bunker, shuttle pad, and ammo dump. And, based on hours of careful scrutiny, Colonel Six knew that the hostages weren't free breeders but law-abiding founder folk. Which put the officer in something of a moral quandary. Because as a soldier it was his job to protect civilians rather than kill them. So what should he do? Break off the attack? So the Ramanthians could kill more civilians? Or attack the base, knowing full well that POWs would die along with the enemy, in hopes that other innocent lives would be saved?

It was an extremely difficult decision, but one the founder had anticipated, and provided for in her book, *The Great Design*. "When forced to choose between genetic lines," Hosokawa had written, "the hierarchy must always choose the action that will benefit the greatest number of people. Because society *is* the organism—and the organism must survive."

The carefully memorized words gave Six some comfort as he low-crawled from position to position, checking to make sure that all of the Seebos were ready. And he had just arrived at tube three, and given the crew a few words of reassurance, when a bright light stabbed down out of the night sky. The mortar crew was fully illuminated as a synthesized voice gave orders in Ramanthian. The words were cut short as the clone fired his submachine gun. The bullet-riddled robot fell not four feet from the mortar and burst into flames. "Fire!" Six shouted into his lip mike. "Let the ugly free-breeding bastards have it!"

And fire the clones did, with the 81mm mortars, which began to drop bombs into the camp with monotonous regularity, crew-served 5.56×45mm light machine guns, and extremely accurate sniper rifles. Which, unlike the .50-caliber weapons preferred by the Legion, fired bolts of energy. They were visible but eerily silent.

The result was a hellish symphony in which the staccato *rattle* made by the light machine guns provided a sharp counterpoint to a series of percussive *booms* as the 81mm mortar rounds marched across the compound. Those sounds were punctuated by the steady *bang, bang, bang* of semiautomatic weapons, shrill screams as dozens of hostages were killed, and a chorus of strident whistles as Ramanthian noncoms attempted to rally their troops. There was outgoing fire, too, but it was spotty at best, because only a third of the Ramanthians had been awake when the attack began and dozens were cut down as they emerged from their bunkers to join the fight. All of that was clear to see because, for some inexplicable reason, the lights were still on!

Then the executions began. The Ramanthian officer was armed with a sword. And given the volume of incoming fire, was either very brave, or very fanatical, as he made his way from one group of POWs to the next, his weapon rising and falling with a terrible regularity as he slaughtered the helpless prisoners.

"Kill that officer!" Six ordered, as his targeting laser wobbled over the Ramanthian's chest. The alien looked up, as if to see where the red dot was coming from, and it was the last thing he ever did, as a bolt of coherent energy left one of the sniper rifles, shot across the intervening space, and blew the bug's head off. Light rippled along the length of blade as the bloodied sword flew into the air, flipped end over end, and landed point down.

The outgoing fire died down shortly after that, but Six knew Ramanthian reinforcements were on the way, and ordered the mortar teams to take their weapons and withdraw before the enemy reaction force could arrive. Then, accompanied by a squad of heavily armed Seebos, Colonel Six entered the camp through one of many holes in the security fence. Once inside the clone was amazed, and to some extent sickened, by the full extent of the slaughter. The 81mm mortar rounds had pretty much leveled everything that stood more than a couple of feet high as they sent shards of sharp metal scything across the compound to dismember Ramanthians and POWs alike. The ground was covered with a gruesome jumble of intermixed body parts that lay like pieces to a macabre jigsaw puzzle.

Shots rang out as Colonel Six and his men executed wounded Ramanthians, and there was an explosion as an alien holdout tried to throw a grenade, but was killed before he could bring his arm forward. Then Six was standing on the landing pad at the very center of the base. The can of spray paint *hissed* as the clone made his mark, a Seebo yelled, "The charges are set, sir!" and it was time to run.

Seven adults and two children had somehow survived the slaughter, and were herded through the wire, and into the darkness beyond as a *thrumming* sound was heard. The key was to gain the relative safety of a cave located more than a mile away *before* the enemy shuttles could sweep the area for heat-emitting targets. So the clones ran, and ran some more, as the ominous *thrumming* noise grew steadily louder.

Then the fugitives were there, being passed from hand to hand into the back recesses of a natural cave, as the alien reaction force circled the now-devastated camp, and began to land. The first pilot to reach the scene had the good sense to land *outside* the wire, but the second put down right on top of the numerals "666," and the noise generated by his engine triggered two carefully positioned satchel charges. The resulting explosion blew the aircraft apart, killed seventeen Ramanthians, and confirmed what General Akoto already knew: The clones were down—but not necessarily out.

PLANET ALPHA-001, THE CLONE HEGEMONY

It was nearly noon, but thanks to a decision made by bureaucrats in the Department of Harmonious Weather, rain had been allowed to fall during the daylight hours, thereby reducing the view beyond the water-streaked window to layerings of gray. Which was the way Vanderveen felt as another sad-faced official left President Nankool's temporary office, and thereby cleared the way for her. Something was clearly wrong—but what? Rumors were running rampant, but none of those who knew were willing to say, so that the chief executive could notify each staff member personally.

So it was with an understandable sense of foreboding that Vanderveen entered the dimly lit office, crossed the wooden floor to stand in front of the utilitarian desk, and waited to be noticed. Nankool, who was staring out through a large picture window, heard the footsteps and turned. The smile was forced and the words had a rehearsed quality. "Christine . . . I'm sorry to pull you away from your work, but I have some bad news to impart, and I felt I should do so personally. Especially given the fact that you have family on Earth."

The words caused the bottom to fall out of Vanderveen's stomach. Her diplomat father, Charles Winther Vanderveen, was stationed on Algeron, but her mother was living on the family estate in North America. It took an act of will to control her voice. "Earth, sir? What happened?"

So the president told her, and because he'd been practicing, the story of how the home fleet had been destroyed unfolded rather smoothly. Which led to the inevitable question. "What will the Ramanthians do now?" Vanderveen wanted to know. Her lower lip had begun to quiver, but that was the only sign of how the young woman felt, as Nankool rounded the desk. She was strong, *very* strong, as the chief executive had learned firsthand on Jericho. But the possibility that her mother might be in danger had shaken her.

"We don't know for sure," Nankool said kindly, as he placed an arm around Vanderveen's shoulders. "But based on what General Booly told me, not to mention common sense, it seems likely that the Ramanthians will invade Earth and attempt to occupy it. . . . Because if it was their intention to glass the planet, they would have done so by now."

"What about the ships we sent to Gamma-014?" the diplomat inquired. "Could we divert them to Earth?"

"It was a trap," the chief executive said regretfully. "And they sucked us in. . . . It's too late to abort the attack on Gamma-014 now. And, given the attack on Earth, we need the alliance with the Hegemony all the more. I'm sorry," Nankool added lamely. "I promise to do everything I can."

Vanderveen left the office with those words still ringing in her ears, made her way down to the first floor of the building, and from there to the street. It was still raining as she turned to the left and began to walk. Office buildings rose around her, their windows eyeing the street, while their walls channeled what little foot traffic there was. But unlike Los Angeles, where multitudes crowded the streets day and night, there were only a few pedestrians to be seen. That was how it would remain until the end of the workday. A strategy intended to keep productivity high—and limit the amount of time available for "counterproductive" activities.

But none of that applied to Fisk-Three, Four, or Five, all of whom were born revolutionaries. They were average-looking men, with uniformly light brown skin, even features, and nondescript clothes. And, as Christine Vanderveen turned a corner, they followed. Because here, after two weeks of patient surveillance, was the opportunity the Fisks had been hoping for. "She's northbound on ninth, headed for Q Street," the lead operative said into his sleeve mike. "Let's take her."

Vanderveen, whose mind was focused on Earth and what was about to unfold there, was completely unaware of the white box truck until it swerved over to the curb. That was the moment when a side door whirred open and two Fisks grabbed her from behind. They took control of the diplomat's arms, lifted Vanderveen off her feet, and carried her toward the truck. She tried to call for help, but there wasn't enough time, as the men threw her inside. The whole evolution consumed no more than twenty seconds. Three more seconds than the Fisks would have preferred, but well within the margins of safety, as the young woman struggled to free herself.

Number four pressed a pistol-shaped injector against Christine's shoulder and pulled the trigger. Vanderveen felt a sharp pain as powerful sedatives were injected through both the weave of her jacket *and* into her bloodstream. There was a moment of dizziness, followed by a long fall into an ocean of blackness, and a complete cessation of thought. When Vanderveen came to, she found herself flat on her back, looking up at a blur. It gradually resolved into the face of a man who had a bar code on his forehead, intensely green eyes, and a three-day growth of beard. Judging from his expression, he was clearly concerned. "Ms. Vanderveen? How do you feel?"

The diplomat blinked her eyes experimentally, tried to sit, and felt a sharp pain lance through her head. "I feel terrible," the diplomat answered honestly. "Where am I? And why am I here?"

"You're in a safe place," the man said evasively. "As to why, well, that's simple. . . . We want to talk to you."

The diplomat should have been frightened. But somehow, for reasons she couldn't put a finger on, she wasn't. "Next time just call and make an appointment," Vanderveen said thickly. "I promise to clear my calendar."

The man laughed as a young woman appeared at his side. She had black hair, bangs that functioned to conceal the bar code on her forehead, and was very pretty. She offered a white pill with one hand—and a cup of water with the other. "It's a pain pill," the woman explained. "For your headache."

Vanderveen looked from the pill over to the man. "It's safe," he assured her. "Had we meant to do you harm, we would have done so by now."

That made sense, so the diplomat took the pill, and chased it with two gulps of water. "Thank you," she said. "Sort of. Who are you people anyway?"

"My birth name is Trotski-Four—but my free name is Alan," the man answered.

"And my birth name is Yee-Seven, but you can call me Mary," the woman added.

Vanderveen nodded, forced herself to sit up, and was pleased to discover that the pain was starting to abate. Now, being able to see more, she realized she was in some sort of utility room. Shelving occupied most of one wall, a utility sink stood against another, a robo janitor sat in a corner. The machine's green ready-light eyed them unblinkingly. "Don't tell me, let me guess," the diplomat said sourly. "I'm being held in the world headquarters of the Freedom Now party."

Mary frowned, but Alan laughed. "Very good! That isn't what we call ourselves, but that's our goal, and we need your help."

"Sorry," Vanderveen replied, "but you put the snatch on the wrong person. I'm a lowly FSO-2, and what you want is a 1, or an assistant secretary of state."

"We tried to establish contact with Secretary Yatsu, but either the secret police were able to block our communication, or she chose to ignore our message."

"Not to mention the fact that she has bodyguards," Mary put in. "That's why we settled on you."

"That's right," Alan said enthusiastically. "You can carry a message for us!"

"Gee, thanks," Vanderveen responded dryly. "I'm honored. What sort of message?"

There was something about the intensity of Alan's expression, and his obvious sincerity, that Vanderveen found appealing as the clone paced back and forth. "Our people live under what amounts to a hereditary dictatorship," the clone said disparagingly. "And they want a say in government."

"Including the right to have free-breeder sex and babies," Mary said firmly.

"That's already taking place," Alan added matter-of-factly. "There was a time when ninety-eight percent of all babies were sterilized, but that number continues to fall, as people bribe med techs to skip the procedure, in hopes that future generations can reproduce normally. In the meantime many of those who can are having babies. In spite of the fact that the death squads track some of them down."

Vanderveen's eyebrows rose. "Death squads?"

"*Yes,*" Mary said emphatically. "Most of the police are members of the Romo line, and primarily interested in keeping the peace, but about ten percent of them are Nerovs. And they are completely ruthless. Some say they take their orders from the Alphas—others claim they kill on their own. It makes very little difference," she finished soberly. "Dead is dead."

Vanderveen looked from the woman, who stood with arms folded, back to Alan. The revolutionary had stopped pacing by then and was staring at her with his electric green eyes. "I'm no expert on your culture," the diplomat said carefully. "But why would the founder and her advisors authorize a line like the Nerovs?"

The male clone answered so quickly it was as if he'd been waiting for the question. "Because Dr. Hosokowa was interested in creating the perfect *society*," he explained. "Not perfect people, because that would be impossible. So countervailing forces were put into play. That's why she commissioned *my* line, to make sure someone would stir things up, and thereby keep the Alpha Clones on their toes. And Mary's line, to provide the two percent of the male population that hadn't been sterilized with a sexual outlet, but one that wouldn't produce children."

"*Couldn't* produce children," the woman said sadly, as a tear trickled down her cheek. "Even though the first Yee was chosen because she was sexually attractive."

"All so the great society could survive," Alan concluded. "Which, when you think about it, was Hosokowa's child."

"So you're doing what you were created to do," Vanderveen mused out loud. "Doesn't that mean your efforts are doomed to failure? Because other lines are dedicated to canceling you out?"

"Not this time," Alan said grimly. "There's too much unhappiness. The people are ready to rise up and take control of what is rightfully theirs!"

Vanderveen had been skeptical at first. But the more the diplomat listened, the more she began to believe that a revolution was possible. And with that belief came certain questions. Important questions that could have a bearing on the war with the Ramanthians. If the clones were to rise up, and overthrow the existing government, how would that affect the new alliance? Because if that came apart, Nankool's strategy would crumble, and the Confederacy would teeter on the edge of defeat. "You mentioned a message," the diplomat said cautiously. "What did you have in mind?"

"Go to President Nankool," Alan instructed. "Tell him that the revolution is about to begin, and when it takes place, there will be an opportunity. By recognizing the new government quickly, and allowing it to join the Confederacy without delay, he will be in a position to replace the existing alliance with something far more valuable: a member state."

It was a stunning opportunity, or would be if the population actually rose up, but before Vanderveen could respond to the offer the door slammed open and Fisk-Three appeared. He was dressed in homemade body armor—and armed with a machine pistol. "The Nerovs are here," the clone said matter-of-factly. "Take her out through the sewers. . . . We'll hold them off for as long as we can."

Suddenly, Alan had one of Vanderveen's arms, and Mary had the other, as they hustled the diplomat out of the store-room and down a hall. Off in the distance the muted *rattle* of automatic fire could be heard, as the secret police attempted to search the building, and the Fisks sought to delay them.

Then Vanderveen was propelled through a doorway, down a flight of metal stairs, and into a room filled with what appeared to be the building's heating and cooling equipment. Machines *rumbled*, *whined*, and *purred* as the threesome jogged between them. The floor-mounted access hatch was made out of steel, and protected by a three-sided tubular railing and a length of bright yellow chain. The sign that dangled from it read, "Danger! Authorized personnel only!" But that didn't stop Alan from unhooking the chain—and motioning for the women to enter the restricted area. Mary turned the wheel mounted on top of the hatch, pulled the dome-shaped closure upwards, and motioned with her free hand. "Down the ladder! Quick before the Nerovs come!"

Part of Vanderveen wanted to stay, and thereby free her-self from captivity, but another more professional persona said no. The alliance with the Hegemony was clearly impor-tant, and if the revolution that Alan spoke of actually took place, a preexisting relationship could be extremely advanta-geous. So the diplomat nodded, turned, and grabbed hold of the protective railing. Once Vanderveen's right foot found the top rung of the ladder, the descent began.

The shaft went down about twenty feet or so, and it wasn't long before Mary's body blocked much of the light from above, and the smell of raw sewage rose to envelop the diplomat. She had been dressed for work when snatched off the streets, but something told her that the pantsuit was destined for a recycling chute, as her pumps came into contact with the duracrete below.

Mary was only a few feet above her, so Vanderveen hurried to get out of the way, and found herself on a raised walkway that ran parallel to a river of sewage. The odor was so strong it made the diplomat gag as she wondered where she was relative to her hotel. The ceiling was curved, oppressively low, and equipped with recessed lights. There weren't all that many though, not more than one every fifty feet, and some were burned out. That contributed to the dark, claustrophobic feel of the tunnel, and caused Vanderveen to question the decision made minutes before.

"The place stinks!" Alan acknowledged cheerfully, as he appeared at her elbow. "But it's reasonably safe. The Nerovs don't come down here unless they absolutely have to—because they know at least half of them will get killed if they try. That doesn't prevent them from sending robots, though—some of which are quite nasty. So keep your eyes peeled."

On that cheerful note, the three of them set off. Alan was in the lead, with the two women following. The stench was nauseating, so Vanderveen tried to breathe through her mouth, and memorize the route. But there were too many twists and turns, so it wasn't long before the diplomat was forced to give up.

Then they passed under a low arch, and arrived in front of a gate guarded by two seemingly identical men. Both had stocky bodies, appeared to be quite strong, and stood no more than four feet tall. The sentries were armed with pistols appropriated from Nerovs who had been brave enough, or stupid enough, to enter the maze of tunnels under Alpha Prime. "They're Lothos," Mary explained. "The founder chose their progenitor, Lars Lotho for both his engineering expertise, and small stature. It's easier to work down here if you're small." The history of the Lotho line was especially interesting, since unlike Alan and Mary, the Lothos hadn't been born into the role of outsiders. But were there more mainstream rebels? Or were the Lothos the exception? Time would tell.

A mesh barrier barred the way, and metal clanged as one of the guards opened a door that allowed the fugitives to enter the holding area. "That's one of our habs," Alan explained, as he pointed to the brightly lit area that lay beyond a second mesh wall. Vanderveen saw that sections of solid flooring had been laid over the open sewer, and the duracrete walls were covered with idealized murals, plus a variety of slogans. "Before we show you around," the clone continued, "we'll need to visit the clean rooms."

"It's annoying," Mary added apologetically, "but necessary. Please follow me."

So Vanderveen followed the prostitute through a doorway and into a room equipped with two standard gynecological tables. That was enough to stop the diplomat in her tracks—but Mary had already begun to strip. "It's almost impossible to visit the surface without picking up half a dozen robots," the clone explained. "Most can't harm you directly, but the Nerovs can track them, and that's a problem. It's difficult for low-power signals to reach the surface from down here, and we have scramblers, but it pays to be careful."

Mary was nearly naked by then—and Vanderveen could see why the first Yee had been chosen for her job. The prostitute had large breasts, a flat stomach, and a nicely rounded bottom. A female nurse entered the room, and Mary was quick to climb up on the examining table and spread her long slim legs. Then, as the diplomat began to remove her pantsuit, the cleaning process began. It consisted of examining the clone's body through a pair of high-tech goggles, removing the tiny machines with a pair of tweezers, and dropping each of them into an acid bath.

Ten minutes later it was Vanderveen's turn. But at least

the naked diplomat knew what to expect, even if the process was embarrassing, and seemed to last forever. Finally, having been declared "clean," Vanderveen was free to get down off the table and put on a new set of clothes. They were at least one size too large and anything but fashionable. Alan and Mary were waiting outside. After the threesome were cleared through the second barrier, the diplomat was taken on a tour. Strangers were a rarity, so people had a tendency to stare. Vanderveen tried to ignore that, as she was led through a brightly painted cafeteria, family-style living quarters, and into a school full of free-breeder children. "This is what we're fighting for," Mary said tightly, as the visitors looked in on a room full of preteen children. "It's too late for people like Alan and me— but they will be able to lead normal lives."

"But only if we win," Alan said harshly. "Otherwise, the death squads will find the children and kill them."

"So, you'll do it?" Mary wanted to know. "You'll take our message to your government?"

Vanderveen eyed the room and the children before turning back to Alan and Mary. "Yes," the diplomat assured them. "I will carry your message to my government. But, will they listen? That's anybody's guess."

6

There is many a boy here today who looks on war as all glory, but, boys, it is all hell.

—Union General William Tecumseh Sherman
Speech at Columbus, Ohio
Standard year 1880

PLANET GAMMA-014, THE CLONE HEGEMONY

The assault boat shuddered as it bucked its way down through the atmosphere, and the men, women, and cyborgs of Alpha Company, 2nd Battalion, 1st REC waited to find out if they were going to live or die. Because in spite of the fact that the invasion of Gamma-014 was less than six hours old, the attack had already been described as a "fucking disaster" by General Kobbi, who was certainly in a position to know. The opinion had not been shared with the troops, lest it erode their morale, but Captain Antonio Santana was cognizant of it. All because Commanding General-453 was an idiot.

The campaign to defeat the Ramanthian navy, or chase it away, had gone smoothly. Perhaps *too* smoothly in the opinion of some, who were aware of General Oro Akoto's reputation, and wondered if the wily Ramanthian *wanted* the allies to land. But General-453 had been quick to categorize all such theories as "defeatist nonsense," as he and his mostly clone staff hurried to harvest what they felt certain would be a quick and painless victory. The only problem was that most of the people in the first wave, which was almost entirely comprised of Jonathan Alan Seebos, were slaughtered as they landed—in large part because they put down in all of the most predictable places.

And so, rather than the victorious battle footage that General-453 had been counting on for consumption back home, he was forced to watch video of his clone brothers being shot down as they stumbled out of burning assault boats, were blown to smithereens by Ramanthian artillery, and crushed by Ramanthian tanks.

But rather than question his strategy, which would have been to admit that he'd been wrong, General-453 chose to throw more troops at the same objectives. Which meant that as the 1st Regiment Etranger de Cavalerie (1st REC), the 2nd Regiment Etranger d'Infanterie (2nd REI), and the 4th Regiment Etranger (4th RE) dropped into Gamma-014's turbulent atmosphere, they were slated to land right in the middle of the same free-fire zones that the dead Seebos had.

And Santana knew that Lieutenant Colonel Quinlan's battalion, which was to say both Alpha and Bravo Companies, had been given a generous slice of a very ugly pie. Specifically, a long, U-shaped valley that had a Class III hydroelectric plant sitting at its south end. Where, thanks to the ingenuity of General Akoto's forces, the electricity intended for the city of Prosperity, which was located some thirty miles to the east, had been redirected to a battery of three surface-to-orbit (STO) energy cannons. These world-class weapons had already been responsible for the loss of a destroyer escort and numerous smaller ships.

The assault boat rocked as an antiaircraft round exploded nearby and the pilot spoke over the intercom. "Sorry about the rough ride, folks. . . . But we're five from dirt, so I'd like to be the first, and probably the only person to welcome you to Gamma-014! Don't forget to take personal items with you, duck on the way out, and give my regards to the bugs."

That produced a chorus of chuckles, as the platoon leaders ordered their people to, "lock and load." The ship lurched as the wash from an exploding rocket hit the hull, sideslipped toward the ground, and seemed to fall the last few feet. There was a solid jolt as the skids hit hard and bullets began to *rattle* against the armored hull as the stern ramp made contact with the ground.

Privates Ivan Lupo and Simy Xiong were slated to exit the ship first and knew how important the next ten minutes would be. Because it was their job to suppress the incoming fire and provide the other legionnaires with an opportunity to exit the ship unharmed. So the hulking cyborgs lumbered down onto the ground, turned in opposite directions, and took up positions to either side of the slab-sided ship. Targeting data was acquired, prioritized, and acted on as both war forms opened fire. And, because each fifty-ton behemoth mounted dual autoloading missile launchers, four gang-mounted energy cannons, and an electronically driven Gatling gun, that was a sight to see! Especially as the cyborgs settled in over their vulnerable legs and transformed themselves into low-profile pillboxes.

As Santana rode Deker out of the ship's cargo bay, he saw that the assault boat had put down next to a burned-out hulk. Judging from the still-steaming bodies that lay scattered about, *all* of the Seebos on that first ill-fated boat had clearly been killed. However, based on the fact that a platoon of clones had taken cover in a fire-blackened crater and were firing on targets to the east, it appeared that a subsequent landing had been more successful. The entire area was littered with half-empty ammo boxes, packaging for battle dressings, and cast-off equipment.

As the Seebos continued to huddle in their shell crater, the quads targeted Ramanthian mortars, artillery pieces, and the deadly multiple-launch rocket systems located on both sides of the valley. Outgoing missiles *roared* off their rails, bolts of coherent energy stuttered across the battlefield, and dark columns of soil were thrown high into the air as secondary explosions echoed between the valley walls. Shortly after that, Santana saw the volume of incoming fire begin to dwindle and knew that Alpha Company was making progress.

Meanwhile the Seebos came boiling up out of the crater, or tried to, but were driven back when Santana ordered Deker to open fire. Three bursts from the T-2's arm-mounted fifty were sufficient to push the clones back. "Take me down into that hole," Santana said over the intercom, and switched to the company push. "This is Alpha Six. . . . Let's get the wounded out of that crater and onto the ship. Watch for fakers though. . . . It looks like some of those guys would like to take the rest of the day off. Alpha One-Four and Bravo One-Four will prepare to board troops. Both platoons will orient on target Alpha and prepare to advance. The first platoon will protect the company's left flank and the second will cover the right. Out."

The entire battalion had been assigned to attack the STO battery, but having seen no sign of either Colonel Quinlan or Bravo Company, Santana knew his unit might have to tackle the objective alone. A scary thought indeed.

The wounded clones had been carried aboard the assault boat by that time and engines screamed as the ship began to lift. "Hey, *you*!" one of the Seebos said angrily, as Deker carried him down into the body-strewn crater. "How dare you fire on us! Bring the assault boat back. . . . The navy is supposed to extract us!"

There was a resounding *boom* as a shoulder-launched missile hit the ship's port engine, blew a hole in it, and caused the boat to roll. It landed upside down, skidded for about fifty feet, and burst into flames. Santana was pleased to see two figures crawl out of the inverted cockpit and scurry away. But the wounded weren't so lucky. The company commander's voice boomed through speakers built into the war form's body as he turned back toward the clone. "And you are?"

"Lieutenant Jonathan Alan Seebo-179,620," the clone officer answered haughtily, as a spent round hit Deker's chest. It made a pinging sound as it bounced off.

"My name is Santana," the legionnaire replied evenly. "And I command Alpha Company, 2nd Battalion, 1st REC.

You and your men can help us take that power plant or die in this crater. Which would you prefer?"

The clone heard a bullet *zing* over his head and scowled resentfully. "We'll come with you."

"Good choice," Santana replied. "Your call sign will be Alpha Two-Zero. Split your men between the quads—and let's get the hell out of here."

The Ramanthian in command of the powerful STO battery at the south end of the valley chose that moment to fire a salvo. The energy cannons were so powerful that the energy bolts they fired broke the sound barrier before they disappeared into space. The recoil caused the ground to shake. The better part of fifteen minutes would pass before the gun emplacement's huge accumulators could store enough power to fire again. "Damn!" Deker exclaimed, as he carried the company commander up out of the crater. "Why don't the swabbies bomb those things?"

"The Intel people say the bugs have more than a thousand civilians locked up under that gun emplacement," Santana replied grimly. "So it's up to us."

Deker chose to accept the explanation, but both legionnaires knew that the bugs might very well execute the POWs, especially if it looked like the STO weapons were about to be captured. As the Seebos scurried aboard the quads, and Deker found level ground, Sergeant Suresee Fareye made his report. Like Dietrich, the Naa had served with Santana before, and had an almost supernatural ability to find his way through any terrain. He was mounted on Private Ka Nhan, and the two legionnaires were concealed in a farm building approximately one mile south of the burned-out crater. "Alpha Six-Four to Alpha Six. Over."

"This is Six," Santana replied, as he glanced at the data projected onto his HUD. "Go."

"Four, repeat *four*, Gantha II tanks are coming out to play," Fareye said, as he peered out through a hole in the south wall of a barn. Six genetically perfect cattle had been left in the building, and they bawled miserably as the Naa continued his report. "The Ganthas are supported by a couple dozen armored personnel carriers all loaded with troops. Estimated time to first contact five minutes. Over."

Santana swore silently. Even though he'd been aware that the Ramanthians would probably throw some tanks at him the legionnaire had been hoping for more time. A quick look at the HUD confirmed that the wind was blowing up the valley toward the dam. "Roger that," he replied. "Pull back, Six-Four. . . . Alpha Six to Alpha One-Six. Send the first squad forward to lay smoke east to west. . . . But I don't want them sucked into a firefight. Out."

"This is Alpha One-Six," Lieutenant Lucy Amoyo replied. "Smoke but don't engage. We're going in. Out."

The last sentence seemed to indicate that Amoyo was planning to lead the evolution personally in spite of Santana's instructions to ". . . send the first squad up." And a quick check of the ITC confirmed that impression. A fraction of a second passed while the company commander considered the pros and cons of pulling the platoon leader back. Then, having decided that no great harm was likely to come of Amoyo's decision, Santana let the matter go.

Alpha Company was up to full speed by that time, closing with the enemy at a combined speed of thirty miles per hour as chits on both sides of the valley continued to fire on them. Having called for air support, Dietrich gave a grunt of approval as a pair of navy Daggers *roared* overhead, and banked over the dam. Triple A burst all around the fighters. One of them lost a wing and tumbled into a cliff, where it exploded. Consistent with their instructions, the second fighter made a run at the tanks. A stick of bombs fell, explosions blossomed, and one of the beetle-shaped monsters took a direct hit. "This is Rover Four-Zero," the pilot said laconically, as she passed over the company. "I'm running on fumes—sorry we couldn't do more. Over."

Dietrich thought about the pilot who had just lost his or her life. "You did good, Four-Zero, *real* good. Thanks. Over."

Meanwhile, having arrived at a point halfway between

the Ramanthians and Alpha Company, Amoyo took a sharp right-hand turn and led the first squad toward the west side of the valley. That was more difficult than it sounded because there were irrigation ditches, dry-fitted stone walls, and other obstacles to leap over. Not to mention the Cyon River, which was a good six feet deep at that point, and moving at a steady five miles per hour.

But the T-2s were more than up to the challenge and were moving so fast that, when the enemy tanks opened fire on them, the chits inside the big, beetle-shaped machines weren't able to traverse their secondary weapons fast enough to catch up with the agile cyborgs.

So as geysers of soil and rock followed the legionnaires across the valley, Amoyo and her bio bods were free to sow smoke grenades like seeds. Each bomb produced a cloud of dense black smoke that would not only prevent the bugs from seeing Alpha Company but block targeting lasers and enemy range finders as well. And, thanks to the tiny bits of burning plastic that were ejected by the grenades, the screen was at least partially effective against thermal-imaging devices, too.

Amoyo swore as her T-2 jumped into the ice-cold river. The water had risen all the way up to her waist before the cyborg made it to the other side, where he splashed up onto the bank. The good news was that her mission had been accomplished, but now she was on the *west* side of the valley, and cut off from the rest of her platoon. Suddenly she understood why Captain Santana wanted Staff Sergeant Briggs to take the first squad out. And, as if to reinforce the lesson just learned, the company commander put Dietrich in charge of the rest of her platoon. His voice flooded the company push. "Alpha Six-Two will take command of the second squad, first platoon. Out."

Amoyo heard Master Sergeant Dietrich say, "This is Six-Two. Roger, that. Out." That left her with no option but to wheel toward the enemy and thereby reinforce the company's right flank.

Santana saw the change on the ITC and grinned as the wall of black smoke gradually blew toward the south. "This is Alpha Six. Let's hook the bastards! Out." Everyone in the company knew what Santana meant, because the "buffalo horns" formation dated back to the Zulu War of 1879, and involved the use of flanking elements or "horns" to at least partially encircle the enemy, while the "chest" or main force came up the middle. In this case, the main force consisted of two badly outgunned quads. Had Bravo Company been present there would have been four quads and something like parity.

Still, it wasn't as if Santana had a choice, given the fact that the bugs weren't likely to surrender. As the Ramanthians rolled into the smoke, the first and second platoons circled around them, turned inwards, and immediately came into contact with the enemy's APCs. The troops weren't all that dangerous, not so long as they remained sealed inside their durasteel boxes, but the vehicles they were riding in carried grenade launchers and machine guns. The automatic weapons *chattered* madly as the T-2s entered a hellish world of drifting smoke, blazing guns, and fiery explosions. A place where Santana, like the bio bods all around him, was reduced to little more than baggage as Deker went to work.

The key to survival inside the war fog was speed and agility. Deker cut between two dimly seen APCs, firing both his fifty and energy cannon as he ran. The bullets failed to penetrate Ramanthian armor, but one of his energy bolts scored a direct hit on a track, which brought one machine to a halt.

In the meantime, even though Santana was being thrown back and forth like a sack of potatoes, it was his job to monitor the ITC and make sure that the melee didn't get out of hand. "Watch for friendlies," the company commander cautioned. "We have enough opposition without shooting at each other. Out."

But the cautionary advice came too late for Private Steelgrip Cutright, who was decapitated by an energy bolt fired by Corporal Bin Han. So that, as Cutright's T-2 continued to fight, his headless body flopped back and forth, spewing blood in every direction. Nor was Cutright the company's only casualty. Because some of the enemy APCs had discharged their troops by then, and bio bod Kai Hayasaki and cyborg Bin Batain both lost their lives when a shoulder-launched missile struck them. Fortunately such incidents were rare thanks to all the smoke and the speed with which the T-2s could move.

But speedy or not, the smaller war forms had been unable to so much as scratch the Gantha tanks as the Ramanthians opened fire. The first rounds fell short of the quads but threw columns of dirt high into the air, which meant that the Seebos riding inside the quadrupeds could hear what sounded like a hailstorm as rocks and soil rained down on the metal above their heads. It didn't take a genius to know that the big war form was being targeted, and that wasn't fair. Not to Lieutenant-620's way of thinking. Because having survived the horrors of the crater—the officer felt that he and his men deserved something better than death in a metal box.

Of course, both Lupo and Xiong had been killed before, and had no intention of dying again, at least not so soon. So they answered the Ramanthian attack with a salvo of four heat-seeking missiles, followed by a blinding fusillade of energy bolts as all eight of their combined cannons began to fire.

One of the enemy tanks exploded as two missiles hit it. A second lost a track, and began to turn circles, but there was no stopping the third. And that was scary, because as high-explosive rounds continued to go off around the quads, they both knew it was just a matter of time before one or both of them took a direct hit.

But only if they were stupid enough to attack the enemy head-on. Much had been written about the advantages and disadvantages inherent in the quad design, but there was one thing that no one could dispute, and that was the fact that the huge cyborgs could step *sideways*. Something tracked vehicles couldn't do.

So the quads began to move *away* from each other—thereby forcing the Ramanthian tank commander to choose between two targets. And, with each step they took, the quads could see more and more of the Gantha's sloped flanks, where the machine's reactive armor was slightly thinner. Then, when a sufficient amount of black metal was visible, the legionnaires loosed another salvo of missiles. The weapons hit, punched their way through the Ramanthian armor, and sent jets of hot plasma into the crew compartments. A powerful secondary explosion sent the Gantha's turret soaring high into the air. It seemed to hang there for a moment, as if held aloft by an invisible hand, before falling on a burning APC.

It was an important accomplishment. Because now, with the tanks out of the way, there was nothing to prevent the legionnaires from attacking the STO emplacement. But before Santana could give the necessary orders an all-too-familiar voice flooded his helmet. "This is Zulu Six. Hold where you are. I'm three minutes north of you and I'll be there shortly. Out."

Santana turned toward the north and saw that a shuttle was coming in low and fast. Where had Quinlan been anyway? "This is Alpha Six," Santana said. "Platoon leaders will reintegrate their forces, check for casualties, and rearm their T-2s. Lieutenant Seebo-620. I would be obliged if you and your men would establish a temporary perimeter around the company and provide security. Out."

There was a series of acknowledgments as the clones exited the quads, and the T-2s were ordered to close with the quadrupeds, so they could take on ammo from the larger war forms. Meanwhile, the shuttle had put down. Quinlan and his T-2 were the first to disembark. Bravo Company's quads followed, along with two platoons of T-2s, and a technical support unit. "Sorry we're late," Quinlan said, as the two men came together. "Our shuttle developed engine trouble after we hit the atmosphere, and we were forced to put down so the swabbies could clear it. But we're here now—and the mission remains the same."

Even though the T-2s were only three feet apart from each other, they weren't privy to the conversation that was taking place on the command channel. "Roger that, sir," Santana replied. "We can use the help. And we need to get under way quickly—before the enemy can reinforce their defenses."

"There's no need to belabor the obvious," Quinlan responded irritably. "Tell your people that the attack will commence in five minutes."

Santana nodded. "Sir, yes sir."

There was an awkward pause at that point, as if the battalion officer wanted to say something more, but wasn't sure how to do so. Finally, having swiveled his body toward the bloody LZ where Alpha Company had put down, Quinlan spoke without looking back. "And Santana. . . ."

"Sir?"

"Well done."

Santana was surprised, but managed a nod. "Thank you, sir. I'll pass that along."

"See that you do," Quinlan said curtly as he turned back, and his normal persona reasserted itself. "Thirty seconds of that five minutes have elapsed. You'd better get cracking."

Meanwhile, ten miles to the south and high atop the dam where the Ramanthian STOs were sited, Force Commander Rundee Homar stood atop a huge gun mount as he peered through a pair of Y-shaped binoculars. Having twice failed to put a significant number of troops on ground, the animals had finally been able to land a company of grotesque cyborgs. And now, having been reinforced by air, the abominations were preparing to attack the STO emplacement. Which, given the way they had defeated the tanks, was doomed. Or that's how it seemed until a truly revolutionary idea blossomed in Homar's brain. What if, rather than destroy the energy cannons and withdraw the way he was supposed to, the Ramanthian were to turn one of the weapons at his disposal on the troops in the valley? And thereby destroy all of the animals with a *single* bolt of energy? That would leave him and his troops with plenty of time to slaughter the prisoners *and* blow the dam prior to an orderly retreat!

But there wasn't much time, so he and his troops would have to work fast if they were to bring a cannon to bear on the valley. Homar lowered the binoculars, turned toward the battery behind him, and began to issue orders.

With twice the number of T-2s and quads lumbering up the valley, Santana felt a renewed sense of optimism, as Quinlan led roughly half the battalion toward the heavily fortified dam. And, truth be told, it had been a relief to surrender overall command. Because even though he wasn't especially proud of it, there was comfort in the knowledge that mistakes, if any, wouldn't be *his*.

In marked contrast to his behavior on Oron IV, Quinlan was leading from the front. Was that the result of his long-delayed promotion? Or a change of behavior that was somehow linked to his daughter's death? There was no way to know as the portly colonel led his troops into battle.

Bravo Company, which had been ordered to lead the way, was within range of the enemy guns by then and opened fire with a vengeance. The legionnaires could lay down another smoke screen, and zigzag back and forth, but there wasn't much more they could do other than pray as shells exploded all about them. Bravo Company took the brunt of the fire, and it wasn't long before what had been an orderly formation was reduced to a ragged group of survivors. One of the quads lost a leg, T-2s were tossed into the air like toys, and bio bods were ripped apart by flying shrapnel. It was a horrible sight and made all the worse by the fact that there was very little the legionnaires could do as the Ramanthians fired down on them.

Meanwhile, Force Commander Homar was having problems of his own. The concept of using one of the STO cannons to destroy the animals with a single shot had been brilliant. But, having turned one of the thirty-foot-long monsters toward the north, his gunners were having trouble depressing the barrel far enough to target the oncoming aliens. The problem stemmed from safeties built into the software used to aim and fire the big weapons, and mechanical stops that were intended to prevent the very thing the Ramanthian officer was trying to do. The first issue had been resolved by switching the control mode from automatic to manual. And now, as Homar looked on, a technician was cutting his way through the last of three six-inch-thick metal tabs that kept the cannons from firing on the planet's surface.

But the humans were coming on fast, and Homar knew that if he and his gunners failed to fire the weapon soon, the animals would be too close to hit. So as the last piece of glowing metal hit the floor, the Ramanthian gun crew hurried to crank the long black tube down as far as it would go, and locked the barrel in place. The accumulators were fully charged, so all Homar had to do was shout, "Fire!" and a blue comet was born.

For the duration of its short life the enormous energy bolt had mass. It was only a foot in diameter as it left the cannon's barrel, but quickly expanded to twelve times that size, so that Santana could feel the heat as the flaming comet passed over his head. Then he heard a loud *shriek*, quickly followed by an enormous explosion, and a flash of light so intense the legionnaire might have been blinded had he been looking north.

That was when an earthquake shook the ground under Deker's feet. A shock wave hit the war form from behind and threw him facedown. Santana fell with him. The cyborg struggled to stand as echoes of the thunderous explosion bounced back and forth between the valley's walls. It took a moment for Santana to process what had occurred, but once he had, the officer realized how lucky the battalion had been. Because rather than strike the legionnaires as intended, the enormous ball of energy had passed over them, and blown a huge divot out of the valley's floor.

But that wasn't all . . . Either because they were as shocked as the legionnaires were, or the Ramanthian gunners had been blinded by the initial explosion, their guns had fallen silent! "This is Alpha Six," Santana proclaimed. "Let's go up and kill those bastards!"

Though not the most precise order the legionnaire had ever given, it was among the most heartfelt, and other officers were quick to echo it—including Lieutenant Colonel Quinlan, who was among the first members of the battalion to close with the dam and start up the access road that led to the top. It was too narrow for the quads to follow and was interrupted by a number of switchbacks, each of which constituted a natural defensive point.

Colonel Quinlan was followed by elements of Bravo Company and Alpha Company, with Santana in the lead. The battalion's ranks were thinner now and the Seebos were hard-pressed to keep up with the fast-moving cyborgs. Santana took advantage of the situation by instructing the clones to seek out and protect the civilian POWs. It was an order he half expected Quinlan to countermand.

But if the colonel heard the interchange, he gave no sign of it, as lead elements of the battalion arrived at the first switchback, where they were confronted by hundreds of Ramanthian regulars. At that point, what had been a largely long-distance duel carried out with high-tech weapons was transformed into a bloody hand-to-pincer brawl that would have been familiar to the legionnaires of the distant past.

Neither side could use hand grenades, lest they kill their own soldiers, but assault rifles used at close quarters could punch through body armor. And some legionnaires, like Master Sergeant Dice Dietrich, carried backup weapons for such occasions. His weapon of choice was a shotgun that made distinctive *boom, clack, boom* sounds as it was fired into the crowd. Often accounting for two or three enemy soldiers with a single shot.

But the battle was far from one-sided. All of Force Commander Homar's officers and noncoms were equipped with power-assisted body armor that could literally rip a human apart. And it was one such trooper who managed to punch a fist through Private Ren Rosato's chest plate, grab hold of some electronics, and jerk them out.

Rosato's brain was still alive, but his body was out of action, which made his bio bod very angry. His name was Private Horu Bora-Sa. And while the three-hundred-pound Hudathan had long carried his father's battle-ax into action, he had never been given an opportunity to use it before. So, having freed himself from his harness as the T-2 fell, Bora-Sa drew the clan's "Ka-killer," and went to work. Light glinted off the two-hundred-year-old ax, and gore flew left and right, as the angry Hudathan shouted the ancient battle cry: "*BLOOD!*"

The shout was echoed by Hudathans and Humans alike, along with cries of "*CAMERONE!*" which was the name of the famous battle in which Captain Jean Danjou and a force of sixty-two legionnaires had taken on thousands of Mexican regulars in 1863. Those cries, plus a renewed effort by the towering T-2s, was enough to push the bugs back as the cyborgs fought for a purchase on the steep blood-slicked road. "After them!" Quinlan was heard to shout, as the Ramanthians began to retreat. "Cut the bastards down!"

"*Hold!*" Force Commander Homar ordered, having raised his sword over his head, and deployed his wings. Noncoms blew their whistles, and their troopers took to the air as well. It was a desperate move, because as a result of the long, slow evolutionary process, all but the young and very fit were limited to only short bursts of flight. But the effort was successful in that it momentarily neutralized the height advantage that the cyborgs had.

Unfortunately for the Ramanthians, however, every fourth T-2 was equipped with a flamethrower in place of the standard energy cannon. Weapons that soon proved to be very effective against the airborne bugs. Wings burst into flames as they beat against the air, and insectoid troopers screamed as they cartwheeled to their deaths.

Homar had accepted defeat by then, but was determined

to take a human with him, and flew straight at Colonel Quinlan. The Ramanthian was a good ten feet off the ground by that time—and so full of naturally produced stimulants that flying was easy.

Quinlan's cyborg could have blown the Ramanthian out of the air, but was engaged in pincer-to-pincer combat with an armored noncom, and couldn't respond. There was a strange moment as the two adversaries locked eyes, the battalion commander raised his sidearm, and Homar swung his blade. Three bullets struck the Ramanthian's face, blew the back of his head out, and sprayed the troopers behind him with gore. The sword fell, but the officer's body continued to hang there for a moment, as his wings fanned the air. So Quinlan fired again. "That's for Nancy, you butt-ugly bastard!"

Homar's body fell, a shout went up as the legionnaires surged forward, and the Trooper IIs began to run. The Ramanthians, none of whom could manage more than a fast shuffle, didn't stand a chance. Even though Santana ordered his men to take prisoners, the legionnaires weren't in the mood. Not after the slaughter in the LZ, the long march up the valley, and the attempt to eradicate them with the STO cannon. They fired until their weapons ran dry, reloaded on the run, and fired again. So that by the time the battalion gained the top of the dam and the gun emplacement was located there, a long trail of dead bodies lay behind them.

Demolition charges had been set, and were about to be detonated, when Dietrich and Fareye arrived. Both of their T-2s were out of ammo by then, but the master sergeant had four shotgun shells left, and the Naa had his knife. Three Ramanthians went down in as many seconds and the dam, not to mention the valley below, was spared.

And, thanks to the efforts of Lieutenant-620 and his See-bos, all of the 1,142 civilian POWs who had been held prisoner next to the huge generators, were secured before the Ramanthians could execute them. A sharply fought action that would probably earn the young officer a medal, assuming he survived long enough to pin the bauble on.

Santana jumped to the ground and walked over to stand next to the STO cannon. It was still aimed at a huge crater in the valley below. The Cyon River had begun to flow into the depression by that time, and it looked as if the resulting lake would be three miles long and one mile wide. Santana knew that the next few hours would be filled with casualty lists, the after-action reports that Quinlan loved so much, and a thousand other things. And once that process began, the assault on the dam would begin the slow fade into history. But right then, at that precise moment in time, a battle had been won. And that felt good.

As the legionnaire looked out over the bloodied valley, and the slowly thickening clouds beyond, a single snowflake came twirling down out of the lead gray sky to land on his navy parka. It was gone a few seconds later. But there would be more to come during the days, weeks, and months ahead. Because the Ramanthians had an ally—and its name was winter.

7

Tora! Tora! Tora! (Tiger! Tiger! Tiger!)

—*Coded radio transmission from Commander Mitsuo Fuchida to the Japanese Fleet just prior to the attack on Pearl Harbor Standard year 1941*

PLANET EARTH, THE CONFEDERACY OF SENTIENT BEINGS

With no fleet left to protect it, Earth was nearly defenseless, as the Ramanthian battleship *Regulus* and her consorts left hyperspace, and arrowed in toward the blue planet. There were *thousands* of them. By far the largest fleet ever assembled, even during the first and second Hudathan wars. About 25 percent of the warships were Sheen vessels that had been stolen from the Confederacy, which made the occasion that much more enjoyable from a Ramanthian perspective. Still, even though the once-mighty *Stern-Krieger* and most of her escorts had been destroyed, elements of the human armada remained. And rather than flee, as Admiral Ru Lorko fully expected them to, the "animals" came out to fight.

The counterattack wasn't a smart thing to do, since the Confederacy's ships were doomed from the start, but it *was* incredibly brave. And that was something Old Iron Back wasn't expecting to see from the humans. Not after the way the animals on the *Gladiator* surrendered months before.

But it seemed that *these* aliens were more honorable, and rather than live as cowards, had chosen to die like warriors.

It was an honor that Lorko, like any member of the fanatical *Nira* cult, was duty-bound to grant them. So as destroyers, gunboats, and even tugs threw themselves at the Ramanthian fleet they were snuffed out with methodical precision. Not even lifeboats were spared. A magnificent slaughter that Lorko would never forget.

But as thousands of humans died, and the admiral took pleasure in his victory, the Queen felt the first stirrings of worry. Because rather than surrender, as she had been assured that they would, the surviving elements of the home fleet had chosen to fight. In order to buy time? So that those down on the planet's surface could better prepare their defenses? Or for some other reason? The monarch feared the latter. What if the animals were less indolent than they appeared to be? What if somewhere, buried deep within their self-indulgent culture, there was a core of steel? That could be very dangerous indeed!

The monarch couldn't afford to let such doubts show, however, as the leading elements of her fleet swept the last remnants of resistance aside and began to trade salvos with the planet's orbital-defense platforms. The human habitats were massive affairs, each housing more than six thousand animals, and possessing a vast array of weaponry. According to intelligence reports each of the four battle stations was armed with a massive Class I energy cannon, plus two dozen lesser gun emplacements, and an equal number of missile launchers. This meant that, so long as all the platforms were operational, it would be difficult if not impossible to put a significant number of troops on the surface of the planet.

Impressive though the orbital fortifications were, however, they had a major weakness. And that was the fact that while the ring of battle stations could lose *one* platform and still bar access to the planet below, the destruction of a neighboring habitat would open a hole large enough that invading ships would be able to pour through. And because the battle stations couldn't direct their weapons downwards without running the risk of hitting Earth's surface, once enemy ships managed to penetrate the human defenses, there was nothing to fear from above.

The remaining battle platforms could launch fighters, however—a threat that the Ramanthians would have to counter. For that reason Admiral Lorko planned to put most of his capital ships against Battle Stations III and IV, while sending a swarm of smaller craft to suppress the aerospace fighters from I and II. If all went well, both platforms would be effectively sidelined.

Meanwhile, aware that there were fortifications on the moon, Old Iron Back planned to neutralize the batteries in the fastest and most expedient manner possible—nuke them. And that was the way the human colonies on Mars and Jupiter's moons would be dealt with as well. While Earth had value as a bargaining chip, the rest of the solar system's settlements weren't worth occupying, and could be dispensed with.

Yes, the Queen knew that the humans would make use of the new hypercom technology to call for help, which was why a significant portion of the fleet was being held in reserve. But given the alliance with the Clone Hegemony, plus conflicts elsewhere, it wasn't clear if the Confederacy would be able to respond in time. The coming hours and days would tell.

In spite of whatever minor doubts she had, the Queen believed the strategy would work as she looked down upon the jewel-like planet that hung below her. Animals lived on it now. But someday, perhaps thirty years in the future, all of them would be dead.

BATTLE STATION III, IN ORBIT AROUND PLANET EARTH, THE CONFEDERACY OF SENTIENT BEINGS

"All civilian and supernumerary personnel will report to the mess deck, where they will receive combat support assignments. . . ." Battle Station III's primary Command & Control (C&C) computer's soft, dispassionate voice was supposed to communicate a sense of calm, even if that didn't match what was going on. A flight of three enemy missiles struck the station within yards of each other. And the nearly simultaneous explosions caused a shield generator to overload. That created a momentary hole in the space station's defenses, which one of the Ramanthian fighters managed to exploit by firing a torpedo through it. The entire habitat shuddered as the missile penetrated the hull and killed 216 people. Within seconds the surrounding airtight compartments sealed themselves off and prevented what could have been an even larger catastrophe as the C&C computer delivered the latest piece of bad news. "The battle station's primary weapon system is off-line," the computer intoned emotionlessly. "Secondary and tertiary weapons have been delegated to local control. All damage-control parties will report to . . ."

Lieutenant JG Leo Foley didn't care where the damage-control parties were going to report. All he wanted to do was to escape the battle station's brig, round up some sort of transportation, and get the hell off the platform before the bugs began to board it. Because there wasn't a man or woman in the navy who hadn't heard about the slaughter that took place aboard the *Gladiator* once the crew put down their arms and surrendered. Some of the POWs had been taken off the battlewagon to serve as slave labor, but many had been murdered, or left to die when the ship blew. And, assuming the stories were true, the chits were especially hard on officers. Which Foley still was, for the moment at least.

Foley's thoughts were interrupted as a hatch opened and a first-class petty officer appeared. His arms were full of printouts, and it looked as though the rating had been ordered to feed the pile of documents into a shredder bolted to the opposite bulkhead. All things considered, that was *not* a good sign. "Jonesy!" Foley said imploringly. "You've got to let me out of here! You know what the bugs will do if they board. Give me a fighting chance!"

"Yeah!" a neighboring prisoner agreed loudly. "You heard the loot—give us a fighting chance!"

The shredder made a grinding noise as the jailer fed sheaves of paper into it. "How stupid do you think I am?" Jones inquired rhetorically. "Rather than fight, you eight balls would run for the nearest escape pod!"

Foley had something more comfortable than an escape pod in mind, but knew better than to say so, and continued to plead his case. "No way, Jonesy. . . . Let us out of here, give us weapons, and we'll make the bugs pay!"

There was a chorus of agreement from the other holding cells as the petty officer fed the last sheets of paper into the shredder. The battle station shuddered as something blew, and the deck started to tilt as 12 percent of the habitat's steering jets went off-line. Perhaps it was that, as much as anything else, that caused the noncom to pause and reconsider. Foley was a thief by all accounts, although the charges against the officer had yet to be proven, which meant he was theoretically innocent. The rest of the prisoners were enlisted personnel who had been charged with offenses ranging from sleeping on duty to running a distillery down in the battle station's engineering spaces. All of which were serious offenses, but they didn't justify the death penalty. And none of them deserved to be killed like rats in a trap. Because, based on what Jonesy had heard, Foley was right. The Ramanthians were merciless. "I'll probably regret this," the PO said, as he rounded the duty desk. "But what the hell? I never expected to make chief anyway."

A meaty finger stabbed at the touch-sensitive screen, six indicator lights went from red to green, and there was a metallic *clang* as all the doors slid open. The prisoners were free! Or so it seemed. But moments after rushing out of their cells, and milling around inside the detention facility, a *new* announcement came over the PA system. And, rather than the well-modulated tones typical of the C&C computer, this voice was human. Thereby raising the possibility that the

Command & Control computer was belly-up, too. "This is Lieutenant Commander Nidifer," the female voice said. "All hands will stand by to repel boarders. I repeat, *all* hands will stand by to repel boarders."

Foley swore. It didn't take a fleet admiral to figure out that if the main battery was off-line, and most of the secondary armament was down, then the bugs were going to come aboard and clean house. And, worse yet from his perspective, the five pounds of stardust that he'd been willing to sacrifice his navy career to steal was locked up where he couldn't get at it!

But there wasn't anything Foley could do about it, so the larcenous officer made his way out into the main passageway. It was a madhouse. Horns, Klaxons, and smoke detectors continued to *honk*, *bleat*, and *buzz*. The sick bay was full, and had been for some time, which explained why a long line of wounded sailors and marines lay on stretchers next to the outboard bulkhead. Medics were trying to help them, but there weren't enough hospital corpsmen to go around, so it was already too late for some of the patients.

Most of the people who were jogging, limping, or being carried past Foley were dressed in pressure suits, a reminder that, because Foley didn't have one, and wasn't likely to get his hands on one, he could wind up sucking vacuum. Especially if the chits blew a really big hole in the hull. Foley felt someone touch his arm and turned to find that a dozen brig rats were standing behind him. A second-class petty officer stepped forward. The name on his jumper was Tappas. He was thirty or so, had boyish features, and intelligent eyes. "Okay, sir," Tappas said calmly. "What do we do now?"

Foley's plans, such as they were, didn't include anyone other than himself. But the sailors looked so forlorn that he couldn't bring himself to refuse them. "It sounds like the chits are about to board," Foley said. "So we're going to need some weapons."

Tappas nodded. "Yes, sir. Then what?"

Foley, who had been planning to steal a six-person lifeboat, was forced to change his thinking. "Once we have the weapons we'll make a run for the flight deck, grab a shuttle, and head dirtside for some well deserved R&R."

It was exactly the kind of plan that Tappas and the rest of the brig rats wanted to hear. So they were quick to follow as Foley led them up corridor toward access way P-8. The corridor would carry the group in toward the lift tubes that were clustered around the battle station's hollow core, a twelve-deck-tall structure that was home to the habitat's fusion reactor, the power accumulators that fed the main battery, and the argrav generators.

Thanks to the confusion, no one thought to ask Foley where he was going. With an officer in the lead, the brig rats looked like a work detail as they jogged single file along the main corridor, accumulating weapons along the way. Which wasn't all that hard to do given that the wall-mounted arms lockers were open and rows of neatly racked weapons were there for the taking. Energy rifles for the most part, since they were less likely to punch a hole in the battle station's hull, and let the habitat's atmosphere out.

But, having made good progress for a while, Foley and his men ran into a roadblock as they approached Lock 8. There was a flash of light as an energy grenade went off, followed by a concussive *bang*, and the staccato *whine* of energy weapons as blue energy bolts stuttered back and forth. "It's the bugs!" a wild-eyed marine captain announced, as he lurched out of the drifting smoke. Foley saw the bandage that had been tied around the other officer's head was red with blood, and one of his arms hung uselessly by his side. "Come on!" the leatherneck urged. "Follow me!"

So Foley followed, knowing that if he and his men were going to reach their objective, they would have to pass the lock. And, having very little choice, Tappas and the rest of the brig rats followed. Bodies lay in heaps where an earlier attempt to board the battle station had been repulsed. But just barely, as was obvious from the fact that most of the casualties were human, and only a handful of marines remained to defend the lock as another assault began.

A hail of energy bolts sleeted back and forth as a file of heavily armored Ramanthians surged out, firing as they came. And, had the jarheads been forced to battle the aliens alone, the bugs would have been able to break through. But that was when Foley and the brig rats arrived, crouched behind the makeshift barrier that had been established earlier, and opened fire. A Ramanthian trooper went down as energy bolts from a half dozen weapons punched holes in his armor.

The contest was far from one-sided, as the enemy troopers turned toward their tormentors and fired. They were using projectile weapons, and one of the brig rats was snatched off his feet, as a slug hit him in the chest.

That made Tappas angry, and the petty officer rolled an energy grenade into the enemy formation, as his companions continued to spray the aliens with energy bolts. There was a bright flash of light, three Ramanthians were blown apart, and pieces of shattered chitin whirled through the air. The bugs appeared to waver, started to fall, and were subsequently cut down as the sheer volume of defensive fire punched holes through their armor. The battle ended three minutes later.

Having never fought an infantry action before, the brig rats were impressed by their achievement, and were busy high-fiving each other when Tappas noticed that Foley was twenty yards up the corridor and gaining speed. "Come on!" the petty officer shouted. "Follow the loot!"

The sailors were quick to respond, as were the jarheads, who had their company commander sandwiched between them as they carried the officer along. "Follow me!" the wild-eyed marine exclaimed. "Let's kill the bastards!"

Foley saw markers for access corridor P-8, took a glance over his shoulder, and was amazed to discover that the group behind him had grown even larger! Not a good thing from the fugitive's perspective since it didn't make sense to go

AWOL with the equivalent of a brass band and a couple dozen witnesses along for the ride. But it was too late to worry about such matters as Foley rounded the corner and pounded down the corridor toward the lift tubes beyond. The battle platform shook as if palsied, and Foley heard the sound of muted thunder, as a *new* voice came over the PA system. It was male this time. "This is Lieutenant Simmons . . . All hands prepare to abandon ship. I repeat, all hands . . ."

Foley swore as he skidded to a halt in front of the tubes. It had been his intention to leave the ship *before* the rest of the crew were ordered to do so. Because there were only so many escape pods, lifeboats, and other small craft for people to use. That meant the competition for flyable vessels was about to become a lot more intense. Something that could already be seen in the crowd gathered in front of the large personnel lifts.

By that time Tappas knew that unlike the marine captain, Lieutenant JG Foley was never going to shout something like, "Follow me!" That made it necessary to keep a close eye on the slippery officer or risk losing track of him. And sure enough, without so much as a "by-your-leave," Tappas saw Foley break away from the steadily swelling mob and start to run. "This way!" Tappas shouted, as he waved the brig rats and the marines forward.

But others heard the order as well, and being desperate for leadership, were quick to follow. So that by the time Foley arrived in front of the lift tubes normally reserved for freight, more than a hundred people were trailing along behind him. The officer swore as they flooded onto the enormous platform, and repeatedly stabbed the DOWN button, as valuable seconds ticked away. Finally, after what seemed like an eternity, the platform began to descend.

Three long minutes passed before the gates opened, and the mob flooded out onto the walkway that circled the vast hangar deck. Plastisteel windows kept the vacuum out but permitted the crowd to look out at the vessels parked on the blast-scarred deck. Even as they watched, a navy launch rose on its repellers, turned toward one of two huge openings, and accelerated away.

"We're going to need something *big*," Tappas said, as he shouted into Foley's ear. And the officer realized that the sailor was correct. And, while there weren't many vessels that qualified as "big," the officer saw one that did. A freighter, which judging from the activity around it, would soon depart. The problem was that the ship was of Hudathan rather than human design. And while the big aliens were allies, they were more than a little insular, and somewhat unpredictable. Would the alien crew allow humans to board their ship? Especially a *mob* of humans? There was only one way to find out.

Foley took off, with Tappas hot on his trail. The rest followed. Their feet made a *thundering* sound as the group followed the curving walkway past a number of locks to the one where two armed Hudathans stood guard as a train of heavily laden carts passed between them. Were the aliens loading something that already belonged to them? Or stealing what they could? There was no way to know, and Foley didn't care as he came to a stop in front of a hulking guard. Both Hudathans raised their weapons and aimed them at the mob. At least half the humans responded in kind. A fact that provided Foley with some welcome leverage.

"Hi there," Foley began. "We need transportation to the surface. . . . You can invite us aboard, or we'll shoot you and commandeer the ship. Which would you prefer?"

There was a pause while one of the aliens spoke into a lip mike. And another pause as he listened to a response. Then, having been ordered to do so, he lowered his weapon. His voice sounded like a rock crusher in low gear. "You can board—but do so quickly."

Foley was the first one through the hatch, and the mob surged in behind him. A short flexible tunnel led between a pair of pressure doors and into a well-lit hold. A series of loud *clangs* was heard as muscular Hudathans wrestled the cargo modules off the carts and secured them to D-rings set into the deck. A Klaxon began to *bleat* as the last humans managed to squeeze themselves into the hold, and massive pressure doors slammed closed behind them.

With no warning whatsoever, the alien ship lifted free of the deck, turned on its axis, and began to accelerate. Foley, who was being crushed from all sides, closed his eyes. The naval officer had a good imagination, which meant he could visualize the scene *outside* the battle station, where the Ramanthians would be lying in wait.

And sure enough, as the boxy freighter shot out through one of two enormous hatches and entered space, the bugs opened fire on her. The Hudathan vessel's screens flared, and the ship shook like a thing possessed, as the captain took evasive action. But rather than be thrown around as they could have been, the refugees were so tightly packed, that they held each other in place.

What happened next was wonderful and horrible at the same time. Wonderful, in that the fugitives were spared, but horrible because thousands of people were killed when Battle Station III exploded. Later, after there was time to reflect, some would maintain that the devastating explosion had been triggered by members of the space station's crew, who, having defeated all of the reactor's safeties, had intentionally pushed the device into overload. The action destroyed both the platform *and* the Ramanthian troopships that were alongside it.

Others took the position that such theories amounted to wishful thinking and amounted to jingoistic nonsense. The truth, they claimed, was that Battle Station III, like IV, had been destroyed by the enemy. This meant the loss of their troopships was the result of poor judgment rather than a suicidal act of heroism.

One thing was clear, however, and that was the fact that the fleeing freighter had been able to escape during the aftermath of the blast, saving more than a hundred lives. That meant Foley could open his eyes, give thanks for the fact that he was still alive, and ask himself a very important question. Given the fact that the Ramanthians seemed in-tent on occupying Earth—how could an entrepreneur like him profit from such a horrible calamity?

NAPA VALLEY, PLANET EARTH, THE CONFEDERACY OF SENTIENT BEINGS

It was dark in the western hemisphere, so when Battle Station III exploded, it was like the birth of a small sun. Light strobed the surface of the planet below, which caused people such as Margaret Vanderveen to look upwards and gasp in surprise. Because even the most pessimistic of news commentators had been telling the citizens of Earth to expect a battle that would last weeks, if not months, ending in a draw if not an outright victory for the Confederacy's navy. That was why many people were still in a state of denial even as the Ramanthians destroyed the last ships sent up to oppose them.

But not everyone. As the newly formed sun was snuffed out of existence, Margaret not only knew that thousands if not hundreds of thousands of people had died, but what would happen next. Because her husband, Charles Winther Vanderveen, was a senior government official presently stationed on Algeron. And her daughter, Christine, was a diplomat, and more than that, a survivor of many months spent in a Ramanthian POW camp. That meant the society matron not only knew what was coming, but what to do about it, starting with the very thing that most of her wealthy Napa Valley neighbors would be most reluctant to do. She must leave the lovely three-story Tudor-style house, not to mention all of the treasures within, and run like hell. Because if safety lay anywhere, it was to the northeast, along the border with what had once been the state of Nevada. A place where the Vanderveen family had a rustic vacation home.

The problem was that the potential refuge lay hundreds of miles away. And while the vast majority of the population were still in a state of shock, that wouldn't last for long. Once they went into motion, all the freeways and roads would be transformed into hellish parking lots. So even though Margaret's heart was heavy with grief for those who had given their lives attempting to defend Earth, she knew it was important to get moving. And do so quickly.

The family had six full-time servants. And having polled them, Margaret discovered that while four wanted to join their families, two preferred to remain with her. They included Thomas Benson, who served as the estate's maintenance man, and Lisa Qwan, a young woman who was married to a naval rating currently serving aboard the *Epsilon Indi*. Wherever that ship might be . . . And, since John, the family's domestic robot wasn't sentient, he had no choice but to come as well.

So in keeping with the needs of her party, as well as the likelihood that they would be on their own for a sustained period of time, Margaret chose the estate's sturdy four-wheel-drive pickup truck as being the best vehicle for the trip. Her employees were instructed to load the truck with food, tools, and her husband's gun collection.

Then, having already selected a pistol for herself, Margaret went upstairs to the master bedroom. The safe was located at the back of the closet. She and her husband typically kept a few thousand credits on hand, which should be spent first, since they could be rendered worthless later on. That was when Margaret's jewelry, and her husband's coin collection, might very well come into play.

Then, having slipped a computer loaded with all of the family's records and photos into her pocket, the society matron took one last tour of the house in which her only child had been raised. There were dozens of beautiful vases, boxes, figurines, hangings, mementos, and paintings to choose from. But in the end it was the carved likeness of Christine that Margaret chose to take with her. Not only because it was beautiful but because Captain Antonio Santana had given it to her. And, if the legionnaire managed to live long enough, he might become her son-in-law one day.

With the box clutched under one arm, and towing a suitcase loaded with toiletries with the other, Margaret left through the front door. The air in the entryway was thick with the odor of spilled fuel. The heavily loaded truck was waiting in the driveway. A big horse trailer was hooked up behind it. "Are you sure about this?" Benson wanted to know, as Lisa took charge of the suitcase. "What if we're wrong? What if the bugs never come?"

"Oh, they'll come," Margaret predicted darkly. "And looters, too . . . So let's get this over with. We need to cover a lot of ground before dawn. The Ramanthians will be hunting by then. . . . And a lot of people are going to die."

So Benson lit the old-fashioned lantern that had been sitting in the barn for generations. The buttery light served to illuminated his craggy, weather-beaten face from below—and made his normally benign features look stern. Having walked up to the front door he threw the lantern inside. There was an audible *whump* as glass shattered and the open flame made contact with the fuel-soaked carpet. The smoke alarm began to *bleat* as fingers of fire explored the interior of the house. Soon the entire house was engulfed in flames as a lifetime of memories went up in smoke.

But the truck was on the road by then, and Margaret refused to look back, as the headlights bored twin holes into the night. "Look!" Lisa exclaimed, as she peered through a window. "Shooting stars!"

Margaret knew that the bright streaks weren't shooting stars. They were pieces of wreckage that, having hit the upper atmosphere, were starting to burn. The battle for Earth had been lost.

ABOARD THE BATTLESHIP *REGULUS*, NEAR PLANET EARTH, THE CONFEDERACY OF SENTIENT BEINGS

Everyone aboard the battleship *Regulus* had something to do. Everyone except the Queen, that is, who stood with her back to the ship's wardroom, looking out over the planet below. Based on reports received by hypercom, the Mars colony had been destroyed, efforts were under way to hunt the Jovian prospectors down, and not a single Confederacy ship had been sent to help Earth. And, as far as Earth orbit was concerned, the former moon base was little more than a radioactive crater, two of the battle stations had been bypassed, and two had been destroyed, thereby opening a path along which her aerospace fighters and troop transports could safely reach the surface. Thousands of these ships were already entering the atmosphere. During the next few hours, they would begin a systemized attack on the planet's surface installations. Military bases first, followed by civilian power plants, and targets of opportunity. Because without electricity, the humans would quickly turn on each other, thereby saving her troops a lot of casualties, and hastening victory. Which, based on preliminary reports, would come within a matter of days.

There had been grievous losses, of course, well in excess of the more optimistic estimates. Not the least of these were the troopships that had been destroyed along with the human battle station, the loss of two destroyers during ship-to-ship combat, and the almost incomprehensible destruction of the carrier *Swarm*. It had been rammed by a Class III container ship nearly twice her size. Not a *military* ship, but a civilian vessel, named the *Maylo Chien-Chu*. The freighter had been destroyed, but more than a thousand Ramanthians had also been killed.

Even with those losses in mind, the attack was still a success given that Earth was not only exposed for the taking, but the Queen's larger goal had been realized. Which, when complete, would eventually turn human beings into an endangered species. With little more than a few million of the disgusting creatures eking out a marginal existence along the rim, and constantly on the run from the Ramanthian navy, as they were pushed farther into the unknown. The thought brought the monarch a moment of pleasure as a bright light blinked down on the surface and half the city of Chicago disappeared.

8

My business is stanching blood and feeding fainting men; my post the open field between the bullet and the hospital.

—Clara Barton
Nurse and founder of the American Red Cross
Standard year 1863

PLANET GAMMA-014, THE CLONE HEGEMONY

Marine Firebase 356 (MF-356) was situated on top of a softly rounded hill that had been denuded of all vegetation and crowned with a multiplicity of improvised bunkers. MF-356's purpose was to keep an eye on the highway that twisted snakelike through the valley below and, if necessary, bring it under fire from a pair of 105mm howitzers and a surface-to-surface missile launcher. There were mortars, too—which would raise hell with anyone stupid enough to attack the hill. But MF-356 was more than a tube farm. It was also home to the 2nd Battalion, 3rd Regiment, of the Marine Expeditionary Group. Which meant the base had its own landing pad, a supply dump, and a small field hospital. All of which made 356 interesting to Colonel Six and his Seebos. Because as far as Six was concerned Confederacy free breeders were only one rung above the Ramanthian free breeders, and the Alpha Clones had been wrong to enter into an alliance with them. Which meant if it became necessary to kill some marines to obtain supplies for his men, then so be it.

Having watched the firebase for the better part of three days, Six knew that the time to strike was at hand. Two of battalion's rifle companies, along with roughly half the weapons company, had been airlifted off the hill that morning. Judging from the full load-outs that the off-world troops were packing as they boarded the assault boats, the marines were going to be gone for a good two or three days. That left one rifle company, half a weapons company, and a variety of rear-echelon types to hold what the jarheads sometimes referred to as "Motherfucker-356," which, if subjected to a conventional infantry assault, they would probably be able to do. Especially if air support was available.

But Six and his company of seventy-six men had no intention of launching a conventional attack. Having seen everything he needed to see and confident that his plan would work, Six lowered his glasses and pushed himself back into thick brush. The Seebos were waiting.

A raw, two-lane dirt road led down from the top of the hill that the firebase sat on to the paved highway below. But, with the exception of the foot patrols that the marines sent out to keep an eye on the surrounding neighborhood, the path was rarely used because just about everything came and went by air. That was a quicker, and for the most part safer, way to move equipment and personnel around, now that the allies owned the sky. All those conspired to make sentry duty especially boring for Lance Corporal Danny Tovo and his best buddy, Private Harley Haskins, as they stood guard at the main gate. Both were dressed in summer-weight camos, even though it was almost freezing, and the weather wizards were predicting snow flurries for later in the day. The long johns that the CO had purchased for them helped some, but what the leathernecks *really* needed was the parkas General-453 had promised, but never delivered.

Still, the CO *had* authorized a makeshift heater, which consisted of a fifty-gallon drum filled with fuel-soaked dirt and whatever wood scraps happened to be available. It was positioned next to the largely symbolic pole gate, about a hundred yards outside the ring of razor wire and the constantly shifting crab mines that were supposed to keep the bugs out.

Primitive though the device was, the additional heat was welcome, and both marines were standing right next to the barrel when Haskins frowned. "Hey, Tovo," the private said. "What the hell is *that?*"

Tovo followed the other jarhead's pointing finger, looked downhill, and spotted a column of troops marching up the dirt road. Clones from the look of them—all dressed in cold-weather gear. That impression was confirmed when Tovo raised his glasses to take a second look. "Call the captain," Tovo instructed. "And tell him that we've got company."

Fifteen minutes later Marine Captain Arvo Smith was standing next to the burn barrel, warming his hands, when the first of the clones arrived. Jets of lung-warmed air drifted away from nearly identical faces, and their gear made gentle creaking sounds, as the Seebos came to a halt. Colonel Six was at the head of the column and waited as the marine officer came out to meet him. "Good afternoon, sir," Smith said politely, as he delivered a crisp salute. "I'm Captain Smith. . . . And this is Marine Firebase 356."

"It's a pleasure to meet you," Six lied. "I'm Colonel-420, and this is A Company, 102nd Airborne. That's what we're calling it anyway. . . . The truth is that my men were originally part of five different units. All of which got chewed up and spit out when the bugs landed."

"I'm glad that you and your men made it through," Smith said sympathetically. "Here's hoping things improve soon."

"Not for *us*," Six replied inclusively. "Not unless we join the navy."

That got the expected laugh. "So, how can I help?" Smith wanted to know. "We weren't expecting you—so I don't have any orders."

"We're on our way east," Six said truthfully. "To harass

the enemy. We know this country, and they don't. So once we close with the bastards, we'll have an advantage."

The plan sounded iffy to Smith. Especially given the number of troops the clone had at his disposal. But who was he to argue with a full bird? "Sir, yes sir," Smith said respectfully.

"So what we need is some MREs, a few thousand rounds of ammo, and medical treatment for a couple of men who have infected wounds. Then, if you'll let us stay the night, we'll be out of here in the morning."

Everything the other officer said made sense, and the clones were allies, so Smith was tempted to approve the request himself. But the battalion commander could be an asshole at times, especially where command prerogatives were concerned, so why take a chance? Having put the clones on hold, Smith walked a few yards away and activated his radio. It took the better part of five minutes to get an okay from the CO along with a lot of unsolicited advice—most of which Smith planned to ignore as he went back to speak with the man he knew as Colonel-420. "Sorry about the delay, sir. . . . Lieutenant Colonel Suki told me to welcome you to Firebase 356 on his behalf, and invited you to use his quarters. So, if you and your men will follow me, we'll get you settled."

Six nodded politely, let out an inaudible sigh of relief, and waved his men forward. The computer-controlled crab mines, which were located to either side of the zigzagging road, made scrabbling sounds as they crawled back and forth. Six knew that the potentially lethal devices would flood the path during the hours of darkness, thereby preventing enemy forces from finding their way into the firebase. Hopefully, assuming that everything went according to plan, there would be no need to deal with the self-propelled explosives on the way out.

Having gone through a *second* defensive perimeter, Six felt a sense of satisfaction as he and his Seebos passed the stilt-mounted observation tower and stopped just short of the circular landing pad beyond. It consisted of rock-hard heat-fused soil that resembled volcanic glass. A variety of sand-bagged enclosures marked weapons emplacements and the bunkers that lay below. To the clone's eyes the firebase looked like a well-stocked supermarket that could supply his troops for weeks to come. Not with some MREs, and a few thousand rounds of ammunition, but with all of the things that the free breeders would refuse him were he to ask. Like the shoulder-launched missiles he and his men were going to need in order to fulfill the next part of his plan. A rich harvest indeed! But first it would be necessary to play a part.

All of the marines knew about the Seebos, but very few had seen any of the clones close-up, so there was a tendency to stare as the Hegemony's soldiers topped the hill. One of the onlookers was Lieutenant Kira Kelly. She was a doctor, and like all of the medical staff assigned to the Marine Corps, she belonged to the navy. And with most of the battalion in the field, and having held sick call earlier that morning, she was sitting outside her surgery, enjoying a cup of hot caf when the clones arrived.

It was strange to see so many virtually identical men—the only difference being variations in age. Having read up on the subject, Kelly knew that appearances were deceiving, because each soldier had a different personality, which was obvious from the wide variety of expressions that could be seen on their faces, the manner in which they held their bodies, and the way some of them stared at her.

Kelly noticed that one man had a pronounced limp and went out to meet him. But, before she could speak to the soldier, a colonel stepped in between them. "Don't you have some work to do, Lieutenant?" Six demanded. "Because if you don't, I'll speak with Captain Smith, and I'm sure we can find some."

Kelly had short, flaming red hair, piercing blue eyes, and what most people agreed was a two-second fuse. So when she turned to confront Six, the physician gave him what her subordinates generally referred to as "the look." It consisted of a narrow-eyed stare that was normally reserved for incompetents, slackers, and other assorted miscreants. That, plus the way her hands rested on her hips, was a sure sign that the shit was about to hit the fan. Two marines close enough to be privy to the exchange looked at each other and grinned. "First, Colonel whatever your number is, I don't report to *you*. Second, I don't report to Smith either. And, third, I *am* doing my goddamned job! And if you try to interfere with me, Chief Kibaki will blow your motherfucking head off!"

"Sorry," a deep basso voice said from somewhere behind the clone. "But Dr. Kelly is correct. If you try to interfere with her, I *will* blow your motherfucking head off. . . . Except you don't have a mother. . . . Do you, sir?"

That caused every marine within earshot to laugh. And Six turned to discover that a huge black man was pointing a pistol at his head while grinning from ear to ear. The Seebos didn't like that, and were reaching for their weapons, when Lieutenant-44 snapped, "As you were!" Because he knew that one wrong move could start an all-out shooting war. One the clones would lose.

Six was thunderstruck. Partly because the free-breeding female was the first person to question his authority in a long time, but also because Kelly was so pretty it took his breath away. That made the officer ashamed, because such reactions were *wrong*, and he of all people was supposed to control himself.

But when the clone turned back, ready to deliver a stern rebuke, it was to find that the doctor was helping 81 over to an ammo crate so he could take his right boot off. There was an audible *click* as Kibaki let the hammer down and returned the pistol to its shoulder holster. "Don't let the doc get to you, sir. . . . Dr. Kelly has a lot of edges, but there ain't none better! Especially when the casualties start to roll on in."

Smith came to the clone's rescue at that point by offering Six a lukewarm shower, and a hot meal. But Lieutenant-44 had witnessed the whole thing, and knowing his commanding officer the way he did, wondered if that would be the end of it. Everyone knew Colonel Six was a horny old bastard. Everybody except *him* that is. . . . Which was what made the whole thing interesting. Four-four grinned and went in search of something to eat.

The night was cold, and a light snow was falling, as the clone noncoms made their rounds. There was a chorus of groans as the soldiers extricated themselves from their sleeping bags, pulled their boots on, and checked their weapons. Once the Seebos were ready, they left the relative comfort of the bunkers to which they had been assigned for the freezing cold air outside. Each squad had a separate objective—but the same basic orders: Take control of the base, prevent communications with the outside world, and keep casualties to a minimum. And the effort went well at first. Four-Four led a squad into the Bat HQ bunker, where they took Captain Smith, the duty sergeant, *and* the RT (radio tech) prisoner. Meanwhile, other teams took control of the weapons pits, the observation tower, and the supply dump.

In fact, the entire operation might have gone off without a hitch had it not been for the fact that Private Harley Haskins had a bad case of the runs. The problem forced the jarhead to exit his sleeping bag in a hurry, grab his weapon, and dash out into the night. The partially screened four-holer was located about twenty-five feet away, and it seemed like a mile. Having dropped trou, Haskins was forced to plant his formerly warm ass on slushy plywood as a regiment of snowflakes parachuted out of the sky. And that's where he was, shitting his guts out, when a group of clones paused just beyond the privacy screen. Then, as one of the Seebo sergeants paused to remind his brothers "To use knives rather than guns," Haskins hurried to wipe himself. Having hoisted his pants, and grabbed his weapon, the marine did what any good leatherneck would do: He followed the clones to the front gate, saw them take a sentry down, and opened fire. And, because Haskins was a good shot, all six of the clone bastards fell.

But the sound of gunfire set off what could only be described as five minutes of hell, as Haskins tried to warn his buddies over the companywide push, and those marines who hadn't already been taken prisoner opened fire on anything that moved. That resulted in two deaths from friendly fire—and triggered the predictable response from the Seebos. Having lost six brothers to the free breeders, the clones went on a killing rampage, even going so far as to kill a marine who was already bound hand and foot. Lieutenant-44 ran from position to position ordering his men to stop, but that took time and a number of people were killed in the interim.

In the meantime the sound of gunfire caused Kelly to sit up and start to push the sleeping bag down off her legs when a figure loomed over her. A single light had been left on inside the surgery, and because the man was backlit, it was impossible to see who the visitor was. "Chief?" Kelly inquired. "Is that *you?*"

"No," Colonel Six replied flatly. "The chief never made it out of his sleeping bag. My men roped him to his cot."

As Kelly continued to work herself free, she heard a half dozen shots followed by a profound silence. "What's going on?" the doctor demanded angrily. "We're supposed to be allies!"

"Not in my book," Six responded darkly, as the woman's feet hit the rubber mat. "Once we push the Ramanthians back into space, it will be *your* turn. In the meantime, we need supplies, and that's why we're here. Gather your things. You're coming with us."

Kelly had her boots on by then and she stood. Her eyes flashed and Six felt her presence so strongly he wanted to push the free breeder down on the cot and rape her. But that would be wrong, *very* wrong, so the officer held himself in check. "I'm staying here," Kelly said tightly. "Now get the hell out of the way. People could be dying out there."

"People *have* died out there," Six replied grimly. "And how many more of them die will depend on you. Choose one medic. Anyone other than the chief. Pack enough supplies to support an infantry company for a month. Don't worry about weight. You won't have to carry it."

Kelly folded her arms and looked up into his heavily shadowed face. "No," she said defiantly. "I won't do it."

The clone stared down into her eyes. "Sergeant . . ."

"Sir!" a noncom said, as he stepped out into the half-light.

"Go get one of the marines. *Any* marine. Bring him here."

"Sir, yes sir," the Seebo said obediently, and disappeared.

"Will one be enough?" Six inquired. "Or will it be necessary to shoot more?"

Kelly stared into the clone's hard, implacable eyes. "You're crazy."

"No," Six replied calmly. "I'm a soldier engaged in a war against a ruthless enemy that will do anything to win. In order to beat them, we will have to be equally ruthless. Our survival depends on it."

As luck would have it the person the clones dragged into the surgery was Hospital Corpsman Third Class Sumi. A small man, with black hair, who was clearly pissed off. "What's going on, ma'am?" the medic wanted to know. "The clone bastards shot a whole lot of our guys—and they won't let me help them!"

"Here's the deal," Kelly said grimly, as she stood with hands on hips. "You let Sumi and I treat all of the wounded, yours included, and we'll go with you. Otherwise, you can go ahead and start shooting. And you'd better start with *me!*"

It was a good suggestion. Six knew that. But even though it made sense, he couldn't bring himself to shoot the doctor and thereby deny her services to his men. That's what he told himself anyway as the officer took a full step backwards. "Okay, Doctor, have it your way. But hurry. I'll give you one hour to treat the wounded *and* pack. Then we're leaving. And we'll be watching you. Step out of line, and the chief dies."

The next hour was a living nightmare as Kelly and one of

her medics sought to save as many lives as they could while Sumi packed their gear. Which, thanks to the fact that all their equipment was *designed* to be portable, was fairly easy to do.

The total number of casualties was shocking, and as a badly wounded marine died in Kelly's arms, more than fifty sturdy civilians plodded up the hill. All of them wore homemade pack boards. One by one the Ortovs stepped up to the mountain of supplies that had been assembled for them, accepted their eighty- to one-hundred-pound loads, and made their way back down the hill. Even *children* could be seen through the drifting snow, bent nearly double under twenty-five-pound packs, as they followed the adults into the darkness.

Finally, at exactly 0300, Kelly was forced to break her efforts off as the last loads of medical supplies were carried away. "It's okay," Lance Corporal Danny Tovo said, as the doctor stood. "My leg feels pretty good all things considered. Don't worry, ma'am, we'll come looking, and once we find these bastards, *all* of them are going to die."

Kelly wanted to say that there had already been enough dying, but knew Tovo wouldn't understand, and nodded. "Tell the chief I said to change that dressing every eight hours. Do you read me?"

The marine grinned. His teeth looked unnaturally white in the glare produced by one of the pole-mounted lamps. "I read you five-by-five, ma'am."

Kelly wanted to cry but didn't as Sumi helped her into her jacket, and the two of them marched downhill. The battle for Firebase 356 was over.

PLANET ALPHA-001, THE CLONE HEGEMONY

Christine Vanderveen was standing. She couldn't see anything through the blindfold, but she felt the truck start to slow, and knew it was about to stop. Fisk-3 and Fisk-5 held the diplomat upright as the truck jerked to a halt. "Remember," the clone called Alan said, as a side door slammed open. "Tell Nankool that the revolution is coming. Tell him that if the Senate will recognize the new government *quickly*, we'll join the Confederacy."

Vanderveen had heard the argument at least a dozen times by then, and wasn't likely to forget, but she nodded. "And," Alan added softly, "*please* take care of yourself."

Before the diplomat could make any sort of response, she was literally lifted out of the truck, and placed on the sidewalk. The blindfold came off as the truck *roared* away. The bright sunlight caused her to blink. It was well into the workday by that time, so very few clones were out on the street, but those who were eyed the female as she hurried away.

The orderly grid-style streets made it easy to navigate. So it was only a matter of minutes before Vanderveen located the hotel to which Nankool and his delegation had been assigned. As Vanderveen entered the lobby, she was planning to contact Nankool's secretary and request an appointment. But that wasn't to be as someone recognized the FSO-2, shouted her name, and triggered all sorts of attention.

Within moments Vanderveen was hustled away and sequestered in a conference room, where she was questioned by a succession of security teams. Starting with the beings assigned to protect Nankool, who were followed by three stern-looking clones, including two Romos and a hard-eyed Nerov. The latter were the genetic line which, if Alan and Mary had told her the truth, hunted free breeders as if they were animals. So Vanderveen was careful to be as vague as possible regarding her abductors, what their motives were, and where she had been held. All of which frustrated the policemen, who were used to browbeating the citizenry into submission but couldn't use such tactics on a foreign diplomat.

That was when a *second* team of Confederacy security people arrived. They escorted the recently freed diplomat to one of the "clean rooms" that had been established a few floors above, where they intended to interrogate her all over again. Partially to clarify what had occurred, but mostly in an attempt to protect senior officials from a similar fate, especially the president himself.

So they were far from happy when a mere FSO-2 refused to answer their questions until she could sit down with Nankool and give the chief executive a firsthand report on what she had learned. An assistant secretary of state tried to talk Vanderveen out of her plan, but she was insistent, and due to the nature of her relationship with Nankool the official thought it best to back off rather than risk the president's ire.

That was why three hours after her unexpected return, Vanderveen finally found herself standing outside the conference room that the president was using as his office, waiting for the undersecretary of defense to leave. And eventually she did. Vanderveen noticed that the retired colonel, whom some people referred to as "the Iron Lady," closed the door gently, as if letting herself out of a hospital room. The two of them made eye contact, and Undersecretary Zimmer forced a smile. "Hello, Christine. . . . It's good to have you back safe and sound. You should have seen the president's face light up when the news came in. He actually smiled!"

Vanderveen searched the older woman's face. It was common knowledge that Nankool had been depressed ever since the attack on Earth. But the last comment seemed to hint at something more profound. "It's that bad?"

Zimmer was silent for a moment. Then, having come to some sort of conclusion, she gave a single nod. "Yes, I'm afraid it is. . . . Take it easy on him." And with that she left.

Nankool had always been a tower of strength, but never more than during the months the two of them had been held in the Ramanthian POW camp, and to see someone like Zimmer so obviously concerned about Nankool's emotional well-being came as a shock. Vanderveen knocked on the door, heard a nearly inaudible "Come in," and palmed the access plate. The barrier *whispered* softly as it slid out of the way.

As Vanderveen entered Nankool sat with his back to the semidarkened room. He was staring out the only window at the angular cityscape beyond. "The bugs destroyed most of Chicago," Nankool said flatly. "And all of Paris, Rio, and Sydney. All because of *my* stupidity. Gamma-014 was the bait, Christine. And I took it. Hook, line, and sinker. Now we're bogged down in the Clone Hegemony, fighting on some slush ball, while the bugs rape Earth. People are fighting back though, killing as many chits as they can, waiting for a fleet that doesn't exist. That *can't* exist, unless I break my word, and pull our forces out of clone-held space. And that's what Zimmer thinks I should do. Hell, that's what *most* of my staff thinks I should do. What about you Christine? What do *you* think?"

Vanderveen thought about her mother, and wanted to ask about San Francisco, but held the question back as Nankool turned to face her. Vanderveen was shocked by what she saw. Though once overweight, Nankool had shed at least thirty pounds during the months spent in captivity. But the slimmed-down version was nothing compared with the way he looked now. The president's eyes stared out at Vanderveen from blue-black caverns. His nose was like a blade that divided his gaunt face into halves as a clawlike hand came up to rub a furrowed brow. "I think you made the right decision," Vanderveen said, desperately hoping that she was right. "And based on what I learned over the last few days, there's a very real chance that you could cement something better than an alliance with the Hegemony. Because if certain things play out the way I expect them to, and if we take appropriate steps, it might be possible to incorporate the Hegemony into the Confederacy. Which would result in *full* rather than qualified military cooperation. And that could turn things around! Or at least level the playing field."

Nankool's cadaverous face seemed to brighten slightly. "Really?" he inquired hopefully. "I could use some good news. . . . Tell me more."

So Vanderveen told Nankool about Alan, Mary, and the free breeders who lived under the city. Then she told him about the revolution, what it could mean, and how the Confederacy could take advantage of it. But as she spoke, the diplomat saw the hope disappear from Nankool's eyes and a frown appear. So as her presentation came to its conclusion, Vanderveen already knew what the president's decision would be, even if she didn't know why.

"Thank you," Nankool said, "for keeping your head, and continuing to do your job under what were clearly trying circumstances. But no, I don't think we should pursue the course you recommend, and for a variety of reasons. First, because the chances of a successful revolution are slim, but the chances that the Alpha Clones would find out about our meddling are high . . . Which means we could lose whatever benefits may derive from the existing relationship. And believe me—the situation is tenuous already. General Booly wants to shoot most of his clone counterparts.

"Second, even if such a revolution were successful, a period of internal instability would almost certainly follow. And instability runs counter to our interests.

"Third, the whole idea represents a distraction at a time when it's very important to keep our focus. I'm sorry, Christine, I really am, but I want you to forget this particular idea."

The diplomat felt her spirits sink. Was Nankool correct? Or was he so depressed regarding the war with the Ramanthians that his judgment was impaired? And if that was the case, what if anything, should she do about it? Having never been invited to sit down, Vanderveen was still on her feet. "Thank you for seeing me, sir. . . . I know how busy you are."

Nankool nodded and watched Vanderveen leave the room. Something was missing from the transaction, something important, but he couldn't quite put his finger on it. Not until the door closed behind her and the truth dawned on him. Rather than agree to his request as Christine normally would have, she had chosen to leave. Did that mean something? Or was it her way of expressing disappointment? There was no way to know. Nankool allowed himself a protracted sigh, turned his back to the room, and looked out through the window. It wasn't supposed to rain, not during the day, but hundreds of water droplets had appeared on the glass. That made it difficult to see.

The security people were waiting for Vanderveen when she left Nankool's makeshift office. They took her to a clean room, where she was debriefed all over again. The people who were responsible for the president's safety were primarily interested in the abduction, the people Vanderveen had interactions with, and their ostensible motives. But the intelligence types, both of whom were listed as "support personnel" on documents submitted to the Hegemony, chose to focus their questions on the underground society, the possibility of a popular revolution, and which individuals might come into power should such an event take place.

Vanderveen couldn't answer questions like that, but told the debriefers everything that she could, in hopes that Madam Xanith, who was in charge of the Confederacy's intelligence organization, would find the information to be credible and pass it along to Nankool. Thereby putting the possibility of a revolution in front of the president again.

Finally, having been squeezed dry, Vanderveen was allowed to go to her room. It was dark by then. Vanderveen took a hot shower, ordered dinner from room service, and ate it while watching a government-produced news show. Earth lay in ruins, but thanks to thousands of brave Seebos, the battle for Gamma-014 was going well. Or so the nearly identical smooth-faced coanchors claimed. Once again Vanderveen was reminded of her mother—and wondered what had become of her. Was she lying dead in the ruins of the family estate? Had she been thrown into some sort of POW camp? Or been attacked by looters? There were so many horrible possibilities.

Having eaten half her dinner, and being totally exhausted,

she went to bed. The streetlights made patterns on the ceiling, but rather than fall asleep, Vanderveen found it impossible to turn her brain off. No matter how hard she tried, Vanderveen couldn't get Alan, Mary, and the rest of them off her mind. Especially Alan—and that troubled her. Both because of promises made to Santana and the possibility that her interest in the clone had clouded her judgment. Did she *really* believe that a revolution was possible? Or was she trying to please Alan? And how did *he* feel about her? Did his parting words carry a special meaning? Or were they just a nice way to say good-bye?

Dozens of possibilities, problems, and questions swirled through her mind, all seemingly part of a giant puzzle that she couldn't quite make out or fully understand. Eventually, at some point, sleep took over and carried Vanderveen into a land of troubled dreams. A place where every hand was turned against her.

But six hours later, when Vanderveen's alarm began to chirp, and her eyes popped open, Vanderveen awoke to a sense of clarity. It was as if her subconscious had sorted through the problems and come to some conclusions. If not about her relationship with Alan, then about the political situation and the action she should take. Which, if things went wrong, would not only end her diplomatic career, but result in charges of treason. The possibility of that caused a knot to form in her stomach, but in no way sapped her resolve, as Vanderveen went to the table where the comset was waiting.

The nine-digit number had been memorized at Alan's urging, and for reasons she hadn't been entirely sure of at the time, withheld from the debriefers. But it was safe, or so the Fisks claimed, so long as Vanderveen followed their instructions: Dial the number, provide a time, and hang up. That was the procedure. So Vanderveen entered the correct sequence of numbers into the keypad and waited for someone or *something* to answer. The device at the other end rang three times before a synthesized voice came on the line. The little video screen was blank. "Leave your message at the tone," the voice said, and a *beep* followed.

Vanderveen said, "Ten this morning," and broke the connection.

It was 8:37—and there was a lot to do. Not the least of which was to write a carefully worded memo to the assistant secretary of state in which Vanderveen put forth her arguments in favor of a relationship with the free-breeder underground and made clear her intention to act as an unofficial liaison between the revolutionaries and the Confederacy.

Then, with that chore out of the way, it was time to tend to other more routine matters. Like cramming as many necessities as possible into her briefcase, which she should be able to carry out of the hotel without generating any suspicion. Then, having sealed the memo in an envelope that she intended to slip under the secretary's door, Vanderveen left her room.

The park, located four blocks from Vanderveen's hotel, was a popular place for retirees to congregate during the day. Especially given the fact that the dormitories that the clones lived in were rather bleak. That was why the Fisks had gone to considerable lengths to disguise themselves as harmless Hornbys, and were seated around a concrete table playing chess, when the free-breeder female entered the park, took a long look around, and sat on a bench. There were cameras in the park, *lots* of them, and the clock was running.

But, unlike the old days when the Fisks had been forced to work alone, they had help now. Based on a signal from a Fisk, one of the Hornbys began to argue with an Ortov, and it wasn't long before fists flew. That caused all of the security cameras to swivel toward the disturbance. And they were still focused on the fight when the police arrived. The conflict came to an end at that point, but when the Romos went looking for the free breeder who had been spotted just prior to the fight, the woman was gone. And none of the retirees remembered seeing her. FSO-2 Christine Vanderveen, daughter of Charles and Margaret Vanderveen, confidante to President Nankool, and the recipient of numerous awards for distinguished service to the Confederacy, had gone AWOL.

9

The reason we have always advocated a policy of luring the enemy to penetrate deeply is because it is the most effective tactic against a strong opponent.

—Mao Tse-tung
On Protracted War
Standard year 1938

PLANET GAMMA-014, THE CLONE HEGEMONY

It was cold. The temperature had fallen thirty degrees during the last twelve hours, a persistent ten-mile-per-hour wind was blowing down through the long mountain pass, and a curtain of snow limited visibility to half a mile. Which would have been bad enough for troops who had proper gear. But unlike the 1st REC, most of the legionnaires, marines, and Seebos who had been sent up into the mountains were dressed in multiple layers of summer clothing. Because instead of winning the battle for Gamma-014 in a matter of weeks, as General-453 had predicted they would, the allies were bogged down. Rather than leapfrog ahead, and engage the main body of General Akoto's forces *before* they could retreat into the At-Sak Mountains, the clone general insisted that isolated pockets of Ramanthians be eradicated first. An error made worse by the fact that as the weather continued to deteriorate, the allies soon lost one of the few advantages they had, which was air superiority. That was in spite of

General Bill Booly's repeated attempts to offer Four-fifty-three counsel.

And, as if that wasn't bad enough, the knowledge that Earth was under attack ate at everyone's morale as Santana and Alpha Company followed other allied units up the long, twisting road that led to Tow-Tok Pass. Because even though people like Santana had no family there, all of them had friends on the planet, and still felt a special affection for Earth even if they had been born elsewhere.

For his part, Santana knew that Margaret Vanderveen was probably on her own, and he was worried about her. And Christine would be frantic—but unable to help.

Santana's thoughts were interrupted by the sudden *shriek* of an incoming artillery round, followed by an earthshaking *carump*, as a column of frozen soil was lifted high into the air two hundred yards ahead. And there, suspended within the geyser, the cavalry officer could see darker forms that might have been bodies. Clone civilians, most likely, who until moments before, had been trudging along at the tail end of a CVA labor battalion. Santana yelled, "Incoming!" over the company push, but knew it was unnecessary, as more Ramanthian shells fell up ahead.

Lieutenant Lucy Amoyo ordered the first platoon off the right side of the highway—even as Second Lieutenant Gregory Zolkin led the second platoon to the left. It was better than continuing to march right up the center of the two-lane road, but still far from safe. Because even though the Ramanthian gunners couldn't actually see that section of road from their positions high in the mountains, they had coordinates for every inch of the highway. That, combined with targeting data fed to them by computer-controlled drones, allowed the aliens to lay down effective fire along both margins of the crowded road—the only place to go since cliffs, steep slopes, and carefully laid minefields kept the allies hemmed in. That's why Route 1 was frequently referred to as "blood alley." It was a long ribbon of wreck-strewn duracrete, every mile of which had to be paid for with lives, as the allies were sucked into Akoto's trap.

The chits weren't free to fire on their pursuers with total impunity, however. Because even though the weather was keeping most of the allied air force on the ground, there were other ways for the allies to strike back. This was where the company's quads came in. Both of the fifty-ton monsters opened fire at once. Blue energy bolts stuttered up into the snow-laced sky as onboard computers tracked the incoming shells and soon started to intercept them. The sound of explosions echoed back and forth between the surrounding mountain peaks as the incoming weapons were detonated high in the air. Which was good—but not good enough. Because some shells managed to get through, and the quads couldn't fire indefinitely.

"This is Alpha Six to Alpha One-Four, and Bravo One-Four," Santana said, as Sergeant Omi Decker carried the officer off the ice-encrusted pavement and into an area of well-churned snow. The theory being that any piece of ground that had already been stepped on was probably free of mines. "How 'bout it?" Santana demanded. "Have you got a fix on the bastards? Over."

"Yes, sir," Private Simy Xiong replied confidently. "Stand by for outgoing. Over."

Having tracked the incoming rounds back to their source—the quads were ready to strike at the Ramanthian artillery battery responsible for the bombardment. Missiles *roared* off rails, vanished into the swirling snow, and sought the enemy. "Got 'em!" Private Ivan Lupo exclaimed triumphantly, as a series of overlapping explosions was heard, and thunder rolled down the valley. "You can scratch one bug battery. Over."

"Well done," Santana said. "That'll teach the bastards a lesson!"

That was true, but as Alpha Company, 2nd Battalion, 1st

REC continued to follow the CVA unit up the wreckage-strewn road, the impact of the barrage was clear to see as Santana and his T-2 rounded a curve. A half-track loaded with civilians had taken a direct hit, killing most of those on board, and reducing the armored vehicle to little more than a pile of burning scrap. A survivor, the only one from all appearances, was kneeling next to a dead body. His hat was gone, and one arm was bloodied, but he didn't even look up as a medic arrived to treat him.

A hundred yards farther on, Santana saw eight marines laid out in a row along the left side of the road where two androids had paused to inspect them. Both robots had the initials "GR," painted on their alloy bodies, which meant they were members of a graves registration team. Each machine had a scanner that could be used to read the bar codes inked onto each clone's forehead and the back of each marine's neck. Data regarding the casualties would be uploaded to a satellite in orbit above *and* stored on the android's CPU.

Later, assuming that everything worked the way it was supposed to, trucks would travel the length of the highway and collect the dead. In the meantime bodies from both sides were routinely stripped of clothing, weapons, and food so that piles of partially clothed corpses were a common sight.

It was growing dark by then, and it was dangerous to travel at night, which meant the company was going to need a place to bivouac, just like all the rest of the allied units strung out along two hundred miles of bloody road. So when scout Suresee Fareye spotted the turnout, and the jumble of burned-out vehicles that had been pushed into it, he was quick to alert Santana. "Alpha Six-Four to Alpha Six. Over."

Santana looked up the road, toward where the Naa and his T-2 should be, but couldn't see either one of them through the swirling snow. The front portion of his body was toasty warm, thanks to the heat produced by his cyborg, but his ass was ice-cold. A strange phenomenon—but one the bio bods were already getting used to. "This is Alpha Six. Go. Over."

"I have what might make a good bivouac," Fareye said, as

a track loaded with miserable looking CVAs ground past him. "It's on the left side of the highway. Over."

"Good," Santana replied, as he eyed the display on his HUD. "We'll be there in ten minutes or so. Don't let anyone take it. Over."

"Roger," the Naa confirmed. "Alpha Six-Four, out."

There was no such thing as a sunset in the wintry At-Sak Mountains. Just a quick fade into darkness. And the light had already started to dim by the time Santana arrived at what had probably been a scenic lookout back during better times but had since been transformed into a nightmarish salvage yard piled high with scrap, much of which had been mangled by explosions and blackened by fire. As Deker carried the officer over to where Fareye and his T-2 stood waiting, Santana saw that a frozen Ramanthian, his face obscured by a mask of ice, still sat at the controls of an alien crawler. "There isn't much room," Santana observed cautiously, as he eyed the area around him.

"That's true," Fareye agreed. "But what if the T-2s were to rearrange this junk? They could use it to build defensive walls and windbreaks."

Santana directed Deker around the pile and over to the edge of the road. But rather than the steep drop-off that Santana had been hoping for, he saw a long, gentle slope, that led to the valley below. It was difficult to see, given the blowing snow, but it seemed logical to suppose that a river lay somewhere below. The incline *looked* innocent enough, but as Akoto and his troops had been forced to withdraw across Tow-Tok Pass, groups of fanatical warriors had been left behind. And, having gone to ground for days or even weeks, they could attack at any time. Often from above, which gave the bugs a tactical advantage, but sometimes from below. Which was the scenario that Santana feared as he looked down across the pristine snow.

Fareye and Nhan had come around to join Santana by then and stood two feet away. "I think you're right," Santana confirmed. "We can make it work. But this slope bothers me.

Take a couple of bio bods down and check it out. See if you can find a good spot for an OP. Something with a clear line of retreat."

Like all Naa, Fareye had been born and raised on wintry Algeron, and was covered with fur to boot. So the prospect of taking a downhill stroll through the snow didn't bother the legionnaire in the least. But when the noncom ordered two members of the first squad, first platoon to join him, there was plenty of good-natured bitching as the threesome disappeared over the edge.

With that process under way, Santana directed the rest of the first squad to set up a security screen around the company, while the rest of the legionnaires went to work carving out a place to camp. And, thanks to how strong the T-2s were, it wasn't long before an oval-shaped enclosure had been created, with a quad anchoring each end of it.

Special attention was paid to securing the outside slope, which, given the sheer cliff wall on the opposite side of the highway, was the point of greatest vulnerability. Then, as darkness settled over the mountains, and traffic dwindled to almost nothing, the first squad of the second platoon took over responsibility for security as the rest of the company began to settle in.

And that was the moment when the legionnaires were grateful to be cavalry. Because even though the quads carried tons of ammo and supplies inside their cargo bays, there was still enough room for two squads of bio bods to get in out of the cold, and grab some sleep. For a few hours at a time, anyway, because people were constantly rotating on and off guard duty, which meant that cold air flooded into both cargo bays on a regular basis. But all of them knew that the occasional wintry blast was nothing compared to the subzero temperatures the infantry had to cope with.

Still, if the legionnaires were privileged in some respects, those benefits were offset to a great extent by the maintenance the cyborgs required. Because fluids that flowed freely at thirty-six degrees, became viscous at sixteen degrees, and started to clot at ten below. And metal parts that would normally last for years would sometimes weaken and break as they were heated during the day and allowed to cool by as much as thirty or forty degrees at night.

So once a variety of carefully shielded fires had been started, and the bio bods had been given a chance to wolf down some half-warmed MREs, it was time to pull out the tools and get to work. Because, having been served by a T-2 all day, it was time for each bio bod to return the favor.

Some of the legionnaires were certified techs, but all of them had at least nominal skills, and were expected to inspect their cybernetic mounts looking for worn actuators, leaky hydraulics, and loose fittings. Then, assuming that everything was in good working order, it was time to rearm their T-2s. That activity included replenishing each cyborg's magazines, cleaning the Trooper II's .50-caliber machine gun, and running diagnostics on any other hardware their particular unit was packing, including energy cannons, flamethrowers, and missile launchers if such were authorized. All of this sucked up at least an hour and a half each evening, and was carried out with very little light, and half-frozen fingers.

Meanwhile, the med techs were expected to keep an eye on all of the cybernetic life-support systems, tweak them if necessary, and give medical care to their fellow bio bods on top of that! This was why the techs were rarely if ever assigned to guard duty.

Nor were the NCOs and officers exempt from such duties. So Santana was kneeling in the snow, fitting a new coupler to Deker's left foot pod, when Private Volin emerged from the surrounding gloom. "The colonel wants to speak with you, sir. He's on channel two."

"Roger that," Santana said, as he came to his feet and stuck both hands under his armpits. He had gloves, but it was difficult to perform fine motor tasks while wearing them. Santana knew that the persistent needles-and-pins sensation in his fingers was a warning of impending frostbite.

"I'll finish up," Volin offered, and went to one knee in

order to work on the coupler. Captain Antonio Santana might be tough, but he was fair, and everyone in the company felt the same way. "If we take care of him—he'll take care of us."

"Thank God," Deker rumbled. "Some competent help for a change!"

Santana gave the T-2 a one-fingered salute, and left both legionnaires laughing, as he crossed the narrow compound to the point where Xiong had settled in over his legs. The quad was off-line at the moment, grabbing some sleep, but that didn't prevent the bio bods from using the cyborg's cargo bay.

Santana slapped a pressure plate, which caused a side hatch to cycle open, and produced the usual chorus of groans as a blast of cold air invaded the otherwise-warm interior. The forward section of the cargo bay was taken up by cargo modules, but there were various nooks and crannies, all of which had been colonized by off-duty bio bods. Lines had been rigged so that hand-washed socks and underwear could dry, and the air was thick with the pungent odors of sweat, wet clothing, and gun oil. "Sorry, sir," Staff Sergeant Pool said, as she looked up from peeling pieces of dead skin off her toes. "We didn't know it was you."

"Can't say as I blame you," the cavalry officer said mildly, as he stepped over Private Gomyo's supine body. "Although it would be a good idea to air this place out once in a while. I wish there was some way to capture the smell so we could use it on the bugs."

That generated some laughter as Santana made his way back to the tiny cubicle that was supposed to function as a command desk but was far too cramped to be of much use. He pulled a swing-out seat into position, sat down, and put a pair of large can-style headphones over his head, not so much for enhanced audio quality as for privacy. There was no way to know what subject Quinlan wanted to talk about. Quinlan's face filled most of the screen, but judging from what Santana could see in the background, the other man was in an office environment somewhere. "There you are," Quinlan said waspishly. "It's about time."

"Sorry, sir," Santana said neutrally. "I came as quickly as I could."

Quinlan sniffed, as if to say that he had doubts about that, but left them unsaid as he made use of his leather-covered swagger stick to scratch his left temple. "General Kobbi put in a request for your services," Quinlan said disapprovingly. "I can't say that I appreciate losing an entire company to a wild-goose chase, but there isn't much I can do about it, so be ready at 0800 tomorrow morning. That's when the weather wizards predict that we'll see a break in the cloud cover. A fly-form will pick you up. Tell Amoyo to proceed to Waypoint 27 and wait for you there. And don't be late."

Santana was about to say, "Yes, sir," when the transmission came to an abrupt end, and electronic snow filled the screen. So Santana removed the headset, made his way over to the door, and pulled his gloves back on. Then, having warned those in the immediate area, he slipped out through the hatch as quickly as he could. Quinlan clearly had reservations about whatever mission Kobbi had up his sleeve, and Santana did, too. Even though Amoyo was a good officer, the legionnaire didn't like being separated from his company for more than a few hours at a time. But there wasn't anything Santana could do about the situation except load his XO down with well-intended advice and reinspect the perimeter before grabbing some shut-eye.

Some company commanders made it a habit to sleep in one of their quads, seeing that as a privilege of rank, but Santana preferred to spend every other night out in the open the way his troops had to. That was one of many reasons why the legionnaires respected him and looked out for him. As evidenced by the fact that anonymous individuals had already prepared a place for their captain between a crackling fire, and a sheet of scorched metal that was angled to reflect some of the heat back at him.

Having spotted his gear, Santana made a face. "*What?* No turn-down service?" This served to let his benefactors know that the company commander appreciated what had been done and generated a chorus of chuckles as well. The legionnaires who were gathered around that particular fire were already in their bags as Santana entered his. Each legionnaire had his or her own theory about the best way to set up a Legion issue "sleep system." The innermost layer of Santana's "sack" consisted of a slick liner, commonly referred to as a "trash bag," that allowed a soldier to slide into the bag with his or her boots on. And, if necessary, could serve as a body bag, too.

The liners also served to keep the inside of the actual bag relatively clean. That was nice after it had been used for a couple of months. But, rather than insert a blanket or some other type of liner into his sack to provide extra warmth, the way some people did, Santana had chosen to shove his sack into a Hudathan-sized bivvy bag "borrowed" for that purpose. All of which provided enough warmth so the officer could sleep—which was what he was doing when the Ramanthians attacked.

Having made his way downslope earlier, and located a pile of boulders that could serve as a forward observation post, Fareye had volunteered to stay while a steady succession of other legionnaires came and went. That was why the Naa and a bio bod named Purdo were huddled behind the rocks, sipping lukewarm caf from a thermos, when the first sounds were heard. The disturbance began with a series of *crunching* noises as feet broke through crusty snow, soon followed by the occasional *clink* of unsecured gear, and muted bursts of click-speech.

That was more than enough to bring Fareye out of hiding. And one look through his night-vision goggles was sufficient to confirm the Naa's worst fears. Dozens of heat blobs were visible downslope and there was no question about who they belonged to. Fareye ducked, felt for the flare pistol, and pulled the device out. Purdo, who had complete faith in the noncom's judgment, waited for orders. "Get ready to throw your grenades," the Naa said. "Then, once those are gone, run like hell. And don't stop."

Purdo had questions, *lots* of them, but never got to ask any as Fareye pulled the trigger. The flare soared high into the sky, went off with a distinct *pop*, and began to drift downward. The device flooded the slope with eye-aching bright light and shrill command whistles were heard as Ramanthian noncoms urged their troops forward.

When Purdo stood, he saw that at least a hundred white-clad alien soldiers were fighting their way upslope. Fortunately, the jungle-evolved bugs weren't designed for traveling uphill through deep snow. "What the hell are you waiting for?" Fareye demanded, as he brought his assault rifle to bear. "Throw your grenades!"

So Purdo threw his grenades in quick succession, and was proud of the fact that he had remembered to pull the pins, as a series of four loud explosions was heard. Enemy bodies were ripped apart as gouts of snow, blood, and broken chitin were hurled high into the air. The rest of the Ramanthians were forced to march through a grisly rain as the remains of their comrades fell around them.

More alien soldiers went down as Fareye began to fire three-round bursts from his CA-10. Then, having emptied a magazine, the noncom turned to Purdo. "Okay! Now's the time! Run like hell!"

The explosions woke Santana from a deep sleep. All three of the sleeping bags were equipped with rip-open closures. They came apart one after another as bursts of automatic fire were heard. Within seconds, both the officer and his legionnaires were out of their sleep sacks, on their feet, and ready to fight. "The hill!" someone shouted. "They're coming up the hill!"

So Santana made his way over to the edge of the turnout, where Master Sergeant Dice Dietrich and others had taken cover behind the improvised barricade and were firing downhill. "Keep it high!" the noncom roared. "Or you'll answer to me!"

Santana saw why. Purdo and Fareye were only halfway up the incline. Ramanthian bullets kicked up spurts of snow all around the legionnaires, as they fought for purchase on the slippery slope, and lost their footing time after time. Darkness fell as the pistol flare burned out, but two even brighter lights appeared, as the quads sent 110,000-candlepower illumination rounds arcing over the valley below. The flares glowed like miniature suns and swayed under small parachutes as they spiraled toward the ground.

"Run, goddamn it, run!" Staff Sergeant Briggs shouted from above, as Purdo managed to arrest the latest slide and start upwards again. But the bio bod hadn't gone more than five feet before a slug hit him between the shoulder blades. The legionnaire's body armor was sufficient to stop the projectile, but the force of the impact threw him forward. And that was when a burst of sustained machine-gun fire ate Purdo from below.

Santana swore as the heavy-caliber bullets followed the cavalryman's legs up his waist and literally cut the bio bod in two. The good news was that Fareye had made it to the top of the slope by then, where Dietrich reached out to grab the Naa, and pulled him over the top of the barricade as bullets *rattled* on metal.

Amazingly, given the amount of fire they faced, approximately fifty Ramanthians were still on their feet and battling their way upwards. No longer constrained by the need to worry about their fellow legionnaires, the company opened fire with a vengeance. And with half a dozen T-2s standing almost shoulder to shoulder the sheer volume of outgoing fire was something to see. A lethal mixture of red tracer and bright blue energy bolts stuttered downslope, cut the advancing soldiers down, and washed the slope with their blood.

That was sufficient to produce a certain amount of satis-

faction where the legionnaires were concerned. But Santana
felt differently. Not only had one of his troopers been lost
but the seemingly mindless ferocity of the attack worried
him. What did it bode for the future? His people were
good, very good, but would they march uphill into certain
death? Would *he*? Maybe, but maybe not, which meant the
chits would always have an advantage. At least some of the
bugs *wanted* to die. And he, like those around him, wanted
to live.

The regimental weather wizards were correct. The snow ta-
pered off around 0400, the skies began to clear, and by 0730
the sun was out. But with no clouds to hold some heat down,
the air grew even colder as the legionnaires struggled to boil
water and ready themselves for the coming march.

Santana battled the desire to reiterate all of the orders already given to Amoyo, took one last tour of the company,
and was ready to depart when the fly-form appeared. Like
both the T-2s and the quads, the streamlined aircraft was
piloted by a living brain in a metal box. The cyborg was
connected to both its flyable body and the outside world by
a complicated system of computer-assisted electronics. Fly-
forms came in a wide variety of shapes and sizes. This one,
which was clearly intended for the sort of mission to which
it had been assigned, was equipped with helicopter-style rotors and a two-person in-line cockpit. "Watch your six, sir,"
Amoyo said, as the aircraft landed on the road. "And have a
hot shower for me!"

Santana waved as he ran for the fly-form, put his right
boot into a recess intended for that purpose, and pushed
himself up so that his shoulders were level with the cockpit.
The backseat was empty, so Santana threw his AWOL bag in
there, before taking a second step that allowed him to enter
the front passenger seat. A few seconds later he was strapping
himself in as the canopy slid closed and a female voice came
over the intercom. "Welcome aboard, sir," the cyborg said
respectfully. "My name is Lieutenant Pauley. The estimated

flight time to Division HQ is one hour and twenty minutes. The surrounding peaks are too high for me to fly over—so we're going to follow Route 1 out of the mountains. The bugs took a few potshots at me on the way in—so they'll probably do the same thing on the way out. But don't worry because I'm feeling lucky today! Please let me know if there's anything I can do to make your flight more comfortable." And with that the fly-form took off.

Santana spent the first five minutes of the flight looking for signs of ground fire and marveling over how beautiful the surrounding mountains were, but having logged only a few hours of sleep the night before, and having been freed from any sense of responsibility for what took place around him, it wasn't long before Santana's eyelids grew heavy and the drone of the engine lulled him to sleep. When the skids touched ground, the resulting jolt came as a surprise and served to wake the officer up. "Welcome to Division HQ," Pauley said over the intercom. "And watch that first step. It's a lulu."

The canopy slid back, and the rotors went *whop, whop, whop* as they began to slow. By the time Santana retrieved his AWOL bag, and lowered himself to the ground, a couple of techs had arrived. "It looks like you took three rounds," one of the legionnaires observed cheerfully, as he stuck his forefinger into one of the .50-caliber-sized holes located just aft of the passenger compartment. "I'll bet that got your attention!"

Santana smiled politely, and thought about how long his nap *might* have been, as a six-wheeled utility vehicle (UV) pulled up next to the chopper. A rather plain clone was at the wheel and barely acknowledged his passenger as Santana tossed his bag into the back and climbed in next to her. The UV jerked into motion, *whirred* loudly, and pursued a serpentine course out across a vast expanse of duracrete.

Assault boats, shuttles, and fly-forms were lined up all around them. But way off in the distance, half-obscured by the yellow-gray ground-hugging smog, a row of spaceships could be seen. There was a muted *roar* as a navy transport rose on its repellers, swiveled into the wind, and began to gather speed. It was gone moments later, as the ship began to climb, and was soon lost in the blue-gray haze.

Judging from what he could see, Santana got the feeling that the Ramanthian navy wasn't considered to be much of a threat. Because while there were plenty of antiaircraft batteries, lots of aircraft were parked close together and would normally constitute a class-A target.

The UV left the vast expanse of heat-fused tarmac a few minutes later and entered a complex maze of tents, inflatable shelters, and makeshift shacks built out of anything that was handy. Unlike the orderly manner in which the Legion's base on Adobe was laid out, it appeared as though Division HQ's twisting-turning streets had been allowed to evolve naturally, which meant that a lot of time would be wasted as newcomers got lost. There was no apparent rhyme or reason to the way the various military units were grouped either. Rather than put a company of tanks next to a maintenance facility, which would make sense, Santana noticed that some bozo had assigned a battalion of Seebos to camp there instead! Which raised another question. Given that most of the fighting was taking place hundreds of miles to the east— why were so many resources sitting around Division HQ?

There was no way to know, as the UV was forced to stop for a security check, before being allowed to approach what had once been the spaceport's terminal building. It was one of the few structures General Akoto had spared so his forces could use it. But having driven the bugs out, the clones had taken over, and it soon became clear that a bunch of REMFs (rear-echelon motherfuckers) were in charge. Was that General-453's fault? Or was the Confederacy to blame? There was no way to know.

As Santana exited the UV with AWOL bag in hand, a brace of smartly uniformed Seebos crashed to attention. Once inside the building, Santana was required to check in at the duty desk, where a spit-and-polish NCO located the visitor's name on his screen, and summoned a young Seebo who might have been better employed at the front. Having received his orders, the soldier preceded Santana up a stair-well. The Ramanthians had nailed sheets of plywood over the stairs to make ramps, but most of it had been torn off by then, allowing both men to proceed unimpeded.

The door to conference room 302 was open, and when Santana looked in, he saw that Colonel Quinlan, General Kobbi, and a Jonathan Alan Seebo were waiting for him. General Kobbi was the first to come over and shake hands. "You look like hell," Kobbi said cheerfully. "And I mean that from the bottom of my heart."

"Thank you, sir," Santana replied. "Fortunately, I feel better than I look."

"And *smell*," Quinlan said disapprovingly, as he came over to shake hands. "I believe you know Major Seebo-1,324?"

As it happened the legionnaire *did* know three-twenty-four. Both men had been stationed on LaNor during the Claw Rebellion, although Santana had been a lieutenant, and the clone a captain. "Of course!" Santana said enthusiastically. "It's good to see you, sir."

"And *you*," the major replied sincerely. "Although I wish it were under more pleasant circumstances."

"I think we can promise you a hot shower and a drink at the O club later on," Kobbi said, "but lunch is on the way. In the meantime I want you to meet someone else."

So saying, Kobbi pointed a remote at a big wall screen, and touched a button. Video swirled, then locked up. The picture that appeared was that of a Jonathan Alan Seebo. Who, based on the name printed at the bottom of the frame, had been given the number: 62,666. "He's a handsome devil," Three-twenty-four put in. "You have to give him that!"

Kobbi laughed along with the others, but the general's eyes were serious as he turned toward Santana. "Good looks aside, the man you're looking at led a company of Seebos up to an allied firebase, where he and his men not only murdered twenty-three marines, but took hostages, and stole two tons' worth of supplies. Prior to that, eyewitnesses claim that Colonel Six, as his subordinates refer to him, knowingly slaughtered civilians during guerilla-style attacks on enemy forces."

"And that's why you're here," Three-twenty-four added soberly. "Based on your combat record General Kobbi and I believe you're the right man to track Six down and bring him in."

"Or kill him," Quinlan said offhandedly. "Which, all things considered, might be the better course of action. It looks like the food arrived. Let's have lunch."

10

Be careful what you wish for—you might just get it.

—A human saying of uncertain origins
Standard year circa 2000

PLANET EARTH, THE CONFEDERACY OF SENTIENT BEINGS

The humans called it Death Valley. Which the Ramanthians found amusing since they thought the long, low, mostly barren depression was rather pleasant—not to mention the fact that it was safe from ground attack. Because there was nowhere for humans to hide. Which was why the invaders had chosen to establish a temporary base in the area called Stovepipe Wells, a mostly flat area that was home to the Third Infantry Division. The division consisted of more than ten thousand combat troops, two thousand support personnel, and more than one thousand aircraft. It was one of twenty such bases that the Royal Expeditionary Force had been able to establish on the planet. All of which made the Queen feel good as her shuttle swept in over a makeshift parade ground and hundreds of perfectly aligned habs to land a few hundred feet north of the inflatable headquarters structure erected the day before.

The landings generated a miniature sandstorm that was still swirling when a hatch whirred open, and the Queen shuffled down a ramp and onto the surface of the planet where the human race had evolved. It was pleasantly warm, which was to say 110 degrees in the shade, and the Queen's ceremonial body armor glittered as she paused to look around. Members of the prestigious Imperial Guard lined both sides of the carpeted walkway that led to the headquarters structure. Behind them, still other soldiers supported T-shaped poles from which rectangular flags hung. One for each of the swarms that had been combined to form a single society hundreds of years earlier.

It was a historic moment, which having been captured by the usual bevy of flying cameras, would be beamed to planets throughout the empire so bedazzled citizens could see their warrior queen symbolically taking possession of Earth. The air was thick with the smell of wing wax, chitin polish, and mood-altering pheromones as the Queen nodded to a group of officials, who had been waiting for the better part of an hour, and preceded them into the headquarters structure.

All of which was quite impressive but not enough to quell the misgivings that Chancellor Ubatha felt. Especially when he was well outside the influence of the psychoactive chemicals that perpetually surrounded the royal and impelled even her most ardent critics to do her bidding. Because even though the human fleet had been destroyed, and the planet's orbital defenses had been breached, the battle for Earth was far from over. The civilian population had proven to be a good deal more combative than anticipated, and that made it difficult to settle in.

In fact, rather than simply allow themselves to be slaughtered, as many high-ranking officials originally believed they would, the animals continued to fight back! And rather effectively, too. . . . Which was one of the reasons why the invaders were camped in such a remote location. Because every time they attempted to occupy a city, the soldiers came under fire from the surviving elements of various military organizations, newly formed guerrilla groups, and heavily armed criminals. All of which meant that the Queen's plan to occupy Earth without destroying it was still in question.

It wasn't too late, however. Victory of a sort was still within reach if only the Queen and her advisors would listen to Ubatha's ideas. So as the royal disappeared from sight, and her staff passed between the rows of Imperial Guards, the Chancellor knew a different but no less important sort of battle was about to begin.

The Queen was waiting by the time her staff entered the room prepared for her use. It was square. There was a platform to one side where the monarch was seated on a saddle chair and backed by two bodyguards, a security precaution she objected to but her generals insisted on so long as portions of the planet's surface remained unsecured.

The area directly in front of the royal remained open to accommodate holo projections should any be required. A semicircular table, at which seven of her advisors were invited to sit, had been set up facing her. And, since Chancellor Ubatha was senior to all the rest, he was at the center.

The Queen made a brief opening statement thanking those present for a job well done, and lauding, ". . . the brave warriors upon whom all of us rely." Most of the troops would see the statement within the next day or so.

What followed was a long, and to Ubatha's thinking, overly detailed series of reports about every theater of the war *except* Earth. Based on reports put forth by various military officers, it seemed that rather than lose the battle for Gamma-014, as everyone expected him to, General Akoto might actually *win it.* Especially if the navy could intervene at exactly the right moment. All thanks to the massive incompetence of General-453, who in the words of one admiral, was "the best officer the Ramanthian Empire had!" Even the Queen found that concept amusing and signaled her merriment with a flurry of *clicks.*

There had been some reverses of course. . . . Because even though the Confederacy's forces were stretched thin, they remained potent, as evidenced by a chance encounter off Imiro VI. Having run into a task force consisting of a Ramanthian cruiser, two destroyers, and three heavily loaded transports, a human destroyer and two destroyer escorts not only engaged the larger force, but won the ensuing battle! A sad day indeed. But such narratives were few and far between as Ubatha's peers continued to brag about a long list of unalloyed victories.

Finally, once the glowing reports were over, it was time to discuss Earth. This prompted a long series of reluctantly negative reports. Because even though the empire had a large number of troops on the ground, only 10 percent of the planet's surface could be classified as pacified, and the Queen wanted answers. Half a dozen possible solutions were put forward. All of them called for *more* ships, *more* troops, and *more* supplies. Eventually, having heard from the military, the Queen called upon Ubatha. "You've been uncharacteristically silent, Chancellor. Yet you're rarely short of opinions! What would *you* have me do?"

It was the moment Ubatha had been counting on. "You will recall my original advice, Majesty," the official intoned carefully. "I felt it would be best to glass Earth and thereby deny the humans their ancestral home."

At that point some of the individuals seated to either side of the Chancellor began to squirm uneasily. If Ubatha was preparing to chastise the Queen for failing to follow his advice—then they wanted no part of what would almost certainly be a career-ending moment of self-justification!

But Ubatha had risen to high rank for a reason, and while he sincerely believed that a mistake *had* been made, the bureaucrat wasn't so foolish as to say that publicly. "But I was mistaken," the official admitted humbly. "Because as you pointed out at the time of our discussion, the destruction of Earth could precipitate an attack on Hive, and Earth constitutes a valuable bargaining chip as well."

By that time the officers and officials seated to either side of Ubatha were wondering where the Chancellor's comments were headed. But if the Queen was concerned, there was no sign of it in the position of her antennae or the set of her wings. "But there's a danger," Ubatha continued. "If we continue to throw more and more resources at Earth in what may be a futile attempt to pacify the planet, Earth could become *our* Gamma-014. That is to say, an expensive diversion that saps our strength even as the enemy continues to grow stronger."

That was too much for General Ra Ool—who felt honor-bound to protest. "Excuse me, Chancellor," the old warrior said. "But that's absurd! You heard the reports. With few exceptions, our forces are winning every battle they fight!"

"Yes," Ubatha agreed soberly, "that's true. But what lies ahead? Even if we win the battle for Gamma-014, who's to say whether such a mutual defeat will weaken the relationship between the Confederacy and Hegemony, or strengthen it?"

"This is ridiculous," Ra Ool objected contemptuously. "I really must object—"

"And you have," the Queen put in sternly. "But, if Chancellor Ubatha plans to make a fool of himself, why not give him every opportunity to do so?"

In spite of the royal's words, Ubatha knew he had almost total control of the room. "But let's say I'm wrong about Gamma-014," the bureaucrat continued, with a nod toward the disgruntled General Ra Ool. "Here's something I know for sure . . . Thraki intelligence agents tell us that an effort is presently under way to recruit and train Confederacy militia units out along the rim. Specifically, three brigades of mostly human troops. And all of them are likely to be twice as tough as the animals encountered here.

"And if *that* doesn't concern you," Ubatha continued urgently, "then consider this. . . . Having joined the Confederacy, the Hudathans are no longer prohibited from raising an army. And, based on reports from our agents, that's exactly what the barbarians are doing!"

The words produced a veritable click-storm of concern, because a number of Ramanthian planets had been badly mauled during the Hudathan wars, making it necessary for the race to briefly ally itself with the Confederacy in order to survive. Because the Hudathans had been cut off from all trade for many years, it was widely assumed that years would pass before the aliens would represent a threat again. A period during which the empire could defeat the Confederacy without being forced to deal with the Hudathans at the same time.

It was important information, intentionally withheld to produce maximum effect, and the Queen couldn't help but admire the skill with which the strategy had been executed—even if Ubatha was guilty of hoarding intelligence that should have been shared the moment it became available. She would chide him for the omission later. But privately—because it was in her interest to keep him strong. "That's interesting," the royal allowed calmly. "So tell us, Chancellor, how many Hudathans should we expect to face?"

"There are roughly two billion of them," Ubatha replied soberly. "And every male under the age of sixty qualifies as a potential warrior. Which means that within a year we will face another 750 million soldiers. And not just any soldiers, but *Hudathan* soldiers, of the sort who have laid waste to our planets before."

"So what would you suggest? the Queen demanded. She was beginning to tire of the way in which Ubatha had manipulated the meeting, and he could literally smell her dissatisfaction in the air. "We should try to hold what we have," Ubatha answered succinctly. "For the reasons already given. But under no circumstances should we expend additional resources on Earth—knowing what will face us soon."

There was a long period of silence, followed by a sequence of approving clicks from the Queen, and a discharge of pleasurable pheromones. A decision had been made.

Like thousands of other small towns in North America, Mill Valley, just north of San Francisco, had come under attack by the Ramanthians. But without any military bases to threaten the aliens, or heavy industries to attract their attention, the community had escaped relatively unscathed until a wave of urban refugees poured across the latest in a succession of four

Golden Gate Bridges, and laid waste to everything in their path. And that included Mill Valley's shopping mall.

What had been a beautiful state-of-the-art five-story building complete with huge skylights, plant-filled atria, and hundreds of retail sales outlets had been destroyed. Each and every shop had been broken into and looted, tons of shattered glass covered the floors, and bits of worthless merchandise lay everywhere. There were even uglier things, too, including dead bodies, or what was left of them. Because thousands of previously privileged pets had been abandoned in the mad rush to escape the Bay Area and were quickly turning feral, with a tendency to spread bones far and wide.

In spite of all the damage that had been done to the mall, and all the theft that had taken place since, one monument to capitalism remained untouched. And that was the low, squatty structure called the Mill Valley Security Deposit Building. Though part of the mall complex, it stood like an island in the middle of a vast wreck-strewn parking lot. The depository wasn't a bank in the regular sense of the word, because there hadn't been much need for brick-and-mortar financial institutions for a long time, but it was a descendant of such buildings. Because the one thing rich people couldn't do via their personal computers was to store their gold bullion, expensive jewelry, and other valuables anywhere other than within their vulnerable homes. So chains of fortresslike buildings existed to meet that need, most of which contained at least a thousand safety-deposit boxes, which could normally be accessed twenty-four hours a day by anyone having the correct code, retinal pattern, and voiceprint.

When the Ramanthians attacked, and looters swept through the community, the computer in charge of the Mill Valley Security Deposit Building had gone to the deep defensive mode. This resulted in a shutdown so complete that not even bona fide customers could get in. And that explained why either a looter or a frustrated customer had attempted to drive a beer truck through the front door. That attack, like dozens of others, had been unsuccessful. Even the Ramanthians had taken a crack at the depository without any success.

None of that troubled Lieutenant JG Leo Foley, because he and his brig rats were armed with something no other looters had access to. And that was the Mark IV Cutting Torch, which the group had "liberated" from the wreckage of a Confederacy shuttle shortly after being dumped onto the planet's surface. A truly awesome tool that they, as navy personnel, were very familiar with. Which was how they knew the torch could cut a hole through the depository's front door and give them access to the riches within!

Getting inside was only half the battle. Because human society had been reduced to predators and prey, and even though they were armed, plenty of other people were carrying weapons as well. The last thing they wanted to do was attract attention and be forced to fight for what they already regarded as theirs. And that was why the would-be thieves were hiding inside a stolen delivery van, waiting for darkness to fall, when one of the sentries called in. He was crouched on top of the depository's flat roof and his voice had a nasal quality. "Uh-oh. A Ramanthian transport is coming in from the south. . . . It's traveling low and slow. You'll see it in a minute or so."

Foley swore. There was no telling what the bugs were up to, but one thing was for sure: It would be stupid to leave the protection of the van and tackle the depository just as the chits arrived. "Get down off that roof," Foley ordered. "And take cover. Chances are they'll keep on going so long as we don't give them a reason to stop."

But the bugs had other plans, which quickly became obvious. "There it is!" Tappas exclaimed, as the sailor peered up through the van's windshield. "I think the bastards are going to land!" The comment proved prophetic as a loud *thrumming* noise was heard and a black shadow slid across the parking lot. Jets of bright blue energy stabbed the ground, and metal creaked as the transport settled onto huge skids. Foley was worried by that time. He and his companions couldn't drive away, not without drawing attention to themselves, but it would be crazy to stay. "The main hatch is opening," Tappas observed gloomily. "That can't be good."

Foley agreed, as two files of Ramanthian troops shuffled their way down a ramp and onto the debris-strewn asphalt. Rather than heading straight for the van, as Foley feared they would, the aliens came to an abrupt halt. Then, just as Foley was starting to feel hopeful, an officer brandished his sword and ordered the soldiers to form two ranks. The first of which dropped to one knee. "What the hell are they doing?" Tappas inquired, as he continued to peer out through the windshield.

Foley was just about to say, "I don't know," when a flood of humans poured out of the ship. Some glanced back over their shoulders as if fleeing someone. The crowd included men, women, *and* children. That was when the navy officer felt something cold trickle into the pit of his stomach. Because judging from the way the troops were positioned, they were about to open fire!

"Check *your* weapons," Foley said grimly, "and start the engine. Kill the officer with the van. We'll shoot the rest."

"But what about the depository?" one of the men inquired plaintively. "Aren't we going rob it?"

"Not today," Foley said, as he turned to Tappas. "Hit it!"

There was a loud *roar* as the engine came to life, followed by a *screech* as the tires fought for traction, and the vehicle shot forward. The Ramanthian officer was just turning toward the van when the vehicle struck him and threw his body high into the air. It was still falling when Tappas plowed into the troopers beyond and skidded to a stop. Foley hit the door release, and it slid out of the way. "Kill them!" the navy officer yelled as his boots hit the ground. "Kill *all* of them!"

There were six brig rats in the van, plus two slightly mystified sentries, all of whom opened fire on the Ramanthians. And, having been taken by surprise, a dozen aliens went down before their comrades could return fire. But there were at least thirty aliens, so it might have been over then, except that the seemingly helpless civilians weren't all that helpless.

A woman yelled an order, and the civilians charged. Five or six staggered and fell, but the Ramanthians were forced to divide their fire, and that made the crucial difference. Two brig rats had been killed by the time all the combatants collided. Sheets of blood flew as one of the alien noncoms made use of his power-assisted armor to rip a man's arm off. But the same Ramanthian was brought down a few moments later and dispatched with a captured rifle. That was when Tappas pointed at the transport. "Look! They're getting ready to lift!"

Foley saw that the sailor was correct. Vapor outgassed as the transport's engines began to spool up. Having seen the Ramanthian troops cut down by a group of animals, the ship's pilot was pulling out. That was fine with Foley, but one of the civilians took offense. "Oh, no you don't," the man said, and ran toward the van.

Tappas had left the engine running, so all the civilian had to do was put the vehicle in drive and take off. The van bucked wildly as it rolled over three or four dead bodies, swerved to avoid a derelict car, and began to pick up speed. Then it was on course, headed straight for the transport's ramp, which was in the process of being withdrawn. The vehicle bounced as it hit, but still found enough traction to run up the ramp, and bury itself in the open hatch. It was too big to pass through the rectangular opening. And the driver was trapped inside. But the additional weight caused the ship to wobble, and while the pilot struggled to compensate, one of the civilians tossed a grenade in under the van. It was an act of bravery that cost the woman dearly as the resulting explosion triggered two more, the transport rolled over, and crashed on top of her. There was a loud *whump* as flames enveloped the ship, and the battle was over. "Damn . . ." Foley said respectfully. "That woman had balls."

"Not exactly," a man with a beard said. "But Marcy is

with her husband now. . . . My name's Utley. Marvin Utley. And you are?"

A huge paw enveloped Foley's hand as the civilians began to execute wounded Ramanthians. One of them had taken possession of the officer's sword. Blood flew as the blade rose and fell. "Lieutenant Foley," the officer replied automatically.

Utley nodded approvingly. "The Legion or the Marine Corps?"

"Navy."

"Well, you and your boys did one helluva job, Lieutenant. Most of us are members of the resistance," Utley explained. "The bastards captured the whole bunch of us night before last, sentenced us to death, and brought us here for execution. It's all part of a calculated effort to intimidate the population. They like to fly prisoners to remote locations, kill them, and leave the bodies. It makes for a pretty effective warning. What were you doing here anyway?"

"I'm glad we were able to help," Foley replied evasively. And was surprised to discover that he meant it. "We'd better get the hell out of here, though. Because a quick-reaction force may be on the way."

"You're right about that," Utley said fervently, before turning to yell at the rest of his group. "Take their weapons and follow Lieutenant Foley!" And that was the moment when a new and rather unlikely guerrilla leader was born.

Even though all of the traffic on the two-lane road was headed east, and vehicles that ran out of gas were routinely pushed off the highway by the motorists behind them, the densely packed mass of vehicles was traveling at no more than one or two miles per hour when the Ramanthian fighters attacked. They came out of the sun, just as they had been trained to do, and swerved back and forth as they followed the serpentine highway west toward the cities from which the people below were trying to escape.

Vehicles exploded, rear-ended each other, and ran off the

road as energy bolts tore them apart. Margaret Vanderveen was driving, and managed to stop the truck without hitting the car in front of her, but could do little more than close her eyes and pray as the alien fighters passed overhead.

Then the Ramanthians were gone. It wasn't the first time that the slow-moving column had been savaged. Margaret couldn't remember how many attacks there had been as she opened her eyes to discover that she and her three companions were still alive. Others weren't so fortunate, however, as could be seen from the flames that enveloped three vehicles farther up the road. Horns were honking, and people were shouting orders at each other, as the cars just ahead of or behind burning wrecks struggled to put a few feet of space between the conflagration and whatever they were driving. Margaret turned to the maintenance man seated next to her. "Okay, Thomas," Margaret said. "You win. We'll take the next turnoff."

Lisa Qwan, and the robot named John, were in the backseat. Both were familiar with the ongoing debate, and neither chose to intervene. All of the humans agreed it would be necessary to abandon the truck and trailer at some point, but the question had always been "when?" Margaret favored staying on the road as long as possible, because she felt they could make better progress on the road, even at a slow crawl.

Benson understood that point of view but felt highway travel was too dangerous. Especially given attacks from the air. That perspective was reinforced by the sight of the still-smoldering vehicles that a group of volunteers was pushing off the road. There would be no burial for the blackened bodies that remained inside of them. Just the slow-motion decay Mother Nature provided to all of her creations.

It took the better part of an hour for the mob of cars and trucks to get under way again, but once they did, Margaret and her party were on the lookout for a turnoff. *Any* turnoff, so they could get off by themselves and unload their supplies without attracting the wrong sort of attention. Because while only a minority of the refugees were thieves, they were a dangerous minority, and would happily prey on anyone they could.

The opportunity to part company with the metal river came an hour later, as a dirt road appeared on the right, and Margaret put the wheel over. "Here we go," she said. "For better or for worse."

"Let's stop after half a mile or so," Benson suggested. "And put on a show of force. The truck, trailer, and contents are so valuable that there's a high probability someone will try to follow us."

Margaret knew it was true and felt a knot form in her stomach as the truck continued to *rattle* along. There were evergreens on both sides of the road, which judging from their height, had been planted fifteen years earlier. "Okay," Benson said, as the truck-trailer combination came to a halt. "Everybody grab a gun, and make sure it's loaded. You know the kind of people we're dealing with. So if it comes to that, show no mercy. They won't. Agreed?"

Unlike some military androids, John's programming included specific prohibitions against the taking of human lives, so that left only three of them to face down whoever chose to pursue them, and that was downright scary. There was reason to worry, because even as the cloud of dust generated by the truck-trailer combination began to blow away, *another* one appeared behind them.

"Here they come," Benson said grimly, as he pumped a shell into the shotgun's chamber. "Remember, if I fire, *you* fire, and don't stop until they're dead."

What the burly maintenance man *didn't* say was what the rest of the party should do if he were killed? But maybe that was obvious. They could fight, or they could die.

Because Benson had no intention of making his way down the middle of the road so the oncoming thieves could simply run him over, he walked next to it instead. So when the dusty yellow cab came to a stop, and two men got out of it, Benson addressed them from behind a thin screen of trees.

"Get back in the car," Benson ordered in a loud, clear voice. "And do it *now.*"

Both men carried hunting rifles and turned toward the sound. One of them had a narrow face, hollow cheeks, and a two-day growth of black stubble. He was dressed in an olive drab T-shirt and filthy jeans. He smiled engagingly. "Hey, take it easy, pops. . . . It ain't like that. Larry and I saw you turn off and figured you could use some help. Especially with two women and all."

"Thanks," Benson said, grimly. "But *no* thanks. Now get in the car and turn it around."

"Or *what?*" Larry demanded belligerently. He was wearing a blue bandana on his head, had a sheath knife dangling from the lanyard he wore around his neck, and sported knee-length shorts worn over a pair of scuffed combat boots. Larry was holding a rifle with his left hand, but as his right hand began to drift toward the pistol located at the small of his back, a shot rang out. The .300 Magnum bullet struck Larry between the shoulder blades, blew a hole through his bony chest, and hit a tree to Benson's right.

As the dead body continued to fall forward, the first man attempted to bring his weapon up and took half a load of double-ought buck from Benson. He dropped to his knees and appeared to be praying when the maintenance man shot him again. Blood sprayed the dirt and immediately began to dry.

Margaret stepped out onto the other side of the road at that point, still carrying a scope-mounted rifle. She looked pale, and Benson understood why. "You did a good job, ma'am," the maintenance man said gruffly, as he stepped over one of the bodies. "The only problem being that you were firing in *my* direction. But all's well that ends well."

Margaret didn't answer. She threw up instead. Qwan led her employer off to get cleaned up, while John stripped both dead men of potentially useful items, and Benson fired up a chain saw. It made quick work of two trees and it wasn't long before both were lying across the road. Not an impossible barrier by any means, but one calculated to slow pursuers down, and buy the group some additional time. Strangely enough, it was Margaret's idea to drag the bodies over and prop them up against the fallen trees. A clear message if there ever was one!

Then, encouraged by the fact that there hadn't been further signs of pursuit, Margaret and her companions reentered the truck and continued on their way. Having pored over all of their maps, the socialite had identified a hiking trail that cut across the road roughly two miles ahead. If they followed it toward the northeast, they would eventually connect with a *second* trail, which would take them to a point only a few miles from their ultimate destination. And sure enough, it wasn't long before they saw the trail sign they were looking for, and Benson braked to a stop.

"Okay," Benson said, as they prepared to get out. "The horses won't be able to carry all the stuff we have—so let's sort everything into two piles. The 'gotta have it to stay alive pile'—and the 'it would be nice to have pile.' We'll load the most important stuff first and add more if we have room. Any objections?"

There weren't any objections, so they piled out, and work began. By unspoken agreement, it was Margaret's job to coax the horses out of the twenty-eight-foot trailer, check the animals over, and prepare them for the trail, an activity that was likely to come as a shock to the pampered beasts since they were intended for riding and had never been used as pack animals.

The most spirited, and skittish, horse was the Arabian that belonged to Margaret's daughter Christine. As the society matron worked to put one of Benson's makeshift pack saddles on the mare, she took comfort from the fact that her daughter was with President Nankool and therefore safe from harm.

Meanwhile the other three sorted through everything they had, remembering that each horse would only be able to carry about one hundred thirty pounds of gear. That, plus the additional three hundred pounds of tools and supplies the humans and John could carry, added up to slightly over eight hundred pounds of freight.

So there were tough choices to make, and some arguments as a result, but there was general agreement where weapons, ammo, and medical supplies were concerned. The same was true of nonperishable food, although Qwan was forced to give up some of the canned items she was fond of, and the suitcase full of beauty products that Margaret wanted to take was voted down. Benson, by contrast, was allowed to keep almost all of his carefully selected hand tools and hardware, plus a quantity of liquor, for what he called "medicinal purposes." The rest of the carefully packed loads consisted of tents, tarps, and kitchen equipment. Clothes were limited to three outfits each. Except for John—who could go without if necessary.

It was evening by the time everything was ready, and rather than tackle the trail in the dark, the decision was made to stay where they were until morning. So a fire was built, and the humans gorged themselves on canned food, while John stood sentry duty. Something the android could do all night without experiencing fatigue.

Margaret thought it would be difficult to sleep that night, but she surprised herself by dozing off almost immediately, in spite of the fact that she had killed a man earlier that day. And when she awoke, it was to the smell of canned hash frying over the fire, and coffee perking in a fire-blackened pot.

Margaret discovered that she was sore from sleeping on a thin backpacking mat, but otherwise fine, as she set about caring for the horses. It was an endless task even under the best of circumstances, but was made even more demanding by the need to load and unload the Arabians every day, plus find something for the animals to graze on.

As the three of them sat down to eat, Benson suggested they destroy the items they couldn't take with them. But Margaret refused. "People are desperate," she said soberly.

"Who knows? The extra supplies could save a few lives. Let's put them in the back of the truck and leave it unlocked. We're all in this together."

Benson knew that the supplies could just as easily fall into the hands of people who didn't deserve any charity, but chose not to say anything. So everything they couldn't carry went into the truck. And an hour later they were gone. More exposed in some ways, but safer in others, as the forest closed around them.

The succeeding days were hard, even harder than Margaret had expected. For even though she was in better shape than many her age, Margaret was sixty-one years old and used to a life of privilege. And it was hard work leading an often-recalcitrant horse all day, carrying a pack, and battling rugged terrain. But Margaret became tougher with each passing hour as her body grew stronger.

There were worse things than the rigors of the trail, however. Like the day when a loud *thrumming* noise was heard, and a Ramanthian shuttle passed directly above them before they could hide, but, inexplicably, continued on its way.

And there were three encounters with other groups of refugees, one of which involved a party of twelve heavily armed men who could have easily taken everything they had. Fortunately, all of them were would-be resistance fighters, on their way to join forces with a group called the Earth Liberation Brigade, which was determined to throw the bugs off the planet.

But the moments all of them dreaded most were when the trail passed remote homes, a large number of which were clearly occupied, or crossed highways, which was even worse. On one occasion it had been necessary to wait until nine in the evening for a seemingly endless Ramanthian convoy to pass. Then, like ghosts in the night, the foursome led their pack animals across the pavement and into the woods on the other side.

Finally, after what seemed like an eternity, the group came up over the saddle between two hills and were able to look down into Deer Valley. Something they did with great care, having learned how important stealth could be over the last week or so. John took charge of the horses while the rest of them elbowed their way forward to look down from the cover of some sun-warmed rocks.

There had been a gold mine on the property hundreds of years earlier. After that played out, the valley had been used as a cattle ranch, a private estate, a bed-and-breakfast, a religious retreat, and a hunting preserve, before turning into a private estate once again when Charles and Margaret Vanderveen purchased it twenty-one years earlier.

At that point the spread included a sprawling two-story ranch house, a guest cottage, an elevated water tank, an old barn, and the new stable Margaret had commissioned two years before. But as Margaret looked down into the valley, she saw little more than fire-blackened rubble where the house and barn had once stood. There was no way to know how the fire had been started or by whom. The obvious suspects were Ramanthians and/or looters.

It was a terrible blow, especially after working so hard to get there, and Margaret felt a rising sense of despair as Qwan put an arm around her shoulders. "I'm sorry, Margaret," Benson said, as he eyed the valley through a pair of binoculars. "It looks like the place was looted. Wait a minute. . . . What have we got here? Kids, that's what, a couple dozen of them."

Margaret wiped some of the tears away with the back of her hand. "Children? No adults?"

"Nope," Benson replied. "Not so far as I can see. Here, take a look."

So Margaret accepted the glasses and eyed what remained of the family retreat. There had been a caretaker, of course, but there was no sign of him, which was certainly understandable given the circumstances.

From what she could see it appeared that some of the children had made themselves at home in the guest cottage, with the rest living in the stable. The oldest looked like she was fifteen or sixteen and the youngest about four or five. "Come on," Margaret said, as she backed away. "We need to get down there. . . . Those children need our help."

"I was afraid you were going to say something like that," Benson grumbled. But he came nevertheless—and was right beside her when Margaret made her way up a dirt road and onto her property. A ragged-looking teenage girl was positioned on the cottage's front porch. The youngster pointed a .22 rifle at Margaret as she and her companions made their way up a gentle slope. The teenager was flanked by twin boys and a blond girl with a runny nose. "We don't have anything worth stealing," the girl said tightly. "So go away."

"My husband and I own this ranch," Margaret said calmly. "Not that such things mean much anymore. . . . But you need to know that my friends and I plan to stay. And we'd be happy to have you and the other children stay, too. This was a self-supporting ranch at one time, and if we work hard enough, it can be again."

The teenager was silent for a moment before lowering the rifle. Margaret could see what might have been relief in the girl's eyes. "I'm sorry about your house, ma'am. . . . It was already burned when we got here. My parents are dead, at least I think they are, and that's the same for all the rest. I started out with the two I was babysitting—and the rest kind of glommed onto us. I couldn't tell them no."

"No, of course not," Margaret said understandingly. "My name is Margaret Vanderveen, the young lady is Lisa Qwan, the man with the scruffy beard is Thomas Benson, and the android is named John."

"My name is Christine," the girl said. "But the kids call me Chris."

Margaret felt a lump form in the back of her throat but managed to swallow it. "That's a very pretty name. Well, Christine, there's a lot of work to do, so we might as well get started."

As night fell two days later Margaret took a flashlight and made her way up an overgrown trail to the hilltop where she and her husband liked to sip hot chocolate and watch shooting stars flash across the sky. And now, even though she knew that a lot of what orbited the planet was evil, she chose to look beyond that and talk to her husband. "We've got a lot to do," Margaret said, as she stared up into the night sky. "The ranch will continue to attract trouble so long as it looks habitable. So we're moving everything of value into the old mine shaft. Benson says all of the supports are in good shape, and I trust him. Once that work is complete we'll burn the guest cottage and the stable. We'll keep everything hidden after that.

"The children are going to need help, Charles. . . . Lots of help—and lots of food. So that will be the next thing to worry about. But right now I'm just thinking of you. . . . On cold, cold, Algeron, worrying about me. Well, I'm fine, Charles, just fine. And someday, when you can come home again, I'll be here waiting."

There was no reply of course, there couldn't be, but what might have been a shooting star chose that exact moment to streak across the sky, and Margaret took it as an omen. Darkness would hold sway for a while—but a new dawn would surely come.

11

Given that most of our forces are not equipped for arctic conditions, and the fact that there is every reason to believe that the enemy is drawing us into a trap, I recommend that we suspend the push into the mountains until we can equip all of our troops with appropriate clothing and winter conditions abate. It is my considered opinion that the existing strategy will lead to a significant and unnecessary loss of allied forces.

—*An extract from COMFORCES Command Memo 2842.417 from General Mortimer Kobbi to General Jonathan Alan Seebo-785,453 Standard year 2842*

PLANET GAMMA-014, THE CLONE HEGEMONY

Colonel Six, the surviving members of his company, two hostages taken from Marine Firebase 356, and roughly fifty heavily laden Ortovs had been hiking all day. And everyone was tired. But, before the clones could eat and crawl into their sleeping bags, Dr. Kira Kelly insisted on screening them. Her office consisted of an open space next to a roaring fire. It warmed her right side but did nothing for her left, as the snow continued to fall. The big fluffy flakes *hissed* as the fire consumed them. "Next!" Kelly said, and a brawny Ortov made way for a teenage boy. "How do you feel?" the doctor inquired, as the youngster took his place on her guest rock.

"Fine," the clone replied flatly. His features were impassive, which was typical of the Ortov line, but the doctor

could see the curiosity in his eyes. Chances were that she was
the first off-world free breeder he had ever been allowed to
talk to. There was something innocent about the clones—a
quality that Kelly found refreshing.

"So why are you limping?" the doctor wanted to know.

"I wasn't," the teenager countered evasively.

Kelly sighed. The Ortovs were tough, and took pride in
that, sometimes to their own detriment. "Remove your left
boot."

The boy did as he was told.

"Now the sock." Kelly noticed the careful manner in which
the sock was removed and soon saw why. The teenager's toes
were black and swollen. It was a sure sign of gangrene stem-
ming from frostbite. But which kind? The dry type, which she
and Hospital Corpsman Sumi might be able to treat without
having to amputate, or the wet kind? Also known as gas gangrene, which is caused by a dangerous bacteria, and can follow dry gangrene if left untreated.

Kelly cupped the boy's heel, brought the dirty foot up
within inches of her nose, and immediately caught a whiff of
the foul-smelling gas associated with wet gangrene. She lowered the foot, got out a roll of gauze, and began to apply it.
"I'm sorry I have to tell you this," she said kindly. "But your
toes are badly infected—and at least some of them will have
to be removed. We'll take care of that as soon as we arrive
wherever it is we're going."

Now there was fear in the boy's eyes. His voice quavered
when he spoke. "Will I be able to walk afterwards?"

"Yes, you will," Kelly said gently. "But it will be difficult
at first—and it's going to hurt."

Two adults were summoned to help the boy—and Kelly
told them that a stretcher would be required to transport
him. Then, just as they were about to carry the teenager away,
he cleared his throat. "Doctor?"

Kelly looked up. "Yes?"

"Thank you."

Kelly said, "You're welcome," and watched the other

Ortovs carry the lad away. *It must be strange to live with people so similar to yourself yet not have parents,* Kelly thought to herself. But with more potential patients waiting to be seen, there was no opportunity to consider the complexities of clone society.

Kelly was *still* screening the Ortovs when a visibly angry Colonel Six appeared fifteen minutes later. Snow went *crunch* under his combat boots, and his breath jabbed the air in front of him. "There you are!" Six said accusingly, as if Kelly had been trying to hide from him. "What's this I hear about a stretcher? The Ortovs can't carry each other around on stretchers. Who will haul the supplies?"

Kelly was disinfecting a cut and didn't bother to look up. The truth was that Six frightened her—but she was determined not to show it. "Beats me. It looks like you have me confused with someone who gives a shit."

Blood rose to suffuse the clone's face. "I rate a sir!"

"Not in my book you don't," Kelly replied matter-of-factly, as she secured a dressing over the small laceration. "You're the one who wanted a doctor, and here I am. Please feel free to turn us loose anytime you want to."

What Colonel Six *really* wanted had nothing to do with Kelly's status as a doctor, but the Seebo couldn't say *that*, so there was very little for him to do but turn and stomp away.

Kelly watched him go out of the corner of her eye, let her breath out, and was surprised to learn that she'd been holding it. She was afraid of the clone, and appalled by his ruthlessness, yet strangely fascinated by the man as well. That frightened her all the more.

Even with some two dozen fires, tarps to keep the worst of the snow off, and some high-quality clone-issue mummy bags, it was a long, cold night. When morning finally came, each member of the party was given a large portion of mush, along with a mug of unsweetened tea. Once breakfast was over, it was time to reshoulder the heavy packs and follow the soldiers into the silent, snow-shrouded forest. Kelly made a point of checking to ensure that the boy with the gangrenous toes was being transported on a stretcher and was pleased to discover that he was. Could that be interpreted as a peace offering from Six? And if so, why did she care? It wasn't a subject Kelly wanted to think about, so she pushed it away.

The trail wound between stands of three-hundred-year-old trees, and crossed a dozen icy creeks and streams, before eventually coming to an end at the foot of a flat-topped butte. That seemed strange since all the other hills and mountains in the area had rounded if not jagged tops. The mystery deepened as Colonel Six led the column up a slanted walkway that ran along the west face of the butte. A *uniform* walkway that was far too wide, and far too well engineered, to have been created recently. What might have been round windows appeared at regular intervals. Many were open, but some had been sealed, using a variety of materials. So there was no telling *what* the structure was.

Kelly had some friends by that time—one of whom was the Ortov female who had been assigned to carry about a third of the doctor's medical equipment. The clone explained that the complex was believed to be contemporaneous with similar ruins found on about 10 percent of the planets that had been surveyed so far, which suggested it was the work of the mysterious civilization generally referred to as "the Forerunners."

Regardless of its origins, the butte offered local civilians a place to take shelter after their town had been destroyed, which was why Six had decided to take his troops, hostages, and stolen supplies there to rest and regroup. When the people in front of her came to a sudden stop, Kelly was forced to do likewise, and took the opportunity to look around. The sky was pewter gray, and her breath fogged the air before a light breeze blew it away. Now that she was standing still, Kelly could feel her body temperature start to drop as sweat cooled her skin—a phenomenon that could lead to hypothermia unless the column began to move again.

Kelly's thoughts were interrupted by a sudden flurry of

gunshots, distant yelling, and a physical response as the entire line recoiled in response to whatever was taking place at the top of the incline. Some of the Ortovs stood on tiptoe, trying to see what was going on, but none of the clones ran. Moments later a Seebo appeared, skidded to a stop, and waved Kelly forward. "Come on! They shot Three-Three!"

Kelly had no idea who "they" were, but followed the Seebo up past the long line of Ortovs, with Sumi bringing up the rear. Two minutes later they arrived on a landing, where a Seebo lay sprawled on the bloodstained snow. Six was there, pistol in hand, kneeling beside the fallen soldier. Other clones, weapons at the ready, were clustered in front of a metal door. "Hurry!" Six said urgently, as he waved Kelly over. "They shot Three-Three in the chest!"

Kelly was struck by the obvious angst in the officer's voice—and the expression of concern on his normally stern face. He was clearly upset, and even though the doctor disagreed with the Seebo's approach to almost everything, she felt sorry for him. And a little bit pleased to discover that there was something the cold-blooded bastard cared about. Even if it was an exact replica of himself! Yet this same man was responsible for killing more than a dozen marines. . . . So liking him was wrong. *Very* wrong.

"Get out of the way," Kelly said, as both she and Sumi moved in to displace Colonel Six. "It's a sucking chest wound," Kelly said, as she removed a blood-soaked battle dressing and heard the characteristic hissing sound. "Where is this man's body armor?"

"The idiot left it unzipped," Six replied darkly. "Can you save him?"

"Of course I can," Kelly answered confidently, as Sumi handed her a sterile patch. Three of the edges bore adhesive, so that when the dressing was placed over the purple-edged hole, air could escape the chest cavity. But air couldn't enter the chest cavity when the Seebo inhaled. Which was important because the bullet had passed through the Seebo's lung and caused it to collapse. It was a life-threatening injury if not treated immediately.

"Okay," Kelly said. "Let's get him inside, where it's warmer. We'll put the chest tube in there."

"They won't let us in," Six responded angrily. "A group of revolutionaries took control of the complex."

Kelly stood. "Revolutionaries, as in people who want to overthrow the government?"

"Yes!" Six answered emphatically. "And when I ordered them to let us in, they shot Three-Three!"

"Did you try asking instead of telling?"

"I don't have to ask!" the soldier insisted loudly. "They are *required* to obey me!"

"Let me give it a try," Kelly said reasonably, as she approached the door. The metal was dimpled where bullets had struck it, but the door was otherwise intact. A small portal located about chest high was closed at the moment, but could obviously be opened. Kelly felt sure that someone was standing just beyond the door listening and perhaps peering through a crack. "This is Lieutenant Kira Kelly," the physician said loudly. "I'm a navy doctor. . . . You don't trust the Seebos, and I understand that. But it doesn't alter the fact that we have a wounded man out here—and he's going to die unless you let us in! So, here's what I propose. . . . Colonel Six and three of his men will offer themselves up as hostages against the good behavior of everyone else. Then, when the Seebos are ready to leave, you'll let them go."

"*What?*" Six objected. "I never agreed to that!"

"No," Kelly said reasonably, as she turned to look at him. "But you should. . . . Unless you want Three-Three to die."

"*Damn you!*" Six said fervently. "I should never have brought you!"

"On that we can agree," the doctor said sweetly. "So what's your answer? Yes? Or no?"

"*Yes*, blast you," the Seebo said disgustedly.

"Did you hear that?" Kelly inquired, as she turned back toward the door. "The offer stands."

There was a long pause, as if some sort of debate might be taking place within. Then came a *clang* as the smaller portal opened, and a bland-faced Fisk appeared. "Tell the hostages to put their hands on top of their heads," the anarchist said brusquely. "And no funny business."

The larger door opened moments later and was quickly slammed shut after Six and three of his Seebos went inside. A long, agonizing five minutes passed before the door swung open for a second time. A Fisk armed with a submachine gun motioned for them to enter. "There's a room down the hall on the right. All weapons must be placed there, but two Seebos can stay to monitor them."

Kelly looked at Lieutenant-790,444, who nodded in agreement. "Okay," the doctor said as she turned back toward the door. "It will be as you say."

"Good," the Fisk said. "Welcome to the Sanctuary."

The Forerunner complex was so huge that the approximately five hundred clones who had taken refuge in it occupied less than 5 percent of the available space. But given the bitterly cold weather, there was no incentive to spread out since doing so would require more fuel for the makeshift fireplaces.

There was no heat source in the cell-like room that Six had been placed in, however. Just a built-in bench made out of the same material as the butte itself. So the Seebo was sitting on the bench, huddled inside his sleeping bag, when he heard the sound of voices. The door *rattled* and opened to admit Kelly. She was holding a brown ceramic bowl, a spoon, and a tubby thermos bottle. Even though Kelly was a bit grubby, and clearly tired, she was still beautiful. That's what Six thought anyway, as one of guards pulled the door closed, and Kelly presented him with the bowl. "Here, hold on to that while I serve you some soup. It's actually quite good."

Six held the bowl with both hands while the doctor

opened the thermos and poured a generous serving of chunky soup into the waiting container. It was steaming hot, and the rich odor made Six realize how hungry he really was. "Dig in," Kelly said understandingly. "And have some of *this*." So saying, Kelly removed a big chunk of crusty bread from a cargo pocket and brushed some lint off it. "Sorry," she said. "Bon appétit!"

Six said, "Thank you," as he accepted the bread. "For the food *and* for coming. How is Three-Three?"

"He's going to be fine," Kelly assured him, as she took a seat on the other end of the bench. "We reinflated his lung, closed his wounds, and gave him a broad-spectrum antibiotic. The Ortov boy is doing well, too. . . . Although it's going to take him some time to recover."

"I'm glad to hear it," Six said, as he paused between spoonfuls. "So what's going on?" he wanted to know. "Will the rebels let us leave? Or was that a lie?"

"The sooner the better is the impression I get," Kelly responded. "I know very little about Hegemony politics, but if I understand correctly, the revolutionaries want to overthrow the Alpha Clones in favor of a democracy. And they see the Seebo line as part of the problem."

"They're wrong," Six said sternly. "Dr. Hosokowa's plan is *perfect*. All we need to do is follow it."

"Well, it's good to see that you have an open mind," Kelly replied lightly. "No wonder they want to get rid of you!"

"They're free breeders," Six said accusingly. "And there's no place for free-breeder children in the plan! So what they want won't work."

"It will if you change plans," Kelly said mildly, as she came to her feet. "And let people be whatever they *want* to be. Or are capable of being. My father is an accountant, my mother is a teacher, and I'm a doctor. That may not be all neat and tidy, but it works! Sorry," she said, "but they want me to return the bowl."

Six gave her the bowl but kept what remained of the bread. "Tell me something. . . ."

Kelly raised her eyebrows. "What?"

"In your society, where people choose each other, can a soldier be with a doctor?"

Suddenly Kelly knew something she should have understood all along. In spite of all his straightlaced posturing, the Seebo was as horny as all the other men she knew, but he felt guilty about it! The schoolboy crush might have been endearing except that she had been abducted. Yet where was her anger? And why had she come to visit him? She felt guilty, confused, and strangely compassionate all at the same time. "Yes," she answered soberly. "A soldier *can* be with a doctor. But only if *both* people want to be together." And with that she left.

Kira Kelly was thousands of light-years away, sailing her father's boat across a sparkling lake, when a hand shook her shoulder. "Wake up," Six said urgently. "Get dressed! We have to leave."

Kelly looked at her watch and groaned. It was 0126. "Why? It's dark outside."

"Because a battalion of Seebos is trying to get in! I'm not sure yet, but it's my guess that at least one of the radios we stole has a tracking device in it, which revealed our location. The rebels claim that government forces want to arrest me."

Kelly struggled to kick the sleeping bag off. "Arrest you? Why?"

"Because I chose to fight the Ramanthians *my* way instead of *their* way."

"But what about the perfect plan?" the doctor wanted to know. "If it's perfect, you should follow it."

"The plan *is* perfect," Six replied defensively. "But some of the people who are supposed to implement the plan aren't. General-453 is an idiot."

"So you're a revolutionary," Kelly said, as she fastened her boots. "Just like the people you detest."

"Don't you ever stop talking?" Six demanded. "Hurry up."

"No," Kelly said firmly, as she stood. "There's no need for

me to hurry since I'm staying here." It wasn't what the doctor *wanted* to do, but it was what she *should* do, and Kelly was determined to take a stand.

"We have Sumi," Six replied evenly. "And the revolutionaries want you to leave in spite of what you did for them. So get ready."

Kelly felt a strange sense of relief knowing that the situation was beyond her control and went off to pack her things.

Twenty minutes later a Fisk led the soldiers plus twenty-five heavily laden Ortovs through a maze of passageways, down what seemed like endless flights of stairs, and out into the freezing cold. The pursuing Seebos were on the other side of the butte, and the chase was on.

PLANET ALPHA-001, THE CLONE HEGEMONY

Consistent with Founder Hosokowa's master plan, every city of any size had an elaborate water-recovery and purification system designed to take advantage of rainfall and runoff, thereby reducing the need for dams, wells, and expensive pipelines. Once collected, the water had to be stored, which was why the lake-sized reservoir had been constructed before the city was built above it, and had subsequently been capped with a one-foot-thick duracrete lid. That, for lack of a better location, was where the Revolutionary Council was about to hold its first and possibly last public meeting.

Even though the space wasn't intended for such gatherings the high-arched ceiling, and the lights that twinkled like distant stars, gave the place a majestic feeling. Folding chairs had been placed on top of the lid, a temporary PA system was up and running, and a ring of pole-mounted spots threw light onto the seats.

Security was extremely tight. Having been given only an hour's notice prior to the meeting, the attendees were subjected to DNA analysis as they entered and were processed through a receiving area. The precaution was intended to make sure none of the attendees were surgically altered

Romos or Nerovs. Once that formality was out of the way, the representatives were funneled into twelve cleaning stations, where dozens of tiny robots were removed from each delegate and they were given new clothes. Then, and only then, were the men and women who had been chosen to represent the various lines allowed to file out onto the concrete lid and take their seats.

Christine Vanderveen hated the cleaning process, but was willing to go through it, in order to be present at the very start of the revolution. Assuming Alan and the rest of the Council could muster the votes necessary to start a revolt. Because in order to succeed, the would-be revolutionaries knew they would need support from *all* of the genetic lines, and at least 70 percent of the overall population. Many of whom were satisfied with their lot in life—or too afraid to oppose authority. Still, Alan believed sufficient support was available, and the Council did as well.

So once Vanderveen had clothes back on, she was in a hopeful frame of mind as she walked out onto the lid. Because if the revolution was a success, and the Council kept its word, the Confederacy of Sentient Beings would have a new *member*. Which would be qualitatively different from the lukewarm alliance currently in place. Could that impact the battle for Earth? Vanderveen certainly hoped so, because her mother, and billions of other humans, were in desperate need of help.

Speed was of the essence, lest the Romos and Nerovs get wind of the gathering, so the last of the incoming delegates were still getting dressed when the meeting was called to order. Vanderveen, who was the only foreign dignitary present, had been given a seat in the first row, where she had a good view of the seven-person council. Though not allowed to record the proceedings or take notes, Vanderveen did the best she could to memorize what went on for inclusion in the report she planned to write later. But would anyone be willing to read a document authored by a renegade diplomat? Yes, Vanderveen thought they would, but *only* if the revolution was successful. Because at that point Nankool and his senior staff would be desperate for an "in."

With the preliminaries out of the way, Alan rose to speak on behalf of the governing council. In terms of appearance, he was almost the polar opposite of Antonio Santana. Because where Alan had light-colored hair—Tony's was midnight black. And where Alan was idealistic—Tony was cynical. And where Alan was a man of ideas—Tony was a man of action. Yet there were commonalities as well. Both men were intelligent, caring, and funny. So how to choose? Promises had been made to Tony—but the two of them weren't engaged. All of that was going through the diplomat's mind as Alan began to speak.

"Welcome to what may very well be a historic meeting. We are gathered here to consider the first step on a very uncertain path. Which, when you think about it, was the very thing the Founder sought to avoid. Because she believed that all of humanity's problems, reverses, and tragedies stem from uncertainty. To remedy that, Dr. Hosokowa and her advisors created a plan, a blueprint by which predictable people would do predictable things and produce predictable results."

Alan paused at that point. As his bright green eyes made momentary contact with hers, Vanderveen felt something akin to electricity jump the gap. "And it worked," Alan continued soberly. "Not perfectly, not in every case, but across society as a whole. The pain previously associated with familial relationships was eliminated. The massive gap between the rich and poor was closed. Everyone had equal access to health care. Each person had useful work to do. And even nature was tamed to some extent.

"So, why give that up? Well, the answer is simple, if somewhat counterintuitive. A predictable existence may be safe, but it's also boring, and stultifying, and colorless, and joyless. Because without pain there is no pleasure, and without challenge there is no success, and without freedom there is no opportunity to fail! And ultimately to learn from failing.

"That's why the Council and I invited you here," Alan

continued earnestly. "To tell you that the time has come. Conditions will never be better than they are right now! Let's take back our lives, and the right to live them as *we* see fit, even if we suffer as a result. If you authorize us to do so, we will strike a blow for freedom, and the revolution will begin. I cannot tell you when, where, or how for reasons of security. But I can assure you that once the blow is struck, you and your line will recognize the event for what it is. And that will be the moment when you must lead your brothers and sisters to the ramparts—where those who worship the status quo will defend it to the end. Thank you for listening. The voting process will begin now. No one will be allowed to leave the area until all votes have been submitted and counted."

There was a stir as monitors began to make the rounds, and individuals representing the various lines began to cast their votes. Vanderveen was proud of both Alan, and the speech, and felt sure that Nankool would approve as well had the president been present to hear it.

The results were available fifteen minutes later. Vanderveen felt a sudden emptiness in the pit of her stomach as the results of the vote were brought forward for review by the Council prior to the formal announcement. Because if those seated all around the diplomat had a stake in the outcome, then so did *she*, and those she had chosen to represent. Whether they wanted her to do so or not!

Vanderveen watched carefully as the piece of paper was passed from person to person. She tried to read the Council's faces, searching for the slightest glimmer of joy or disappointment, but without success. Because one of the hallmarks of the perfect society was the need to conceal one's emotions. It was something all of the clones were extremely good at. So when Alan rose to read out the results, the diplomat had no idea of what to expect. "The votes have been counted," the rebel said gravely as he looked out over the assemblage. "And your decision is clear. You chose freedom—and all it entails. The revolution has begun."

There were cheers as the delegates came to their feet, and somehow, in all the hubbub that followed, Vanderveen found herself in Alan's arms. There was pleasure in the long, tender kiss that followed, but a sense of guilt as well. Because promises had been made on planets far, far away. Promises that echoed through her mind, robbed the kiss of its sweetness, and left the diplomat confused, for the memory of the legionnaire was bright and clear. He was smiling down at her as they lay together on the hill above her parents' estate, toying with a lock of her hair, while a hawk wheeled high above. Then a cheer went up, the embrace came to an end, and the vision disappeared.

It was a sunny day, and as Vanderveen followed Alan and a team of Fisks along a busy street toward Bio-Storage Building 516, she was struck by how unassuming the drab one-story structure was. Except that description wasn't really accurate. For Building 516 was an inverted skyscraper that extended hundreds of feet down below the planet's surface—a design intended to protect both the structure and its contents from everything up to and including an orbital attack. Because there was nothing more precious to the Hegemony's hereditary social structure than the sperm and ova stored in the carefully maintained bio vaults below. There were duplicate facilities, of course. Two of them. Both located on other planets. But neither had the symbolic and emotional heft that 516 had, which was why it was the perfect place to start the revolution. And why it was heavily guarded.

But the freedom fighters had a number of things going for them, including the element of surprise and a cadre of revolutionary sympathizers who were waiting *inside* the building. The assault was timed to coincide with the morning rush hour, a time when it was perfectly natural to see lots of people on the street. Normal, that is, until a hundred of them suddenly broke away from the main flow and turned in toward the storage building.

Vanderveen heard the staccato *rattle* of gunfire as the shock troops at the head of the column took submachine guns out from under their trench coats and opened fire on the Seebos stationed in front of the main entrance. Only one of the six soldiers managed to fire a shot, but it was deadly, and the diplomat had to step over a dead Fisk as she followed the others into the building. She felt sorry for casualties from both sides of the conflict.

The second line of defense consisted of four Romos. They were in charge of the security checkpoint located in the lobby beyond the front door, and having already been alerted by the sound of gunfire, were waiting with guns drawn. But as the policemen turned their attention outward, and prepared to fight the invaders, two female Crowleys attacked the men from the rear. The gentechs were armed with pistols that had been smuggled into the facility piece by piece over a period of weeks. And even though the women weren't experienced with firearms, they didn't have to be, since the unsuspecting policemen were only a few feet away.

Most of the Romos *weren't* members of the hated death squads, but some were, which was justification enough as the Crowleys emptied their weapons. There was no way that body armor could protect the policemen's heads, which appeared to explode as the high-velocity projectiles hit them. As Alan, Mary, and Vanderveen followed a phalanx of Fisks into the lobby, they were forced to pass through something resembling a slaughterhouse. The diplomat had seen a lot of violence during her relatively short career, and even been forced to take some lives herself, but she had never experienced anything worse than the sight of the blood-drenched walls, the smell of suddenly released feces, and the pathetic whimpering noises that the single survivor uttered as he lay fetuslike in a pool of his own blood.

A Fisk pointed a gun at the Romo, as if preparing to finish him off, but Alan intervened. "No," the Trotski said firmly. "He was doing what he was bred to do. . . . Just as *you* are."

The anarchist gave Alan a strange look and turned away.

"We need a medic!" Alan shouted, and one paused to help, as more rebels pushed in off the street. Many were carrying supplies in case of a siege.

"All right!" Fisk-3 shouted. "The alarm has gone out—and government troops are on the way. . . . So let's get some people up onto the roof! And watch your backs. . . . There are still plenty of Romos and Nerovs *inside* the building."

At that point, all of the measures intended to protect Building 516 from external threats were turned against the authorities, as they were forced to set up a security cordon around the now-impregnable fortress, and try to come up with a plan to force their way in. Except that the people inside had hostages, *billions* of them, in the form of frozen sperm and ova.

Meanwhile, as heavily armed revolutionaries worked to block all of the street-level entrances to the building, specially designated teams went looking for Romos and Nerovs who had already gone into hiding. Except that hiding was difficult to do, because the Crowleys knew where to look, and it wasn't long before the remaining security men were killed or captured, leaving Bio-Storage Building 516 secure—for the moment at least.

All of which was bad enough from the government's point of view. But what happened next took the loss of Building 516 and multiplied the disaster by a thousand times as the enterprising revolutionaries tapped into the planetwide communications system and took control. Suddenly, out of nowhere, both the Alpha Clones and millions of citizens found themselves looking at a man who's official name was Trotski-4, but introduced himself as "Alan."

As the revolutionary began to explain why Building 516 had been taken, one of Nankool's aids rushed into the president's temporary office to tell the chief executive about the live feed. It was only moments later, as Nankool's staff gathered around to watch the impromptu newscast, that Undersecretary Zimmer said, "Look!" And pointed at the screen. "It's Christine Vanderveen!"

And sure enough, standing behind the clone named Alan, to his right, was the missing diplomat. "Well, I'll be damned," the president was heard to say. But Nankool had a smile on his face—and that was a wonderful sight indeed.

12

Every mile is two in the winter.

—George Herbert
Jacula Prudentum
Standard year 1651

PLANET GAMMA-014, THE CLONE HEGEMONY

The snow had stopped, the clouds had blown away, and the sun was out. So as the fly-form circled Marine Firebase 356 (MF-356), Captain Antonio Santana and Lieutenant Mitch Millar had an excellent view of the hilltop fortification below. However, because Millar was a cyborg, and therefore capable of plugging in to the fly-form's circuitry, the recon ball could enjoy what amounted to a 360-degree sensaround, while the bio bod was left to peer out the window next to him.

Still, Santana could see that MF-356 was well positioned to put fire on the highway, and serve as a staging point for local area patrols. And, should the bugs attempt to take it, the hill would be a tough nut to crack. Although the firebase's considerable weaponry had been useless in the face of Colonel Jonathan Alan Seebo-62,666's act of cold-blooded treachery. An armed invasion that cost the lives of twenty-three marines and resulted in the loss of two ton's worth of supplies. And now, having narrowly escaped arrest some fifty hours earlier, the renegade would be even more wary than before. And that would make him difficult to catch.

Especially since the clone was an expert at cold-weather survival techniques and familiar with the local terrain.

But, as the fly-form came in to hover above the hilltop landing platform, Santana thought he had a fix on the renegade's critical weakness. Or strength, depending on how one chose to look at it. And that was Colonel Six's determination to close with the enemy and kill as many of them as he could. That desire, that determination, would make the fugitive somewhat predictable. Or so Santana hoped.

There was a palpable *thud* as the fly-form put down. Servos *whined* softly as Millar extruded two skeletal tool aims, which the cyborg used to release the tie-downs that secured his sphere-shaped body to the seat. The cyborg's war form incorporated four high-res vid cams, a variety of weaponry, and the capacity to fly long distances at low altitudes—which was one of the primary reasons why Santana had requested one of the much-sought-after scouts. While no one could beat Fareye on the ground, and recon drones had their uses, nothing could surpass a flying brain when it came to collecting and distributing real-time battlefield intelligence. Having freed himself from the tie-downs, Millar hovered in midair, as Santana got up and made his way forward. In spite of whatever special capabilities the cyborg might have, he was a lieutenant and the bio bod was a captain.

Even though the sun was out, it lacked any real punch, and the air outside the aircraft's cabin was bitterly cold. *So* cold that the legionnaire could feel the moisture freeze inside his nose as he descended the fold-down stairs and snapped to attention. He held the salute until a short, stern-looking lieutenant colonel saw fit to return it. "I'm Captain Antonio Santana, sir . . . And this is Lieutenant Mitch Millar. We're both with the 2nd Battalion, 1st REC." The cyborg had exited the fly-form by that time—and was hovering four feet above the landing platform.

"Welcome to Firebase 356," the marine officer said gruffly. "My name's Suki, Lieutenant Colonel Suki, and we were told to expect you. Tell me something, Captain. . . . Why would a Legion officer show up wearing navy cold-weather gear?"

"Because we had the foresight to steal all the cold-weather gear we could lay our hands on, sir," Santana answered truthfully. "And it belonged to the navy."

When Suki laughed, the sound came out as a loud guffaw. "You report to General Kobbi. . . . Is that right?"

Santana nodded. "Through Colonel Quinlan . . . Yes, sir."

"Kobbi's a good man," Suki said. "So good he could have been a marine! So you're the officer they selected to go after Colonel Six."

"Sir, yes sir," Santana said evenly.

"Well, do me a favor," Suki growled. "Once you find the bastard, shoot him! Because if you bring him back, there will be a court-martial, and who knows what would come out of that. Especially once the politicians get wind of it."

"You're not the first person to make that suggestion," Santana answered noncommittally.

"I'm glad to hear it," Suki replied. "Come on. . . . Let's get in out of the cold."

Five minutes later, the legionnaires were in the firebase's heavily sandbagged command bunker, which though warmer than the air outside, was still too cold for comfort, despite the combined efforts of chemical stoves that sat crouched in opposite corners. One plastic-draped wall was taken up with com equipment, while a second was obscured by a bank of video screens, on which helmet-cam video from foot patrol "Joker-Four" was currently displayed. There was also a rack of assault weapons, a two-burner field stove with two pots sitting on top of it, and a long, narrow worktable, which consisted of two cargo mods, topped by a sheet of locally manufactured plywood. Positioned on that were four milspec computers—two of which were currently being used by marine noncoms. "Okay," Suki said, as the two bio bods took their places on upended ammo crates. "I'm going to assume you did your homework—and read the reports we sent in. So, since you know what we know, why the visit?"

It was a somewhat contentious question. But because the legionnaire knew how frustrating it was to play patty-cake with fact finders, touring politicians, and other forms of lowlife REMF scum, he wasn't offended. "Don't worry, sir. . . . The lieutenant and I didn't come all this way to participate in a cold-weather circle jerk. We need information that wasn't available at the regimental level."

That was news to Millar, who knew that junior officers were meant to be seen and not heard. That was why the cyborg continued to hover off to one side, half-hidden in the shadows. "Okay," Suki responded. "What are you after? We'll do whatever we can to help."

"Colonel Six came here to steal supplies," Santana began. "That much seems clear. Based on the reports that Captain Arvo Smith filed, the decision to take hostages was clearly made on the fly. Plus, the Seebos had about fifty civilians on call, which further substantiates that premise. But," Santana continued, "according to what I read, Colonel Six and his men were rather choosy about what they took. A list of the stolen items was included in the report submitted by Captain Smith. What wasn't available at the regimental level, was a list of what Colonel Six *could have taken*, but *didn't*. If we compare the two lists, we should be able to get a pretty good idea of what the clone bastard plans to do next."

"Well, I'll be damned," Suki said admiringly. "You're smarter than you look! Sergeant Diker! You've been listening in—and don't pretend you weren't. Pull up a list of the supplies that were on hand the day the clones arrived—and put that side by side with what they actually took."

A corporal brought the officers mugs of hot caf while Diker summoned the data Santana had requested, formatted the results, and sent the product to a printer. Millar plucked his copy right out of midair by tapping into the low-power wireless network.

With hard copy in hand, Santana began a systematic review of both lists. Most of the stolen items were what any guerrilla fighter would want, including food, ammo, and com gear. One piece of which included the locator beacon that had been used to track him down a couple of days earlier. Of course, other things had been stolen as well—including a significant quantity of medical supplies.

But of more interest were *ten* Shoulder-Launched Multipurpose Assault Weapons (SMAW), and sixty 83mm High-Explosive Dual-Purpose (HEDP) Rockets, which was twice, if not *three times*, the number of SMAWs a company of Seebos would normally carry. The question was why? Because the weapons were available? Or to equip the guerrilla fighters for a specific mission?

Now that he had it in front of him, Santana could see that the *other* list, the one that laid out what Six *could* have absconded with, included six 60mm mortars, which would be perfect for guerrilla fighting, a generous quantity of high explosives that would be just right for blowing bridges, and four surface-to-air missile launchers with heat-seeking rockets. Weapons that would have given the Seebos the theoretical capacity to knock fighters out of the sky. But rather than select any of those items, Six chose ten SMAWs.

It soon became apparent that having reviewed both lists, and having given the matter some thought, Suki was thinking along similar lines. "I never thought about it before," the senior officer admitted reluctantly, "but why steal so many shoulder tubes? Unless the bastard plans to go tank hunting."

"I think that's exactly what he has in mind," Santana responded grimly. "Though not in the way you mean. Sergeant Diker . . . Please pull up all of the holding areas or similar facilities where Colonel Six could potentially lay his hands on allied armor. That includes tanks, APCs (armored personnel carriers), and anything else you can think of."

"How far, sir?" the noncom wanted to know, his fingers already tapping away.

"One hundred miles around this firebase," the legionnaire answered. "Prioritize those facilities located to the east of us—and those that have the smallest footprint. After all," Santana observed thoughtfully. "Why attack a *big* base, if you can get what you need from a small one?"

There was barely enough time to take another sip of coffee before the answer came back. The light from the computer screen gave Diker's face a bluish tint. "Using those parameters the most likely location would be Refueling Station 32, which belongs to the 3rd Force Support Group. It's located about sixty-four miles east of here—at the point where the road starts up toward Tow-Tok Pass. There aren't any armored units based at RS-32, but plenty of tanks and APCs stop for fuel there, before heading up over the hump. Both the second and third hits are relatively large battalion-strength repair and maintenance outfits."

There was a loud *thump* as Santana's fist hit the surface of the table. "Yes! That's exactly the kind of place Six would choose! Especially now that everyone is on the lookout for him. Assuming RS-32 is the same one that I'm thinking of, we passed it a few days ago, and a squad of half-drunk store clerks could take it!

"All Six would have to do is sneak up on RS-32 with his SMAWs at the ready, wait until the depot was empty, and put the first rocket into the com mast. The second, third, and fourth rounds would be used to neutralize weapons emplacements if necessary. Otherwise, he would simply walk in! What would a refueling depot have?" the legionnaire wondered. "Six bio bods and an equal number of robots? They wouldn't stand a chance. The next vehicles to arrive might, or might not, be to his liking. If not, he would let them go. But if they met his requirement, Colonel Six would commandeer them, top off their tanks, and drive them up over the pass. Because that would not only get his Seebos into combat sooner—but give his troops an edge once they arrive!"

Suki was clearly impressed. "Not bad, Captain, not bad at all. . . . Of course there are some big ifs in your plan, but assuming the bastard wants to kill bugs, then that's where he would go."

"Let's get Station 32 on the horn," Santana suggested. "So we can warn them."

Five long minutes passed while a com tech repeatedly sought to make contact with the tiny base. But there was no response. "I think you'd better get ahold of Regimental Command," Santana said as he came to his feet. "Tell them to send a rapid-response force to RS-32. . . . And tell them to be very careful once they arrive."

Then, having tossed a salute toward Colonel Suki, Santana made for the surface. Millar was right behind him. And, because the cyborg had already been in radio communication with the fly-form, the other legionnaire's engines were beginning to spool up as Santana entered the passenger compartment. The boxy transport was airborne four minutes later and headed southeast. Millar was strapped in by that time. "You nailed that one, sir," the recon ball said. "But I have a question. . . ."

Santana's thoughts were miles away, and he had forgotten all about Millar. "Yes? What's that?"

"Well, sir," Millar said hesitantly. "What if we arrive *before* the rapid-response team? And Colonel Six is still there?"

It was something Santana should have considered but hadn't. He smiled. "Then we'll land and order the sonofabitch to surrender!"

Millar laughed, but when Santana didn't, the junior officer wondered if the cavalry officer was serious! And that was scary, because the special ops officer had been killed in action once, and had no desire to repeat the experience.

But Millar needn't have worried, because by the time the fly-form arrived over Refueling Station 32, an armed shuttle and rapid-response team were on the ground. And, judging from all of the troops that were milling around, and the smoke still pouring out of what remained of the depot's com hut, some sort of action had already taken place. "Put us down," Santana ordered grimly, and the fly-form hurried to obey. The station wasn't much to look at. Just a mound inside a defensive berm, two opposing gates so that vehicles could pull through without backing, and what was left of the smoking hab. Half of the com mast was missing, which was why the com tech at MF-356 had been unable to get through.

A lieutenant from the 13th DBLE's recon squadron was there to greet the cavalry officer as his boots hit the frozen ground. She had brown skin, wide-set eyes, and a scar that ran diagonally down across her face. "Lieutenant Bamik, sir," the woman said, as she tossed Santana a salute. "I have orders to provide you with whatever assistance I can. But we arrived too late to stop him."

Santana swore. "How many people did the bastard kill?"

"One, sir, when the HEDP round hit the com shack. A company of Seebos stormed the place immediately after that."

"What about the hostages?" Santana wanted to know.

"Colonel Six has them," Bamik answered glumly. "A navy doctor and a navy medic. Both appeared to be in good condition. The doctor dropped this on the ground."

Santana accepted the small piece of paper. Judging from how wrinkled it was, the note had been wadded up into a ball. "To whom it may concern," the message began. "I have reason to believe that Colonel Six plans to take us over Tow-Tok Pass." It was signed, "Lt. Kira Kelly, Medical Officer, CSB Navy." That was promising. Not only did it serve to confirm the cavalry officer's hypothesis, it meant the doctor had her wits about her.

Santana looked out toward the highway as two heavily loaded trucks growled past. Both were loaded with glum-looking CVA conscripts. The officer was struck by how empty the two-lane road was compared to the bumper-to-bumper traffic that he and his company had been forced to deal with as they entered the mountains. That seemed to imply a break-through of some sort, a victory that had allowed allied forces to cross Tow-Tok Pass and head for the town of Yal-Am beyond. So maybe General-453 had been right all along. Maybe the bugs were on the run.

Not that it made much difference to Santana. What mattered to him was that the highway was open. Which meant that the renegade and his Seebos would be able to make good time. "So what kind of vehicles did they steal?" Santana wanted to know as he turned back toward Bamik.

The junior officer consulted a scrap of paper. "Two Hegemony hover tanks, five half-tracks, a six-by-six, and a fueler. All taken from a company of Seebos. All the colonel had to do was order them to exit the vehicles, and they obeyed," the legionnaire said disgustedly. "That's the clones for you!"

"So he's got plenty of go-juice," Santana commented. "Okay, let's see if we can cut the bastard off. I need a com link."

"I can take care of that," Millar said, thereby reminding Santana of his presence. "Right," Santana replied. "Thank you. See if you can raise First Lieutenant Lucy Amoyo for me. . . . Call sign, Alpha One-Six. My company is on hold at Waypoint 27. Maybe, just maybe, they can block the road and cut Six off. Assuming you can raise Amoyo, tell her what to look for, and tell her I'm on my way."

Millar bobbed up and down by way of an acknowledgment, attempted to make contact, and failed. That wasn't unusual in and around the mountains, so the recon ball shot straight up, and leveled off at one hundred fifty feet. And from that altitude the cyborg had better luck. He was able to make contact with Alpha Company within a matter of minutes, introduce himself to Lieutenant Amoyo, and relay Santana's message.

Having accomplished his mission, the scout dropped to a point only four feet off the surface, where it was necessary to hurry over to the fly-form, which was preparing for takeoff. The transport flew only one hundred feet off the highway as it followed the ribbon of concrete up into the mountains. The cyborg kept a sharp "eye" out for the fugitive vehicles but saw no sign of them. Even though it had taken Alpha Company days to make their way up to Waypoint 27—it took the cybernetically controlled aircraft less than fifteen minutes to make the same trip.

Back before the invasion, Waypoint 27 had been little

more than a wide spot in the highway. A place where civilian truckers could pull out to let faster vehicles pass, take a bio break, or make some minor repairs. But during the long, hard-fought push up toward Tow-Tok Pass, the flat area had been used as the site for everything from a field hospital to a forward repair-and-maintenance company. Of course, those units were gone, leaving the piece of godforsaken real estate to some forlorn wrecks, and the legionnaires of Alpha Company.

The fly-form's repellers generated a cloud of steam and blew a layer of powdery snow sideways as the cyborg came in for a perfect landing on the big red X that Master Sergeant Dietrich had spray-painted onto the ice-encrusted ground. By the time the engines began to spool down, and the fly-form's steps had been deployed, Santana's T-2 was there to meet him. Ten minutes later, the two of them were out on the surface of the much-abused road, where the company's quads were half-blocking the highway. Which should be enough force to stop Six given that he wouldn't be able to deploy more than two hover tanks side by side or run any flanking maneuvers. Millar followed ten feet behind them.

The moment Santana saw Amoyo's force he knew something was wrong. The platoon leader's face shield was up, her cheeks were ruddy from the cold, and the set of her mouth was grim. Both legionnaires were mounted and therefore eye to eye. "Welcome back, sir. . . . I wish I had better news to report."

Santana felt his spirits fall but was careful to keep his expression neutral. "They got by?"

"Sir, yes sir," Amoyo said miserably. "It was my fault, sir. . . . I gave orders to watch for two tanks, five tracks, a truck, and a tanker."

There was a brief pause while Santana considered the way the report had been phrased. Then he understood. "But you didn't give orders to be on the lookout for a tank, two half-tracks, and a six-by, or some other combination of vehicles."

"Eventually, I did," Amoyo added apologetically. "But it

was too late by then. They had already passed in three seemingly discrete groups. And the unit designators on the vehicles had been changed."

"That's too bad," Santana allowed sympathetically. "But don't let it get you down. . . . Colonel Six is one smart bastard! That's why they chose us to catch him! Come on, let's pull the company together, and give chase. Maybe one of his vehicles will break down or something. We'll catch up with him eventually."

And they tried. But there was no sign of the renegade or the stolen vehicles as the company topped Tow-Tok Pass four hours later and started down the other side. It became increasingly difficult to see because a winter storm had blown in from the west and was about to dump a foot of fresh snow onto eastern slopes of the Hebron mountain range. So it wasn't long before visibility was reduced to fifty or sixty feet. That was when Santana sent Lieutenant Millar forward to scout the road ahead and provide advance warning if something was blocking the highway.

But it wasn't long before the recon ball came across something a lot more serious than a stalled APC blocking the road. The ground was fairly level at that point, forming a broad shelf in the mountainside, where the ice-encrusted concrete disappeared into a nightmarish landscape of wrecked vehicles. There were *hundreds* of them, both Ramanthian and allied, all mixed up with each other in a way that suggested a close-quarters battle between two armored units.

It would be easy to lose one's way inside the steel maze, especially given the gathering gloom, and Millar was about to call that in when a flare lit the sky ahead. A lacy curtain of gently falling snow caused the light to flicker, as it threw ghostly shadows toward the west, and the steady *pop, pop, pop* of rifle fire was heard intermixed with the cloth-ripping sound of automatic weapons. "Alpha Six, this is Alpha Six-Six," the cyborg said, as he hovered next to an overturned truck. "There's a huge junkyard directly in your path—and the snow is making it very difficult to follow the road.

Based on that, plus the firefight under way up ahead, I recommend that the company stop short of the battlefield and wait for morning. Over."

"Roger that," Santana replied. "Can you give me any additional intel on the firefight? Over."

"Negative," Millar answered. "Not without going forward. Over."

"Hold your position," the company commander ordered. "I'll bring the second platoon up to join you in a few minutes. Out."

"Roger," Millar confirmed. "Alpha Six-Six out."

Santana ordered the company to halt, told Deker to find Amoyo, and was soon close enough to open his visor and talk to her off-line. Cold snow flakes began to kiss his face. "Let's circle the wagons, Lieutenant. . . . You can use both of the quads in the perimeter—but keep all your people combat-ready until the firefight is over. I'll take the second platoon forward to see what's going on."

Having allowed Colonel Six to get past her, Amoyo was feeling down, and would have welcomed an opportunity to redeem herself. More than that, she wondered whether Santana had lost faith in her—or was simply exercising his right to carry out the mission himself. Not that it made much difference, because all she could say was, "Yes, sir."

Confident that Amoyo would do a good job, and worried lest Second Lieutenant Zolkin blunder into a situation he wasn't prepared to handle, Santana went looking for the other platoon leader and found the young man raring to go. Even if his tired legionnaires would have preferred to stay back. "We're ready, sir," Zolkin said enthusiastically. "Just say the word."

Santana grinned behind his visor. "Thank you, Lieutenant. . . . I'm glad to hear it. Please put Staff Sergeant Pool and Corporal Torrez on drag. . . . And tell them to stay sharp. It would be easy for someone to get in behind us on a night like this."

Because the orders had been delivered face-to-face rather than by radio, the instructions would seem to originate from the platoon leader thereby strengthening Zolkin's position with the troops. Santana knew squad leader Pool wouldn't like walking drag, but it was a very important slot, and would become even more so if both officers were killed. In that situation, it would be her responsibility to assume command.

With the second platoon strung out behind them, Santana and Deker followed Fareye and Ka Nahn into the maze of wrecked vehicles. Another flare went off, and cast an eerie glow across the battlefield, as the muted *thump, thump, thump* of a heavy machine gun was heard. "Try all of the allied frequencies," Santana ordered. "We need to warn those people that we're coming in. It would be a shame to get shot by someone on our side."

Deker was well aware of the dangers involved. He said, "Yes, sir. I already have. *Twice.* But I'll keep trying."

It would have been nice to turn on their helmet lights in order to see where they were going, but that would be suicidal. So Santana was thankful for the steady succession of flares that kept the area at least half-lit as Fareye led the column forward. They passed between a half-slagged hover tank and a burned-out truck, made their way down into a trash-strewn gully, and up the other side. A frozen human, his weapon still aimed at an invisible enemy, marked the edge of the flat area beyond. There was no way to know if he had been killed by a bullet or frozen to death.

"Alpha Six-Four to Alpha Six," Fareye said, as he and his T-2 paused. "I see heat signatures up ahead. *Lots* of heat signatures. All of which appear to be Ramanthian. They seem completely unaware of our presence. Probably because they're busy assaulting a big pile of wreckage. Over."

"Roger that," Santana answered, as Deker carried him down into the gully. "Hold your position. Bravo One-Six. Position your platoon in a line abreast. Use Alpha Six-Four as your center marker. Prepare for a sweep of the area ahead—but caution your troops to keep their fire off the pile of wreckage where the friendlies are holed up. Over."

"This is Bravo One-Six," Zolkin replied. His voice was tight with either excitement or fear. "I read you. . . . Out."

Santana eyed the display on his HUD, waited for the second platoon to swing into position, and was pleased to see the speed with which the evolution was executed. Zolkin had come a long way since the landing on Oron IV and was shaping up to be a good officer. "Still no response on any of the allied frequencies, sir," Deker put in over the intercom. "Either they don't have a com set, or they aren't listening."

"Thanks," Santana said, as he eyed the constantly shifting blobs of heat in front of them. "Alpha Six to Alpha Six-Six. We've been unable to make radio contact with the allied unit up ahead. . . . Once we engage the enemy, I want you to go forward, and get in touch with the people in that pile of wreckage. Tell them who we are, take command if they will allow you to do so, and serve as liaison officer if they won't. Your first responsibility is keep them from firing on *us*. Do you read me? Over."

"Sir, yes sir," Millar answered affirmatively. "Alpha Six-Six out."

"Alpha Six-Five will prepare to fire two flares, and the second platoon will prepare to charge," Santana continued. *"Readddy, fire! Readddy, charge!"*

Deker was up and out of the gully before the additional flares went off. *Real* cavalry charges were a rarity given the way most high-tech battles were fought, but the sudden attack out of the surrounding darkness could have taken place on the plains of Mongolia, in the Crimea, or at Gettysburg. Except that *these* steeds were sentient, could see in the dark, and were armed with weapons that would have been unimaginable two thousand years earlier.

Someone yelled, "Camerone!" over the company push, and all hell broke loose. Having been caught by surprise, the bugs were forced to turn their backs on the pile of wreckage as the cyborgs swept toward them. Now, as Deker opened fire with both his fifty and his energy cannon, Santana realized there were more Ramanthians than he had bargained for. In addition to the enemy soldiers that had been visible before, *more* of the aliens came swarming up out of shell holes, emerged from hiding places in the surrounding wreckage, and returned fire.

All of which caused the officer to wonder if he should call upon Amoyo for reinforcements. But the quads would take a long time to arrive—and were too big to operate effectively within the confines of the metal maze. Plus, were he to strip the big walkers of the protection offered by the first platoon's T-2s, it would make the cyborgs vulnerable to an infantry attack. So, having considered the alternatives, the officer decided to leave the first platoon where it was.

Even though it was the officer's job to lead the legionnaires, that became impossible as the cyborgs passed through the enemy's ranks, and the members of the second platoon found themselves inside a nightmarish world of speeding bodies, stuttering weapons, and shrill command whistles. Because of the chaos, and the speed with which the battle was being fought, all of the tactical decisions had to be made by the T-2s regardless of whatever rank the bio bod they were carrying might hold. There simply wasn't enough time for the process to work any other way.

That meant that as Deker circled a burned-out APC in an attempt to get the drop on a Ramanthian rocket team—it was Santana's responsibility to provide the cyborg with security. So when a Ramanthian fired at Deker from the right, the officer was there to gun the bug down, even as the borg ran over an alien soldier. Chitin crackled as it shattered, and the alien uttered a nearly human scream, as Deker kept going.

Though busy trying to protect Deker's six, Santana noticed that the volume of fire coming out of the pile of wreckage had fallen off, suggesting that Millar had made contact with the people within. But if that was good, other things *weren't* so good, as a shoulder-launched missile struck Private Mary Volin between the shoulder blades and blew up. Her body must have shielded Private Shalo Shaley to some extent, because the T-2 survived the hit, even if the cyborg didn't want to. Because Shaley had been in love with Volin, and the bio bod's death spurred the Trooper II into a frenzy of killing.

With the bio bod's grisly remains still flapping around on her blood-spattered back, Shaley went looking for any Ramanthian she could find, killing each with the ruthless efficiency of an avenging angel. Most of the alien soldiers were already dead by that time. In fact, so many of them had been killed that their bodies lay in drifts, like the snow that was already beginning to cover them, as the raging T-2 ran out of ammo and stomped a wounded Ramanthian to death.

Sergeant Ramos had a zapper in hand as he went to intervene. None of the other legionnaires knew what he said to the cyborg, since it was off the push, but whatever it was worked because the noncom was able to lead Shaley away without having to zap her. Which was the only way a bio bod could bring an intransigent cyborg under control.

Meanwhile, as bio bods dismounted to search the dead for anything that might be of interest to the intelligence people, they also collected anything that might be of use to the company in the future. Not the Ramanthian assault rifles, because they were awkward to fire, but energy grenades, which were better than CSB issue in certain situations, plus the highly prized grain bars that many of the bugs carried in their packs, and which tasted like honey. Their helmet lights bobbed and swayed as they probed the battlefield for loot, adding yet another otherworldly element to an already-surreal scene.

And that was the situation that Santana was presiding over as an additional light appeared and Millar emerged from the surrounding murk with a woman in tow. A knit cap covered her hair. She had a softly rounded face, a snub nose, and generous lips. The clothing the woman wore consisted of a mishmash of Hegemony-issue items that had been altered as necessary and layered to create the semblance of a winter uniform. That was overlaid by a combat vest at least one size too big for her, and the whole outfit was dusted with snow. But there was nothing amateurish about the Marine-Corps-issue carbine cradled in her arms or the look in her brown eyes. It was hard and calculating. "This is Hoyt-11,791," Millar announced. "She's in command of the CVA company that the bugs were working so hard to eradicate."

"It's a pleasure to meet you," Santana said as he jumped to the ground. "My name is Santana. I'm in command of Alpha Company, 2nd Battalion, 1st REC."

"Thank you for coming to our rescue," Seven-ninety-one said soberly. "We wouldn't have been able to hold out much longer." Her voice had a husky quality that Santana found attractive.

"At some point our forces tried to clear the area of wreckage by making a big pile," Millar explained. "Having been ambushed as they passed through the battlefield, the Hoyts crawled inside and fought back. It made a pretty good fort."

"I'm sorry we didn't arrive earlier," Santana said. "How many of you are there?"

"Fifty-seven when the battle began," the clone answered succinctly, "and thirty-one now."

"I'm sorry," Santana said sympathetically. "But you were right to put up a fight. They would have slaughtered you otherwise. Where were you headed? And what were you supposed to do?"

"We have orders to join the 181st Labor Battalion," Seven-ninety-one answered. "As for what we're supposed to do, well, no one told us that. We're office administrators from Alpha-002. So it's hard to imagine what they had in mind for us."

Santana swore, then caught himself. "Sorry, ma'am, but sending office workers into a combat zone has got to be one of the stupidest things I ever heard of. Have you got any transportation?"

"No," the woman replied. "Our truck was destroyed in the ambush."

That was a problem because Santana knew the bio bods wouldn't be able to keep up with the cyborgs and would be extremely vulnerable if left on their own.

"Some of them could ride in the quads," Millar put in helpfully.

"I suppose," the cavalry officer allowed. "But what about the rest?"

"They could ride on *top* of the quads, and jump off if we take fire," Millar answered.

The legionnaire eyed the Hoyt. Snowflakes caught in her eyelashes and forced her to blink. "You and your people would be exposed to both the weather and enemy fire up there," Santana cautioned.

Seven-ninety-one shrugged. "We were exposed in the truck," she said fatalistically. "And riding beats walking."

"Okay," Santana agreed. "Do you have any objections to taking orders from Lieutenant Millar here for the duration of your stay with us?"

The Hoyt looked at the hovering recon ball and back again. If the prospect of reporting to a cyborg bothered the woman, she gave no sign of it. "No, sir," she said formally. "That's fine with me."

The cavalry officer nodded. "All right, Lieutenant, take care of your people. Make sure they scrounge all the good stuff they can find. I have a feeling everything is going to be in short supply up ahead. Perhaps Seven-ninety-one would be good enough to help identify the dead. And let's lay them out where the graves registration people will be able to find them. Dismissed."

By the time the second platoon, and the newly designated third platoon pulled back into the relative security of the encampment that Amoyo and her people had prepared, a full-fledged blizzard was under way. Weather so cold it was necessary for sentries to work the actions on their weapons every two to three minutes or risk having them freeze up. But there was one good thing about the storm however. . . . And that was the fact it would be just as hard on the enemy. Because no matter how many battles the two sides fought— winter would always win.

13

Tragedy is by no means the exclusive province of the lowly.

—Paguumi proverb
Author unknown
Standard year circa 120 B.C.

PLANET EARTH, THE RAMANTHIAN EMPIRE

It was raining as the Ramanthian task force swept in over Seattle. What had once been a discrete city was now part of the sprawling metroplex that began in the old nation-state of Canada, and ran all the way down to Baja, California.

For reasons not entirely clear, the Seattle area had been especially hard to pacify. This meant it had been necessary to repeatedly punish the animals who lived there. A process that eventually turned what had been gleaming high-rises, floating sea habs, and carefully manicured streetscapes into a cratered wasteland. The destruction was plain to see as the Queen watched the vid screen on the bulkhead before her. Though capable of in-system spaceflight, the *Reaper* was classified as a combat assault platform, and intended for use inside planetary atmospheres. As such the flying fortress was heavily armed and, thanks to a spacious flight deck, could launch and retrieve smaller vessels at the same time. As the airborne fortress approached the city from the south it was traveling at a scant twenty miles per hour, a fact that somehow made its presence over the city that much more ominous.

As the monarch looked down onto the surface, she saw an arrow-straight line of craters, each measuring exactly one hundred feet across, which had been etched into the planet's surface by OTS (orbit-to-surface) cannons firing from outside the exosphere. Thousand-foot-high skyscrapers had been cut down like trees. So what remained looked like a thicket of fire-blackened stumps, many of which were still smoking, because of fires that continued to burn below street level.

What resembled old lava flows were actually rivers of previously molten metal and glass, which followed streets down to a large bay, where cold water transformed them into something resembling stone. Everything else was a sea of fire-blackened wreckage occasionally interrupted by islands of miraculously untouched buildings. As the *Reaper* began to slow, the royal spotted tiny pinpricks of light down below, followed by an occasional spurt of light-colored smoke. "What," the monarch wanted to know, "are the animals doing?"

Captain Ji-Jua was standing at the royal's side. He was a serious-looking officer with a reputation for probity. "The humans are firing at us, Majesty," the naval officer replied gravely. "They have a quantity of shoulder-launched missiles looted from human military bases—and it may have been a lucky shot from such a weapon that brought the transport down."

"I find it strange that when *we* manage to destroy an enemy ship it's always ascribed to skill—but when *they* do it we refer to it as 'luck,'" the Queen observed tartly. "And where *is* the transport? I expected to see it by now."

"It's difficult to see because of the rain," Ji-Jua replied tactfully. "The stern is half-submerged in that lake—but the bow is resting on dry land."

The *Reaper* shuddered gently as a surface-to-air missile exploded against her screens. The ship's combat computer ran a lightning-fast series of calculations and fired an energy cannon in response. The blue bolt slagged everything within twenty feet of the point from which the rocket had been launched.

But the royal was oblivious to such details as the crash site came into full view. There were hills to the left and right as the task force slowed and hovered above the wreck. The Queen knew, as did everyone else, that roughly half of the three hundred troops traveling on board the transport had been killed on impact. The survivors were not only alive, but still fighting, as wave after wave of murderous humans attacked them.

And, as smaller ships spread out to suppress enemy fire, a task force led by the Queen herself was about to rescue the beleaguered troopers. Video of that was sure to raise morale throughout the empire. Pictures that would look even better if taken on the ground rather than inside a warship. The Queen stood. "I will lead the rescue party myself," she announced. "I'll need my armor and a rifle."

Captain Ji-Jua reacted to the statement with undisguised alarm. "Majesty!" the officer said. "Please reconsider! The situation on the ground is extremely unstable. . . . I could never allow you to risk your life in such a manner!"

"You not only can, you *will*," the royal responded sternly. "Or I can replace you here and now. . . . Which will it be?"

Ji-Jua *wanted* to resist what he believed to be an extremely poor decision, but the force of the monarch's personality combined with a sudden flood of pheromones, was more than the officer could overcome. "I'm sorry, Majesty," he said contritely. "It shall be as you say."

Thirty minutes later the Queen was aboard an assault boat headed for the surface. The plan was to secure a landing zone, hold it long enough to load the beleaguered soldiers, and take off as soon as possible. Which, given total command of the air, should be relatively easy to do.

Thanks to the monarch's reassuring presence, plus their natural feelings of superiority, morale was high as the boat put down three hundred feet west of the wreck. The stern ramp made a loud *thud* as it hit the ground. A trio of flying vid cams went off first, followed by the Queen and four members of the Imperial Guard. As the Ramanthians shuffled out into a cold rain, the lake was only twenty-five feet to their left, which should have been a good thing. Except that sixteen SCUBA-equipped freedom fighters chose that moment to surface and open fire! Half of the humans had never fired a weapon in anger, and their bullets kicked up spurts of dirt and rainwater, as they held their triggers down.

The original plan had been to attack the downed transport from the water side, but with a group of Ramanthian soldiers directly in front of them, the humans had no choice but to attack or be attacked. The Queen was wearing body armor, but one of the first bullets the animals fired found the seam between the stiff collar that protected her neck, and the material that cloaked the rest of her elongated body. The projectile punched a hole through the royal's chitin and nicked her posterior nerve bundle before exiting through the other side of her body, where it slammed into her armor.

The whole thing came as a complete surprise to the Queen, who being all-powerful in every other respect, believed herself to be invulnerable on the battlefield as well. There was no pain, just a sense of disbelief, as she collapsed and lay helpless in a large puddle of muddy water.

There was a great deal of shouting, pincer clacking, and confusion as the royal's bodyguards grabbed what they feared was a dead body, and attempted to carry the limp burden toward the assault boat. But they were under fire the entire time, and two of them fell, thereby dumping the already-wounded monarch onto hard ground. So two of the rank-and-file soldiers stepped in to help, got hold of the inert body, and helped drag it up the ramp.

Once the royal was on board, the pilot lifted, thereby leaving the rest of the file to be slaughtered, as those on the *Reaper* subjected the aviator to a nonstop flow of frantic orders. Ten minutes later the assault boat and its special cargo were safe inside the warship's launch bay, where a team of medical personnel was waiting. They rushed on board and, having made an initial assessment, delivered the good news: "The Queen lives!"

That was true, but it quickly became apparent that while conscious, the royal was paralyzed from the neck down. The effort to rescue those trapped on the surface continued as a despondent Captain Ji-Jua took the actions necessary to transfer the royal to the battleship *Regulus*, where a team of medical specialists would be waiting to receive her.

Chancellor Ubatha was present as the Queen was brought aboard the battleship some three hours after the injury. He shuffled alongside the high-tech gurney as the monarch was wheeled into a waiting operating room. A consensus had emerged by then. All of the doctors agreed that initial efforts should focus on stabilizing the monarch, so they could evacuate her to Hive, where the empire's foremost surgeons would be brought in to evaluate her condition.

For that reason, the initial operation was mostly exploratory in nature and didn't last long. It took the Queen half an hour to recover from the effects of the general anesthetic, but once she did, Ubatha was summoned to her side. Although the royal lacked the ability to move her body, she could talk, albeit with some difficulty.

Ubatha felt a genuine sense of affection for the warrior queen, and that, plus the chemical cocktail that permeated the air around her, caused a genuine upwelling of sympathetic emotions as the official looked down on her. "I'm sorry," the Queen croaked. "But it looks like I was in the wrong place at the wrong time. But even *that* can serve our purposes. . . . Make sure video of what took place is seen throughout the empire. Along with assurances that I'm still alive. I think I can assure you that the Ramanthian people will fight even harder after what happened to their Queen!"

"Yes, Majesty," Ubatha said gently. "The people love you. . . . And your sacrifice will show them the way."

"And that brings us to *you*," the monarch put in.

"*Me*, Majesty? How so?"

"Until such time as I regain the full use of my body, you

will serve as my surrogate. That will be difficult for both of us—but we have no other choice."

"Yes, Majesty," Ubatha said obediently.

"We can discuss all of the procedural difficulties during the trip to Hive," the Queen added. "But, first I want you to find Captain Ji-Jua, and check on his mental state. He attempted to dissuade me from participating in the rescue, but I overrode him, and I'm afraid he will blame himself."

"Yes, Majesty. Right away, Majesty," Ubatha said, as he backed away. "I'll take care of it."

"I knew you would," the Queen said, as she allowed her eyes to close. "Thank you."

Ubatha was as good as his word, and immediately went in search of Ji-Jua, who had been thoroughly chastised by then, and summarily relieved of his command. So the Chancellor located the cabin assigned to the visiting officer, announced his presence via the intercom, and waited for a response. When none was forthcoming he pushed a pincer into the access slot and heard servos *whir*, as the hatch opened. It was dark inside, but there was no mistaking the body that lay on the deck, or the pistol that lay inches from the dead officer's outstretched pincer. Having failed in his duty to protect the Queen, Ji-Jua had taken his own life. A terrible waste—but useful nevertheless. Because once the news of the Queen's injury became public, there would be an overwhelming desire to place blame. Knowingly, or unknowingly, Captain Orto Ji-Jua had volunteered to go down in history as the officer responsible for the monarch's disabling wound. And for that, Chancellor Ubatha was grateful.

METROPLEX, SAN FRANCISCO

The old warehouse stood because no one had gotten around to knocking it down. Shafts of sunlight slanted in from windows high above and threw pools of light onto the much-abused duracrete floor below. And there, seated behind a beat-up metal desk, was a very troubled man. Because one of the many problems associated with heading the Earth Liberation Brigade was the amount of work that the newly created position entailed. It was work that Lieutenant JG Foley found to be especially onerous since much of his life had been dedicated to evading responsibility rather than trying to embrace it. And now, having been transformed from would-be thief to resistance leader, the officer was faced with all the issues natural to any large organization. Which was to say recruiting, stroking, and retaining good people, while simultaneously trying to obtain scarce resources like food, medical supplies, and weapons.

Such problems weighed heavily on Foley, as the woman in front of him rose to leave, and one of his underlings brought a man forward to replace her. There were at least twenty-five people waiting for an audience, which meant that his so-called office hours were sure to extend well into the evening, at which point brigade headquarters would be moved to another location.

"Thank you for agreeing to see me," the man with the blond hair said, as he sat down opposite Foley. He had a medium build, a woodenly handsome face, and appeared to be about twenty-five years old. Unlike Foley, whose face was covered with a two-day growth of beard, the visitor was clean-shaven. His clothing was nondescript but sturdy—perfect for urban warfare. "You're welcome," the resistance leader said automatically. "What can I do for you?"

"It's more like what I can do for *you*," the blond man answered with a sardonic grin.

"I really don't have time for word games," the officer said dourly, as he examined the list in front of him. "I'm sorry, there must be a mistake. . . . Would you mind giving me your name?"

"Chien-Chu," the blond man said. "Sergi Chien-Chu. But given that you're a lieutenant, and I'm an admiral, feel free to call me *sir*. I don't pull rank very often—but there are times when it makes sense. And this is one of them."

Like most humans, Foley was familiar with the name. It

was hard not to be, since the *real* Chien-Chu was not only the billionaire owner of Chien-Chu Enterprises, but the man many called "The Father of the Confederacy," and was rumored to be well over one hundred years old. Or his brain tissue was anyway, since his original bio body had worn out decades before, and been replaced by a succession of cybernetic vehicles, which were said to come in a variety of shapes and sizes.

But was Foley looking at one of them? That seemed very doubtful. . . . Because rich people had space yachts, and thousands of them had escaped Earth orbit during the early days of the invasion. So rather than feeling awestruck, as he otherwise might have, Foley was angry. "Right, you're Sergi Chien-Chu, and I'm President Nankool. . . . You can leave now. . . . Or should I have some of my men *throw* you out?"

Sergi Chien-Chu thought of the file he wanted and watched the electronic document appear in front of his "eyes." "Before you do that, Lieutenant, consider this. . . . Who, but an admiral, or someone similar, would know that your military ID number is CFN 204-632-141? Or, that you have a heart-shaped birthmark on the upper surface of your left arm? Or, that you were in Battle Station III's brig, accused of grand larceny when the Ramanthians attacked? Which is when you found your way to the surface—and wound up in command of the Earth Liberation Brigade. And you've been riding the tiger ever since."

Foley realized his mouth was hanging open and closed it. Even though it was theoretically possible that someone other than a genuine admiral could assemble the information the stranger had at his disposal, it was unlikely, given the circumstances, and deep down the officer knew that the blond man's claim was true. Somehow, impossible though it might seem, one of the most remarkable people in the history of the Confederacy was seated there in front of him! "Sorry, sir," the officer said apologetically. "But this is something of a surprise. . . . A welcome one, however—since you're far more qualified to run this organization than I am!"

"Nice try, son," Chien-Chu said dryly. "But you accepted your commission—and by God you're going to earn it! In fact, given that it would be unseemly to have such a junior officer in charge of a soon-to-be-powerful army, I'm jumping you up to commander! It's a temporary rank, of course, but who knows? *If* you can control your larcenous instincts, and *if* you show up for work every day, we might make the promotion permanent when this is all over. And drop the charges against you . . . Sound good?"

Foley looked around, saw that his underlings were staring at him with open curiosity, and knew why. He had already spent more time with Chien-Chu than the people who had preceded him. "Sir, yes sir. Would you be willing to drop the charges pending against my men as well?"

"Yes," Chien-Chu answered. "We'll drop any charge short of murder, assuming that they take your orders, and remain loyal until Earth has been liberated."

"Okay," Foley said. "It's a deal."

"Good," the entrepreneur replied. "Now here's the problem. . . . We, which is to say the Confederacy's military forces, are spread very thin at the moment. The truth is that we won't be able to send a fleet here for months to come. And that's if things go well! If they don't, it could be as much as a year before help arrives. Meanwhile, as is typical in such situations, all sorts of criminals are busy feeding off the chaos."

Foley remembered his plan to rob the Mill Valley Security Deposit Building and felt a sense of shame. Chien-Chu saw the expression on the other man's face and grinned knowingly. "Shocking isn't it? And, making a bad situation worse, is the fact that some of these criminal organizations are pretending to be freedom fighters as a way to solicit popular support. At least one of which is being led by a retired general. It will be necessary to deal with him eventually, but given the fact that his people would kick your ass right now, that will have to wait. In the meantime we're going to strengthen your group until the Earth Liberation Brigade is felt increasingly nauseous. Not Chien-Chu, though, who had just finished explaining how the yacht had been "borrowed" from a wealthy acquaintance of his, who was among those who had fled the planet. The crew consisted of Chien-Chu Enterprises employees, who wore black hoods and were heavily armed. A group which, Foley suspected, would be assigned to keep an eye on him.

"We're getting close," the admiral promised, as another wave broke over the plunging bow. "Earth is two-thirds water you know. . . . That makes for a lot of surface area to keep track of. And even though they have to drink the stuff, the bugs aren't all that partial to H_2O. That's because they evolved on a planet that doesn't have any oceans."

All of that might have been more interesting to Foley had his stomach felt better. As it was, the naval officer was battling the urge to vomit, which for reasons he wasn't altogether sure of, he didn't want to do while Chien-Chu was looking on. "Okay," the cyborg said, as a stream of data continued to scroll down the right side of his "vision." "Here it comes!"

There was a clap of thunder as whatever "it" was broke the sound barrier, followed by a tremendous explosion of water as something big smacked into the surface of the ocean a thousand yards off the port bow. "There's our fish!" the businessman proclaimed enthusiastically. "Now to reel it in!"

It took the better part of twenty minutes to bring the yacht alongside the heaving object, hook on to a submerged tow-point, and begin the process of hauling the object ashore. The boxy container would have been very difficult to tow had it not been for extendable hydrofoils that provided the same amount of lift the yacht enjoyed.

"You can sink it, too!" Chien-Chu said proudly, as he looked astern. "And program it to surface whenever you want! That feature will become increasingly important once the bugs realize what's going on. There's a whole lot of ocean out here—and even with orbital surveillance they can't track

the big boy on the block. . . . And that's when you'll I
ready to throw your weight around. But only for the bene
of the Confederacy. Do you read me?"

The truth was that Foley wasn't sure he could live
to all of the admiral's expectations. But Chien-Chu kn
about his personal history and hadn't been deterred. So p
haps he *was* capable of leading the Earth Liberation Brig
and just didn't know it. "Yes, sir," Foley said. "I read yo

"Good," the other man said. "Tell me something, son.
Are you an angler?"

Foley thought it was strange to have someone who
peared to be the same age he was call him "son." "No, sir,
officer replied. "I grew up the city, so I never went fishin

"Well, it's never too late to learn," the businessma
served. "Go ahead and finish what you were doing. The
cept of meeting with citizens on a regular basis is a
thing to do by the way. . . . And it makes you different
the pretenders who would like to set up shop out the
once you're finished, we're going to take a run down
bay. You know the huge hab that Homby Industrie
just off Angel Island? Well, the condos took a beatin
the bugs, but there's nothing wrong with the mar
cated underneath the complex. And that's where our
boat is hidden."

Foley thought that the whole notion of a fishing
strange, *very* strange, but nodded anyway. "Yes, sii
need some sort of pole?"

Admiral Chien-Chu smiled indulgently. "No,
won't."

It was nearly pitch-black off Point Bonita, but
some light from the moon, as large swells passed
yacht. The ride out had been relatively smooth,
the winglike hydrofoils that lifted the hundred
boat out of the water and enabled speeds of up to f
knots. But now that the vessel was hull down, it v
to the motion of the waves like any other boat,

everything that goes on. Plus, we're going to throw empties at them, just to keep the bastards busy!"

Now that the yacht's foils were deployed, the ride was a good deal steadier, which allowed Foley to focus on something more than his stomach. "That's amazing, sir. May I ask what's in the container?"

"Yes, you may," Chien-Chu replied cheerfully. "This one contains automatic weapons plus lots of ammo. . . . Just the sort of thing that an up-and-coming resistance leader like yourself would ask for if he could! Future loads will include heavy weapons, medical supplies, and food."

Foley felt a steadily rising sense of hope. "That's terrific, sir. . . . Can I make a suggestion?"

"Of course," the cyborg said indulgently, as the boat passed under the partially slagged Golden Gate Bridge. "Suggest away."

"Some or all of those dummy containers could contain bombs," Foley said. "That would not only inflict casualties— but slow the chits down."

"*And* discourage any criminals that might get a hold of one!" Chien-Chu added gleefully. "I can see that we chose well! I will forward your idea to the proper people. They'll love it."

Foley nodded. "Thank you, sir. But one more question . . . The last time I was up in orbit, the bugs were in control. Won't they intercept and destroy our ships before they can drop more containers into the atmosphere? Frankly, I'm surprised this one got through."

"No, they won't be intercepted," the admiral answered confidently. "Because there aren't any ships! Not in the conventional sense anyway. . . . We're using specially designed drones, each of which has its own hyperdrive and onboard NAVCOMP. Rather than exit hyperspace six planetary diameters out, the way all incoming traffic is normally required to do, the drones are programmed to drop hyper *inside* the moon's orbit! That means the chits have very little time in which to respond before the vehicle enters the atmosphere, opens up, and dumps up to four individually targetable cargo modules into any body of water we choose.

"Oh, sure," the entrepreneur continued matter-of-factly. "The Ramanthians will nail some of them. And others will go astray for one reason or another. . . . But we calculate that about sixty-three percent will reach the designated target area even after the chits have come to expect them. That means your organization will have more supplies than all the rest of the gangs and armies forming up out there. So make good use of your advantage. . . . Because it's your job to keep the bugs from settling in and to prevent the criminals from becoming too powerful while the government regroups. Got it, Commander?"

Foley looked back along the bar-taut tow cable to where the matte black cargo module was skimming the surface of the moonlit sea. Admiral Chien-Chu made it all seem so obvious, so simple, but he knew better. Even though the yacht's power plant was shielded, there was the possibility of a heat leak that would attract attention from above. Or that a passing aircraft would spot them—or that one of a hundred other calamities could occur. Which meant that every time someone went out to retrieve a cargo module it would be a crapshoot. But there was only one thing the officer could say: "Yes, sir, we'll do our best."

DEER VALLEY, EAST OF SAN FRANCISCO

As the sun rose and Margaret Vanderveen emerged from the old mine shaft to look down on the valley below, she marveled at how beautiful it was, in spite of the charred ruins of what had once been her second home. Some of the buildings had been torched by looters. And, after stripping them of everything that might be useful during the coming weeks, months, or, God forbid, years ahead, Benson had set fire to all the rest. Because any signs of habitation, or prosperity, would serve as an open invitation to both the Ramanthians and the human looters—a breed the society matron had come to fear more than the insectoid aliens.

A doe and a fawn were grazing on what had once been Margaret's front lawn as she took a sip of tea and considered the day ahead. Having taken in the teenager named Christine, and the orphans in her care, the three adults had their hands full trying to feed all the hungry mouths, keep the youngsters halfway clean, and prevent them from attracting the wrong sort of attention. The latter was the most difficult task because the children had lots of energy and hated being cooped up inside the mine.

The answer was to take small groups of them on expeditions like the one planned for that morning, where they could get some exercise while foraging for edibles, and checking Benson's artfully concealed snares. There were lots of rabbits in the area, and they were a welcome source of protein.

Such forays were dangerous, not only because the group might be spotted from the air but because it took constant vigilance to avoid etching trails into the hillsides. Visible paths that, if allowed to develop, could lead the inquiring eye straight to the mine shaft.

Such were Margaret's thoughts as an ominous *thrumming* noise was heard—and she automatically backed into the jumble of boulders that helped conceal the entrance to the mine. There was a cord there, which the matron pulled three times to alert her companions to the possibility of trouble.

Both of the deer bolted as the *thrumming* sound stopped, then started again. And that was when the small two-seat Ramanthian scout ship passed over the valley headed west. It was trailing a stream of black smoke, and as the engine continued to cut in and out, the aircraft lost altitude and disappeared from sight as it passed over the opposite ridge. "It looks like the bastards are going to crash," Benson said heartlessly, as he appeared next to Margaret with a rifle clutched in his hands. "Here's hoping they die a painful death."

Margaret understood how Benson felt, but couldn't bring herself to wish anyone a painful death, even a Ramanthian. "We'd better keep everyone inside," she said. "It seems safe to assume that they radioed for help. That means a rescue party is on the way."

Benson nodded. "Thank God we don't have anyone out there at the moment," he said. "It looks like we caught a break."

Margaret was inclined to agree, but as the day wore on, and the adults took turns on sentry duty, there were no signs of a Ramanthian rescue party. Or anyone else for that matter. Although there was always the possibility that ground troops had been ordered to respond from the west—something the humans wouldn't be able to see because of the intervening hill. That was Benson's theory—and it made sense.

When darkness fell, and the evening meal was over, the adults took turns telling stories until it was time for the children to go to bed. Since John could stand sentry duty all night without fatigue, and could see in the dark, the rest of them could get a good night's rest knowing that the android was on duty.

That's why Margaret was sound asleep when the robot came to wake her. A beam of light washed the walls around the socialite, and she held up a hand to protect her eyes. John spoke with the same calm tones he might have used to announce the arrival of a guest at the Napa Valley estate. "I'm sorry to disturb you, ma'am," the android said formally. "But it's my duty to inform you that a life-form bearing a strong resemblance to a Ramanthian entered the valley from the west and is presently taking a nap where the house used to be."

Margaret was up by then and pulling her clothes on. "A Ramanthian. You're sure?"

"Yes, ma'am," John responded gravely. "I'm sure."

"And there's only one of them?"

"Yes, ma'am," the robot replied patiently. "There's only one of them."

"Did you tell Benson?"

"Yes, ma'am, I did," the android confirmed.

"Good," Margaret said, as she strapped a gun belt around her waist. "Go back and tell Lisa to stay with the children. I'll be with Benson."

The group had a pair of night-vision binoculars they had appropriated from the men who attempted to kill them immediately after they left the highway. And Benson was already using them when Margaret emerged from the mine to stand next to him. "So," she wanted to know, "was John correct?"

"He sure as heck was," the maintenance man answered. "It's weird. . . . But here, take a look for yourself."

Margaret accepted the binos, brought them up to her eyes, and swept the area below until a greenish blob appeared. Then, after she fiddled with the controls, the picture came clear. There, lying on his side as if sound asleep, was a Ramanthian soldier, or aviator, if this particular bug had been aboard the ship they'd seen the previous day. "It looks like he's asleep or dead," the socialite commented. "Maybe they weren't able to get a message out. Maybe he was injured, left the crash site looking for help, and couldn't walk any farther."

"Maybe," Benson allowed grimly. "But regardless of what happened he's a problem. If the chits see him, they'll land right in our front yard. Maybe they'll spot the mine, and maybe they won't. But why take the chance? I say we go down and deal with him before the sun comes up."

The plan made sense. So Margaret went to tell the others, ordered John to come along, and followed Benson down into the valley below. They were careful to step on rocks wherever possible in order to avoid creating a trail.

Once in the valley, the humans circled the body, before approaching it with weapons at the ready. Margaret noticed that a faint odor of formic acid hung in the air around the Ramanthian as Benson prodded the body with his rifle. There was no response so Margaret decided that it was safe to move in and examine the corpse more closely.

Margaret had seen Ramanthians before, and even spoke with some during prewar diplomatic functions, but never under circumstances such as these. The first thing she wanted to do was search the body for any objects or bits of information that might prove useful. Then, just to satisfy her own curiosity, Margaret was hoping to establish the cause of death. With those objectives in mind, she forced herself to grab hold of the aviator's harness in an attempt to roll the alien over. And that was when the trooper uttered a groan. Margaret jerked her hand away as Benson raised the rifle. "Holy shit! The bastard is alive!"

"You know I don't like that kind of language," Margaret said primly. "Come on. . . . Let's prepare the sling you were talking about."

"But it's alive!" Benson objected. "I should shoot it first."

"You'll do nothing of the kind," Margaret replied firmly. "Is that the way you would like them to treat us? Now, hurry up. Or would you like to have a Ramanthian patrol find us out here?"

It was that argument as much as anything that convinced Benson to take the coil of rope off his shoulder and work with John to prepare a sling. Then, once the carefully knotted rope was laid out next to the aviator, it was a simple matter to roll the alien onto it. That produced another groan, but the bug was still unconscious insofar as Margaret could tell, and that was good. Because she had nothing to offer the Ramanthian for his pain.

Margaret led the way as Benson and the android carried the aviator up the hill to the mine, where Lisa was waiting. "We'll take him back to one of the side galleries," Margaret instructed, and turned to lead the way. The main shaft ran straight back into the hillside. The gradient slanted upwards, so the miners could move their fully loaded carts more easily, but the iron rails were long gone. Lights, all powered by carefully camouflaged solar panels, lit the way. Side tunnels, some of which had been enlarged over the years, provided rough-hewn rooms for sleeping, eating, and storage. And it was in one of the latter where a table had been placed so that the Ramanthian could be laid on his side. The same position he had been found in and the only one that would accommodate the alien's wings.

The first task, to Margaret's mind at least, was to assess the extent of the alien's injuries in case there was something that she or her companions could do to help. Benson wanted no part of the activity, but Lisa was willing, and having rigged some lights, the two women conducted an inch-by-inch examination of the alien's body. And that was when they discovered that a section of the Ramanthian's exoskeleton was not only broken, but pressing in on the aviator's internal organs, which had most likely been damaged as a result.

Margaret knew that the question of why the scout ship had crashed, and why there hadn't been any signs of a search, would probably go unanswered. But one thing she *did* know was that the alien in front of her had gone down in what he no doubt saw as enemy territory, had suffered a terrible injury, and still found the courage to try and walk out. So while she hated the Ramanthians as a group, the matron couldn't help but admire the being in front of her, as she pressed her fingers against the alien's reddish brown chitin.

And that was when Margaret noticed something she thought was strange. Although she could have been wrong—since she knew so little about bug physiology. But based on her efforts to move the Ramanthian, it seemed as though his chitin, and therefore his exoskeleton, was very thin. If true, that might have had something to do with the extent of his injuries. The problem was that Margaret had no way to know how thick normal chitin was. Still, if the aviator's shell-like covering was especially fragile, the question was why?

The issue was academic, of course, but continued to linger in the back of Margaret's mind, until the Ramanthian died six hours later. Benson was there, as was Lisa, when the socialite made her announcement. "We have some work to do before we can bury him," Margaret said. "I want to take samples of his exoskeleton and major organs."

Both of her companions were amazed. "Whatever for?" Lisa wanted to know.

"I think the aviator was sick before the crash," Margaret answered firmly. "That's why his exoskeleton was so fragile."

"So what?" Benson inquired cynically. "Humans get sick; Ramanthians get sick. That's how it is."

"You're probably right," Margaret admitted. "But what if other Ramanthians are suffering from the same disease? And what if a lot of Ramanthians were suffering from the disease? Wouldn't our intelligence people want to know that?"

"They might," Lisa conceded. "But how would you get in touch with them? Algeron is a long ways off."

"I don't know," Margaret replied. "But we've got to try."

"I think the whole discussion is a waste of time," Benson said dismissively. "We don't have the means to preserve tissue samples once you take them."

"Oh, but we do!" Margaret proclaimed, with a wicked smile. "You went to some lengths to bring liquor along, as I recall—claiming that we might need it for 'medicinal purposes.' Well, it looks like you were correct!"

"*No,*" Benson said, as he looked at her aghast. "You wouldn't!"

"Oh, but I *would*," Margaret assured him. "Lisa, please find some containers. Plastic would be best. Thomas, please fetch a saw. We have work to do."

14

Swift, blazing flag of the regiment,
Eagle with crest of red and gold,
These men were born to drill and die.
Point for them the virtue of slaughter,
Make plain to them the excellence of killing
And a field where a thousand corpses lie.

—Stephen Crane
War Is Kind
Standard year 1899

PLANET GAMMA-014, THE CLONE HEGEMONY

Having successfully led his troops and their stolen vehicles
up over Tow-Tok Pass, and down onto the plain beyond,
Colonel Six stood on top of a three-tiered main battle tank,
and surveyed the battlefield ahead. Various types of data
scrolled down the right side of the viewfinder, including the
range of each object that fell under the crosshairs, the preva-
lent wind direction, and the temperature—a skin-numbing
twenty-six degrees.

But Six barely noticed the discomfort. His mind was on
carnage spread out in front of him. Knowing that the allies
would have to come down out of Tow-Tok Pass, General
Oro Akoto had chosen to dig hundreds of north–south
trenches intended to block access to the city of Yal-Am beyond. And, thanks to the canyon that bordered the battlefield to the north, and a densely packed minefield to the

south, the Ramanthian had been able to keep his enemies right where he wanted them, which was bogged down a good ten miles short of their goal.

Deep ditches were connected by communication trenches that ran east and west. Carefully sited bunkers, pillboxes, and machine-gun nests were positioned to put the allies in a lethal cross fire whenever they attempted to advance. All of that would have been worthless in the spring, summer, or fall, when allied aircraft would have pulverized the Ramanthian army. But thanks to very bad weather, and thickets of surface-to-air missile launchers, Akoto had been able to neutralize what should have been an overwhelming advantage.

Rather than wait for better weather—it appeared that General-453 was pushing ahead, relying on superior numbers to overwhelm the bugs and force entry into Yal-Am. And, judging from what Six could make out, the results had been nothing short of disastrous. As far as the eye could see there was nothing but fire-blackened craters, wrecked hover tanks, and thousands of unrecovered allied and Ramanthian bodies.

As the officer continued to scan the war-torn landscape ahead, *another* chapter in the bloody conflict began to unfold. Thunder rolled as the artillery pieces that had been dug in along the west side of the city began to speak. That sound was followed by a freight-train *rumble* as the big shells passed through the atmosphere. Then came a series of concussive *booms* as the high-explosive rounds landed among the allied troops and threw columns of earth, snow, and raw meat high into the air.

Even as the bloody confetti fell, Six saw thousands of white-clad Ramanthians boil up out of distant trenches and surge forward. Not to be outdone, the allies fired their howitzers and multiple-rocket launchers. And with devastating effects, too. . . . Dozens of red-orange explosions rippled along the Ramanthian trenches, and hundreds of bugs fell, as they battled to retake the north–south trench they had been forced to vacate the previous day.

Then the allied artillery barrage stopped as thousands of Seebos, marines, and legionnaires swarmed up out of their hiding places and rushed forward. Most of the clones wore winter white and gray, but all too many of the free breeders were dressed in layered summer uniforms, or ponchos made from blankets. The darker uniforms made excellent targets, and the people who wore them began to die as boots slipped on ice, robots struggled to cut paths through a maze of razor wire, and officers waved them forward. The soldiers fell in waves, their lives harvested like wheat, as the yammering machine guns cut them down. Mortar fire added to the madness, as men and women scrabbled through clods of falling earth to capture another few inches of bloody ground. And for what? Nothing that the Seebo could see and understand. It was a battle conceived by a conceited fool who, brother or not, was a mass murderer.

Having seen all he could stomach—Colonel Six lowered his binos. He had to stop the madness. . . . But how? Suddenly a mad, crazy idea occurred to him. A plan that *shouldn't* work, but could work, given the unusual circumstances. But would Dr. Kira Kelly be willing to cooperate? Maybe, the clone concluded, *if* she saw what he'd seen. The clone spoke into his lip mike. "This is Six. . . . Fetch the doctor. There's something I want her to see."

As the sun sank in the west, and powerful flares drifted down out of a lead gray sky, both sides settled in for a night of bitterly cold weather. The darkness was punctuated by occasional cross-trench raids as the adversaries sought to claim or reclaim precious inches of frozen ground they had been denied during daylight hours. A brutal, frequently close-quarters, business that rarely produced the sort of results that General-453 and his officers were looking for.

But that didn't keep them from trying, so any number of fanciful plots were hatched as General-453 and his mostly clone staff took their usual dinner within the cozy warmth of the command bunker located underneath his inflatable hab. The soft-sided structure was located fifteen miles west of Yal-Am, which put it safely beyond the reach of the biggest tubes General Akoto was willing to waste on a planet he expected to lose to the enemy.

Having consumed a hearty meal in the company of his cronies, the clone went up to his office, where it was his intention to respond to General Kobbi's latest memo. A missive the Seebo wanted to ignore, but couldn't, because of the way the free breeder consistently copied General Bill Booly. Still, the legionnaires were dying at a prodigious rate, and there was an excellent chance that Kobbi would take a bullet during one of his frequent trips to the front lines. *I'll give the asshole a posthumous medal,* the officer thought to himself, *and send my condolences to General Booly!*

The thought brought a thin smile to General-453's face as he entered his office only to discover that another Seebo was waiting for him. Even though the clone soldiers looked identical except for differences in age, they could frequently tell each other apart thanks to nuances of dress, posture, and inflection. Not this time however, because even though they were roughly the same age, Four-fifty-three couldn't remember meeting this officer before. "Is there some sort of emergency, Colonel?" the general wanted to know. "Because if there isn't, I would prefer that you see my adjutant, and make an appointment to see me."

Colonel Six stood. Thanks to his obvious status as a Seebo, and his relatively high rank, it had been absurdly easy to find out where the general was and await his return. The renegade put the time to good use by studying the schematics on the walls, reviewing a thick stack of intelligence reports, and skimming through the correspondence stacked on one corner of the collapsible desk. "I'm afraid it *is* an emergency, sir," Six assured the senior officer. "But we'll have everything under control in a moment. Isn't that right, Lieutenant-44?"

General-453 opened his mouth to say something, but never got a chance, as Lieutenant-44 took him from behind. The senior officer struggled, but couldn't counter the combination of a full nelson, and the younger man's strength. "Okay," Colonel Six said. "You can come out now."

That was Dr. Kira Kelly's cue to step out of General-453's washroom. "How dare you!" General-453 spluttered, and the medic crossed the room. "I'll have you arrested! I'll have you court-martialed! I'll have—"

"Make him shut up," Colonel Six said disgustedly, as Kelly knelt next to Four-fifty-three.

"This should do it," the doctor said calmly, pressing the injector against one of the general's meaty thighs. There was an audible *pop* as a gas cartridge forced a powerful sedative through the weave of Four-fifty-three's trousers and into his bloodstream. Lieutenant-44 was there to support the older Seebo as the strength left his legs.

"Let's put the general to bed," Six said, moving in to help. With Four-Four supporting Four-fifty-three's torso, and the others lifting his legs, the Seebo was carried into his sleeping compartment and strapped to his cot. With that accomplished, Six turned to Kelly. "Thank you, Doctor. You know what this means, don't you?"

"No," Kelly answered. "What does it mean? Outside of the fact that I must be crazy?"

"It means you're one of *us*," Six said meaningfully. "Because now you're part of what amounts to a mutiny."

Kelly remembered the view from the top of the tank, as thousands of brave men and women were sent forward into what constituted a meat grinder, and knew Six was correct. By giving the sedative, she had knowingly crossed the line from victim, to criminal, and aligned herself with a man who, if not a murderer on the scale that General-453 was, still qualified as such. Not that it mattered much, because Kelly had already lost her way, and knew it. Her resolve had weakened since leaving the note at the refueling station. Serious mistakes had been made, and there was no going back. "Yes," Kelly agreed fatalistically. "We're on the same side."

"Good," Six replied evenly. "The next part is going to be tricky. Very tricky indeed. And I need your help."

General Mortimer Kobbi had his combat gear on, and was about to go out into the flare-lit trenches, when the summons arrived. "You're sure?" the tough little legionnaire demanded, as the com tech faced him under the glare produced by the overhead strip lights. Their breaths fogged the air, a series of distant explosions sent tremors through the frozen ground, and a nearly spent bullet *pinged* as it flattened itself against one of the metal shutters.

"Yes, sir," the corporal said steadfastly. "General-453 wants to see you right away."

"It was probably that last memo you sent," a major named Perko said sardonically. "The firing squad is ready."

The com tech thought that was funny—but knew better than to smile. "*All* of the regimental commanders were invited," the corporal put in. "The meeting is scheduled for 2100 hours."

Kobbi waited until the enlisted man had left before turning to Perko. The major was a big man, with broad shoulders, and a long, lugubrious face. "Who knows?" the general said rhetorically. "Maybe the bastard will listen to someone other than his clone suck-ups for a change."

Perko shrugged. "Here's hoping. I'll take care of the tour for you."

"Keep your head down," Kobbi cautioned. "You'd look damned silly without it."

The makeup job was far from perfect, but by putting on three sets of General-453's underwear in order to better fill out one of his uniforms, and by inserting a couple of Kelly's two-inch-by-two-inch gauze pads in his cheeks to make his face look puffier, Colonel Six was able to approximate the other officer's appearance. Would any of Four-fifty-three's subordinates notice discrepancies? Probably, especially where subtle mannerisms were concerned, but it wouldn't make any difference unless they had the courage to challenge the supreme commander. And that was unlikely.

So that was the man who entered the underground command bunker at 2100 hours. It was a long narrow space that had been scooped out of the ground with a tank-mounted dozer blade, tidied up by hand, and spray-sealed to keep moisture out. Self-adhesive strip lights had been attached to the ceiling, two folding worktables took up the center of the room, and folding chairs were slotted all around. The floor consisted of locally produced wood planks that were painstakingly scrubbed each morning consistent with General-453's standing orders.

About half of the officers who came to attention were Seebos, and the rest were free breeders, including Mortimer Kobbi. The clone's face looked more bloated than usual, but that was of little interest to the legionnaire, who was hoping for some sort of breakthrough. Anything other than another suicidal attack against an entrenched enemy. And, much to Kobbi's amazement, that was what he got! "At ease," the imposter said, as he eyed those around him. "Please take your seats. Our present strategy isn't working—so get ready to take notes. We're going to try something new."

Though not identical to the way the legionnaire would have planned it, the strategy that Four-fifty-three presented was similar, especially where the use of armor was concerned. "As you know," Six said, "the battlefield is strewn with wrecked hover tanks. That's because the Ramanthians knew we would use them—and knew they wouldn't work very well over deep trenches."

Kobbi was amazed. As were the other Confederacy officers seated around him. It was like listening to a different man! Or himself for that matter—because everything Four-fifty-three was saying could be found in the memos he'd sent in.

"But, thanks to our brave allies, we have an answer!" Six proclaimed. "Because the Legion's quads can *walk*, rather than float across the battlefield, engaging multiple targets as they do so, thereby clearing the way for the Trooper IIs and bio bods who will follow."

Now it was the Seebos' turn to look at each other in amazement. Because on all previous occasions, when no free breeders were present to hear, the supreme commander had consistently referred to the Legion's cyborgs as "freaks, weirdos, and criminal scum." Military curiosities at best who weren't fit for serious combat. Which was why none of the cavalry units had seen any action yet—in spite of the fact that the Legion's infantry had taken part in assault after assault. But such was their fear of the general, and his notoriously short temper, that none of the clone officers wanted to challenge the apparent about-face. Especially with so many free breeders present.

So the battle plan was finalized, and all of the regimental commanders were sent out to prepare their troops, which were slated to attack the Ramanthian positions just before dawn. Not with the goal of taking a few trenches, but in an effort to wipe the bugs off the battlefield, and capturing the town beyond! Kobbi was whistling by the time he made his way down the slippery ramp and entered his command bunker. And that, as all of his subordinates knew, was a very good sign.

Rather than the chance to rest, which Santana and his company had been hoping for, they came down out of Tow-Tok Pass to discover that they would be at the forefront of an all-out attack scheduled for 0500 the next morning. The cavalry officer got the news in person, as people bustled about the 1st REC's command bunker, clearly preparing for something. "I'm sorry," General Kobbi said, once Santana had delivered his report. "But we've got to put the Colonel Six matter aside for the moment. I know you and your people deserve a break, but I can't give you one. Finally, after all this time, General-453 has come to his senses! We're going to launch a major attack in the morning—I'm going to need every cyborg we've got. So rearm your people and get them ready. God willing, we'll take Yal-Am in time for lunch!"

Santana had known the diminutive general for quite a while by then and couldn't recall seeing him quite so enthusiastic before. "That sounds good, sir," Santana replied. "I'd better get back to my company."

"One thing before you go," Kobbi said thoughtfully. "I was going to assign this task to someone else, but you have more combat experience, and you know what that means."

Santana made a face. "Is this some sort of shit detail, sir?"

"Yes, it is!" Kobbi replied cheerfully. "Much to everyone's surprise General-453 wants to lead this assault from the *front*. But given the speed with which we're going to advance, the only way he can possibly keep up is to ride a T-2. Which he's never done before."

Santana groaned. "So you want *me* to babysit him."

"No," Kobbi countered. "I want you and your company to *guard* him. But I won't insist. Colonel Quinlan misses you terribly—and will be quite happy to bring Alpha Company back into the fold."

There was a moment of silence as the men stared at each other. It was Santana who spoke first. "Permission to speak freely, sir?"

"Granted."

"You are one rotten bastard. Sir."

Kobbi grinned from ear to ear. "That's what they tell me. So, we have a deal?"

"Yes, sir," Santana agreed grimly. "We have a deal."

"Good. I'll send word to the general. Which cyborg will you partner him with?"

"Private Shalo Shaley, sir. We lost her bio bod up in Tow-Tok Pass."

"I'm sorry to hear that," Kobbi replied soberly. "Well,

tell the private she's about to become a corporal if she can get Four-fifty-three into Yal-Am with his clone ass intact."

Santana came to attention. The salute was smart and crisp. "Sir, yes sir."

Kobbi returned the salute. "Dismissed."

The senior officer's face was impassive, but as Santana turned, and made his way up the ramp Kobbi sent a thought after him. *Take care of yourself, Captain. . . . Your father would be proud.*

The entire front line seemed to hold its collective breath as the final seconds ticked away, and General-453 yelled "Charge!" over the division-level push. Except that it *wasn't* Four-fifty-three, because he was still being held under Dr. Kira Kelly's supervision, as dozens of simultaneously launched flares transformed night into day, artillery shells screamed downrange, and the huge quads lumbered out onto the battlefield.

The fifty-ton cyborgs were *big* targets, and therefore almost impossible to miss, but they could take a lot of punishment, and did, as the Ramanthians opened up with everything they had. The legionnaires fought back as missiles raced off their rails, energy cannons sent pulses of blue death stuttering across no-man's-land, and powerful legs tore through coils of barbed wire. And there were others besides Lupo and Xiong, sixteen quads altogether sweeping across the icy moonscape.

The big monsters weren't alone. The smaller, more agile T-2s were all around them. Jumping over trenches, flaming machine-gun nests, and firing shoulder-launched missiles. The rockets sleeted across the cratered landscape to strike at enemy artillery positions. Some were neutralized, while others continued to fire, their barrels nearly parallel to the ground.

That was when Colonel Six, AKA General-453, realized his mistake. Rather than *lead* allied forces, the way the renegade had imagined that he would, the clone had been reduced to little more than a piece of living luggage strapped to a T-2's back! And not very skilled baggage, because if it hadn't been for the harness that held him in place, Six knew he would have been thrown clear by then. So all the imposter could do was hold on, fire his pistol at targets of opportunity, and hope things were going well.

And things *were* going well, or so it seemed to Santana, who was advancing parallel to General-453, roughly fifteen feet away. Even though he understood the theoretical advantage that the big walkers had when fighting on broken terrain, Santana had never been exposed to trench warfare before, and was proud to see how easily the quads could advance across a battlefield littered with burned-out hover tanks. And not just advance, but *destroy* the enemy with overlapping fields of fire, as the seemingly unstoppable behemoths continued to plod forward.

Unfortunately, the big cyborgs *could* be stopped, and even though they hadn't had any practice, the Ramanthian officers understood the theory. Every weapon system involves a series of trade-offs. One of which is the ratio of weight to speed. And speed was very important. So rather than use the same thickness of armor *underneath* the quads, as they had everywhere else, the cybernetic engineers put less metal there. That meant the way to kill a quad was to send infantry in *under* it, find a way to attach a demolition pack to the cyborg's belly, and run like hell! Or, if that wasn't possible, then attack a spindly leg. Of course the Legion's tacticians understood how vulnerable the big machines were, which was why a platoon of T-2s was typically assigned to guard each quad against infantry attacks.

But where there's a will, there's a way, and as Xiong moved forward her "torso" passed over a group of dead Ramanthians. Except one of them *wasn't* dead. His name was Koga Noo, he was a member of the fanatical *Nira* cult, and eager to sacrifice himself to the cause. Especially if he could take one of the big walkers with him!

War involves luck, both good and bad, and as luck would

have it a demo pack lay four feet away. It had been brought onto the battlefield for the purpose of blowing a hole in the allied wire, but the engineers assigned to place it had been killed. So it was a simple matter for Noo to grab hold of the container and leap into the air as the quad passed over him. The cyborg's thinly armored belly was too high for the soldier to touch, but the Ramanthian had wings and was quick to deploy them. Seconds later, before the deadly T-2s could intervene, Noo was hovering just below Xiong's closely packed cargo bay. That was when the enemy soldier pinched the switch.

There was a brilliant flash of light, followed by a resounding *boom*, as the charge went off and Noo was vaporized. Less than half the force generated by the explosion was directed up and into the cyborg's belly, but it was sufficient to burn a hole through the relatively thin armor, and send a jet of superheated gases into the compartment above. That triggered a series of secondary explosions, which not only killed the twelve Seebos seated in the cargo bay but ripped Xiong apart.

Santana swore, and attempted to contact the cyborg via the company push, but there was no answer, as what remained of the legionnaire toppled onto one of Bravo Company's T-2s, thereby raising the death toll to fifteen.

However, there was no time to stop and grieve as the rest of the allied line continued to surge forward. Colonel Six had grown somewhat used to the violent rocking motion by that time, and could be seen at the very front of the allied army, shouting encouragement to every unit he passed. This came as something of a surprise from an officer better known for his cutting criticisms than unreserved praise.

The allied formation had cleared no-man's-land by that time, and was well within Ramanthian lines, which had broken before the onslaught. Santana, who was busy guarding General-453's right flank, saw what was taking place and urged Alpha Company forward. "Run the bastards down!" he shouted. "Remember Xiong!"

There were shouts of "Camerone!" and "Blood!" as the Hudathan legionnaires uttered their traditional war cry. Then they were through to the Ramanthian rear lines, where the enemy tanks and artillery pieces were trapped in their own revetments, as the alien soldiers continued to pull back into the devastated city of Yal-Am.

Rather than remain where he was, and die an ignominious death at the hands of the animals, one of the tank commanders sent his beetle-shaped Gantha straight at Deker and Santana. The cavalry officer saw a flash of light as the big 120mm gun went off, followed by a potentially deafening *boom*, as the big shell *roared* past him.

Then the T-2 was in the air! Metal clanged on metal as Deker landed on the Gantha's lower deck. Santana looked up to see that the helmeted tank commander was trying to bring a heavy machine gun to bear on the threat below him. Santana brought his CA-10 up, pulled the trigger, and felt a sinking sensation when nothing happened! The goddamned piece of crap had frozen up!

The machine gun continued to swing around as Santana worked the action, brought the weapon up for a *second* time, and pulled the trigger again. The Ramanthian's head jerked backwards as two of the slugs smashed through his face shield, pulped his brains, and blew what was left out through the back of his fiber-composite helmet.

"Good one, sir!" Deker said approvingly, as he began to climb higher. "Got any grenades?"

"Two," Santana replied, fumbling for them.

"That should do it," Deker said cheerfully, as he arrived next to the turret. "But mind the chit, sir. . . . He's in the way!"

The two of them were so close that Santana was able to reach out, grab the dead Ramanthian's harness, and pull him to one side. That opened a hole large enough to accept both grenades. They were still falling into the compartment below, when Deker took to the air, hoping to put as much distance between himself and the Gantha as he could. The ensuing explosion lifted the turret off the top of the tank, sent a gout of flames into the air, and produced a wave of hot air that washed around both legionnaires. Deker made a perfect landing, absorbed most of the impact with his mechanical knees, and was about to reenter the fray when a frantic call was heard.

"Alpha Six! This is Bravo Three-Three! The general is missing! I can't find him anywhere. Over."

"*What?*" Santana demanded, incredulously. "What do you mean you can't find him? He was strapped to your back! Over."

"I mean the bastard bailed out," Shaley answered angrily. "And I can't find him. Over."

"Alpha Six to Alpha Company," Santana said. "Form on me! Alpha One-Four will provide security while we search for the general. Execute. Out."

Meanwhile, as the surviving members of Alpha Company gathered to look for the allied commander, General Akoto was deep beneath the city of Yal-Am, preparing to deliver the *Kiyo*—the killing stroke. Because everything, including the retreat up over Tow-Tok Pass, and the way the ongoing battle was being fought had been leading up to *this*: the moment when the allies would enter the killing ground and give themselves over to the final slaughter. Thanks to massive incompetence on the part of their military leaders, the process had taken much longer than anticipated, thereby extending the amount of time available for the purpose of conquering Earth. Thus, the most important aspect of Akoto's mission had already been accomplished.

The general was too old for active service in the minds of many, as was apparent from the age spots on his chitin, and the many maladies for which the doctors were treating him. But there was nothing wrong with his mind, which was sword bright, and as keen as a thrice-honed blade. This was why he knew that, even as a seemingly unstoppable juggernaut rolled toward the depopulated city of Yal-Am, a unique opportunity lay before him. Rather than simply stalling the allies, as the old warrior had originally been ordered to do, it was his intention to defeat them! More than that, to drive the degenerates back into space—where others could deal with them.

The navy would have to do its part, of course. But the hypercom call had been sent, and even as Akoto's servant strapped his sword to the old warrior's back, a battle group was emerging from hyperspace. Soon, within a matter of hours, all of the allied warships presently in orbit around Gamma-014 would be fighting for their lives.

While that battle took place, Akoto, plus ten thousand heavily armed Ramanthian regulars, were going to pour up out of the natural caverns located below the city of Yal-Am and *consume* the five thousand allied troops presently rushing to their deaths. Because exhausted from the battle just fought—the badly outnumbered humans would be easy meat. And Akoto was known for a hearty appetite. The warrior took pleasure in his joke—and that was the moment when the *real* battle began.

Because the Ramanthians had been swept from the field of battle, Alpha Company was pretty much on its own, as the legionnaires completed the third, and what would have to be final, search for General-453. Or, failing that, what remained of his body. But there was no sign of the officer so far, and Santana was just about to wrap up the effort, when a voice came over the division push—a rarely used com channel that was reserved for extreme emergencies since it had the effect of smothering communications at the battalion, company, and platoon level. "This is General-453," the voice proclaimed. "I was held prisoner until fifteen minutes ago. . . . The man who led the assault is a renegade who calls himself Colonel Six. Seize the imposter and place him under arrest! I will arrive in Yal-Am shortly. Out."

The announcement was like a bolt out of the blue. It

seemed that the Seebo who had reformulated allied strategy, and led the successful assault against the Ramanthians, had been none other than the clone Santana had been ordered to track down! Knowing that his impersonation would have to end, he had taken his leave just short of the final goal.

That was shocking enough, but what took place over the next few minutes was even more so. It began with a sudden flurry of confused radio traffic, soon followed by frantic calls for help, and a storm of gunfire. Santana ordered his unit forward, but hadn't traveled more than a hundred feet when Kobbi came over the regimental push. His voice was calm but urgent. "It was a trap! Thousands of Ramanthians were hiding underground. The 1st REC will fall back toward the west. Bravo Company, 1st Battalion, will escort the wounded. Alpha Company, 2nd Battalion, will provide covering fire—"

Santana overrode the transmission to give orders at that point. By repositioning his remaining quad, and surrounding it with Trooper IIs, the cavalry officer was able to create an island of steel in the middle of the horrific battlefield. And that was important, because as the badly mauled allied troops streamed back along both flanks, the company could keep the pursuing aliens from overrunning them. As other units fell in next to the legionnaires, what had been an island was transformed into a defensive wall—a barrier that fell back every ten minutes or so, giving more survivors an opportunity to escape, and denying the bugs the slaughter they had been looking forward to. But many of the cyborgs had run out of ammunition by then, as had the foot soldiers, which meant that orderly though the retreat was, it couldn't hold. That reality became horribly clear as the allies were pushed back through what had been their rear lines, where unit cohesion began to break down, and everything came apart.

Official records would eventually show that General Kobbi attempted to call in an orbital bombardment on his own position, hoping to kill *everyone* in the area, but couldn't find a navy ship that wasn't already fighting for its life. Total chaos ensued as more than three thousand allied troops and civilian volunteers began the long, cold march up over Tow-Tok Pass, toward the bases beyond. The battle of Yal-Am had been lost.

15

Allies are enemies who intend to attack you later.

—*Triad Hiween Doma-Sa*
In a speech to the Sa clan
Standard year 2841

PLANET ALPHA-001, THE CLONE HEGEMONY

The last three days had been hellish. And as Alpha Clone Antonio-Seven entered the Emergency Operations Center normally reserved for natural disasters, he felt sick to his stomach. Suddenly, seemingly out of nowhere, a general uprising was taking place. Not just on Alpha-001, but if reports could be believed, on *all* of the Hegemony's most important planets. Millions of formerly law-abiding citizens had gone on strike, and with no work to keep them occupied, had flooded out onto the streets, where the treacherous Trotskis and Fisks were waiting to exhort them.

That was when the mass demonstrations began, some of which had evolved into riots, as the Romos and Nerovs tried to disperse the crowds. The riots produced casualties on *both* sides. But when a worker was injured, or killed, rebel leaders referred to that individual as a "victim." Whereas dead Nerovs were hung from lampposts and their dead bodies pelted with rocks.

Of course, Antonio knew some of that treatment was due to the fact that so many Nerovs had participated in the death squads his "brother" Pietro had conceived of as a way to "keep the lid on." The strategy had been successful to some extent. Except that now, in the wake of all that had taken place, Antonio had come to realize that it had been a mistake to push the discontent deeper underground, where it could fester and spread. It was a key lesson but one that had come too late.

The mood within the heavily secured Emergency Operations Center was somber, which made sense given the nature of the data that continued to stream in, and what Antonio could see with his own eyes as he sat down between his brothers. Even though Marcus had recently been the recipient of new lab-grown lungs, he was having trouble with them for psychological reasons, and couldn't stop coughing. And, in spite of all that was at risk, Pietro came across as bored. "Okay," Antonio began. "What have we got?"

The briefer was a social engineer named Santo-212. "The situation remains critical," the Santo said, "as you can see from the incoming video."

The curvilinear walls were covered with a mosaic of video screens, *hundreds* of them, most of which bore bad news. Everywhere Antonio looked, he could see demonstrators on the move, bodies lying in the streets, and every kind of chaos. "That much is obvious," the Alpha Clone said impatiently. "The question is what, if anything, can be done about it? Should we bring the Seebos in to restore order?"

Santo-212 was a handsome man with black hair, large, expressive eyes, and an unwrinkled countenance. Up until then his entire life had been dedicated to keeping everything the way it was, even though instability had been introduced into the system by the founder herself, as a way to prevent the perfect society from becoming overly complacent. "No, sir," the social engineer replied confidently. "Though excellent warriors, the Seebos feel an ingrained loyalty to Hegemony as a whole, rather than to its leadership as individuals. Which means any attempt to use them against the general population could have unpredictable results. In fact, depending on circumstances, they could turn *against* the government."

"All right, then what would you suggest?" Pietro wanted to know.

"I have a plan, sir," Santo answered eagerly. "And it starts *here!*"

The social engineer pushed a button on a remote, and the picture on the largest screen dissolved from a demonstration on the far side of Alpha-001 to a shot of Bio-Storage Building 516. Like his brothers, Antonio was well acquainted with both the structure, and its importance. The low one-story building had been attacked more than once over the last few days, and as an airborne surveillance camera circled 516, the Alpha Clones could see that hundreds of unrecovered bodies lay in the streets around the repository. Some wore uniforms, but most were dressed in civilian attire. The corpses had begun to decay and were covered with brown rot birds. Most of the scavengers had already eaten their fill, and could barely lift off as the flying camera interrupted their feast.

And there, at the very center of the grisly tableau, was the building itself. Because of its symbolic importance, 516 occupied an open area, far enough away from other buildings so that the police had been unable to fire down onto it, or advance using surrounding structures for cover. The southwestern corner of the repository had been blackened by fire. Every exposed surface was riddled with bullet holes and a wrecked assault boat could be seen on top of the much-disputed roof. "The revolution started in Building 516, Santo added grimly. "And, based on what we've been able to learn, rebel leader Trotski-Four is still there, along with a force of two dozen other criminals. I propose that we launch a final attack on the building and either take this Trotski prisoner or kill him. The assault will be televised, and once the disaffected workers see their leader go down, the uprising will end."

Marcus started to speak, paused to cough, and held up a hand. Finally, when the coughing fit was over, the Alpha Clone managed to get the words out. "And what about other leaders? Need I remind you that all of the Trotskis look alike?"

"There were only 1,112 at the beginning of the uprising," Santo replied confidently, "and according to the statistics maintained by my department, 998 of them have been killed over the past few days. That leaves only 114 individuals to deal with. And, because 56 of them are in prison, that takes us down to a pool of only 58 people, 52 of whom are living on planets other than this one."

"But what about further damage to the facility?" Pietro wanted to know. "As well as the DNA stored there?"

"That's a possibility," Santo admitted soberly. "Especially if the rebels carry out their threats to deactivate the freezers. But the backup facility on Alpha-002 is being guarded by Romos—so the lines are secure."

There was a long moment of silence after that, as everyone looked toward Antonio and waited to see what he would say. The Alpha Clone stared at the image up on the screen as he wrestled with the variables. Would the proposal work? And even if it did, would the additional deaths be worth it? Because even though the original Antonio and he were different people, both had the same DNA and common tendencies. One of which was a genuine affection for the people they were supposed to lead.

But in the final analysis, order was superior to chaos, or so it seemed to Antonio. "I say, 'yes,'" the Alpha Clone announced. "But I sense we're at a tipping point, a moment when either side could win. So this had better work."

"It will," Santo said confidently. "Just leave everything to me."

Having successfully negotiated the military alliance on Alpha-001, and been caught there when the Ramanthians invaded Earth, Nankool and his staff were preparing to depart for Algeron when the revolution began. A development that was none of their business in one way, but all-important in another, because the Hegemony wasn't going to be much of an ally unless the government was stable. So, over the objections of his security people, Nankool insisted on staying a few more days in hopes that the situation would stabilize. But now, as the president and his staff sat among dozens of half-packed cargo modules, even *more* bad news was in the offing.

And, like it or not, Military Chief of Staff Bill Booly was the person who was forced to deliver it. The legionnaire had returned from Gamma-014 only the day before, and looked the way he felt, which was exhausted. Those present included the undersecretary of defense, Zimmer, the assistant secretary of state, Tumbo, and the Confederacy's ambassador to the Hegemony, Marcy Cowles. All of them listened intently as Booly spoke.

"A report from General Kobbi just arrived from Gamma-014," the military officer said glumly. "General-453 successfully led allied forces up over a strategic mountain pass. But, while attacking a city called Yal-Am, they ran into a trap. Unbeknownst to General-453, General Akoto had a reserve of some ten thousand troops hidden in caverns under Yal-Am, and as our forces started to enter the city, the chits boiled up out of the ground. General-453 is missing in action, and assumed to be dead, while what remains of our army is retreating to the west with the Ramanthians in hot pursuit."

"But how can that be?" Nankool demanded incredulously, "We own the sky! Surely our ships can pound the bugs to paste!"

"I'm afraid things have changed," Booly reported grimly. "You'll recall that once Gamma-014 had been secured, we withdrew most of our ships to protect the inner planets, and left only a handful in orbit around 014. So, when a Ramanthian battle group dropped hyper about twenty hours ago, our ships were outnumbered two to one. Although they were able to inflict significant casualties on the bugs, there was never any doubt as to the eventual outcome, and the surviving vessels were forced to withdraw into hyperspace or face certain annihilation."

The news elicited a chorus of dismayed comments and some heartfelt sobs as the reality of the situation began to sink in. "So it was timed?" Zimmer inquired, her eyes bright with anger.

"Yes," Booly confirmed. "As General Akoto's troops came up out of the ground in Yal-Am, the Ramanthian ships were dropping hyper."

"That kind of coordination would have been impossible prior to the advent of hypercom technology," Nankool observed darkly. "It seems as if the bastards are always one step ahead of us."

"So what's going to happen to our troops?" Tumbo wanted to know. He was a burly man, with close-cropped gray hair, and a broad moonlike face. Everyone present knew that one of his sons was a major in the Marine Corps. Presently on Gamma-014—and right in the thick of it.

"They're cut off," Booly answered grimly. "And we lack the means to reinforce them quickly enough to prevent what will almost certainly be a slaughter if they are forced to surrender."

Nankool nodded. He had firsthand knowledge of what could happen to those who surrendered. "We can't abandon them," the politician said steadfastly. "I won't allow it."

"So, what's the solution?" Cowles inquired hopefully.

"The Ramanthians made effective use of hypercom technology, and so can we," Booly replied. "All of you are acquainted with my wife, Maylo Chien-Chu, and her company. If you approve, I'm going to ask Maylo to coordinate an effort in which civilian boats and ships will land on Gamma-014 and evacuate our forces. Anything that has both a hyperdrive and a willing owner will be pressed into service."

"But they'll be slaughtered!" Cowles objected.

"Some will be," Booly admitted sadly. "But, if there's enough ships, and they drop hyper about the same time, the bugs won't have enough resources to chase all of them."

There was a long silence as the group contemplated the general's words. It was Nankool who spoke first. "It's a desperate strategy, but unless one of you has a better alternative, then we'll have to go for it." There was no response, which caused Nankool to nod. "That's what I thought. . . . General, if you would be so kind as to contact your wife, the government would be most grateful."

"I will," Booly promised. "And we'll work out the details as quickly possible."

There might have been more discussion, except that the door to the conference room slammed open at that point, and Christine Vanderveen attempted to enter. Two members of the president's security detail grabbed the diplomat, and were about to hustle the young woman back outside, when Nankool spotted the familiar face. "Christine? Is that *you*?"

"Yes, it is," Vanderveen replied firmly, as the security operatives were forced to let go of her arms. "I'm sorry to interrupt your meeting, sir, but it's very important."

"It had better be," Nankool said grimly. "It turns out that you were correct about the possibility of a revolt, but that doesn't make up for the fact you went AWOL, and entered into unauthorized negotiations with a group of people who are trying to overthrow a legally constituted government."

Most of the officials agreed and said as much. "That's right," one of them commented. "Who does she think she is?" another wanted to know. "The president should bring charges against her," a third put in, as the wayward diplomat made her way to the front of the room.

Vanderveen's appearance was anything but professional. Her hair was matted, her face was covered with grime, and her clothes were caked with dried blood. *Other* people's blood for the most part—acquired while working in the makeshift aid station inside Building-516. But some of the crusty matter belonged to her as evidenced by the battle dressing wrapped around the young woman's right biceps as she turned to face the president and his staff. "I don't blame you for being angry," the FSO-2 said contritely. "But desperate times call for desperate measures. And, with all due respect, Mr. President, what many considered to be a legally constituted government was overthrown in order to make way for the Confederacy!"

"She has you there!" Zimmer put in lightly, and that elicited some appreciative chuckles.

"And I didn't negotiate with the rebels," Vanderveen put in carefully. "All I did was offer myself as a point of contact, a person who could carry a message to the Confederacy when and if the time was right. And that's why I'm here."

"All right," Nankool said wearily. "Say your piece."

Vanderveen glanced at her wrist term. "The rebels will announce a new government in one hour and forty-six minutes. The offer I brought earlier still stands. *If* you recognize the new government as legitimate, the provisional leadership will agree to *full* membership in the Confederacy, and place the Hegemony's military under centralized command. *Your* command."

"That could make a *big* difference," Undersecretary of Defense Zimmer put in. "Our generals counseled against fighting a winter campaign on Gamma-014, General-453 ignored them, and now look where we are! We *need* the Seebos. And the shipbuilding capacity that the Hegemony has."

"That's all very nice," Ambassador Cowles put in cynically. "But what if the rebel leaders get killed in the next hour or so? Or, they make their announcement, and the population fails to respond? Some sort of alliance is better than none, and if you come out for the rebels only to see them go down, we'll wind up with nothing. Or, worse yet, a *new* enemy! Because at that point the Alpha Clones could become so angry they would be tempted to cut a deal with the bugs."

It was a danger, a very *real* danger, and everyone in the

room knew it. Even FSO-2 Vanderveen. Nankool looked from face to face, made a fateful decision, and opened his mouth to speak.

The sky was clear, the air was still, and it was hot. Sirens could be heard in the distance, as the badly overtaxed Romos rushed to cope with still another demonstration. But the Bio-Security Building was surrounded by a cocoon of silence until a long string of airborne surveillance cams snaked out of the city beyond and began to circle 516 like a necklace of black pearls. Taken together, they generated a loud *humming* noise that caused a tremendous flutter of wings as hundreds of rot birds left the bodies they had been perched on and took to the air. *Don't go far,* Alan thought to himself, as the scavengers lifted off. *There will be more to eat soon.*

"Okay," Fisk-Five said, as he aimed a small handheld camera at the rebel's face. "Say what you've got to say—and hurry up! We don't have much time."

The government had done everything possible to keep the rebels off the main com channels, but that was hard to do, so long as all the technicians continued to side with the rebels. "My fellow citizens," the rebel began. "My clone name is Trotski-Four. But my *new* name is Alan Free-man. As I speak to you, the forces of oppression are preparing to attack Bio-Storage Building 516. If the Alpha Clones are successful in their efforts to kill, and thereby silence us, they will insist that they did so in an effort to protect *you*. But what they are really trying to protect is the status quo, which is to say *their* power, so they can pass it along to replicas of themselves. Not power conferred on them by the people, but power they are born to by virtue of a plan, handed down to them from a dead scientist, which no one is allowed to change.

"Well," Alan said, as he stared into the camera. "If you're happy with things as they are—then this is nothing more than a day off from work. But if you, like so many others, would like the freedom to choose another line of work, or to have a sexual relationship, or to produce natural children, then take to the streets and support the new Clone Republic! A provisional government, led by me, will prepare the way for a constitutional democracy, which will take over one year from today.

"But in order to accomplish that, it will be necessary to show the Alpha Clones that the new government has the support of the people," Alan said urgently. "So take control of your lives! Be whatever you want to be! And demonstrate your power by continuing to strike until a member of the provisional government announces some sort of settlement. At which point I want you to remember that we are at war with the Ramanthians. Our citizens are fighting on distant planets, and it's important to support that effort by running our factories and other institutions as efficiently as possible. And that means it will be necessary for most of us to remain in our present functions during the ensuing transition period. Thank you for your support," Alan finished. "And let this be our first day of freedom!"

"Good job," Fisk-Five said, as he lowered the camera. "But I think we just ran out of time. Look at that!"

Alan turned to look in the direction of the other man's pointing finger. Though not an expert on military spacecraft, the clone didn't have to be to know that the ship coming their way was *big*! At least twenty times larger than the police assault boats that were circling the building. And, given the weaponry the warship carried, it could destroy both Building 516 and half the city if those on board chose to do so. That suggested the Alpha Clones were prepared to sacrifice the DNA repository in order to kill the rebel leaders.

The ship was only two hundred feet off the ground, which made it all the more impressive, as repellers *roared* and the destroyer escort drifted in over the building. The downdraft blew debris every which way, and the air was thick with acrid stench of ozone, as a huge shadow fell over Alan. The rebel thought about running, knew it would be pointless, and saw Fisk-Five aim the camera at him. To record how brave he was? Or document the end of the Clone Republic? There was no way to know.

As Alan waited to die, one of the Crowleys pointed upwards. Her hair was flying, and it was necessary to yell in order to make herself heard. "Look at those markings!" the woman said. "That ship belongs to the Confederacy!"

As an assault boat parted company with the larger vessel, the rebel realized the woman was correct! Did that mean what he thought it meant? Alan felt a sudden surge of hope as the assault boat circled the building and came in for a perfect landing. A hatch opened, stairs were deployed, and a familiar figure appeared. But rather than rush forward and embrace him, Foreign Service Officer-2 Christine Vanderveen took up a position next to the stairs, as a *second* woman appeared. And it was *she* who came forward to shake hands with Alan Freeman.

"Hello," the woman in the tidy business suit said. "My name is Marcy Cowles. *Ambassador* Marcy Cowles. On behalf of President Nankool, and the Confederacy, please allow me to be the first to congratulate you and your fellow freedom fighters on the creation of a new government. I know you're busy, but considering the circumstances, this might be a good time to have lunch with the president."

Alan turned to eye his surroundings. Once the warship arrived, the police boats had been forced to back off. He could imagine the frantic radio traffic between them and various government agencies as hundreds of bureaucrats were forced to confront a problem the founder hadn't prepared them for. He and his fellow revolutionaries were safe for the moment, but that would end once the ship left, so the choice was really no choice at all. "Are my friends invited as well?" the rebel wanted to know.

"Of course," Cowles responded blandly. "We look forward to meeting *all* of the brave freedom fighters who will go down in the annals of history as having founded the Clone Republic."

Alan looked over to where Vanderveen was standing. Her

blond hair was whipping in the downdraft from the warship overhead, and despite the condition of her filthy clothes, she looked regal somehow. He wanted to take her into his arms, but knew he couldn't, and nodded instead. "Thank you," Alan said, as he turned back to Cowles. "It would be an honor to join the president for lunch."

There was a sense of purpose within the conference room, as Booly made arrangements to evacuate the president under fire should that become necessary, and senior staff members took furious, and in some cases, frantic calls from individuals inside the Hegemony's government. It quickly became apparent that while some of the clones were trying to hold things together, others had capitulated, and were seeking asylum within the Confederacy.

That left Nankool and a handful of others to watch video provided by both the rebels *and* the Confederacy's destroyer escort, as Cowles, Vanderveen, and the rebel leaders entered the assault boat and were subsequently taken aboard the warship that was hovering above. That left the Romos and Nerovs to reoccupy an empty building. A victory of sorts, but not the one the Alpha Clones had been expecting, as their carefully organized society crumbled around them. The process continued to accelerate as a *new* video clip appeared on the rebel-dominated com channels.

"There it is!" an aide said excitedly, and Nankool turned to look at a screen off to his right. "Good afternoon," the digitized version of himself said. "My name is Marcott Nankool and, as president of the Confederacy of Sentient Beings, it is my pleasure to formally recognize the Clone Republic, and assure its citizens that not only will the existing military alliance remain in force so far as we're concerned, but we look forward to having even closer ties with your democracy during the days ahead. I will meet with Provisional President Alan Freeman within the next few hours and provide him with whatever assistance he requires." The last phrase was directed more at the Alpha Clones, than the citizenry, and amounted to a thinly veiled threat. Now that the Confederacy was committed, it couldn't back off, even if that meant a clash with the police.

Nankool watched his likeness smile—and knew what was coming. "For all too long the two major branches of humanity have been divided by a social system that could deliver peace and prosperity, but at a very steep price, that being the loss of personal liberties. Foremost among them was the right to vote, the right to choose a profession, and the right to procreate. Congratulations on the acquisition of your newfound freedom—and the responsibility it entails! Because, like us, *you* are at war. . . . And the future of *all* humanity is at stake, along with the well-being of other sentients as well. It will be up to you to chart the exact path that your new government will take, but the Confederacy will be there to help in any way it can, and to celebrate your accomplishments. Thank you." And with that the screen faded to black.

Meanwhile, even as Nankool's message was delivered to the population, half a dozen protest groups converged on the building that housed the Chamber of Governmental Process and became a single mob. That was when Alpha Clones Antonio and Pietro boarded a shuttle, and were transported up into orbit, where the admiral in command of the Hegemony's home fleet agreed to take them aboard his flagship, but only as prisoners. Not because he hated them, but out of fear of the political consequences, were the military to take sides.

As that was taking place, Marcus went out to confront the mob. It was common knowledge that an earlier version of himself had not only fallen in love with a free breeder, but produced a child by her, believing the birth would trigger systemic changes within the Hegemony. But that Marcus had been wrong. The other Alpha Clones had been able to keep things under control, eventually forcing the visionary and his family into exile, thereby leaving all the existing problems unresolved.

But the historical connection meant that would-be free breeders had come to see any Marcus as a potential ally even though the current replicant had been a faithful and unwavering enforcer of the founder's plan. For that reason, Marcus believed that the workers would listen to his pleas to stop rioting and return to work. So even as his clone brothers fled, he went out to greet the riotous mob. There were hundreds of them, representing dozens of lines, all mixed together. And it was an ugly sight to behold.

The workers could hardly believe their eyes at first, as one of the normally reclusive Alpha Clones came out to speak with them, and did so without any Nerovs to guard him. That was why the crowd actually let him speak a few paragraphs of what they saw as government mumbo jumbo before surging forward.

In a bloody denouement that was televised for all to see, the workers tore the Alpha Clone apart. And that, in the judgment of the historians who would write about the revolution later, was the moment when the old government truly came to an end.

Christine Vanderveen was naked. More than four hours had passed since Antonio and Pietro had fled, Marcus had been killed, and Alan finished his lunch with Nankool. The Clone Republic was a wildly chaotic reality by then, and the new president knew there were thousands of things that he should do, and eventually would do, but only after what he *wanted* to do—which was to spend some quality time with Christine Vanderveen. A private meeting which, thanks to his new title, he'd been able to insist upon.

And now, as the blond encircled him, Alan was lost in the smell of her freshly washed hair, the softness of her lips, and the urgent thrust of her hips. He wanted to please her, but knew very little about how to do so, and feared he would lose control.

But Vanderveen's passion was a match for his, and it wasn't long before the pace of their lovemaking quickened, and both were carried away by successive waves of pleasure that seemed to last forever. And left both lovers wonderfully exhausted.

Alan said things he had never said before, whispering them into her sweat-glazed skin, rubbing them into her pores. And Vanderveen answered, though not with words, because she knew things her lover didn't. She knew the Clone Republic's interim president would be required to travel to other planets, where he would meet hundreds if not thousands of attractive women. More than that, she knew that in spite of the chemistry between them, and the extent to which she admired Alan, there was another. The only man who could truly fill the emptiness inside her, the man with whom so much had already been shared, and the man she had been thinking about when the pleasure had been at its very peak.

Alan fell asleep, and had every right to, given all he'd been through during the previous week. That made leaving easier. Eventually, when the president of the Clone Republic awoke, he would find the note:

My dearest Alan,

Your newfound freedom will bring many challenges, including those posed by the human heart. Mine is filled with gratitude for the time we spent together, as well as admiration for the man that you are, and will be in the future.

But there is another. . . . A man to whom promises were made—and for whom I must wait. But I will remember. . . . Not with shame, but with joy, and the sure knowledge that you will find your way to happiness.

Affectionately,
Christine

16

However skillful the maneuvers in retreat, it will always weaken the morale of an army. . . . Besides, retreats always cost more men and material than the most bloody engagements; with this difference, that in battle the enemy's loss is nearly equal to your own—whereas in a retreat the loss is on your side only.

—Napoleon I
Maxims of War
Standard year 1831

PLANET GAMMA-014, THE CLONE REPUBLIC

Snow was falling, the air was bitingly cold, and the steady *rumble* of mortar and artillery fire could be heard as elements of the Legion's 1st REC, the 3rd Marine Division, and the Clone Republic's 7th Infantry Brigade fought to hold the bugs back. The effort had been successful largely because the trenches intended to bar entry to Yal-Am also made it difficult to leave, so long as they were occupied. But allied forces wouldn't be able to hold the chits back for long, something Legion General Mortimer Kobbi was painfully aware of, as a ragtag collection of battle-weary officers filed into the clone-built structure next to Yal-Am's stone quarry.

There was no heat and the big 155mm-sized hole in the roof allowed snow to filter down into a space that was half-filled with slabs of frosty granite, some of which might very well become grave markers eventually. But the walls were mostly intact, blocking the wind. That, plus four blazing burn barrels, gave the impression, if not the reality, of warmth as the inside temperature hovered at twenty-six degrees.

Rows of makeshift benches offered the attendees a place to sit, and many were so weary that they took advantage of the opportunity to rest even though they knew it was important to keep moving. The officers were a motley group representing the Legion, Marine Corps, *and* the new Clone Republic, which many of them had only recently heard about. And, because of all the casualties suffered during the last few days, Kobbi noticed that captains, lieutenants, and even sergeants had been sent in place of the generals, colonels, and majors who would normally participate in a command briefing.

As the last of them entered, Kobbi was pleased to see that both Santana and Quinlan had survived, the first being a good deal more useful than the second. Although Quinlan had led his troops bravely, if not brilliantly, which was more than some allied officers could claim. By virtue of a small miracle, one of the Legion's supply sergeants had conjured up thermos bottles filled with hot coffee and a "secret ingredient" that was immediately recognizable as rum. Most of the officers carried fire-blackened cups that were critical to a quick "brew-up," and hurried to produce them, as the much-abused aluminum bottles made the rounds. The rest were supplied with mugs, some of which were of Ramanthian manufacture, but still serviceable.

Santana took a tentative sip, and having found the concoction to his liking, took another. A sensation of warmth flooded his belly and seemed to spread out from there. The company, minus a number of casualties, was waiting about a mile away. Zolkin had orders to get a hot meal into the bio bods, and carry out cold-weather maintenance on the cyborgs, while Dietrich went out to scrounge whatever supplies he could. Alpha Company had burned through lots of everything during the past few days and was going to need a lot of ammo, food, and medical supplies if they were going to make it back over the pass. Which, based on the cavalry

officer's limited knowledge of the situation, was what everyone would have to do. Some fly-forms were still in service,
but they were being used to air evac the wounded, and even
that was iffy.

"All right," General Kobbi began, as he stepped up onto
a platform that consisted of two side-by-side cargo modules.
"I know you want to rejoin your outfits, so I'll keep this
meeting brief. First, in case there's someone who hasn't
heard, General-453 is missing in action, and presumed dead.
And yes, the man who led the advance on Yal-Am was a person other than Four-fifty-three."

That announcement produced a good deal of buzz—
since it served to confirm some of the rumors that had been
floating around. Santana felt the first stirrings of concern
when he saw that Kobbi was looking directly at *him*. The
general wouldn't send him after Colonel Six right in the
middle of a full-scale retreat. Would he?

The question went unanswered as the briefing continued.
"So as the most senior officer still on his feet, I assumed command," Kobbi said grimly. "Unless there's another officer
who wants the job—because they sure as hell can have it!"

That generated a chorus of chuckles from the officers
who, better than anyone else, knew how difficult the retreat
was going to be.

"Most of you know that we were suckered," Kobbi said
matter-of-factly. "And not once—but twice! Because even as
the chits boiled up out of the ground in Yal-Am, a Ramanthian battle group dropped out of hyperspace, and tore into
our ships. The swabbies bloodied the Ramanthian beaks
pretty good, but took a lot of casualties, and were forced out
of the system. That left the chits holding the high ground,
which means our line of retreat has been severed, and we're
momentarily cut off. Worse yet, I'm told that thousands of
Ramanthians have filtered in behind us, which means they're
planning to inflict a lot of casualties as we withdraw."

The report produced a symphony of groans, followed by
a more upbeat assessment from a Hudathan major. "Good!"

the legionnaire rumbled. "Now we've got 'em where we want 'em!" Santana laughed along with the others, but knew the reality of it wouldn't be funny, as thousands of soldiers and civilians started the long cold trek up over Tow-Tok Pass.

Kobbi marveled at the fact that the men and women in front of him could still laugh and waited for the noise to die down before picking up where he had left off. "But, thanks to some bug technology, we have real-time communications with General Booly, and he's working on a plan to pull us out. I can't go into the details yet, lest one of us be captured, but I want you to know there's hope. And I want you to communicate that to your troops. But before we can take advantage of the general's plan, we need to get our people over the mountains. So focus your efforts on that. Be sure to get your marching orders from Lieutenant Giles as you leave. And *obey* them. Because if we're going to retreat—then it's going to be the best damned retreat that anyone ever saw! *Do you read me?*"

The answer was a ragged, *"Yes, sir!"*

"Good," Kobbi said. "Now, one more thing before you go out to play in the snow. . . . As many of you have heard, there has been a change of government on Alpha-001. Simply put the Alpha Clones are out—and something called the Clone Republic is in. The new government is going to be a democracy, or so I'm told, and the existing alliance remains in effect. Which, all things considered, is all we need to know!

"All right," the general finished. "Get your orders—and get in gear. I'll be checking in with each one of you during the coming days. Captain Santana—a moment of your time please."

Quinlan frowned. Kobbi's habit of using Alpha Company to run errands for him was starting to grate. Especially now that more than a third of his battalion was either dead or wounded. But there wasn't much Quinlan could do about it except shoot Santana an annoyed look before following the others toward the door.

Santana drank the last of his coffee and rum before folding the handle into the center of the mug and tucking the implement away. Kobbi had stepped off the cargo modules by then, and had just completed a conversation with a major, when Santana made his way forward. Kobbi nodded as they came face-to-face. "So, have you ever seen a bigger screwup than this one?" he inquired lightly.

"No, sir," Santana replied honestly, as his breath fogged the air. "I can't say that I have."

"Nor have I," Kobbi said grimly. "Not even on Savas. But, as we haul our miserable asses back into space, I'd feel a whole lot better if we took Colonel Six along with us. Or, failing that, if we buried the treacherous piece of shit right here. Am I clear?"

The cavalry officer found himself staring into a pair of very dark eyes. They looked like gun barrels. "Yes, sir. You are."

"Good," Kobbi said. "Six and his Seebos are long gone. I want you to pull out before the others, head up the road, and catch the bastard. He has a lot to account for, including dead marines, dead civilians, and a couple of hostages. Not to mention his impersonation of General-453. Although I must admit that I liked *his* version of the general a lot better than the real thing! If it hadn't been for the reserves Akoto had tucked away, we would have kicked their pointy asses.

"Anyway, see what you can do, but don't stray too far. . . . Because when I call for the evac to begin, time will be short—and there won't be any second chances. See Giles on your way out. He'll give you some written orders and a high-priority pass signed by me. Show it to any sonofabitch stupid enough to try and get in your way."

Santana knew that the first troops to go back up the road were likely to run into some of the stiffest resistance, but there wasn't anything he could do other than nod, and say, "Yes, sir. We'll do our best."

Kobbi grinned. "See that you do. . . . Dismissed."

Once again Santana felt grateful for the heat that Deker gave off—even if it did leave his ass out in the cold. The two of them were standing next to the road as Alpha Company began the long journey to the west. Lieutenant Amoyo, Sergeant Matos, Sergeant Telveca, Corporal Han, and Private Xiong had all been killed in action during the assault on Yal-Am. In the wake of the battle, Hoyt-11,791 and fifteen of her thirty-one CVA conscripts had attached themselves to Alpha Company, along with a squad of stray marines, and a Seebo transportation platoon that still had two half-tracks. The vehicles would be extremely useful if the company was going to catch up with Colonel Six.

Lieutenant Mitch Millar passed first, began to pick up speed, and disappeared beyond the veil of softly falling snow. His orders were to scout many miles ahead, keep his sensors peeled for any sign of Ramanthian troops, and find Six. It was something the recon ball was uniquely qualified to do.

Next came Sergeant Suresee Fareye, and his T-2, Private Ka Nhan, who were also acting as scouts and would try to give advance warning of potential ambush sites, road damage, and anything else Santana would want to know about.

The scouts were followed by Master Sergeant Dice Dietrich on Corporal Stacy Subee, and the first squad of the first platoon which, due to casualties, was the *only* squad in the first platoon. It consisted of four bio bods and five Trooper IIs in addition to Dietrich and Subee.

Then came the reassuring *whine-thud* of heavy footsteps as Private Lupo, the company's sole remaining quad, lumbered up the road. The marines were safely tucked inside his cargo compartment, where Santana imagined some were starting to feel the first symptoms of motion sickness. But it beat the hell out of walking—and the officer knew he wouldn't hear any complaints.

The huge cyborg was followed by the half-tracks, loaded not only with supplies, but with Hoyt and her CVA troops. Lieutenant Gregory Zolkin and Sergeant Mark Tebo were right behind them, followed by what remained of the second platoon. Sergeant Jose Ramos was in charge of the rearguard, which included two bio bods, and three reasonably intact T-2s. That force should be strong enough to counter anything that could catch up with the fast-moving company from behind.

It wasn't perfect. Santana knew that. But it was the best he could do. As Ramos marched past, the company commander sent Deker forward on the first of what would eventually be dozens of trips up and down the length of the column. Because that was the only way to enforce the proper intervals, make sure that people were alert, and keep morale up.

Even though the company had traveled the wintry road before, it looked entirely different now, partly because they were going the other way and partly because of the additional snow. And as more of the white stuff continued to fall, visibility was limited to a hundred feet or so, and the monotony of it caused Santana's thoughts to drift. First to Vanderveen, who might be anywhere, then to her mother, who was trapped on Earth. *If* Margaret Vanderveen was still alive—which seemed doubtful.

A couple of hours passed like that, with Santana battling to maintain his focus, while the company covered fifty miles or so. They were up off the flatland and well into the foothills, when the attack came. It was a crude affair, conceived by a group of desperate CVAs, who, lacking any sort of heavy weaponry, managed to roll half a dozen boulders down a steep embankment. The plan was to disable one or more of the vehicles in order to obtain food and ammo. The low-tech ambush had gone undetected because the clones were well hidden. The boulder barrage was followed by the insistent *pop, pop, pop* of small-arms fire as a fusillade of poorly aimed bullets swept the surface of the snow-covered road. But, crude or not, the attack was successful in that one of the bouncing rocks killed Private Sig Gomyo, and disabled T-2 Private Rin Ibo, before it jumped into the air and continued downslope.

The response was swift and uncompromising. A force of enraged T-2s ran uphill, located the CVA bandits in among the rocks, and put them down. Dietrich, who was right behind them, was forced to yell, "Cease firing!" over and over in order to conserve ammunition as some of the legionnaires continued to fire on dead bodies.

One of the bio bods pulled Ibo's brain box, and carried it into Lupo's cargo bay, where the cyborg was hooked up to the quad's life-support system. The entire incident was not only stupid and unnecessary, but a measure of how desperate some of the allied forces were. It was another danger for Santana to worry about.

There was darned little chance that anyone would collect Gomyo's body, not in the midst of a full-scale retreat, so like thousands of legionnaires before him, the bio bod was lowered into a shallow, unmarked grave. The burial was followed by a quick prayer and a flurry of orders as the company resumed its journey. The *other* corpses, those belonging to the clones who had been so thoughtlessly sent to Gamma-014, would soon be covered with a shroud of white snow.

Two hours later the column had covered another fifty miles and it was getting late. Since it wouldn't be prudent to travel at night, Santana wanted to set up a defensive perimeter while there was light left to see by. So when Fareye alerted him to a short side road that led out along the top of a ridge to a spacious lookout spot, the cavalry officer seized on the opportunity. While it might be necessary to camp on the surface of the road before the journey was over, Santana had no desire to do so any earlier than was absolutely necessary. Such spots were hard to defend, and there was no way to know what might come down the road in the middle of the night.

The company followed Fareye and Nhan out along a snow-covered two-lane road onto the hilltop beyond. As Zolkin and Dietrich began to organize the unit's defenses, Santana took a stroll around the perimeter. The snow was unmarked by footprints. That was good. But the slopes that fanned out away from the lookout point weren't very steep, and that was bad. The legionnaire knew from previous experience that the bugs could advance over that sort of terrain at night and were brave enough to do so. Lacking crab mines, all Santana could do was position T-2s around the perimeter, park the quad and the tracks in the middle of the turnaround, and establish an outpost (OP) at the point where the side road intersected the highway. Because the last thing they wanted was to be cut off from the main thoroughfare and isolated on a vulnerable hilltop.

As the temperature continued to drop, and darkness crept in all around them, the men and women of Alpha Company prepared to eat, sleep, and carry out some much-needed maintenance. Given their circumstances it was all they could hope for.

Meanwhile, a hundred miles to the west, Lieutenant Millar was stalking his prey. It was something the cyborg was uniquely qualified to do because he could fly, "see" in the dark, and mask himself electronically. The capabilities that had already enabled the scout to spot three groups of Ramanthians, all hidden within striking distance of the highway, waiting for an opportunity to attack. That was interesting, and well worth reporting, but secondary to his primary mission to find Colonel Six and his band of renegades.

But the clones had a tremendous head start—and Millar had orders to stay within a hundred miles of Alpha Company. So, once darkness descended, and the cyborg found himself a *hundred and twenty miles* out, he was about to turn and head back when there was a brief burst of static, followed by a low-power radio transmission. The exchange was brief, but sufficient to pique the cyborg's curiosity, and trigger a full spectrum sweep of *all* the possible frequencies. That effort revealed more activity, which the recon ball traced to what had been a power transfer station, but was now little more than a pile of bombed-out rubble.

A *useful* pile of rubble, however, because as Millar got closer, it soon became clear that he was onto something. Even though it was dark, and the scout had to rely on infrared imaging, it quickly became apparent that the ruins were being used by a company-sized force of humans.

But were they the humans he was looking for? That was by no means certain given the fact that dozens of military units were strung out along the highway. In fact it was quite possible that this one had been on its way to join allied forces in Yal-Am when the Ramanthian poop hit the proverbial fan.

In order to find out who he was dealing with, Millar began to work himself into the dimly lit ruins, being careful to remain in the shadows whenever possible. There were sentries, but none of them saw the recon ball as Millar passed over their heads.

Having penetrated the inner part of the encampment, Millar caught glimpses of a heat source so intense it had to be a fire, and continued to work his way inwards until he found himself within three standing walls. There was no roof, but the walls served the soldiers as a windbreak, which had been put to good use. Viewed from the cyborg's perspective, eight man-shaped heat blobs were seated around a much brighter heat blob, eating their dinners and talking. All Millar had to do was back his spherical body into a convenient hole and listen in on the conversation below. It quickly became obvious that the humans were clones, who by some means unknown knew about the revolution and were trying to deal with it.

"I don't know," the first soldier said doubtfully. "The founder's plan worked for all these years. Why change it?"

"Because we don't have any say," the second man replied critically. "And if we're going to do all the fighting, we should have a say."

"But what if no one wants to do the fighting?" the first Seebo wanted to know. "What then?"

"Maybe the Santos will want to fight," the third clone put in.

That caused laughter all around. "That'll be the day!" the second Seebo exclaimed. "All they do is go to meetings and boss everyone around."

There was a moment of silence as one of the men put a piece of wood on the fire. A column of sparks shot up into the air and spiraled away. "I'll tell you one thing," the fifth soldier said. "The old man has the right idea. . . . *He* won't be cold tonight."

"That's for sure!" number three said enthusiastically. "How would you like some of *that*? Every single one of us will be free breeders once this is over."

"Odds are that we'll be *dead* once this is over," the fifth man said darkly, as he blew on cold fingers. "General-453 is an idiot."

"*Was* an idiot," the second Seebo said, as he took a sip of coffee. "He's dead by now."

"And a good thing, too," the sixth soldier added. "I wonder what Six is doing?"

"Screwing the doctor's brains out," the fourth man answered cheerfully. "The lucky so and so."

"That would be hypocritical," the first Seebo observed. "Him being a true believer and all."

"Well, you know what they say about the true folk," the seventh clone put in. "They're truly horny!"

That produced gales of laugher and an opportunity for Millar to slip away unnoticed. But not uninformed. Because he not only knew who the clones were—he knew that the female hostage was sleeping with the man who had taken her prisoner! A man who, according to his profile, hated free breeders. Except for *pretty* free breeders. Or so it appeared. But hearing is one thing—and *seeing* is another. So as the snow continued to fall, the recon ball continued to ghost through the ruins, searching for Dr. Kira Kelly.

Kelly was awake—but very uncomfortable. Her bladder was full, so she needed to pee, but was reluctant to leave the relative warmth of the makeshift sleeping bag that she shared with Six. He, in typical male fashion, was not only sound asleep but snoring gently. A quick check with a flashlight revealed that while the tarp over their heads was drooping a bit under the weight of accumulated snow, it was in no danger of collapsing. So there was no need to get up and deal with that.

But the doctor knew she wouldn't be able to get any more rest unless she got up, made her way out of the partially screened "room," and down a short passageway to a freezing-cold closet reserved for her use. Careful to protect the integrity of the air pocket that surrounded Six, the navy officer rolled out from under the blankets and fumbled for her boots. Once those were on, all she had to do was slip her arms into her parka in order to be fully clothed.

Then, with a blob of light from the hand torch to guide her, Kelly made her way back to what had been designated as "the ladies' room." It was a euphemism for a storage closet with a bucket in it. *It isn't fair,* Kelly thought to herself, as she lowered her pants. *Men don't have to do this.*

Three minutes later the officer was busy fastening her parka when a voice came from the darkness three feet away from her. "Excuse me," Millar said softly as he hovered four feet off the floor. "Are you Lieutenant Kira Kelly?"

Kelly reacted with an involuntary jerk and took a full step backwards. "Who are *you?*" the doctor demanded, as her torch came on.

"Turn that thing off!" the recon ball whispered urgently. "Or you'll get me killed!"

Kelly, who had seen the cyborg's markings by that time, did as she was told. The first question to cross her mind, which had to do with whether the recon ball had seen her go to the bathroom, was silly given the circumstances, so she put it aside. "I repeat," Kelly whispered. *"Who are you?"*

"Lieutenant Mitch Millar," came the reply. "I was sent to find you."

Kelly felt her spirits soar only to have them crash again. Here was the rescue that she and Sumi had been hoping for! But what would that mean for Six? Kelly was a doctor, so she was well aware of the fact that even though it isn't logical, some hostages come to have feelings of loyalty toward their captors. Had that happened to her? Yes, the analytical part of her brain said that it had. Did knowing that make her any less concerned for her lover's well being? No, not really. "That's wonderful!" Kelly exclaimed, in what she hoped was a convincing fashion.

"Yes, it is," Millar responded carefully. "Although it's only fair to tell you that the unit I belong to is more than a hundred miles away. It may be a while before we can actually free you."

Kelly felt a sense of relief, knew that was stupid, and silently rebuked herself. "Of course," she said out loud. "I understand."

"Good," the recon ball replied. "How about the *second* hostage? Is he okay?"

Sumi was angry with Kelly for sleeping with Six, the doctor knew that, but saw no reason to discuss it. Not unless she absolutely had to. "Yes," Kelly answered succinctly. "Hospital Corpsman Sumi is fine."

"Excellent," Millar said sincerely. "My CO will be happy to hear it. Here. . . . Take this."

Kelly heard a *whirring* sound as the scout's spherical body extruded a skeletal tool arm. The disk that was held in his grasper was about a quarter of an inch thick and two inches across. "It's a tracker," the cyborg explained, as the woman took the device. "Keep it on your body at all times."

"I will," Kelly promised, as she tucked the disk away. "Thank you."

"Keep my visit to yourself," the scout instructed. "We'll catch up as quickly as we can." Then, having generated no more than a gentle *humming* sound, the recon ball disappeared.

It was pitch-black inside the tiny observation post (OP), the temperature was a face-numbing ten degrees below zero, and more than a thousand Ramanthians were marching along the highway headed east, *toward* the fleeing allies and Yal-Am beyond. The nearest aliens were no more than fifteen feet away, so close Santana could hear the ominous *scrape-thump* of their perfectly synchronized footsteps, the *rattle* of unsecured equipment, and occasional bursts of click-speech as the ever-vigilant noncoms worked to keep the weary soldiers on the move.

More than that, the legionnaire could *smell* the unmistakable mixture of wing wax, chitin polish, and gun oil that was the olfactory hallmark of Ramanthian soldiers everywhere. And by peering out through a hole in the makeshift barricade his company had erected the evening before, the officer could see the enemy formation on his HUD—thanks to the night-vision capability that was built into his helmet. The column was four troopers across and very tight. Tighter than a human formation would be under similar circumstances.

But could the bugs *see* him? Apparently not, given the way they continued to stream past the OP, on their way to a certain confrontation with the lead elements of Kobbi's column. That could be attributed to Santana's having chosen to staff the OP with bio bods, while keeping a quick-reaction force comprised of relatively "hot" cyborgs out on the hilltop, where they could be called upon if necessary. The legionnaire had been summoned by Sergeant Pimm, and the tough no-nonsense marine sergeant had the good sense to keep his jarheads hidden as lead elements of the enemy force trudged past his position.

The question, to Santana's mind at least, was *why* the bugs had been ordered to attack the allied column? Because even though General-453's army had been badly mauled at Yal-Am, they were still capable of defeating a force such as the one in front of him, and rather decisively, too. Unless the real purpose of the impending confrontation was to *stall* the retreating column—which would make sense if Akoto's forces had been unable to overtake the fugitives from the east. Yes, that was logical, and as the last of the bugs shuffled past, Santana gave Pimm a pat on the back. "Well done, Sergeant. I'll send a squad forward to relieve you in about thirty minutes or so. Unless we get new orders. Which wouldn't surprise me."

"We'll be here," the heavily swathed noncom said bleakly, wondering if he would ever be warm again.

Private Ivan Lupo's cargo bay was crammed with sleeping legionnaires, and the hot, muggy air was thick with the stench of unwashed socks, as Santana closed the hatch behind him. There was a communal groan as a blast of frigid air forced its way inside. That was followed by an apology when someone saw who it was, and the officer said, "As you were." It was difficult for the legionnaire to find places to plant his feet without stepping on someone's body as he made his way to the tiny cubicle that was supposed to function as the platoon leader's office in the field. Except that Lieutenant Amoyo was dead and wouldn't be needing it anymore.

The purpose of the unannounced visit was to get on the quad's long-range com set and warn Kobbi. It took the better part of fifteen minutes to talk a succession of protective officers into putting the call through. During that time, Santana was forced to remove layers of clothes in order to deal with what felt like a tropical environment but was actually chilly by normal standards. Finally, a clearly sleepy Kobbi was heard. "This is Six-One. . . . What have you got?"

So Santana told him, and as he did so, the company commander could imagine the look on the little general's face. Because when Kobbi was working a problem, it was like a dog attacking a bone. And, by the time the cavalry officer's report was complete, the general knew what he wanted to do.

Dawn was in the offing as Force Commander Ofay led his troops up a long incline toward the certain glory that lay ahead. Yes, there was danger, and some would fall. But somehow, deep inside, Ofay knew he would be among those who would eventually go home to describe the battle to their admiring mates. Because, from his perspective, that was how life *should* be.

Such thoughts helped warm the soldier, who, being a member of a jungle-evolved species, was not as well equipped to deal with cold weather as a Naa, Hudathan, Thraki, or human would have been. And, Ofay knew that if it hadn't been for the powered warm-suits his troopers wore, they would have been incapacitated within a matter of minutes. Just as so many of the largely improvident animals had been.

Gradually, as daylight filtered down through the clouds, Ofay began to have a better appreciation of the terrain around him. The highway had been engineered to follow the contour of the mountainsides, and having just emerged from a U-shaped curve, was headed higher on a ledge carved from solid rock. That put a cliff to the officer's right, and a drop-off on his left. From his vantage point, Ofay could see that the next right-pincer turn would take his unit around the end of a rocky promontory. The Ramanthian wished he knew what was on the other side of the point, but the cloud cover was blocking orbital surveillance, and his surviving spy-eye was on the blink.

Ofay had scouts, though, both of whom were young enough to fly, so long as they didn't have to carry much gear. So the order went out, and *two* troopers took to the sky and fought to gain altitude. Lung-warmed air jetted away from their beaks, and their wings made a soft *whuffing* sound as the soldiers spiraled steadily upwards. But Ofay, who was still caught up in visions of coming glory, was in too much of a hurry to wait for their reports. Soon, sometime later that day, the War Ofay would collide with animals and hold them. General Akoto would take care of the rest.

The allied column was ten miles long and snaked back through a series of mountain curves, to the point where the rear guard was about to set off some explosives in an effort to block the road and slow their pursuers. The Ramanthians would clear the obstruction of course, but it would take them hours to do so, and hours were precious. Which made the fact that they were standing that much more frustrating.

But General Kobbi was tired of getting his ass kicked. Even though the officer knew the allies were losing the war, he was determined to win a battle. That was why both he and senior members of his staff were at the head of the column staring at two black dots as they topped the promontory ahead. "They sent scouts," Colonel Quinlan commented, as he eyed the airborne Ramanthians. "They know we're here."

The two men were mounted on battle-scarred T-2s. The force around them consisted of thirty-six cyborgs in all, each carrying a heavily armed bio bod, all of whom were combat-ready. Steam rose around them as snowflakes hit warm metal. Half the group had been stripped out of the rear guard, which meant the column would be vulnerable if Akoto came up quickly, but Kobbi was betting on the Legion's ability to engage the force ahead and defeat it quickly. "They know we're here," Kobbi admitted grimly. "But the ugly bastards are still going to die!"

So saying, Kobbi gave a preparatory order, followed by a single word: "Charge!" And, because the legionnaires had been ready for some time by then, they were quick to respond. The width of the highway would allow only five cyborgs to advance in a line abreast. Still, five T-2s supported by an equal number of bio bods represented a lot of firepower, especially when pitted against unsupported infantry.

Ofay knew that, too, and was still in the process of trying to figure out what to do, when a group of murderous cyborgs rounded the promontory ahead and opened fire. They were traveling at about thirty miles per hour by then, and firing every weapon they had. The effect was devastating. Especially since only the first rank of Ofay's troops could fire without hitting the ranks in front of them.

Dozens of Ramanthians fell, cut down by the withering fire, and much to Ofay's horror, the rest began to turn back! They collided with troops to the rear, confusion ensued, and dozens went down. The force commander not only ordered his soldiers to face the enemy, but even went so far as to wade into the mob and shoot two of the retreating troopers. But, rather than restore order as he hoped the punitive measure would, the summary executions caused one of the fear-crazed troopers to shoot Ofay in the face. The projectile blew the back of the force commander's skull out, sprayed blood and brains all over those behind him, and brought Ofay's dreams of glory to an abrupt end.

All constraints having been removed, the badly panicked Ramanthians attempted to flee west. But that was a mistake, because while Ofay's attention was focused on the enemy ahead, Alpha Company had closed in behind them. That, ironically enough, was the fate that General Akoto wanted to impose on the allies.

While Santana didn't have thirty-six T-2s to work with, there was no need to charge, not so long as the bugs were coming toward *him*. And he had a quad, which having already settled over its vulnerable legs, was positioned in the middle of the road with walls of T-2s and bio bods to either side. All of whom opened fire simultaneously.

Even as the chits sought to flee Kobbi and his cyborgs, they were cut to pieces by the force behind them and died in waves. Some staggered like marionettes with palsy as bullets tugged at their bodies. Others were ripped apart by the grenades that Hoyt and her CVAs fired from *behind* the legionnaires and marines. And dozens appeared to melt as bolts of iridescent blue energy plowed bloody holes through the Ramanthian ranks. The only problem was the need to keep their fire down, and on target, lest Alpha Company kill members of Kobbi's force farther up the road.

The slaughter forced the bugs to turn again and run the *other* way, only to suffer the same fate all over again. That's where Quinlan was, right in the thick of it, killing yet another bug for his daughter, when one of the winged scouts landed on his back and went in for the kill. The bug knew he was going to die as he reached forward to jerk the animal's helmet back, but that was fine, so long as he could take a human with him.

Quinlan was reaching back over his shoulders, trying to get a grip on whatever had attached itself to his back, when he saw the sudden flash of steel. That was followed by a burning sensation, an explosion of blood, and a moment of dizziness. Then he was gone.

Kobbi, who was only a dozen feet away, saw the whole thing. He fired a long burst from his CA-10 into the Ramanthian and had the satisfaction of seeing the soldier fall away. But it was too late to save Quinlan, who hung lifeless in his harness, as his blood-drenched cyborg continued to fight.

It wasn't until fifteen minutes later, when all of the killing was over, that the general could dismount and walk over to the place where Quinlan's body had been laid next to the road. Some sort of epitaph was required, or so it seemed to Kobbi, as he knelt next to the dead legionnaire. "You weren't the smartest officer I ever served with," the general said gruffly. "Or even the most dedicated. But you died like a man. Like a legionnaire—of whom all can be proud." And that, coming from General Mortimer Kobbi, was high praise indeed.

17

To illustrate this part somewhat, I shall say that the privileged class may be one of two sorts; either they conduct themselves in such a way as to be under your obligation or not. Those who are, and are not rapacious, must be honored and cherished. Those who are not so bound to you may be of two sorts; either they act as they do out of pusillanimity or natural lack of spirit and in such cases you must use them, especially such as are of good counsel, since in prosperity they do you honor and in adversity you have naught to fear from them; but when they are of the second kind and deliberately refuse to be dependent on you, for their own scheming and ambitious reasons then you may be sure they are thinking more of themselves than you, and a prince should be very wary of such and regard them as open enemies. . . .

—Niccolò Machiavelli
The Prince
Standard year 1513

PLANET HIVE, THE RAMANTHIAN EMPIRE

Hive was perfect. Or so it seemed to Chancellor Ubatha as a government transport carried him over beautifully sunlit fields toward a meeting approximately two hundred miles south of the capital city. Thanks to hundreds of years of hard work, and the fact that all of the Ramanthian power plants, factories, and cities were located underground, the planet's surface was equivalent to an enormous work of art. Rivers had the more-disciplined look of canals, thousands of fruit trees stood in carefully pruned ranks, and well-watered crop circles were thick with green vegetables. All of which stood in marked contrast to what Ubatha had seen on worlds like Earth, where citizens were allowed to rip the surface asunder, pollute the air, and export their garbage into space. It was just one more example of why Ramanthian culture was superior to all the rest.

But as the transport's shadow caressed the well-manicured terrain below, the bureaucrat knew there were other things to focus on, not the least of which was the meeting in which he was about to participate. Given the official's rank, second only to the Queen, most of his days were spent in meetings— some of which were productive while many weren't. The trick was to maximize the former and minimize the latter. A fairly straightforward process for the most part.

There was a *third* category of meetings, however: those that could be dangerous regardless of how productive they might or might not be. While participating in such gatherings might be perilous, it was equally dangerous to ignore them, which was why Ubatha had profound misgivings about the get-together that ex-Governor Oma Parth was hosting.

Though billed as nothing more than "a gathering of old friends," it was clearly more than that, because every person on the guest list other than Ubatha had one thing in common: Prior to the Hive Mother's regrettable death, the invitees had been high-ranking government officials or senior military officers who had been pushed out of their jobs within weeks of the current Queen's elaborate coronation. Even though it was an entirely normal part of the succession process, the displacements could still generate resentment.

That was where the danger came in. Odds were that the gathering was nothing more than an opportunity for disgruntled retirees to get together and talk about the extent to which they had been abused. If so, Ubatha would have to sit and sympathize.

Or, the gathering could represent something a good deal darker. In the aftermath of the wound suffered on Earth, the

Queen was still unable to move her body from the neck down. The condition in no way weakened the strength of her intellect, but put very real limits on what she could accomplish, and made her vulnerable in ways she hadn't been before. That was why Ubatha had agreed to participate in the meeting. He needed to find out what the other attendees were up to—and take action against them should any be necessary.

As the transport circled Parth's immaculately kept country estate, and came in for a landing, Ubatha had plenty to think about—starting with the fact that half a dozen other aircraft were already on the ground in spite of the fact he was early! Being a seasoned politician Ubatha knew the presence of so many transports could imply that a *premeeting* was already under way. If so, it meant that there were matters the other attendees didn't want to discuss in front of him. Still, given that Ubatha was there by invitation, there was no reason to believe that the group saw him as an enemy. Suddenly, as the skids made contact with the heat-fused soil, Ubatha felt lonely and a little bit scared. But the Chancellor kept such doubts well hidden as he shuffled down a ramp onto the sun-parched ground.

Parth's majordomo was waiting to greet Ubatha, and escort the high-ranking official to a broad ramp that slanted down into a series of beautifully appointed underground chambers. Though by no means poor, Ubatha and his mates had nothing like the wealth the Parth clan had accumulated over the last hundred years, and Ubatha was impressed by what he saw.

Ramanthian entry alcoves were generally a good indicator of what lay beyond, and this one was *huge.* And spotlessly clean. Like all members of his species, Ubatha was equipped with two antenna-shaped olfactory organs that protruded from his forehead. Thanks to the input they provided, he knew the air was heavy with expensive incense.

From that point a path led under one of the many shafts,

which brought sunlight down from the surface, past the obligatory rock garden, and down a long corridor. Earthen walls were covered with layerings of expensive fabrics and beautiful pieces of fractal art, all evenly spaced between carefully lit sculptures.

The corridor split three ways after that, and Ubatha followed the majordomo across a glistening water walk, and into the reception chamber beyond. Six males were waiting to greet the Chancellor—and Ubatha knew all of them.

First there was Governor Parth, who immediately came forward to greet Ubatha, his eyes alight with avarice. The Chancellor remembered Parth as a serviceable administrator who, though primarily interested in establishing conditions favorable to his clan's business interests, still found time to represent the rest of his constituents as well.

Also in attendance at the oval-shaped table was Cam Taas, the onetime chief of the Department of Transportation, who was famously hidebound, and completely averse to anything new. That stance, given the Empire's population explosion, was one of the reasons the Queen had been forced to let him go.

Su Ixba, the ex-head of the Department of Criminal Prosecution, and a skillful bureaucratic infighter, was seated next to Taas. Though effective, he had been known for a willingness to use his considerable police powers on anyone who was opposed to his conservative politics.

Tu Stik, Zo Nelo, and Ma Amm were military leaders, and if rumors were true, members of the fanatical *Nira* cult. The group that had been useful in some regards, but was potentially dangerous, since adherents saw themselves as accountable to a spiritual force more powerful than the Queen—a belief system that, while legal, was somewhat unsettling. All of those factors contributed to the steadily growing sense of apprehension Ubatha felt.

Once the traditional greetings were over, and a tray of light snacks had been passed around, Parth made what

amounted to an opening statement. All of the other partici-
pants sought to look disinterested, but Ubatha could *feel* the
tension in the room, and knew something important was in
the offing. "Again, welcome to our little gathering," Parth
said modestly. "We hoped you would join us both because
we enjoy your company—and because you are still in government. Tell me, official pronouncements aside, how *is* our
valiant Queen?"

The Chancellor thought there might be something
slightly sarcastic about the emphasis Parth put on the word
"valiant," but it was a seemingly innocent question, and one
Ubatha would expect any host to ask given the present circumstances. Still, the royal's health was a sensitive matter,
so Ubatha chose his words with care. "I'm sorry to say that
her majesty remains paralyzed. And, while our very best
physicians continue to study the problem, there is no immediate relief in sight. The Queen remains alert, however, and
has been able to carry out the vast majority of her duties,
which is a great comfort to us all."

"Yes, of course," Ixba said politely. "But, with all due respect, we could learn that much from the evening newscasts.
We are patriots, and as such, worried about the empire's
future well-being. We are at war, and as you probably know,
there are some who fear the Queen's paralysis could slow the
governmental process. And do so at a time when quick decisions will be critical to victory."

The comment wasn't treasonous, but it came close, and
Ubatha had no further doubts regarding the meeting's *true*
purpose. Having been displaced, and in their view slighted,
Parth and his cronies hoped to use the Queen's paralysis as a
pretext for replacing her with a *new* monarch. A female of
their choosing, who after taking the throne, would immediately restore them to positions of power. All of that would
be a good deal easier to accomplish if the Chancellor was not
only in on the plot but actively supporting it. Something
Ubatha would never do.

Two courses of action were available. Ubatha could pretend to cooperate, then take the actions necessary to deal with the illicit plot, or he could declare his opposition to it. But would the group allow him to leave if he did so?

Suddenly Ubatha regretted the fact that rather than travel with bodyguards, as he was entitled to do, he had chosen to attend the meeting unaccompanied, as a sign of humility and goodwill. It would be very easy for the group to kill him *and* his pilots, stage a plane crash, and make their move. And, as he looked around the table, Ubatha could sense an increased level of tension. "I see your point," Ubatha said carefully. "Speed *is* important. . . . What, if anything, would you suggest?"

Ixba signaled his approval with a single *clack* of his right pincer. "You're a pragmatist, Ubatha! And that's what we need. . . . A Chancellor capable of looking to the greater good. But, rather than answer your question myself, I would prefer to let someone else speak for our cause. An officer who, having distinguished himself in a number of actions, has been selected to coordinate the military aspect of the transition."

At that point Ubatha realized that the plot was so far advanced that the coconspirators had already chosen a warrior to either suborn the Queen's guards or physically overcome them! This meant there wasn't much time. . . . But, when he looked over at Stik, Nebo, and Amm, the retired officers were silent. So when their heads swiveled toward the doorway, Ubatha turned to see what they were looking at.

What the official saw there was so shocking, *so* terrible, that it felt as if his heart would stop beating. The officer who had been chosen to lead the assault on the monarch's bodyguards, and thereby betray everything that Chancellor believed in, was none other than the War Ubatha! One of his own mates who, judging from the presence of Stik, Nebo, and Amm, was not only a member of the *Nira* cult but an enthusiastic one as well! "Greetings," the soldier said levelly, as his eyes made contact with Ubatha's. "I'm glad it won't be necessary to kill you."

The so-called Summer Palace was located underground, the way any Ramanthian domicile should be, but adjacent to a deep twenty-mile-long river canyon. All of the most important rooms were open to the abyss—allowing whatever breezes there were to flow through unimpeded. Because even though the Ramanthians preferred a warm environment, the equatorial region could be sweltering hot during the summer months, and the palace dated all the way back to preindustrial times.

Of course, all of the monarch's many residences had air-conditioning, so her desire to stay at the Summer Palace had more to do with her affection for the place, than a need for cool breezes. But they were soothing, and as the Queen lay in her specially designed bed, she could see the floor-length curtains sway, and feel the flow of air around her antennae. And that was comforting. Up until the moment the human bullet hit her, the royal had never feared anything other than failure.

But now, in the wake of the latest visit from her doctors, she was terrified. Assuming they were correct, the prognosis wasn't good. Surgery to repair the damage to her posterior nerve bundle *might* work, according to the so-called experts, but could result in death as well. That was why none of the cowards were willing to operate on her.

They didn't say that, of course, but the possibility of being blamed for such a debacle was foremost in their minds. So the answer, or nonanswer, was to leave the Queen as she was. A mind trapped in an unresponsive body. And that, to the monarch's way of thinking, was completely unacceptable. But what to do? She didn't know. And not knowing gave rise to a feeling of helplessness—which was a strange sensation indeed.

The Queen's thoughts were interrupted by a soft *chime*—

and the *swish* of fabric as one of her administrative assistants appeared at the regent's side. "Chancellor Ubatha is here to see you, Majesty," the functionary said. "Shall I show him in?"

"Yes," the monarch replied. "Who knows? Maybe he has some good news."

The assistant withdrew, and no more than a minute passed before Ubatha entered the chamber and crossed the room to stand at the Queen's bedside. Having left Parth's estate, the official had executed a long sequence of carefully thought-out com calls, while flying to the Summer Palace.

Then, having made the necessary arrangements, the rest of the flight was spent mourning the loss of his mate. From the Chancellor's perspective, the being he and the Egg Ubatha loved had been replaced by a hard, ruthless creature who was willing to trade honor for power. Now the functionary was tired, worried, and, above all, frightened. "So, how do I look?" the monarch wanted to know. "Like dinner on a spit?"

The reference to the metal cage that supported her body was an attempt to put her visitor at ease, but Ubatha had seen the contraption before, and was in no mood for levity. "No, Majesty," the official replied, as the usual cloud of pheromones wafted around him. "But there are those who would take advantage of your disability if they could."

So saying, Ubatha launched into a forthright account of the trip to Parth's estate, the ensuing dialogue, and the shocking discovery that one of his own mates was part of the plot to depose her. It was a lot to take in, but the Queen was no stranger to political plots, and, having rid herself of the individuals in question, could understand their motives. Or their *alleged* motives. But what if Ubatha was lying? That was unlikely, of course, given that the official was accusing one of his own mates of treason, and remained subject to her pheromones. But *every* possibility had to be considered. Especially given her condition. "No offense, Chancellor," she said. "But why should I believe you?"

"Because the coup is already under way," Ubatha replied grimly. "Go ahead, request that a shuttle be sent to pick you up, and see what happens."

The royal had access to a voice-operated com system, so she made the call herself. Less than thirty seconds passed before the Queen was piped through to an admiral and a well-known 'member of the *Nira* cult. He listened to the request, apologized for the fact that *all* of the Queen's shuttles were currently undergoing maintenance, and promised to contact the royal the moment one of them became available.

The Queen felt a rising sense of rage, but managed to control it, as she broke the connection. The eyes that sought Ubatha's were black as space. "You were right. . . . I won't forget—and I'm sorry about your mate. You have a plan?"

"Yes, Majesty," Chancellor Ubatha answered. "There are some individuals that we can trust. . . . And insofar as I can tell, the Thrakies are completely unaware of the plot. One of their shuttles will pick us up in roughly thirty minutes. Once we're on board, the conspirators won't be able to strike without attacking a very important ally."

The Queen tried to move her body. *Any* part of her body— but there was no response. "And then?"

"And then we'll be taken aboard a Thraki ship," Ubatha replied.

"But won't that make it easy for them?" the Queen wanted to know. "Once I leave Hive, they'll be free to put their own Queen on the throne."

"No, they won't," Ubatha answered firmly. "Not so long as you are off-planet running the government—and communicating with the population. But it's going to take time to identify all of the conspirators and weed them out. There's reason to believe that the rot runs a lot deeper than the individuals I met with."

What Ubatha said made sense, so the Queen accepted it. "So, where will we go?" the royal wanted to know.

"To a place where you can rest, and no one will think to

look," Ubatha said secretively. "Not at first anyway." And the two of them were gone thirty minutes later.

PLANET EARTH, THE RAMANTHIAN EMPIRE

The slaves had been taken prisoner in places like Petaluma, Fairfield, and Concord before being marched through an urban wasteland to that part of the sprawling metroplex still referred to as San Jose, and what had once been the local convention center. But the huge building had another purpose now, and as Commander Leo Foley watched from a distant rooftop, he knew the long column of raggedly dressed people were about to enter a slave market where men, women, and children were sold to work in underground factories, toil on remote farms, and staff the brothels that had begun to pop up all over the area.

All of which was part of the criminal subculture that had grown up to replace the government structures the Ramanthians had systematically destroyed. It was a feudal system in which gang bosses lived like lords, competing armies fought for turf, and the rest of the population were slaves. The situation was not only barbaric, but helpful to the Ramanthians, who could simply sit back and watch the animals destroy each other.

And that was why Foley and the government-sponsored Earth Liberation Brigade was about to disrupt the illicit economy by taking the slave market down. Assuming the resistance fighters could overcome the mercenary army that Otto Tovar had assembled to protect his business interests. *That* was very much in doubt, because Tovar was a retired general, who theoretically knew more about ground combat than Foley did. It was important to study the complex before attacking it, because unless the guerrillas were extremely careful, their first major battle would be their last.

Strangely, as she and the rest of the slaves were led into the convention center, Margaret Vanderveen was glad to be there. Even if the floor of the main auditorium was covered with filth, a woman continued to utter a series of yelps as a guard whipped her, and the Mozart Requiem's *Dies Irae* was playing full blast over the PA system. Because Margaret was tired. *Very* tired, and looking forward to a rest, even if that was within the confines of a slave market.

The whole thing had begun shortly after a badly damaged Ramanthian scout ship passed over the old mine where she and her companions had been staying and crashed off to the west. Once a badly injured aviator wandered into Deer Valley and collapsed, Margaret and her friends tried to save the Ramanthian, but were unable to do so. Shortly after the warrior's death, Margaret realized that the alien's chitin was abnormally thin. At her insistence, samples were taken and preserved in vials filled with alcohol, *drinkable* alcohol that Benson had been reluctant to part with.

The whole thing could have ended there, should have ended there, given the way things turned out. But that was water under the bridge. Having convinced herself that the dead Ramanthian's medical condition might be of interest to the Confederacy's intelligence people, Margaret left Benson in charge of the mine, and set out to find someone who could convey the tissue samples to the right people.

There were six tiny containers, all of which had been sewn into a specially modified bra, where they would be safe from all but the most intrusive searches. That meant she could travel light, carrying nothing more than a small pack, pistol, and knife.

And things went well at first. Because Margaret was pretty savvy by then—and knew how to move cross-country without attracting attention. Unfortunately, the only way to find some sort of resistance group, and what she hoped would be a link with the authorities on Algeron, was to interact with people. And that was her downfall.

Margaret had covered a lot of ground, and was just outside Dixon, when she stumbled across one of the open-air, country-style markets that were springing up across the land—places where foodstuffs could be purchased, one item could be traded for another, and the latest bits of news could be had. Unreliable information for the most part, but all Margaret needed was a name, and an approximate location. Then, assuming that all went well, she would hand over the samples and return to Deer Valley. So that's where she was, talking to a voluble salt merchant, when the slavers attacked.

It wasn't clear what was happening at first because, even though the *pop, pop, pop* of gunfire could be heard, most of the market goers assumed someone had purchased a gun and was shooting at a target. But then as a woman screamed, and people fled toward the north, Margaret realized something more was taking place. A Ramanthian raid perhaps, which wouldn't have been all that surprising, given the circumstances. Stalls went over, livestock escaped, and people ran away from the gunfire.

So Margaret ran, too, her pack bouncing on her back, only to discover that she and all the rest of the market goers were being driven into a carefully laid trap! Because two converging lines of heavily armed men and women were waiting up ahead and, as the fugitives surged into the open end of the V, they were soon forced to stop. Margaret was no exception. The society matron was armed with a pistol, and tempted to use it, but knew what the outcome would be. Not only would *she* be killed by return fire, but so would many of the people crammed in around her. That was a decision she had no right to make for them.

Seconds later, slavers armed with clubs were in among their victims, beating anyone who tried to resist and taking their possessions. Margaret's pack was ripped off her back, her pistol was confiscated, and a man with bad breath ran greedy hands up and down her body. Even going so far as to grab her crotch and squeeze her breasts. But the little vials escaped his notice, and with younger victims to abuse, the man made no attempt to follow up.

What ensued was like a scene from hell as women were thrown to the ground to be raped, children were hauled away, and the more contentious males were shot. But dead bodies weren't worth anything, except to the crows, so it wasn't long before a man dressed in camos appeared and shouted orders. That was when Margaret caught her *second* look at General Otto Tovar. Because the two of them had met once before.

Rather than tolerate the fringe of hair that would otherwise circle half his skull, Tovar had chosen to shave his head instead. That, plus the fact that he had no neck to speak of, made him look like a fireplug. Because even though the slave master had a big frame, he was overly fond of food, and eternally hovered at the edge of obesity. And that was why the carefully starched militia uniform looked so tight on him.

It had been Veteran's Day, five or six years earlier, when they had met. Charles had been home on leave, but the diplomat could never escape work entirely, and having been invited to a government-sponsored Veteran's Day party, felt he had to go. Margaret had agreed to accompany him. Tovar had been at the affair as well, resplendent in a fancy uniform, and pontificating on the second Hudathan war. It was a conflict which, according to Charles, the militia general hadn't fought in other than to help with recruiting.

Quite a bit of time had passed since then, but Margaret remembered being introduced to Tovar, and wondered if the bloated general would remember her as he sat in judgment of his newly acquired merchandise. The slaver's expedition-quality folding chair had been set up on a small rise where a domestic robot stood ready to meet its master's needs as classical music played over a portable sound system. The general had a deeply creased forehead, and deep-set eyes, that were nearly hidden by prominent brows. A heavily veined nose, a pair of thick, sensual lips, and at least three chins completed the picture.

All of the captives had been pushed, prodded, and shoved into the line by that time, and it jerked forward in a series of fits and starts, as human beings were sorted into various categories. Men who were strong enough to perform heavy physical labor went into one group. Women judged pretty enough for the brothels went into another. And there were nonstop wailing sounds as children were taken away. Some to be sold and some to be used for even darker purposes.

That was shocking enough, but there were even less fortunate people as well, who were shunted off into a group Tovar didn't want to feed. Less robust people for the most part, who couldn't be harnessed to a plow, and would be of no interest to the brothels. They were shot, and male slaves were forced to drag the bodies away.

Each gunshot sent a ripple of fear down the line. Older people, Margaret included, had reason to be especially fearful since they clearly had less value to potential customers than younger people did. So Margaret had mentally reconciled herself to being executed, and was trying to deal with that, as the woman directly in front of her was sent to join the work group. Having accepted her fate, the society matron took two steps forward, and looked into Tovar's piggy eyes.

But there was no glimmer of recognition there, and that made sense. Because the woman the militia general had met years before had been wearing expensive jewelry and fashionable clothes, unlike the sunburned, travel-worn specimen who presently stood in front of him. So Margaret was nothing more than a piece of meat insofar as Tovar was concerned. However, thanks to some skillful plastic surgery, and the fact that Margaret kept herself fit, the society matron looked ten years younger than she actually was. That saved her life. "Put her in with the workers," the slave master ordered harshly. "She won't fetch much—but something is better than nothing."

So Margaret survived. But it was a long walk from Dixon to San Jose, and by the time the column entered the convention center, she was bone tired. And that was why she went in search of a reasonably clean patch of duracrete and lay down. The surface was hard, but she was used to that, and soon fell asleep. There were dreams, *good* dreams, and a smile found her lips.

An entire day had passed since Margaret and the others had arrived in San Jose, and many of Tovar's slaves had been sold. Now it was her turn to enter the center arena, along with five other women who were about to be bid on. Like the others, Margaret had been ordered to strip, but unlike the rest the society matron managed to keep her eyes up as she followed the others out into the artificial glare. Her body wasn't what it had once been, but there was nothing to be ashamed of, and she wasn't. Her clothes, including the all important bra, were clutched in her arms.

Meanwhile, just as the auction was about to start, shouts were heard when a tough-looking slaver led a column of ragged-looking men and women into the holding area adjacent to the arena. It was difficult to tell what was happening, but Margaret got the impression that because the newcomer wasn't a member of the slaver's guild, he wasn't eligible to use the market. Loud altercations weren't unusual, and the socialite didn't think much of it, until the interloper pulled a gun and shot a guard in the face.

Foley saw the man's head jerk backward, as a blue-edged hole appeared at the center of his forehead, and the "slaves" produced weapons of their own. There were lots of people around, most of whom were slaves, but the bad guys were easy to spot. They were the ones who had the guns and, given the element of surprise, Foley's guerrilla fighters had an excellent opportunity to kill them—which is what they proceeded to do.

Margaret hit the floor as the bullets began to fly, heard someone yell something about the Earth Liberation Brigade, and realized the people she'd been looking for were all around her! But in order to deliver the tissue samples, she was going to have to survive, and that was why she decided to roll across the cold slimy floor. Not to get away, but to get her hands on a loose pistol, that lay only inches from a dead man's outstretched hand.

Being no expert with small arms, Margaret had something of an aversion to semiautomatics, which always came equipped with levers and buttons, but this was an easy-to-fire energy pistol. She scooped the weapon up, rolled to her feet, and was looking for a target when a wounded Otto Tovar came lumbering straight at her. The slave master had taken a bullet in the left arm and was clearly in pain as he sought to escape.

Margaret saw the fear on the slaver's face as she brought the weapon up. There was no recoil as the socialite pressed the firing stud and sent an energy bolt straight through Tovar's body. Even though the slave master was effectively dead, he took three additional steps before falling facedown on the filthy floor. Margaret felt pleased with herself, pointed the pistol at Tovar's back, and fired *again*. She knew Benson would approve.

Most of the slavers were down, and there was a very real danger of killing the people they had come to rescue, so Foley yelled, "Cease fire!" over and over again until the firing finally stopped. That was when specially trained teams of civilian volunteers entered to care for the wounded, take charge of orphaned children, and spray-paint carefully phrased warnings onto the walls. "The Confederacy lives. Its laws *will* be enforced. The Earth Liberation Brigade."

And it was during that phase of the operation that Admiral Chien-Chu arrived to inspect his protégé's work. Which, from the billionaire's perspective, had gone very well indeed. Not only had innocent people been rescued, but a line had been drawn, and word of what had happened to the slavers would soon begin to spread.

That's where the industrialist was, giving Foley some orders, when a muck-smeared woman approached them. Chien-Chu was well acquainted with Charles Vanderveen, a man he regarded as a friend, and knew Margaret Vanderveen, too. But not so well that he'd seen her without any clothes on.

"Hello, Sergi," the socialite said calmly. "I'm Margaret Vanderveen, even if I don't look the way I usually do, and I'll bet you're the man I've been looking for! I have reason to believe that at least some of the Ramanthians are dying from a contagious disease. Something they were exposed to here on Earth. And here are some tissue samples taken from a dead pilot."

And with that, Margaret Vanderveen handed Sergi Chien-Chu her bra. It was, and would forever be, one of the few occasions when the Father of the Confederacy was rendered entirely speechless.

18

So long as there is even one brave soul willing to confront tyranny then hope will live.

—Hoda Ibin Ragnatha
Turr truth sayer
Standard year 2202

PLANET GAMMA-014, THE CLONE REPUBLIC

Santana couldn't fly, but felt as if he could, as he looked at the video that was playing on the inside surface of his visor. What he was seeing, and to some extent vicariously experiencing, was what it was like to be Lieutenant Mitch Millar. The cyborg was skimming the surface of the small kidney-shaped lake that separated Alpha Company from the clones on the far side. It was almost dark, which meant there was some light to see by, but not enough to make the recon ball stand out as Millar crossed the opposite shoreline and entered a grove of bristly trees.

Conscious of the fact that Santana could see everything he saw, the cyborg paused to "eye" the area to the south, before firing his repellers, and rising straight up. Though similar to evergreens on Earth in that they had needles—the snow-clad trees surrounding the cyborg were significantly different as well. Because the grove that surrounded Millar was actually a *single* organism. While each vertical trunk had its own root system, it could share nutrients with neighboring structures via a complex system of interconnecting branches.

So as the legionnaire leveled off about fifty feet above the ground, it was necessary to negotiate a maze of crisscrossing branches in order to work his way into the area where the renegades were camped. That made navigation difficult but provided good cover as well. Finally, having arrived at the southernmost edge of that particular grove's territory, Millar came to rest on some sturdy branches. As darkness crept in over the wintry landscape, both the cyborg and his commanding officer had a bird's-eye view of the enemy encampment below. Having located Colonel Six *and* his hostages days earlier, Millar had given a tracking device to Kira Kelly. Which, for reasons unknown, had gone off-line hours later. But Millar was no fool and, having planted a *second* device on one of the half-tracks, he had been able to lead his comrades to the frozen lake where the renegades were camped.

Having chosen an open area, with good fields of fire, Colonel Six had positioned his vehicles to reinforce all four sides of the perimeter. Gaps had been filled with lengths of timber cut earlier in the day, backed by hand-dug firing pits. The defenses weren't fancy, but the officer figured they would be effective against anything up to, and including, a company-strength attack by the Ramanthians.

Four fires had been lit and, as Millar and Santana looked down through a curtain of gently falling snow, they could see dark shapes moving back and forth between the dome-shaped tents as the clones carried out maintenance on their equipment and cooked their dinners. It was a peaceful scene familiar to any soldier.

The problem, from Santana's perspective was how to attack the encampment, especially given the presence of hostages. He could try and take all or part of Alpha Company around the edge of the lake. But groves of interlocking trees barred the way and would prevent his cyborgs from reaching the campsite until well after dawn. Then, if the clones were still in residence, they would be able to see the enemy coming.

Santana knew that a force of bio bods might be able to

arrive quickly enough to carry out a night attack, but Santana lacked a sufficient number of troops to go up against
the Seebos *and* their vehicle-mounted weapons. Not even
with the marines and CVAs thrown in.

So, where does that leave us? the cavalry officer wondered.
The lake was frozen, but the ice wasn't thick enough to support the weight of a T-2, much less a quad. So the direct
route was out. Or was it? It was dark by then, and with his
visor down, no one could see the officer smile.

Even though it was fairly warm inside the sleeping blanket,
it was too cold to take off *all* her clothes, so Kelly was naked
from the waist down, as she pulled Six deep inside her. The
clone hadn't been much of a lover initially, but practice
makes perfect, and he had improved. It felt good to make
love, to participate in an ancient act of renewal, especially
given all the killing that was taking place around them.

But even as the long, steady strokes continued, and the
pleasure began to build, Kelly felt the now-familiar pangs of
guilt, knowing that by destroying the tracking device, Hospital Corpsman Sumi had been sentenced to further captivity.

And, if that wasn't bad enough, Kelly had been unable to
find the strength to tell Six about the recon ball's visit. So
she had been unfaithful to *him* as well.

Her lover's movements became more urgent, causing the
doctor to wrap her legs around his muscular body, and dig
her fingers into his back. There were no thoughts beyond
that point, just a desperate need for release, which came as
an explosion of pleasure. But the moment was soon over, the
afterglow began to fade, and reality seeped in to replace it.
It was then, with Six still inside her, that Kelly began to cry.

Except for the circles of constantly shifting light that surrounded the fires, it was pitch-black outside the perimeter.
So there was nothing for One-O to look at as he sat on top of
the half-track, and waited for the rest of his two-hour watch
to pass. Thanks to the night-vision goggles he was wearing,

the clone *knew* that there weren't any bugs advancing across the surface of the lake, so all he had to do was work the charging lever on the .50-caliber machine gun every five minutes or so, and try to stay warm. That wasn't easy since he couldn't leave the gun. Such were the soldier's thoughts when the ice directly in front of him exploded—and a fifty-ton quad burst up out of lake!

Shards of shattered ice were still raining down on the camp as Private Ivan Lupo took three gigantic steps forward. The first and second carried him up onto the land, and the third came down on top of One-O, as the Seebo battled to bring the fifty into play. Both the clone *and* his half-track were crushed under the weight of the quad's enormous foot pod.

Then, before anyone had time to react, servos *whined* as Lupo lurched forward. Sparks exploded into the air as his left forefoot landed in a fire, and the *rattle* of automatic fire was heard when a sentry opened up on the monster. Water continued to sheet off the cyborg's hull, and steam rose off his back as he fired in return. Both the sentry and the Seebo standing next to him were vaporized as a quick flurry of energy bolts slagged their position.

The ramp was down by that time, which allowed three T-2s, their riders, and six additional bio bods to enter the fray. Santana and Deker were the first to exit the quad and, because all of Colonel Six's heavy weapons were aimed *outwards*, they could enter the encampment without taking fire.

Millar had identified where Colonel Six was sleeping hours before, and put a spotlight on the tent from above, as Deker carried Santana over to it. Thanks to the Integrated Tactical Command system the legionnaire could make himself heard via all four cyborgs at the same time. "Hold your fire! Put down your weapons! You are under arrest!"

And with the huge quad crouched at the very center of the encampment, there was absolutely no doubt as to who the attackers were, or who would win if the clones chose to resist. Slowly, so as not to draw fire, the Seebos laid their weapons on the ground. A force of T-2s and bio bods quickly took charge of the clones and hurried to secure them.

Santana was on the ground with his CA-10 leveled at the entrance of the floodlit tent by the time Six emerged. He was still in the process of fastening his parka. The spotlight forced him to squint, but there was no mistaking the officer's defiant expression. The legionnaire's voice was hard. "Are you Colonel Jonathan Alan Seebo-62,666?"

The clone nodded as he looked around. "I am."

"Pat him down and check his bar code," Santana said grimly. "Let's make sure he isn't playing games again."

It was Master Sergeant Dice Dietrich who came forward to do the honors. A search came up clean, and after scanning the bar code on the officer's forehead, the noncom was able to confirm the Seebo's identity. "It's him all right," Dietrich declared, his breath fogging the air.

"Good," Santana replied. "Stash the colonel inside Lupo, search him again, and chain him to a bulkhead. Put two guards on him—and don't use any marines or CVAs. The jarheads might kill him—and CVAs might listen to his bullshit."

"Roger that," Dietrich said, and led the officer away.

That was when the tent fabric shook and Kelly emerged. Her hair was mussed, her face was pale, and it was her turn to squint into the light. "Don't tell me," Santana said. "Let me guess. . . . You're Dr. Kira Kelly."

Kelly looked into the officer's hard eyes and nodded.

"And Hospital Corpsman Sumi?" the legionnaire inquired. "Where is he?"

"I'm right here," a voice said, and Santana turned to see that a navy medic was standing next to Staff Sergeant Briggs. "The rotten bitch slept with Colonel Six," the corpsman said accusingly. "And did everything she could to help him."

Millar had descended to shoulder height by that time, and the cavalry officer turned to look at him. "Get a statement from this man," Santana instructed. "Record it and make copies. Give one of them to me."

Millar bobbed up and down. "Yes, sir."

Santana turned back to Briggs. "Have one of our females search her. Chain her to a track—and have a legionnaire guard her. Under no circumstances should she be allowed to speak to a marine, Seebo, or CVA without my permission. . . . Understood?"

Briggs nodded. "Yes, sir."

Santana looked at Kelly. She stood with her head hanging, unwilling to make eye contact with those around her, obviously miserable. The legionnaire almost felt sorry for the doctor. Almost but not quite.

ABOARD THE YACHT *PLAY PRETTY*, OFF NAV POINT CSM-9703

The *Play Pretty* was a big yacht. Large enough to carry two shuttles that doubled as lifeboats, fifteen guests in addition to the two owners, and a crew of five. All of which made her special. But now, floating off Nav Point CSM-9703, she was just one of more than six thousand vessels awaiting the order to enter hyperspace. And beauty, or lack of it, wasn't going to play a role in who lived or died. In fact, the only things that were going to matter were speed, agility, and luck.

As befitted a yacht of her status the *Play Pretty*'s control room was not only state-of-the-art but luxurious as well. Frank Simmons was seated in the chair normally occupied by the ship's professional captain, and as the retired businessman looked up at the nav screen, he was amazed by the scene that continued to unfold in front of him. "Look at 'em, hon. . . . *Thousands* of ships. There's freighters, tugs, liners, yachts, luggers, hell, I heard a goddamned garbage scow report in! And that ain't all. . . . During the last half hour I've heard transmissions from clones, Hudathans, Prithians, Dwellers, and a frigging Turr!"

"There's no need to swear," Marsha Simmons replied for what might have been the millionth time. Frank was a rough, tough, self-made man, a miner, who had struck it rich out on the rim, and rarely uttered a paragraph that didn't include at least one swearword. She came from old money, a family that looked down on Frank until the day when his net worth exceeded theirs, and the negative attitudes began to change.

The society matron had carefully coiffed gray hair, big brown eyes, and a sweet face. And when Maylo Chien-Chu had gone looking for volunteers, Marsha was among the first people she called. For when it came to beings with big yachts, Marsha knew everyone worth knowing, and wasn't afraid to call upon them. Which had everything to do with the fact that hundreds of ships like the *Play Pretty* were about to go into harm's way as part of a last-ditch attempt to take as many civilians and troops off Gamma-014 as possible.

Thus, as Frank Simmons stared at the screen, he knew that a lot of the little ships wouldn't be coming back. The strategy was to flood Gamma-014's system with more targets than the Ramanthians could handle and rescue as many people as possible. But even though the bugs wouldn't destroy all of them, they would certainly nail *some of them*, and the *Play Pretty* was going in. Partly because Captain Carly Simmons was down on the planet's surface—but mostly because it was the right thing to do.

"Here comes the feed," Marsha said, as the snow on com channel 3 coalesced into a shot of Maylo Chien-Chu and locked up. "That's a very nice jacket," the society matron observed. "But she looks tired."

And Maylo *was* tired. Her jet-black hair was perfect, as always, but there were dark circles under her large, almond-shaped eyes, and she hadn't been eating much of late. The resulting weight loss, plus her high cheekbones, made the businesswoman look gaunt. "First," Maylo said as she looked into the camera, "I would like to thank each and every one of you on behalf of myself, my husband, General Bill Booly, President Marcott Nankool, the Senate, and the Confederacy's citizens. Because the rescue attempt that you're about to participate in will go down as one of the bravest, most selfless acts of this very important war.

"Now, with that said, let's run through the plan one last time. . . . Be sure to enter the *exact* sequence of numbers you were given into your NAVCOMP, because if you don't, you may exit hyperspace right on top of another ship! And I don't have to tell you how unpleasant that would be.

"Once in-system you're on your own. There won't be any traffic-control system, so watch out for other vessels! The key is to follow a beacon down to the surface as quickly as possible, load as many soldiers as you can, and lift. Once clear of Gamma-014, enter hyperspace as quickly as you can. . . . The bugs won't know where you're going, so they won't be able to follow."

Maylo paused at that point. Her gaze was level, and her voice was calm. "A lot of us won't be coming back. Those who do will find liners and hospital ships waiting to take your passengers. May *all* of our various gods bless this fleet, for in this valiant effort, our hearts beat as one." And with that the video snapped to black.

"That's for damned sure," Frank Simmons said approvingly, and his wife sighed.

PLANET GAMMA-014, THE CLONE REPUBLIC

The allies had crossed Tow-Tok Pass, and were making their way down the other side, when charges that had been placed on slopes above them were detonated, sending an avalanche of snow down across the highway and into the gorge below. That brought the ten-mile-long column to an immediate halt, caused previously well-spaced vehicles to bunch up, and set the stage for the slaughter that General Akoto had in mind.

Upon hearing the initial explosion, followed by a ground-shaking *rumble*, General Mortimer Kobbi swore bitterly. He was a third of the way back along the column at the time, giving one of a thousand pep talks, when the hammer fell. And it didn't take a military genius to know what would happen next, as at least two dozen well-concealed snipers opened fire from the concealment of the snow-covered rocks high above, and Kobbi sent his T-2 racing toward the head of the column. Two crawlers, both equipped with dozer blades had been given the lead to deal with that sort of situation, but Major Perko was waiting with more bad news as the general arrived. "I'm sorry, sir," Perko said, as Kobbi dismounted. "The blast was timed to hit the dozers. One survived—but the other was swept away."

From where he was standing, just in front of the quad that had been positioned immediately behind the crawlers, Kobbi could see the shoulder-high pile of snow and debris that blocked the highway. Trees had been caught up in the avalanche, along with large boulders and a host of smaller rocks. A powerful engine *rumbled* as the surviving dozer attacked the blockage with a big shining blade. What originally had been isolated gunshots escalated into a full-scale firefight as well-hidden Ramanthian soldiers fired down into the column, and legionnaires, marines, and Seebos fired up into the rocks. Slugs pinged off the dozer and made a mosquito-like *whine* as they angled away.

The avalanche was bad luck, *terrible* luck, given what was at stake. The rescue fleet wasn't on the way yet, but they would be soon, and it was imperative to get the column down out of the mountains quickly. Civilians would be taken off first, followed by support forces, meaning those units that hadn't been sent up into the mountains. That was just the nature of things. But Kobbi was determined to evacuate combat troops as well. "Okay," the little general said grimly. "We'll work with what we have. . . . Keep the dozer going. I'll round up a couple hundred CVAs and arm them with shovels. They can pitch in and help clear the slide."

Perko nodded, opened his mouth to reply, and jerked spastically as a bullet smashed through the bridge of his nose. That was when a corporal threw Kobbi facedown on the highway and took the follow-up shot right between the shoulder blades. His body armor was sufficient to stop the slug, but it left a bruise the legionnaire would remember for days to come. Assuming he lived that long.

"Thanks," Kobbi said, as he rolled out from under the corporal. "I owe you a beer. Let me jack into your radio. Those bastards need to die."

Ten minutes later Second Lieutenant Eyeblink Thinkfast and a team of Naa warriors drawn from a dozen units started up the mountainside. It was a development the Ramanthian snipers should have been worried about but weren't. Mainly because the rank-and-file bugs were completely ignorant of the physiological and cultural attributes associated with their enemies.

So they were unaware of the fact that the fur-clad legionnaires considered anything above ten below to be balmy, preferred to fight barefoot because they could sense heat differentials through the soles of their feet, and didn't need to actually see their opponents because they could *smell* chitin polish, wing wax, and gun oil from a hundred feet away. Nor were the insectoid Ramanthians aware of the speed with which the lightly armed Naa could climb, the almost total silence with which they moved, or the mind-numbing ferocity that they brought with them.

Some of the legionnaires fell, plucked off the steep slope by well-aimed bullets, but not many. Because as Thinkfast and half a dozen others came upslope, they were also moving from side to side, utilizing every bit of cover that was available.

Then they were there, on the same level as the Ramanthian sharpshooters, and that was when the *real* bloodletting began. It was knife and pistol work for the most part, carried out by warriors who had not only been raised to kill, but had grudges to settle on behalf of all the legionnaires killed on Gamma-014. They were like ghosts as they slipped between the rocks, slitting throats, and firing from point-blank range. No quarter was asked, and no quarter was given, as more than thirty Ramanthians were systematically put to death. Finally, with his uniform soaked in gore, it was Thinkfast who put in the call to Kobbi. "The heights are ours, sir. . . . We will hold them until relieved. Over."

"Well done, Lieutenant," Kobbi said, as he stared up at the tiny figures above. "Once we get back to Algeron, I'm going to hang every medal I can think of on you and your warriors. Do you have prisoners? Over."

"No, sir," came the answer. "We forgot to take any. Over."

"Well done," the general replied. "Six-One out."

ABOARD THE FREIGHTER *XINGLONG*, OFF PLANET GAMMA-014, THE CLONE REPUBLIC

Maylo Chien-Chu felt a brief moment of nausea as the sturdy *Xinglong* (*Star Dragon*) exited hyperspace and entered enemy-held space. Unlike most of the more than six thousand vessels that were systematically flooding the local system, the boxy *Xinglong* was ideal for the rescue mission, because she had been built for the purpose of transporting cargo to and from Class III planets like Gamma-014. That was just one of the many lines of business Chien-Chu Enterprises was engaged in. Owing to the sometimes lawless conditions out along the rim, the freighter was armed. However, four medium-duty energy cannons and two missile launchers weren't going to make much of an impression on anything larger than a military gunboat.

Maylo had long been a pilot, and a good one, so rather than take up space that a civilian or soldier might otherwise use, she was conning the ship herself. The rest of the skeleton crew consisted of Angie Brisco, her somewhat cantankerous middle-aged copilot, Hal Nortero, the ship's cigar-chomping engineer, and Koso Orlo-Ka, the *Xinglong*'s Hudathan loadmaster, all of whom had volunteered for the mission even if Brisco liked to complain a lot. "Damn," the narrow-faced copilot exclaimed sarcastically, as the freighter emerged from hyperspace one planetary diameter off Gamma-014's surface. "Couldn't you cut it any closer?"

Brisco's lack of tact was the main reason why she had been let go by a dozen companies before finally finding a home within Chien-Chu Enterprises—a company where skill was valued over and above political acumen, not to mention the fact that her shipmates had plenty of quirks themselves. So even though Maylo was president of the company, she responded with a grin. "I would if I could, Angie. Now hang on, we're going in."

The Ramanthians were beginning to respond by then, but not fast enough to stop the steady stream of incoming vessels, most of which were clearly civilian. That didn't make sense to them—and was the source of considerable confusion. That wouldn't last, of course, but Maylo intended to take advantage of the situation while it was possible. The plan was to take clone civilians off Gamma-014 first, ferry them back to Nav Point CSM-9703, and off-load them to the big liners that were waiting there.

Those ships that could would return to Gamma-014 to take military personnel off. Many of whom were still fighting their way down out of the mountains. The whole process was going to take days, and the bugs would be expecting the second, third, and fourth waves, so casualties would be high. "So, what the hell are you waiting for?" Brisco demanded impatiently. "Let's put this rust bucket down. We've got people to load."

The *Xinglong* bucked madly as she entered the atmosphere. "Yes, ma'am," Maylo said agreeably. "We do indeed."

The refugee camp was a huge, sprawling affair, that had originally been a sports complex, before the Ramanthians took control of Gamma-014 and converted the facility into a prisoner of war internment camp. That was where Mama Dee and what remained of her scruffy "family" had been forced to go. Having been locked inside, the POWs were left to find a place for themselves in the muddy field, where thousands of displaced civilians were forced to eat, sleep, and shit within a few inches of each other. A miserable existence but one that most of the so-called accidental people had been able to survive largely because they were used to extreme privation.

Then came what seemed like a miracle at first, as allied forces landed on Gamma-014, and the POW camp was "liberated." The only problem was that while some of the Ramanthians were forced back into space, the victorious Seebos had no use for the Children of Nature, and largely ignored them. Fortunately, the Confederacy's troops, all of whom were free breeders, offered what assistance they could.

So, with no home to return to, Mama Dee and her clan had been forced to remain in what was now a refugee camp. A less-crowded place to be sure—but still just as miserable. Then came the news that the Alpha Clones had been overthrown, which gave the accidental people something to celebrate, until the Ramanthians suddenly reappeared! The bugs hadn't landed in force yet, but clearly had control of the skies, and were said to be winning the ground war over toward Yal-Am.

Now, as the big rawboned Ortov-Chan "mix" and seven members of her "family" stood outside the clan's shabby longhouse, and stared upwards, still *another* shift was under way. Hundreds of contrails were crisscrossing the sky. And it wasn't long before spaceships appeared over the city. These were not the military vessels that the refugees expected to see, but a wild menagerie of yachts, freighters, and other craft, some of which were *very* alien in appearance.

There was a momentary flash of light, followed by a clap of what sounded like thunder, as one of the ships ceased to exist. Pieces of smoking wreckage were still raining down on a spot two miles away when a man in a ten-foot-tall orange exoskeleton approached them. The machine made intermittent whining noises as the petty officer who was at the controls weaved his way between makeshift hovels. The noncom's voice boomed out over the speakers above his head. "Make a hole!" the sailor demanded. "A *big* hole! A ship is about to land. . . . I repeat, a ship is about to land. Gamma-014 is being evacuated. You will board in an orderly fashion. Leave all personal items behind. . . . I repeat, leave all personal items behind."

And as the sailor continued to wade through the crowd, a massive shadow fell over the field, and repellers *roared* as Maylo Chien-Chu brought the *Xinglong* in for a landing. "Be careful!" Brisco cautioned unnecessarily. "There are people down there."

"Thanks," Maylo said dryly, her fingers dancing across the controls. "I'll keep that in mind."

The downdraft from the freighter's repellers destroyed two of the flimsy huts, which were empty by then. That was followed by a noticeable jolt as the skids found solid ground beneath a six-inch layer of semiliquid brown muck. Down in the hold, Orlo-Ka flipped a safety cover out of the way and stabbed a button with a sausage-sized index finger. Metal *groaned* and servos *whined* as the much-dented belly ramp deployed. The big Hudathan was armed with an energy rifle as he stomped down the incline and onto the surface below. That, plus his size, was sufficient to prevent what might otherwise have been a stampede.

Of course, some civilians were suspicious, fearing some sort of trick, and were quick to back away. But the vast majority, the Children of Nature included, figured they had nothing to lose. So as her family surged up the ramp, Mama Dee led the way, her staff thumping on metal.

Fifteen minutes later, a Klaxon began to *bleat*, the filthy ramp came up, and repellers fired. Maylo had to rock the freighter from side to side in order to break the skids out of the mud, but eventually succeeded and accelerated away. There were still lots of people on the ground, but a beat-up ore carrier was circling the camp by then, and was soon on the ground.

It took the *Xinglong* two seemingly endless hours to escape Gamma-014's gravity well, dodge a Ramanthian destroyer, and go hyper. But she made it—and even Brisco was somewhat pleased. "Not bad for an amateur," the crusty copilot allowed. "But the next trip will be harder." And, even though Maylo wasn't ready to think about that yet, she knew Brisco was correct.

It was just after dawn. Santana stood with his back to one of the campfires drinking a cup of hot caf and looking out at the open area to the south of him. At least four or five inches of snow had fallen during the night, and the officer was cold, tired, and dirty. Roughly half of Alpha Company was on high alert, manning the perimeter, while the rest of the outfit was getting ready to pull out. The good news was that the hostages had been rescued, and Colonel Six was in custody. The bad news was that, based on the most recent scouting report from Lieutenant Millar, it appeared as though the previous evening's firefight had been heard or seen because a large force of Ramanthians had infiltrated the area between Alpha Company and the main highway.

So what to do? Santana could marshal his forces, such as they were, and attempt to break out. Or, remain where he was, and let the chits come to him. But one thing was for sure. . . . Kobbi's convoy was busy fighting for its life—so there wouldn't be any help from that quarter. And Santana knew the clock was ticking. Any group that failed to exit the mountains along with the main column ran the risk of being left on Gamma-014. That, given the way Ramanthians treated their prisoners, was tantamount to a death sentence.

Such were Santana's thoughts as he noticed something strange, swallowed the last of his caf, and made his way out to the perimeter. Marine Sergeant Pimm saw the officer coming. He had come to respect Santana over the last few days, which was nothing short of a frigging miracle, since everybody knew the Legion was nothing more than a collection of criminals, wackos, and freaks. Pimm nodded politely. "Good morning, sir."

Santana's eyes were fixed on a point beyond the log barricade. He said, "Good morning, Sergeant," drew his sidearm, and vaulted over the logs. Then, as the mystified noncom looked on, the legionnaire took four paces forward and aimed his weapon at a spiral of wispy vapor. There was a loud *blam, blam, blam* as the officer fired his pistol. Brass casings arced away from the weapon, something heaved under the snow, and blood colored it red.

And that was when all hell broke loose as thirty or forty Ramanthian commandos threw off thermal blankets and rose from the ground. Having concealed their heat signatures with the blankets, the bugs had been able to sneak up on the encampment during the night. Then, once they were within grenade-throwing range of the encampment, the Ramanthians allowed the snow to cover them over. But they had to breathe, and that was what had given them away.

Two commandos were within six feet of Santana. The cavalry officer shot one of the Ramanthians in the face, whirled, and shot the other. Then, as he backed his way toward the barricade, Santana emptied his pistol at a *fourth* commando. That was when Sergeant Pimm grabbed onto the officer's battle harness from behind and jerked him over the barricade. There was a loud *carump* as the first mortar round hit, killed one of the CVAs, and sent a column of blood, mud, and snow up into the air.

The marines were firing by then, as were the legionnaires, but the surviving commandos were only yards away. Grenades sailed though the air, landed, and went off one after another. A Seebo was decapitated by flying shrapnel, a legionnaire went down with a shard of metal in his thigh, and flying fragments *clanged* as they hit the half-tracks. Somewhere off in the distance, shrill whistles could be heard, along with an alien bugling sound, as Ramanthian regulars rushed to join the fray. Daylight attacks were rare, but with the commandos to lead the way, the bugs had been about to launch one. Santana was back on his feet by then—

the decision having been made for him. There was no avenue of escape. Alpha Company would stay and fight.

So as Lupo's onboard computer calculated trajectories for the incoming mortar shells, and the quad sent a volley of short-range missiles racing toward the enemy tubes, Santana offered words of encouragement as the company prepared to defend itself. The legionnaires and their allies had camped inside the perimeter that Colonel Six had established for *his* troops, and thanks to the fact that the cavalry officer had been able to bring the rest of his command around the south end of the lake during the hours of darkness, all of them were in one place. Which was fortunate indeed. Since two separate groups would have been hard-pressed to defend themselves.

Having located Corporal Thain, the officer gave the cyborg a concise set of orders, before turning back toward the center of camp. Millar was there, half-hidden by a track, firing his energy cannon at the enemy. Another defender would have been useful, but Santana had something more important for the recon ball to do, and gave the cyborg new orders. Then, having called upon Dietrich to fire some smoke grenades toward the north, the scout vanished into the resulting fog.

Thanks to Lieutenant Zolkin's earlier efforts, ordnance of all kinds had been unloaded from the vehicles and divided between three widely spaced bunkers to avoid the possibility that a single explosion would destroy all their ammo. So, when the outgoing fire fell off, Hoyt-11,791 and her CVAs rushed to resupply the troops. Especially the T-2s, who couldn't reload their own magazines.

As Santana continued to make the rounds, the cavalry officer realized that insofar as combat troops were concerned, he was down to eight of Alpha Company's bio bods, half a dozen marines, four loyal Seebos from the transportation platoon, and five T-2s. The rest had departed with Thain. Unfortunately, some of his legionnaires were tied up guarding Six, the treacherous Dr. Kelly, and the thirty-six Seebos who remained loyal to the renegade. All of them were seated hip to hip in two rows behind one of their own half-tracks.

But there was nothing Santana could do about that as more whistles were heard and the *real* infantry assault began. "Don't let them reach the perimeter!" Santana shouted, as he brought his CA-10 up to his shoulder and began to fire. "Lupo! Everything outside of a hundred yards belongs to you!"

The quad heard the command via the company push and went to work with all four of his gang-mounted energy cannons. They fired in alternating sequence, but so rapidly that the fire appeared to be continuous, as iridescent energy bolts sleeted across the free-fire zone and carved black swaths through the snow. Dozens of Ramanthians simply ceased to exist, as their bodies were vaporized, and steam fogged the atmosphere.

Meanwhile, closer in, the bio bods, backed by the highly mobile T-2s, were giving a good account of themselves. The vehicle-mounted fifties continued to *chug* methodically, the lighter weapons *chattered*, and exploding grenades threw columns of dirty snow up into the air as clusters of bugs went down. But like the waves of an incoming tide, Santana saw that each drift of bodies was closer to the perimeter than the last had been, and wondered how much longer they would be able to hold.

Suddenly an airborne Ramanthian was there, descending from above to land directly on top of the log barricade, then the trooper was gone in a brilliant flash of light. The payoff for the trooper's act of self-sacrifice was a dead legionnaire and a four-foot-wide hole in the camp's defenses. Both Santana and a force of Ramanthians rushed toward the gap. "Torrez!' the officer shouted. "Hayashi! To me!"

Both T-2s responded, bringing their considerable firepower to bear on a point fifty feet out from the newly created hole, and that's where the oncoming Ramanthians seemed to collide with an invisible wall. They staggered, and fell in heaps, which made it difficult for those behind them to advance. But still the enemy came, wave after wave of them, as if willing to absorb every bullet the defenders had if that was the price of victory. Sergeant Pimm went down when a bullet smashed through his throat, and Hoyt-11,791 stepped in to take his place on the firing line. Death owned the valley—and the day had barely begun.

Millar's assignment was simple. He could remember Santana's exact words: "Find the Ramanthian sonofabitch and kill him!" By which the cavalry officer meant the bug who was directing the attack on the allied encampment. But that was easier said than done. Even though the recon ball had been able to exit the encampment under cover of Dietrich's smoke screen, his presence had not gone unnoticed. Although the chits didn't believe in cyborgs, they had robotic remotes, which could be used for reconnaissance missions. And the scout hadn't traveled more than a thousand yards before one of the pesky machines locked on to his heat signature and began to follow him.

That forced Millar to waste valuable time turning around and going after the machine, which—though lightly armed—was highly maneuverable and quite speedy. But, after a three-minute chase, Millar had been able to catch up with the robot and destroy it with a single bolt from his energy cannon.

Having resumed his original mission, the cyborg was concealed within a grove of trees peering out into an open meadow located about a mile north of the allied encampment. And what he saw shocked him. Even *more* Ramanthians were streaming into the open area, where they were formed into the equivalent of platoons before being sent south into the fray! That made the task of killing their commanding officer all the more important.

But, while the grouping of what the scout assumed to be officers was within range of his .50-caliber gun, the stubby barrel was way too short to produce sufficient accuracy over the distance required. The obvious answer was to get closer before taking his shot. But with no trees for cover, that wouldn't be possible.

The reality of that sent a trickle of liquid lead into Millar's nonexistent belly as whistles blew, *another* wave of troopers were sent forward, and machines guns *chattered* to the south. The legionnaire had already been killed once, and didn't want to die again, but couldn't see any other option. So the recon ball shot out of the trees, skimmed the snow, and began the long, hazardous run. There weren't any trees, but there were outcroppings of rock, which would provide at least some cover so long as he stayed low.

None of the Ramanthian officers noticed the threat at first, partly because they were preoccupied with what they were doing, and partly because the terrain-following cyborg was hard to see as he weaved his way between boulders and occasional clusters of ground-hugging shrubs.

But right about the time that Millar was halfway to his goal one of the Ramanthians spotted him, *clacked* an alert, and the entire group turned to fire at him. That was bad, but not as bad as it might have been, since the officers were armed with pistols rather than assault weapons.

Still, the legionnaire had no armor to speak of, and felt a sudden stab of "pain" as a well-aimed bullet penetrated his casing and appropriate electronic impulses arrived at his forebrain. The damage triggered electronic warnings as well, which his onboard computer projected in front of Millar's "vision," making it harder to concentrate. The problem was that he didn't know which bug was in overall command. So the logical solution was to kill *all* the bastards and let whatever god the Ramanthians believed in sort them out. Having closed the distance between himself and his targets, the recon ball opened fire.

Having stood their ground against the unconventional attack, the Ramanthian officers were easy meat for the cyborg's fifty and were literally torn to bloody rags as the huge slugs hit them. Body parts cartwheeled through the air, severed wings spiraled down, and a blood mist soaked the snow. But the noise and motion drew the attention of some incoming troops, one of whom was toting a rocket launcher that he was quick-witted enough to fire. Millar "heard" a warning tone, knew there wouldn't be any reprieve this time, and felt an explosion of warmth as the heat-seeking missile weapon caught up with him. Suddenly he was free.

Sending Corporal Thain plus three precious T-2s out of the encampment during the first few minutes of the attack had been a risky thing to do. But now, as the hard-pressed allies struggled to hold on, Santana hoped his gamble would pay off. And it did. Insofar as the chits knew, *all* the animals were directly in front of them. So when four highly lethal T-2s hit their left flank, the Ramanthians were caught entirely by surprise.

Dozens of enemy troopers were swept off their feet as the vengeful legionnaires opened fire on them. The cyborgs were *always* fast, but never more so than when unencumbered by a bio bod, which meant they were difficult to hit. So as the latest wave of Ramanthians turned toward the new threat, it was only to encounter four whirling dervishes, each operating in perfect synchronization with all the rest. Guns *chugged*, energy cannons *whined*, and it seemed as if nothing could stop them until a rocket-propelled grenade hit Private Imbi Yat in the chest.

The force of the resulting explosion blew the cyborg in half, which gave the bugs reason to hope—until Thain and the rest of the T-2s took their revenge. The ensuing slaughter lasted less than three minutes but took nearly a hundred lives. And when it was done, an eerie silence settled over the battlefield as bleary-eyed defenders took a moment to reload, and Santana had time to view the video Lieutenant Millar had sent him. The pictures were truly worth a thousand words—and would be submitted to Kobbi along with a request for a posthumous medal if Santana survived. A battle had been won, but the price had been very, very high. And, as Santana looked out over piles of gently steaming bodies, he knew the worst was yet to come.

19

PLANET GAMMA-014, THE CLONE REPUBLIC

As Santana entered the quad, he quickly discovered that the interior of Lupo's cargo bay was splattered with blood. *Lots* of blood. And there, at the very center of the bay, stood Dr. Kira Kelly. A makeshift operating table had been set up—with her on one side and Hospital Corpsman Sumi on the other. A third person stood with his back to the hatch. The cavalry officer hadn't had time to think about the prisoners during the battle, but as he looked at Kelly, Santana felt a sudden surge of anger. "The doctor is supposed to be under guard. . . . Who released her?"

"That would be *me*," Lieutenant Gregory Zolkin said, as he turned to look at his commanding officer. The word "sir" was noticeably missing from the sentence, and Santana saw no sign of an apology in the other officer's dark eyes.

Santana realized that the platoon leader had been pressed into service as Kelly's anesthesiologist. More than that, the company commander was struck by the extent to which Zolkin had changed since the raid on Oron IV. Somewhere along the line the young, frequently insecure youth Santana had known back then, had been transformed into a battle-hardened lieutenant. Who, in the wake of Amoyo's recent death, was not only a platoon leader but the company's XO. And a man willing to employ the services of the devil herself if that was required to save one of his legionnaires.

It was impossible to tell who the patient was from Santana's vantage point, but the legionnaire's purplish intestines were piled high atop his or her chest. Kelly was sorting through the coils looking for holes. Santana's expression softened. "Who is it?"

Zolkin looked down and back up again. "Private Oneeye Knifeplay, sir. He was standing on a track, firing a fifty, when an incoming slug hit metal and bounced up under his armor. He was going to die, sir. And Dr. Kelly offered to help."

Kelly turned her head toward Santana at that point. Most of her face was invisible behind a blood-splattered surgical mask, but he could still see her eyes. "What I did was wrong," the naval officer admitted bleakly. "But I'm a pretty good doctor. And the only one you have."

Santana saw the determination in her eyes and nodded. "Point taken. Carry on." And with that, the officer turned and exited the quad. It was cold outside, and getting steadily colder, as day gradually surrendered to night. Snow *crunched* under his boots, the moisture in his nasal passages froze, and his cheeks felt numb. But people were working in spite of the cold. Having failed earlier in the day, the Ramanthians were sure to take another shot at their enemies during the hours of darkness, which was why the battle-weary legionnaires, marines, and clones were busy trying to improve the encampment's defenses. Especially the log barricades, which had never been intended for a major battle, and were in need of reinforcement.

But Master Sergeant Dice Dietrich had a solution for that and was busy supervising repairs. Having decided that there wasn't enough time to fell more trees and drag them into position, the noncom was making use of dead Ramanthians instead. There were *hundreds* of them, most of whom were rock-hard, and made excellent building blocks. The trick was to alternate the way the corpses were stacked to add stability.

Of course every now and then the master sergeant's work detail would come across a bug who was badly wounded, and unconscious, or not so badly wounded and hoping to escape notice. The solution was the same in either case. Such individuals were shot before being added to the steadily growing defensive wall, where some of them seemed to stare out at the world through frosty cataracts.

Dietrich was helping one of the CVAs hoist a Ramanthian noncom onto the north section of the barricade when Santana arrived. "There," Dietrich said, as he stepped back to admire his work. "The wall is a lot thicker—and I like a tidy battlefield."

Santana couldn't help but grin. "I'll make a note in your next performance review. 'While often drunk, and frequently disrespectful, Master Sergeant Dietrich insists on a tidy battlefield.'"

"That's a fair assessment," the legionnaire agreed cheerfully. "I'll take it!"

Santana felt a snowflake kiss his nose and shoved his hands farther into his pockets. "They're going to hit us hard."

The noncom nodded soberly. "I know."

"If I fall, give Lieutenant Zolkin all the support you can. And if *he* falls, then save as many people as possible."

The possibility that *he* could wind up in command hadn't occurred to Dietrich until then. It was a depressing prospect. "Don't be silly, sir," the noncom replied lightly. "You're too mean to die! The lieutenant and I will have to get our promotions the hard way."

The conversation was interrupted as Private Kay Kaimo arrived on the scene. She had been assigned to guard the Seebos and was coming off duty. "Excuse me, sir," the legionnaire said politely. "But Colonel Six would like a word with you."

Santana raised an eyebrow. "Really? About what?"

Kaimo shook her head. "I don't know, sir. The colonel didn't say."

"Okay," Santana replied. "Thanks."

"Keep up the good work," Santana said, as he turned back to Dietrich. "Although I would prefer to have the enemy bodies stacked according to regiment next time."

"Screw you, sir," the noncom replied. "*And* the cyborg you rode in on."

Santana laughed and made his way over to one of four well-screened campfires. That's where Colonel Six and his Seebos sat huddled around a crackling blaze. It was dark by then, which meant that more than thirty nearly identical faces were all lit by the same flickering glow. Two legionnaires were present as well—their assault weapons at the ready. One of the clones stood expectantly—and Santana motioned him forward. Six was badly in need of a shave—and snowflakes had started to accumulate on his shoulders. The officer's tone was humble. "Thank you for agreeing to see me."

Santana shrugged. "You're welcome. . . . What's on your mind?"

Six stared into the legionnaire's eyes. "The Ramanthians will attack tonight."

"That possibility had occurred to me," Santana replied dryly.

"And they're going to win," Six predicted. "Unless you get reinforcements—which both of us know you won't. So turn us loose!" he said hurriedly. "We'll fight beside you. And I think you'll agree that thirty-six additional soldiers could make a *big* difference."

"Yes, they could," Santana agreed soberly. "But what happens later on? When the battle is over?"

"We'll lay down our arms," Six promised. "Or keep them if need be—under *your* command."

"It sounds good," Santana admitted. "But no thanks. . . . I wouldn't trust you farther than I could throw a half-track."

"You don't have to trust me," the other man replied earnestly. His voice was pitched so low that the other Seebos couldn't hear. "You have someone that means a lot to me and I wouldn't leave here without."

"Dr. Kelly?"

"Exactly," the clone agreed defiantly.

The offer was tempting. *Very* tempting. Because thirty-six additional defenders would make an important difference. Especially given the fact that the Seebos were crack troops. Literally bred to fight—and tough as nails. But the colonel was accused of murder.

Still, the Legion had the means to keep potentially rebellious cyborgs under control, so why not use a similar technique on Six? Not too surprisingly the clone objected to the concept Santana put forward. But, if the Seebo wanted to live, he had very little choice. Sergeant Jose Ramos was something of a genius where explosives were concerned, and it was he who came up with the combination leg shackle and bomb. A tidy little device that Santana, Zolkin, or Dietrich could trigger remotely anytime one of them chose to do so. It wouldn't kill Six, not immediately, but it would blow his right foot off. Suddenly, what had been a seemingly hopeless situation, was just a little bit better.

The animals had been weakened during the previous day. Subcommander Jaos Nubb knew that. So rather than take the more measured approach that his dead predecessor had—Nubb had chosen to send *all* his troops in at once. The majority of them were members of the much vaunted *Death Hammer* Regiment and therefore among the most valiant soldiers the empire had to offer. So it was with a sense of confidence that the officer led his troops into battle. And simultaneously called upon his secret weapon, which was in orbit one thousand three hundred miles above the planet's surface.

The *Star Taker* had been busy of late, chasing dozens of little ships and snuffing them out of existence, so the ship's crew welcomed the opportunity to settle into orbit and fire on some ground coordinates for a change—even if that meant allowing some civilian vessels to escape. The problem, to the extent that there was one, had to do with the question of accuracy. Because based on data provided by Subcommander Nubb, there was very little distance between his troops and enemy forces. Which meant even a small error could have tragic results. So great care was taken while calculating all of the many variables involved. But finally, on an order from Nubb, one of the destroyer's big guns spoke. An artificial comet was born and slashed down through the atmosphere toward the surface below.

Santana recognized the freight-train *rumble* the moment he heard it. But it was Dietrich who shouted, "Incoming!" and beat the officer into one of the recently improved bunkers. The blue lightning bolt fell on a half-track, blew the vehicle apart, and killed the Seebos who had been stationed at the vehicle's machine guns. The *second* bolt punched a hole in the ice-covered lake, brought the surrounding water to a momentary boil, and sent a geyser of steam fifty feet into the air. The third impact opened a gap in the southern portion of the defensive wall, erased a Hoyt, and opened a grave in which to bury her remains. Dirt and rocks fell like rain. Then while the allies were still taking shelter in their various holes, the Ramanthians attacked. Fortunately, Sergeant Suresee Fareye, who had been sent to scout the enemy, gave the warning. "This is Alpha Six-Four. . . . *Here they come!* Over."

That brought all the troops back up and most were in place by the time the tsunami of chitin and flesh struck. There was no opportunity to think about tactics or give orders because Santana was fighting for his life. A hellish symphony of explosions, gunfire, and alien bugle calls were heard as flares threw a ghastly glow over the scene and began their slow descent. The cavalry officer could see *hundreds* of bugs, all shuffling forward as quickly as they could, determined to roll over the encampment and kill everyone within.

But if the bugs were a wave, the allies were a rock, and the volume of outgoing fire was stupendous. Between the cyborgs, each of whom packed firepower equivalent to a squad of regular troops, and the newly reinforced bio bods, Alpha Company was an immovable object. And with no soldiers left in reserve, there was nothing Nubb could do, but throw *himself* at the wall of dead bodies. A valiant thing to do, but largely meaningless, because he was killed within seconds.

The assault came to an end five minutes later, when the heretofore stationary Lupo lurched to his feet, stepped *over* the grisly barricade, and went on the offensive. With a pack of agile T-2s to protect his flanks, the cyborg went bug hunting. The surviving Ramanthians ran. And the results, as summarized by Master Sergeant Dietrich, were nothing less than: "Goddamned wonderful!" Which, all things considered, was pretty good.

General Mortimer Kobbi had two recon balls left—and made good use of both as the nine-mile-long column snaked its way toward the west. By plugging into what the airborne cyborgs could see, Kobbi could monitor what was happening from his place near the front of the formation. The good news, if one could call it that, was that because the allied force was 10 percent smaller as it left Yal-Am, it was that much speedier. Or would have been, if it hadn't been for a long series of Ramanthian-triggered avalanches, well-conceived ambushes, and cleverly hidden mines.

As the allies waited for the latest rockslide to be cleared, Kobbi raised his binos. Hundreds of Ramanthian troops could be seen streaming along the tops of ridges to the north and south. The bugs were paralleling the allies, waiting for the chance to close in, and that opportunity was coming. Fifteen miles ahead, at a place called the Ordo gorge, the bugs would have the perfect opportunity to converge on the column as it was forced to cross a narrow two-lane bridge.

That was bad enough. But even worse from Kobbi's point of view was the fact that if the span were blown, the allies would be trapped in the mountains, and cut off from the lowlands to the west. That was where Maylo Chien-Chu and her ragtag fleet of yachts, freighters, and other civilian vessels were supposed to pick the soldiers up. But only if the bridge was still in place when the column arrived at the Ordo gorge.

And that was a problem because the little general lacked the fly-forms necessary to airlift troops to the span. All of his attempts to send infantry forward had been blocked by a sequence of well-executed ambushes. So the officer felt a sudden sense of jubilation when a familiar voice was heard on the command push. "Alpha Six to Six-One. Over."

"This is Six-One," Kobbi replied. "Go. Over."

"We have him," Santana said meaningfully. "*And* the hostages. Over."

"That's wonderful," Kobbi enthused, as he lowered his visor. A series of eye blinks summoned the map he was looking for, the blue "snake" that represented the column, *and* Alpha Company's pulsing triangle. Kobbi was thrilled to see that Santana's company was on the highway ahead, only six miles from the Ordo bridge!

It was impossible to conceal the excitement Kobbi felt as he gave his orders. "I'm sure you've been through a lot—but we could use Alpha Company's help. Proceed six miles due west, take the bridge over the Ordo River, and secure it. We will get there as soon as we can. Over."

There was a pause as Santana eyed the map projected on the inside surface of his visor, followed by a laconic, "Yes, sir. Alpha Six out."

Kobbi, who could hardly believe his good luck, removed his helmet and looked up into the lead gray sky. "Thank you, God," the general said humbly. "Thank you for one more chance."

Sergeant Suresee Fareye was on point with Private Ka Nhan. Santana, Deker, and three additional T-2s were half a mile back, closely followed by the quad, two surviving half-tracks, and Lieutenant Zolkin's platoon, a configuration that ensured both halves of the company would have leadership if the formation were cut in two.

Having won the battle at the lake and having covered the four miles back to the highway without encountering any Ramanthians, Santana had been hoping to rejoin the main column. But now, as Alpha Company followed the highway west, he understood the dilemma Kobbi faced. The bridge at Ordo gorge was both a choke point *and* the critical link to the section of the highway that would carry the allies down to the flatlands beyond.

The question, to the cavalry officer's mind at least, was whether the bridge was still in place. And if so, *why?* General Akoto was a smart old bug—and not the sort of officer to forget a strategic choke point. So if the bridge had been left standing, there was a reason. Or *reasons*. One of those could be that having been able to defeat the allies, the Ramanthians might want to preserve the bridge, rather than being forced to construct a new one.

But whatever the truth, Santana knew he would find out soon enough. Meanwhile, of more immediate concern were the Ramanthian troops clearly visible to the north and south. They were traveling along the ridgetops, which, according to the topo map projected onto the cavalry officer's HUD, were going to converge a half mile east of the bridge! Which meant the bugs were going where *he* was going. A very unpleasant prospect indeed. Especially if the chits got there first. Which, had more of them been able to fly, they almost certainly would have. "This is Alpha Six," Santana said, over the company push. "Let's pick up the pace. Out."

There was snow and ice to contend with, plus burned-out wrecks that had to be pushed out of the way so the half-tracks could squeeze through, but the weary troops did their best. Most were operating on no more than three hours' sleep, hadn't had a proper meal in two days, and many had wounds sustained during the battle by the lake.

The legionnaire's thoughts were interrupted by Fareye's

voice on the radio. "The bridge is intact, sir," the Naa said as he examined the surrounding bluffs. "But I'm not sure why. Over."

"Maybe the Ramanthians have plans for it," Santana replied. "We'll be there shortly. Cross over, push two miles down the highway, and settle in. If bugs come in from the west, I want as much warning as possible. Out."

Fareye replied with the traditional double *click* and ordered Nhan forward. He felt exposed on the bridge, *knew* someone was watching him, and wondered if he would hear the shot that killed him.

As Deker rounded a corner, and began to make his way down a 10-percent grade, Santana saw the span up ahead. It was a well-maintained steel-arch bridge. According to the data file that was associated with those coordinates, it was about 3,250 feet long. The structure was two lanes wide, had been constructed twenty-eight years earlier, and was 610 feet high. "Okay," Santana said, as Deker arrived at the east end of the span. "I need a volunteer. . . . Someone with a head for heights. Over."

"That would be any one of us," Colonel Six said, from the passenger seat in the first half-track. "Take your pick. Over." The clones had been allowed to keep their weapons, thanks to the fact that Dr. Kelly was locked up inside Lupo, and Santana had Six on a short leash. "Good enough," the cavalry officer replied. "If you would be so good as to select a couple of your men, and send them down to inspect the underbelly of this bridge, I would be most appreciative. Over."

"So we're looking for explosives? Over."

"Exactly," Santana said succinctly. "Alpha Six out."

Having dispatched Dietrich to help lower the Seebos over the edge, *and* keep an eye on them, Santana turned his attention back to what he saw as the most pressing issue. And that was the defense of the bridge.

But what if that was where Akoto *wanted* the allies to focus their attention? What if the real attack came from the west?

Santana lacked sufficient resources to put a large force on the far side of the span, but Lupo couldn't climb the surrounding slopes, so it made sense to send him across. The cavalry officer gave the necessary orders and held his breath as the huge cyborg began the 3,250-foot-long journey. Lupo was at risk, as were all of those within his cargo compartment, including Kelly and her patients. Thankfully, the trip went off without a hitch, and it was only a matter of minutes before the big cyborg was on the far side of gorge, and marching down the highway.

Having secured the other end of the bridge to the extent he could, it was time for Santana to address the surrounding heights. Rather than wait for the bugs to occupy them, and come swarming down, the legionnaire was determined to cut the insectoid aliens off on the ridgetops, where the flow of enemy soldiers would be severely restricted. It was a made-to-order situation for his T-2s, any one of whom could single-handedly stop such an advance, so long as he or she had adequate cover and plenty of ammo. To avoid any such calamity, Santana planned to place *two* cyborgs on each ridge. That would allow them to rotate in and out of combat while hardworking CVAs humped ammo to them from below.

No sooner had the T-2s been sent on their way than Colonel Six appeared at his side. Santana was standing on the bridge deck by then—having sent Deker up onto the south ridge. So the men were eye to eye as the clone delivered his report. "You were correct," the Seebo confirmed. "Explosives are hidden under *both* ends of the bridge. That's why the bugs left the span in place. They can blow it anytime they want to."

Santana felt the hairs on the back of his neck start to rise. Somewhere, within direct line of sight, a Ramanthian was watching them through a pair of Y-shaped bug binos. Lupo was a high-priority target, but the bugs had allowed the quad to cross in spite of that fact, which seemed to suggest that the chits had an even bigger payoff in mind. So what were they trying to accomplish? Stall the allied column and destroy it just short of the span? And thereby preserve the bridge? Or wait until the allies were streaming across and blow the structure at that point to inflict the maximum number of casualties? There was no way to be sure. "Can we disarm the explosives?" the cavalry officer inquired mildly.

"I don't know," Six said honestly. "They're probably booby-trapped."

"Yeah, that would make sense," Santana agreed.

"But there might be *another* way to deal with the problem," the Seebo put in.

"Yeah? What's that?"

"We could screen the explosives off, so the bugs can't see what we're up to," Six replied. "Then, rather than disarm the explosives, we'll remove the steel beams they're attached to. There's a cutting torch on each half-track."

Santana frowned. "That's a clever idea, but won't it weaken the bridge? Each quad weighs fifty tons."

"There's a lot of structural redundancy in any well-built bridge," Six insisted confidently. "And we won't remove any more steel than we absolutely have to."

Not being an engineer, the cavalry officer wasn't so sure, but couldn't see any alternatives, and knew the main column would arrive soon. "Okay, Colonel," Santana said. "Make it happen."

Six took note of the "Colonel," an honorific that had been noticeably absent up until that point, and knew it was Santana's way of communicating respect. Not approval, but respect, which was more important to the Seebo's way of thinking. He nodded. "Can I ask a favor?"

"That depends on what it is," Santana replied cautiously.

"Look after Dr. Kelly. Get her off Gamma-014 if you can."

"I'll do my best to get both of you off the planet," Santana promised. "So they can put you on trial."

"I'll take that as a 'yes,'" Six replied, and did a neat about-face. And with that, he was gone.

Lead elements of Kobbi's column arrived fifteen minutes

later, but were forced to stop, or risk crossing the booby-trapped bridge. Right about the same time the insistent *rattle* of machine-gun fire was heard, as the Ramanthians attempted to push their way off the ridgetops, only to be met by a hail of bullets when the waiting legionnaires fired on them.

Then, as General Kobbi and his T-2 arrived on the scene, Fareye called in. "Alpha Six-Four to Alpha Six. Four Gantha tanks are coming my way—followed by what looks like a battalion of troops. Over."

Now Santana understood. Rather than simply cut the column off, Akoto planned to eradicate it, and the Ordo gorge crossing had been chosen as the place to accomplish that task. If the column remained where it was, the Ramanthian general would catch it from behind, and if his troops were able to break through, they would attack the allies from above. Meanwhile, if the fugitives attempted to advance, they would collide with the Gantha tanks. Or go down with the bridge. The bugs had all the cards.

Kobbi had access to the company push, so he understood as well. "The bastard has us by the balls," the little officer said, as he dropped to the ground. His breath fogged the ozone-tinged air and ice *crunched* under his boots.

Santana resisted the impulse to salute, knew that could identify the general to any snipers lurking about, and nodded instead as Fareye called in. "Yes, sir. Hold one. I read you, Six-Four. Maintain visual contact but pull back." There was a double *click* by way of a reply.

"Don't tell me. Let me guess," Kobbi put in. The bugs have explosives on the bridge."

"Yes, sir," Santana agreed. "Except that—" The sentence was interrupted by a resounding *boom*, quickly followed by a second, equally loud explosion, and numerous echoes. Both men turned to look at the bridge, but it was still there and apparently undamaged. That was when a dirty, unshaven Seebo hoisted himself up over the rail, spotted the officers, and made his way over. The clone had a big grin on his face.

"It worked like a charm!" he said enthusiastically. "We cut both packages free at the same time, the bugs saw them fall, and blooey! The charges went off about halfway down."

Both of Kobbi's bushy eyebrows rose. "And you are?"

"This is Colonel Six," Santana put in. "Colonel Six—this is General Kobbi."

"Well, I'll be damned," Kobbi said, as he turned to Santana. "The last time we met he was a *general*! You let him run around loose?"

The last was directed at Santana, who smiled grimly. "So long as he behaves himself. And, truth be told, the colonel and his Seebos fought bravely over the last couple of days."

"I'm gratified to hear it," Kobbi said gravely. "And I'm sure that will be taken into consideration during the court-martial. But this is now. Can we cross the bridge?"

"Yes, sir," Six said definitively. "It will hold."

"It better," the little general growled. "I'm sending *another* quad across. Plus two squads of T-2s. Together they should be able to make short work of the battalion that's coming up from the west. Alpha Company will remain in place until everyone is across. At that point you can bring those T-2s down off the ridges and cross the bridge. Once you're on the west side, my people will blow the span. Any questions? No? Well done, Captain. . . . Thank you, Colonel. Let's get to work."

Having been ordered to remain in place until the entire column passed over the bridge, most of Alpha Company played no part in the ensuing battle, as General Kobbi's column went head-to-head with four Gantha tanks and a battalion of Ramanthian regulars. Their job was to keep the bugs from coming down off the ridges, which the T-2s managed to do, until Santana ordered them down onto the highway.

Then, with Ramanthians right behind them, it was time for the legionnaires to withdraw to the far side of the span. A team of demolition experts from the 2nd REI had been left behind to drop the bridge into the river below, which the legionnaires did the moment some overeager chits attempted to cross.

With that accomplished Santana led his company down the twisting, turning highway, and it wasn't long before they began to see evidence of what had been a bloody battle. As expected, the Gantha tanks had been no match for two quads and a pack of voracious T-2s. Santana smiled grimly as Deker carried him past the partially slagged wrecks, one of which was topped by a Ramanthian tank commander who had been cooked in place. A wisp of smoke issued from his hooked beak as the company commander rode past.

What lay beyond was even more gruesome. Because without any armor to protect them from the oncoming cyborgs, and with no avenue of escape, the Ramanthian infantry had been slaughtered. Those warriors who had been killed along the edges of the road lay where they had fallen, their bodies piled in drifts, but all facing the enemy. A testimony to their courage. The rest of the bugs, those who went down toward the center of the highway, weren't recognizable anymore. Not after being crushed by quads and chopped to bits by a succession of tracked vehicles. The result was a bloody porridge made of equal parts blood, chitin, and snow. It was dark red at first, and thick with body parts, but began to thin somewhat as Alpha Company followed the road through a curve. The muck was merely pink by that time, and remained so as they passed through what had been a roadblock but was little more than scattered rubble by then.

The highway turned white after that, as it entered a long series of switchbacks, leading down to the partially forested flatlands below. All of the allies were exhausted, most having fought for days with only hours of sleep, but Santana heard no complaints. The word was out by then. Ships were landing, and everyone who could walk, hop, or crawl to the LZ would be pulled out. And none of the soldiers wanted to be left behind.

So the main column traveled day and night, and Alpha Company did likewise, until finally, after seventeen hours of nearly nonstop travel, Santana led his road-weary troops into what had already been dubbed "the doughnut," by the mixed force of CVAs, legionnaires, and marines who were responsible for the facility.

The doughnut, or landing zone (LZ), was located on mostly level ground and was approximately one mile across. Heavy equipment had been used to dig a deep ditch around the outer perimeter, intended to keep Ganthas out, and slow the Ramanthian infantry. Consideration had been given to building a berm along the circular ditch, which would have been relatively easy to do, given all the dirt removed from what some of the allies called "the moat."

But Kobbi nixed that idea, pointing out that once the allies were forced to fall back, the bugs would cross the ditch, and take cover behind the raised earthworks. So the dirt had been trucked into the landing zone's interior, where a berm made sense, so the troops would have something to hide behind as the size of the overall force continued to shrink. And the evacuation process was already under way as a marine guide led Alpha Company across acres of heavily churned muck. "Look at that, sir!" Dietrich exclaimed, as repellers *roared* and a tramp freighter lowered itself into the so-called doughnut hole. "That ain't no assault boat. . . . It's an inter-system rust bucket!"

"Who cares?" Santana countered, raising his voice so others could hear. "So long as it can fly. And you've been on our troopships. . . . I'll take the freighter!"

That got a laugh, and the comment soon made the rounds. But Santana was concerned. As the civilian ships continued to arrive, he saw that many of them were so old, or so small, that they made the first freighter look like a passenger liner. Still, something was better than nothing, or so the cavalry officer told himself as he was forced to confront the latest challenge.

Alpha Company had been ordered to plug a hole on the east side of the doughnut between elements of the 13th DBLE and the 1st Marine Division, both of which had suffered heavy casualties in Yal-Am. In fact, most of their neighbors looked like hollow-cheeked scarecrows as they interrupted their work long enough to wave at the newcomers and shout friendly insults. There was plenty of work to do, because like the outfits to either side of it, the company was responsible for its own defenses. So with only a few hours of daylight left to them, it was important to dig firing pits, excavate communicating trenches, and fill newly created bunkers with ammo.

Fortunately, the legionnaires could speed the process by replacing the graspers that the T-2s normally wore with "shovel hands" that enabled the cyborgs to dig trenches in a fraction of the time that a team of bio bods would require. So while Zolkin, Dietrich, and Six supervised work on company's defenses, Santana took a moment to climb up onto one of the half-tracks and examine the area through his binos. To call the scene chaotic would have been an understatement.

Ships of every possible description were circling the LZ, waiting for an opportunity to land. Then, when one of them finally managed to do so, a navy beach master was sent to find out how many people that particular vessel could accommodate. An unfortunate necessity caused by the fact that most of the civilians weren't equipped to communicate with the military. Once the ship's capacity had been determined, the petty officer would radio the information in, the correct number of stretcher parties were dispatched, and the loading process began.

According to the orders issued by Kobbi, the wounded were to be evacuated first. Then, once they were gone, enlisted bio bods would go next, followed by the Legion's cyborgs, and the officers. Immediately after each vessel lifted off, another yacht, lugger, or freighter would land, at which point the whole process began again. Or that was how everything was *supposed* to work.

But as Santana and thousands of others looked on, what had once been a thirty-passenger lifeboat took off, and suddenly lost power. It was three hundred feet off the ground by then and fell like a rock. There was a loud *boom* as it hit. Followed by a ball of flame—and a towering column of black smoke.

Fortunately, the boat crashed well outside of the main landing area, allowing the next vessel to settle in two minutes later.

Meanwhile, out along the doughnut's perimeter, work continued. Some sections were well fortified as enterprising officers, and in some cases senior noncoms, sought to strengthen their various positions. Other areas were not prepared either because the troops lacked good leadership or they were too exhausted to do more.

Countless campfires pointed gray fingers up at the overcast sky, where hardworking recon balls zipped back and forth across the LZ, and stoic robots carried stretchers loaded with ammo from one location to another. All this made Santana thankful for the fact that he wasn't a major, colonel, or, God forbid, a general, and therefore responsible for a larger slice of the insanity taking place around him.

Santana was just about to leave his vantage point when a pair of Ramanthian fighters *roared* overhead. The cavalry officer tracked the aircraft as they circled the allied position, vectored in on the incoming rescue boats, and attacked two of them. One of the allied vessels exploded in midair, and rained flaming debris onto the troops below, while the other spiraled into the ground half a mile outside the perimeter. There was a flash of light followed by a muted *boom*.

But victory typically comes at a price, as the bugs learned, when half a dozen quads and twice that number of T-2s hooked up with each other via the Legion's ITC system to create an umbrella of computer-controlled antiaircraft fire. Both fighters were destroyed within a matter of seconds, and the skies remained clear after that.

Santana shook his head sadly and went back to work. There was a lot to do, beginning with the creation of an evacuation list, and the need to get a hot meal into the bio bods. That's what Santana and Zolkin were working on when Kelly appeared. Lupo had been incorporated into the landing zone's defenses a quarter of a mile away, and the doctor had been forced to walk from there, which was why her combat boots were caked with mud. There weren't any guards with her, nor were any required, given the nature of the situation. The naval officer came to attention and delivered a sloppy salute. Santana returned it. There was a continual *roar* as the ships came and went, forcing the cavalry officer to raise his voice. "Dr. Kelly. This *is* a surprise."

"I came to tell you that Private Knifeplay and the rest of your wounded soldiers are still alive," Kelly said. "Or were when we loaded them onto one of the ships."

Santana remembered the lifeboat that had crashed immediately after takeoff and wondered if any of his legionnaires had been aboard it. "Thank you, Doctor. That was very thoughtful of you."

There was a moment of silence as the redhead looked down and back up again. Her eyes were very blue. "You're welcome. Having spent time with Alpha Company, and not being assigned elsewhere, I was hoping you would let me stay."

Colonel Six and his men had been ordered to prepare a position for one of the heavy machine guns. When Santana looked in that direction, he saw Six looking back at him. It didn't take a genius to figure out that the clone had seen Kelly arrive and was waiting to see what would happen.

Santana's first reaction was to say, "No," but when he turned back, the expression on Kelly's face was so hopeful he couldn't bring himself to turn her down. "I'm afraid there will be one more battle to fight," the legionnaire said soberly. "And we'll need your skills."

A look of profound gratitude appeared in Kelly's eyes as she said, "Thank you, sir," and immediately made her way out toward the point where Six stood waiting. The two of them made an odd couple, or so it seemed to Santana, who knew the founder would have agreed with him.

A sleek-looking yacht *rumbled* in from the east, and was forced to pause a few hundred feet south of Alpha Company's position, as another ship rose out of the doughnut hole. The name *Play Pretty* was painted on the side of the ship's hull. The boat's elderly pilots had completed three trips by then—and were back for their fourth. The afternoon wore on.

Night was a long black thing, punctuated by the *roar* of repellers, as the nearly nonstop flow of ships continued. Kobbi stopped by to visit Alpha Company around 0200. He was accompanied by an adjutant, and two bodyguards, all of whom joined Santana, Zolkin, and Dietrich around one of three fires. Colonel Six was off somewhere, with Kelly most likely, although Santana didn't really care anymore. Not so long as they did their jobs.

"There's one helluva battle going on up in space," the little general commented grimly, as a flask of whiskey made the rounds. He'd been talking for hours, and his voice was hoarse. "Our navy is back, and they're doing everything they can to keep the bugs off our backs. So we owe the swabbies big-time."

All of the faces were lit from below as a breeze blew through and caused the fuel-fed fire to waver uncertainly. "But here's the rub," Kobbi continued gloomily. "Every time one of those ships lifts off, we get weaker, and the bugs get stronger! According to my scouts, the chits have us surrounded. I figure they will attack at dawn. So be ready to pull back at 0400. By that time, all the enlisted bio bods will be gone. That means it will be up to the remaining borgs and officers to beat the bugs back. Then, once we get some sort of respite, we'll pull all of the brain boxes and fall back on the doughnut hole. The last ship will be large enough to accommodate everyone. It isn't the way I was planning to leave—but I'm looking forward to a shower and a beer." That got the predictable chuckle, and five minutes later, the general was gone. There were more people to brief, and the clock was ticking.

The pullback went fairly smoothly, all things considered. And by the time a seemingly reluctant sun rose in the east, the allies were hunkered down inside a circle only half a mile across, which, though thinly populated, could still be defended thanks to the Legion's battle-weary cyborgs. The quads were dug in at regular intervals all around the new perimeter, where their war forms would be abandoned when it came time to run. The T-2s, which were sprinkled in between the big behemoths, remained mobile and could shift positions if necessary. Farther out, forming a circle around the ring, were hundreds of crab mines.

That was the scene as a sickly-looking daylight crept in across the land, and what looked like ectoplasm rose to hover spiritlike over the well-churned mud as Santana heard Dietrich say, "Holy shit. . . . Look at that!"

The master sergeant wasn't an officer, but had refused to leave, claiming that *real* officers wouldn't know what to do without him. Six was there as well, as was Four-Four, and Dr. Kelly. T-2s, both armed and ready, were crouched to the left and right, with quads beyond. The scene that Dietrich wanted Santana to look at was hard to miss. During the hours of darkness *thousands* of Ramanthians had closed in on the LZ and stood ready to attack. They stood shoulder to shoulder, fifty deep, in a formation that had lined the far edge of the ditch.

There was a sudden flurry of activity as more *enemy* soldiers came forward through lanes left for that purpose, pushed crudely made footbridges up until they stood on end, and allowed them to fall across the moat. That was the signal for flares to soar high into the air, for bugles to sound, and for noncoms to blow their whistles. Santana expected the soldiers to pour across the bridges at that point, and was surprised when they didn't. As the defenders watched in horror, hundreds of clone civilians were forced to cross the ditch instead—men, women, and free-breeder children who had been captured during the early stages of the Ramanthian invasion and held in remote POW camps until now.

Some of them tripped, a few fell into the moat, but most made it across. And that was when the mines went off. *Boom!*

Boom! Boom! The overlapping explosions circled the LZ, sent columns of bloodied dirt up into the air, and cleared a path for the troops that poured in from behind. But some of the civilians were still on their feet, still stumbling forward, as Colonel Six gave the necessary order. "They're going to die no matter what you do! *Fire!*"

Now it was the enemy's turn to die, as the entire perimeter erupted in flame, and both the civilians *and* the bugs went down like wheat before a thresher. The outer edge of the new, smaller LZ looked like a ring of fire, as both the quads and the T-2s sent blue death stuttering out to slag the half-frozen ground. The officers were firing as well, machine guns for the most part, which sent red tracers out to probe the places where enemy soldiers might hide. And as each rank of Ramanthians fell, their bodies were added to the steadily growing circle of death that was defined by the ditch.

That was the scene that Maylo Chien-Chu saw from the air, as the *Xinglong* circled the embattled landing zone, and fired on the Ramanthians. That support, when combined with the fire being put out by those on the ground, created the sort of respite that Kobbi had been counting on. "This is it!" the feisty little general shouted over the command channel. "Pull those brain boxes. . . . T-2s first. . . . And get them ready to load. The last ship is about to land."

That triggered a mad scramble to jerk each T-2's box, and carry them two at a time to the edge of the so-called doughnut hole, where the *Xinglong* settled into a vapor cloud of her own making. The belly ramp was already in the process of deploying when the big skids touched down. Santana had Deker's box in one hand, and Valario's in the other, as he pounded up the ramp to the point where a very pretty woman stood waiting. The legionnaire was amazed to see that it was General Booly's wife who was waiting to receive the boxes, but there was no opportunity to do anything more than nod as he turned to make another trip.

Ten minutes later, all the T-2s were aboard, and it was time to bring the quad boxes in, as some of the officers fired heavy machine guns and the Ramanthians fired back. Santana ran to where Lupo was dug in, ordered the quad to disengage, and flipped a protective cover out of the way. With that accomplished, all he had to do was grab the T-shaped red handle and give it a full turn to the right. Then, still holding on to the same handle, the officer was able to pull the cyborg's biological support module out into the open. Lupo tried to say "Thanks," but no longer had the means to speak, and felt the world fade as sedatives were pumped into his disembodied brain.

With the box clutched to his chest Santana began the long run back. A bullet plucked at his right sleeve, and others kicked up geysers of mud all around him, as he dodged back and forth. "They know what we're up to!" Kobbi advised over the push. "Pull back! Pull back! It's time to haul ass!"

Santana caught up with Zolkin, who along with Kelly, was supporting Four-Four. The Seebo had taken a bullet in the thigh and was bleeding badly. Other heavily laden officers streamed toward the ship as well even as the *Xinglong*'s energy cannons sent bolts of iridescent blue energy fanning out over their heads. One of the officers threw up her hands and fell facedown when a burst of bullets hit her from behind. The brain box she had been carrying fell, landed in the mud, and was quickly scooped up as one of the surviving bio bods grabbed it.

Metal clanged under combat boots, and the stench of ozone permeated the air, as the officers charged up the ramp and into the freighter. Kobbi was there to count them off. "Twenty-two, twenty-three, where the hell is Colonel Six?" the general demanded.

On hearing that, Kelly turned and made a run for the ramp, only to be tackled by Santana. Both of them crashed to the deck as servos began to *whine*, and Orlo-Ka brought the ramp up. Kelly fought her way clear of Santana and ran over to a bank of screens, where the loadmaster could monitor everything that took place outside his ship. That was when she saw the waves of Ramanthian troopers, and heard the distant *chug, chug, chug* of a .50-caliber machine gun as Six harvested a few more lives. Then he was gone, swarmed under by an angry mob, as thousands of Ramanthian bullets hammered against the ship's hull.

There was a noticeable jerk as the *Xinglong* lifted off and wobbled into the air. One of the bugs was hanging on to a skid, but Brisco shook him loose, and continued to climb. The bug deployed his wings, and was planning to glide in, when hundreds of bullets fired by his comrades ripped his body apart.

Meanwhile, high above the body-strewn LZ, the freighter continued to gain altitude. Most of the passengers were seated by then, if not very comfortably, in fold-down seats. Kelly continued to sob, even as she knelt in a pool of Four-Four's blood, and fought to save a man who *looked* like Six but was actually someone else. Zolkin was there, trying to help the doctor find the big bleeder, and eventually clamp it off.

Santana sat slumped in a web-style seat. His eyes were open but unseeing. A battle had been lost, but the war would continue, and the Legion would be in the thick of it. And, all things considered, that was the only thing he needed to know.

AUTHOR'S NOTE

Though not based on the Korean War, or World War II, some of the events in this novel were inspired by both. In particular, the nature of the wintry battles in which Santana and his company take part would be recognizable to any of the marines who fought in the Chosin Reservoir campaign in 1950, except that what they managed to accomplish was far more heroic than anything in this book. Because in Korea, some 12,000 leathernecks were surrounded by 60,000 Chinese soldiers north of the Yalu River, yet still managed to fight their way out of the wintry mountains, taking their dead and wounded with them. For those who would like to read more about that campaign, I recommend *Breakout* by Martin Russ.

By the same token, those familiar with the Battle of Dunkirk in World War II will recognize the evacuation of planet Gamma-014 as being very similar to the effort by roughly 700 privately owned fishing boats, yachts, and other vessels to remove some 338,000 Allied soldiers from the beaches of Dunkirk in a period of just nine days. Sadly, more than 30,000 British troops were killed, more than 8,000 went missing, and 1,212,000 Dutch, Belgian, French, and British soldiers were taken prisoner by the Germans, who lost 10,000 soldiers during the battle.

These were *real* battles, involving *real* men and women, to whom all Americans owe so much. Their courage astounds me.